Until Death

Nicole Dixon

Copyright © 2021 Nicole Dixon

Lucky Thirteen Publishing, LLC

All rights reserved.

ISBN: 9798754317048

Until Death

UNTIL DEATH

ACKNOWLEDGMENTS

Every book that I write has a special place in my heart. They are bits and pieces of me mixed with a story that is only mine to tell. This book was different. There is something extra special about it. Even more so than usual. These characters are segments of my soul.

I hope you feel what I feel when you read their story.

J. My heart. My inspiration. Your poem is bomb. Thanks for letting me steal it for this book before you even knew its relevance. I love you big. I will always be down for testing out scenes with you as I write them. *wink*

Mom. My biggest fan. I will never get tired of hearing you brag about how cool your kids are to total strangers. We're only cool because we have cool parents.

Beth. My sounding board. To the woman that calls me on all of my bullshit and does it nicely with a smile. I love you.

Kyndall. To the woman that selflessly destroys my books with a red ink pen and does it all in the name of love and family. You will never know how much your help means to me. These books are polished and clean because you wouldn't have it any other way. I couldn't do it without you.

My children. You have no idea the "scary books" Mommy writes on her computer aren't really scary at all. Not really. One day you will be scandalized by your mother and I'm not even sorry. Not even a little. Love you babies.

My readers. Wow. Book six. I can't believe how far we've come together in such a short period of time. Thanks for hanging with me from the very beginning, when I was winging it and praying that I didn't fall flat on my face. Who am I kidding? I'm still winging it. You guys are awesome. Let's keep doing this together. It's fun.

XOXO, Nicole

TIMELINE

This is not the reading order.
This is a chronological order of events.

Silent Hero Series - Until Death
Alex and Emily

Years pass…

Carlton Harbor Series – Mirror Image
Kline and Megan
Carlton Harbor Series – Surprise Reflections
Ryan and Ali
Carlton Harbor Series – For Always
Jason and Olivia
Carlton Harbor Series – Starting Over
Asher and Beth
Silent Hero Series – Devil You Know
Reid and Holly

Until Death

The pain from the past engraves our souls with scars.
We build up walls and protect our hearts with bars.

You try to forget them; you try to tame the beast,
But they always come back stronger like a pack of lions ready to feast.

We all have demons lurking in our deepest thoughts,
Some we have dealt with, others we have never fought.

They say you can't change the past, and those words are distinctively true,
But your future is in your hands. It is all up to you.

Hard days and tough times are forever going to come.
Face each day with courage, and be prepared to lose some.

It's okay to lose a battle, just always win the war.
You will have to face those demons, even the ones that scare you to the core.

Let your scars remind you of just how tough you are,
And render your love so fierce, **until death do us part**.

- J

AEMILIA
AGE – SEVEN YEARS OLD

"Julian, do you feel it?" My mother holds my hand in hers as we walk along the boardwalk near Coney Island.

The hot dogs here are my absolute favorite. Every time we come down to the boardwalk for dinner my dad caves and buys ice cream for all of us, it's mom's favorite. She pretends that she doesn't like it, but she never turns it down when he offers. She usually gets a double scoop of chocolate, just like me. Not to mention, I see the way she peeks over her dripping cone at dad when she thinks I'm not looking.

She totally, secretly loves ice cream.

We take the subway from our apartment and make a trip to the boardwalk at least once a week, even if it's just to dip our toes in the sand. It's our happy place. Mom and dad adore the beach. Mom says it's because they lived near the beach when she was growing up. My parents left their country to start a new life here around the time they found out mom was pregnant with me.

I've never met my relatives in Italy, but sometimes I hear mom talking to them on the phone. She and dad speak Latin when they talk to their family back in their home country, and when they don't want me to know what they're saying, like now, when my dad starts talking quickly in a language that my brain works overtime to try to make sense of.

I pick out bits and pieces of words as he speaks. They think I don't know what they're saying, but I've listened to their conversations all my life, and I'm almost eight! I might not be able to speak the language just yet - give me a break, it's a hard language to learn. But I know when they're planning to meet in secret at bedtime, and I also know when they're getting important phone calls about their work. And, like right now, I know dad is saying something to mom about somebody important at their job.

Dad picks up his pace, and the faster he walks, the looser the strap on my favorite pair of brown sandals becomes. Mom's grip on my small fingers begins to hurt a little as she squeezes my hand tighter the faster we walk together down the long boardwalk.

The newer boardwalk is concrete closer to the water, but the wood of the original boardwalk is brown with weathered gray colors weaved throughout the old wood. I listen to the *slap, slap, slap* of my loose sandal against the weathered slats as I try to keep up with their fast pace.

My tummy is full as it jostles around. We just finished our dinner and ice cream and were taking a walk along the old boardwalk to watch the sunset. But now mom nearly drags me behind her as their words in Latin turn quieter and more serious. Mom's words sound angry, but dad just continues to stare straight ahead. He's on a mission, but I don't know where we're going. I'm the tallest in my class, even taller than the boys, but my legs can't keep up with theirs.

"Mom. Mom!" I yank on her hand as the persistent slapping of my shoe threatens to send it flying into the sand beside us.

But she doesn't hear me.

The tip of a nail pokes out of one of the slats, but it's too late by the time I see it. My shoe catches and slips off of my foot falling behind us.

On instinct I turn to grab it, and that's when I see him for the first time.

Dark hair, so dark that it's almost black, is slicked back to his head. The shininess of it makes it look greasy, like either he doesn't wash it enough, or he uses too much conditioner. His skin is a creamy dark tan, the same color as ours. He wears black slacks with a nice button-down shirt tucked in and a pair of shiny black shoes.

Doesn't he realize he's at the beach? He doesn't much look like he cares as his eyes catch mine, they're black like the night. His eyes are scary, they look mean.

"Aemilia!" My eyes quickly snap back to my mom as she says my name and simultaneously snatches me up in her arms, shielding me from the creepy stranger with her body.

Then we're running. My shoe. Gone, forgotten.

We're running so fast, but mom never drops me. She carries me as dad says words to her in Latin about safe places and hiding, things I can't understand on concept alone, even though I recognize the words they speak.

We take a sharp left as soon as their feet hit concrete, and duck into an abandoned alleyway behind one of the warehouses that are used for storage for the amusement park.

"Listen to me, Aemilia, this is very important baby." My legs wrap around her trim waist as I hold on tightly. One of her small hands presses against my back and the other threads through the tangled strands of my long, dark brown hair.

I don't speak, just listen, because the way her voice shakes scares me. Her breathing is heavy from the running, but her voice quivers because of something else.

"I need you to be brave for me, I know you can. You were born with the bravery of a thousand warriors. I need you to hide when I tell you to hide, and whatever you do, do not come out. Do not make a sound. No matter what you hear, what you think you see, you stay put. Your dad and I will come back for you when it's safe, but it's very important that you follow my instructions exactly. *Promise me*." Her words are rushed as we approach a large green garbage bin in the alley and my dad lifts the lid, his eyes darting around quickly.

Even dad looks scared. I've never seen him scared, he's the biggest, baddest guy I know. He even has all the tattoos, all over his arms and neck, literally all of the tattoos. People give him funny looks at the grocery store, but he's not scared of anything, he says we shouldn't worry what others think of us. My mom says being weird is the new cool anyways.

Or at least I thought he wasn't scared of anything. His eyes meet mine, and I think for a minute he might cry, which is weird. Dads don't cry.

"Daila, in here." He speaks to mom as she lifts me into his arms, even as I try to cling to her, not willing to release my hold on her.

"Aemilia, I love you; daddy loves you. Never forget." His lips brush over my forehead as he hoists my small body like it weighs nothing into the bin. It feels like everything is happening in slow motion as I watch a lone tear run down mom's cheek and fall to the cement below. Dad lowers the lid, and the light is snuffed out, everything bathed in darkness.

"I promise." I whisper the words, but I don't think they hear me. It's too late, they're gone.

It's nasty in this bin, the absolute worst stink I've ever smelt in the history of my life, and my shoe is still missing, so the bottom of my foot touches something slimy, and it takes everything in me not to scream.

I want to scream, but I don't. Because mom said I was brave, and if I did what I was supposed to do, they would come back and get me.

Except they didn't. They couldn't.

ALEX
AGE – FOURTEEN YEARS OLD

My muscles ache from the five-mile run I completed this morning. I watched the sun rise up above the trees before school and simultaneously cussed my best friend for being a freak of nature. Reid insists that we train every single day, rain or shine. He's a junior high school drill sergeant, old beyond our young fourteen years.

I'm an only child, but he's been my brother since our mothers touched wombs while they were incubating us. So, instead of sleeping in like a normal teenage boy, I sack up and slip my sneakers on in the darkness of my bedroom to meet Reid outside my back door for our morning trek through our middle-class neighborhood.

The same back door I walk up the steps to now after a long day of school and a study session at the library with Julie Campbell; she's tutoring me in biology in exchange for my tutoring her in math. Honestly, I don't need a tutor in anything. I just sit next to her and smell her pineapple mango lip gloss as she talks to me about life cycles, and I ask questions that I already know the answer to. I'm weirdly smart like that. I don't try to be, it's just who I am.

I've never had a girlfriend, but our study sessions are

all part of my elaborate plan to ask her to be my date to the Winter Formal. The timing has to be just right, and I've been setting the stage for months. Never let it be said that I'm not thorough. I've been writing out what I'm going to say, planning every detail so she doesn't even consider turning me down. I'm not the type of guy to leave this stuff up to chance. One failed attempt at asking a girl out and you're pegged as *that guy* for the next four years. I'm not going to be *that guy*.

I'm not like Reid, he's loud and confident compared to my quiet and reserved. It's not that I'm shy, it's more so that I don't generally like people, so I don't waste my time speaking to them. I would rather hang out in my own mind or stare aimlessly at Julie's soft locks of hair that fall gently over her shoulders as she turns a page in her textbook.

I left this morning before the sun, and now I come home as it sets, opening the back door and dropping my backpack on the floor just inside. One breath and the immediate stench of alcohol and cigarettes hits me like a punch to the gut.

Dad…not again.

My stomach flips, and the instant nausea from the stress the sickening concoction of those smells induces threatens the protein bar I just snacked on.

My family lives in a nice neighborhood. My dad works at a car dealership; his face is plastered on billboards all over town. My mom's a teacher at the high school, but we never ride home together because she stays late most nights coaching the girls' volleyball team or tutoring students that actually need the help.

My dad is usually home late too, but not tonight. Not on nights when he backslides into a person that I don't know. A guy that isn't my dad at all, but instead is a sad, anxiety ridden hermit with an addiction to cheap liquor and tobacco.

A quick glance around the kitchen tells me that he's not here. But my nose says otherwise, meaning he's probably in the family room.

I rise up onto the toes of my sneakers and tiptoe quietly into the dimly lit family room, my only access to the stairs that lead to my room. The TV drowns on, some old country western movie, but my dad lays passed out in the recliner, eyes closed, an almost empty bottle of Canadian Club in his lap. The bowl I ate my cereal out of on Monday sits on the table to his left, littered with the remanence of cigarettes.

I count my blessings that he's asleep, for now, and snag the cordless phone from behind the couch on my way up the stairs to the safety of my bedroom.

I'll call mom; she always knows what to do when he gets like this. He's not abusive, not in the way you might consider an alcoholic. He doesn't scream or hit. He's depressed. My dad has a sickness that's so often swept under the rug, but every time he appears to be clawing his way back to the top, something happens, and he's back in the bottom of the hole again.

He's tried rehab and done the weekly meetings, but it never lasts. Depression is an unending cycle; it steals the man I know he is on the inside. My mom is the only person that can save him, the only person that continues to hold our family together. My mom is our savior when

I am not enough. His son, I'm never enough.

I top the stairs and stop at the second door on the right. Slowly, I open the door. It squeaks a little too loudly when it reaches the halfway point and cringe a little, hoping the noise didn't wake him. When I determine that I'm all clear, I push the door the remainder of the way open and walk into my bedroom, gently closing it behind me with a soft *click*.

My eyes glance towards the wall on my left, towards the brand-new Apple Macintosh desktop computer that sits proudly on top of my worn wooden desk. It was the only thing I asked for for Christmas, and honestly, I didn't expect to get it. I don't know anyone that has a desktop computer in their house, let alone their own room. I've got dial up internet; it's sweet, but I haven't had much time to use it yet.

Slumping down on top of my small twin-sized bed, I kick my sneakers off and dial the number I know I can reach my mom at. I need her to come home before my dad wakes up, he needs her – I need her.

Two rings and one transfer later I'm connected to the voice of my mother as she breathes heavily like she's been running and yells at a group of girls to do laps while she takes a call.

"Hey baby, did you make it home alright?" I smile hearing her voice, allowing it to calm the shaky nerves that still sit heavy on my stomach.

"Yeah, mom, listen…um…I got home, and dad is having a bad day again." I lean my head back and stare at the ceiling, hating that I have to be the one to tell her this…again.

"How bad is it this time?" I can hear the desperation in her voice. She's tired, but she won't give up on him — she never gives up.

"It smells horrible downstairs, but he was passed out in the recliner, I was kind of hoping you could come home and get him in the bed before he wakes up. I can do it if you want, but…" she interrupts me before I can finish.

"No, not your job, not your responsibility, Alex. I'm leaving now, I will be home in ten minutes, okay? Just stay in your room until I get there or go next door to Reid's house."

"I'll just stay here, make sure he doesn't get up and get into any trouble." My words hold a bravery that I truly don't feel. I've seen too much of his addiction. I know too much, and it scares me. I want to escape from a world where the dark, deep level of depression is slowly stealing my family. Escape from the fear that the cycle doesn't end with him, that somehow it will find its way to me too.

"Ok, I'm on my way, I promise." The dial tone clicks, ending the call. *I love you, mom.* The words are on the tip of my tongue, but she's gone, her mind probably racing a thousand miles an hour.

Promises, yeah — right. Sounds surprisingly like false hopes and broken dreams.

-o-

Ten minutes.

Twenty minutes.

Time passes, but I never hear the back door open from downstairs.

The cordless phone rings on the bed beside me. I pick it up, not realizing that, that one small action will forever change the course of my life. Not that whether I pick up that phone call or not would change the outcome of what happened, it wouldn't. It's already too late.

"Mr. Straton?" A deep voice travels through the line, muffled by sounds of sirens and a flurry of activity in the background. The noises remind me of an active construction site, so much chaos. So loud.

"Um, yeah? This is he." I clear my throat and try to sound older than my fourteen years. Whoever this is doesn't need to speak to my dad in his current condition. This isn't the first time I've had to pretend to be him on the phone, probably won't be the last.

"Mr. Straton, we need to ask you to meet us at the hospital. There's been an accident, and your wife needs you." He's so serious. His voice is cold; free from emotion.

"Mom…my mom?!" Dropping the façade, I feel my voice crack on a cry. Emotion begins to swirl in waves through my gut.

One hit, two hits. I take punch after punch as I feel the core of my world shift beneath my feet. I let the phone slip through my hand and hit the floor as I gasp for air. My chest physically hurts, and in that moment, I know it's bad – the worst.

Someone hit pause on my life, everything from that second forward moving in slow motion.

Leaving my father, who is totally useless, I sprint without shoes to Reid's house. I don't even remember asking, but his mom put us both in her car and drove directly to the hospital.

No matter how fast we moved, we couldn't move fast enough, the confines of time wouldn't allow it – didn't matter.

No goodbye. No I love you. No see you later.

A thick fog of sadness settles in and makes itself at home over my boney shoulders as I continue to sit in the waiting room with my best friend and his mom for what seems like eternity. The longer we wait the more desolate I feel.

My heart is broken, and I feel every incision, every single crack. I made the call; she was in that car at that moment because I couldn't man up and take care of business for our family. She left early because of me. *My fault.*

A police officer escorts a man in a stained white coat over to our small group as we sit huddled together on cold, metal chairs.

I only hear clips of what he was saying, like headers in a newspaper article. I filter through his sentences for words that actually mean something to my chaos riddled brain.

Head-on collision.

Dead on arrival.

Drunk driver.

The sadness was drowning me, so when the anger hit, I welcomed the rage with open arms.

Let me feel the fire, because the crashing waves of the storm were too much to bear.

AEMILIA
AGE – EIGHTEEN YEARS OLD

The music is so loud it vibrates the concrete beneath my feet as I move in the darkness, hiding in plain sight.

I'm invisible, a ghost in the night.

I had a normal life, a great life. I was a normal child. I attended school, played on the playground, and blew out pink sparkly candles on my seventh birthday cake – chocolate, of course.

The world as I knew it was swept away, stolen from me in a matter of minutes. Everything changed the day my parents hid me in a dumpster in an alleyway and ran for their lives. Once my eyes adjusted to the darkness, a sliver of light illuminated a small, rusted opening in the juncture of the corner of the metal dumpster I found my safety inside. If I closed one eye and squinted really hard, I could just see through the hole, but it was enough. Enough to watch the murder of the only family I knew.

The shots were deafening and yet surprisingly silent as I strained to hear them echo through the narrow alley. One shot each, to the back of the head as they ran for cover. My heart jolted and fear spread through my veins as I watched them collapse onto the hard concrete in broad daylight.

I studied the man from the boardwalk, memorizing him as he drug their lifeless bodies away and I did my best to remain silent, hidden. Fulfilling my promise, hoping that if I was good enough, if I was silent enough, they would still fulfill theirs and come back for me – innocent childhood dreams and wishes that never came true.

I was scared to move, terrified that I would be next.

Would he come back to look for me? He saw me with them, he looked into my eyes.

That was the last time I saw my parents.

If we're being honest - and we are - lying is for assholes and people with secrets to hide. Maybe I'm the latter, but I digress. Aemilia died that day too. Aemilia died, and Emily was born. Emily Young to be exact. Or, at least that's the name on the fake ID that I clutch tightly in my right hand as I move through the darkened night towards my destination.

Funny that I chose that last name, right? I'm definitely *younger* than the twenty-one years this phony piece of plastic states that I am, issued by the good state of New Jersey. I'm punny like that. Get it? *Punny.*

At least I didn't lose my sense of humor when my soul fell out of my chest and shriveled up and died in that city issued garbage receptacle.

I maintained my post for three days. Three days I lived with one shoe on my foot and surrounded by filth and decay. It took twenty-four hours for me to break down and begin searching the contents of my new home for food, which I ate, right alongside my new friends the rats that I shared my humble abode with. My introduction to life on the street.

After three days I convinced myself that if I didn't move, I would be found by a city worker and probably sent off to social services. I have no family here, no one would report us missing. I was lost with no one to find me. So instead, I snuck out of my safe haven from the evil and made my way back to my home.

I knew the way well, and while I got some brief glances on the subway, no one stopped to ask the dirty little girl why she was traveling alone wearing only one shoe. Its New York City after all. I would wager that ninety percent of the people I passed never truly saw me, too self-absorbed to acknowledge the broken shell of a little girl mere inches from where they stood.

I finally made it back to our two-bedroom apartment to find the door unlocked, a crack ran alongside the framing that indicated someone forced their way in, but did it well enough that they didn't attract too much attention by breaking the door down completely.

A therapist might say I was still in shock. Maybe I still am, maybe I lost my sanity that day, but I'm convinced therapy is for the weak anyway. I'm a warrior.

I'm not sure what I expected to find when I hesitantly pushed open the door and peeked around the corner. I can't say that anything was surprising after the events of the previous three days, even to my young seven-year-old mind.

I listened to the quiet and said a small prayer that whoever broke in and trashed our apartment was already gone and not hiding somewhere inside waiting for me, as I stepped in and quickly ran to my room.

I couldn't stay. What if they came back? No, I needed

to get some necessities and get out, fast.

In my adolescent mind, that meant changing clothes, slipping on a pair of sneakers and searching for the only thing that might give me the answers I needed.

Quickly, I hurried down the short hallway that connected my room to my parents. The room was barely recognizable. It looked like it had survived a category four hurricane and hardly lived to tell about it. Clothes littered the floor, furniture was overturned – they were searching.

I walked to the built-in window seat and knelt down, just as I'd seen my mother do so many times before. The cushions were now on the floor across the room, but the hand carved wood was untouched, a solid fixture in a room of anarchy. Sliding my tiny hand under the lip of the wooden bench my fingers hit the small metal latch - still locked.

I opened the hidden latch and gently lifted the lid on the bench seat, revealing a book with frayed pages covered in worn leather: my mother's journal. My road map to redemption.

Without hesitation I grabbed the journal then closed and locked the hidden compartment back once again. Not that it mattered; there was nothing else of value in the hidden compartment. But to my young mind it was meant to be locked, so I locked it anyway. Straightening from where I kneeled on the floor, I stood to leave my parents room for the last time. I took a deep breath, trying to smell them over the stench that still coated my skin, committing their scent to memory. I allowed myself one single moment to be sad, to rid myself of the cloak of bravery my mother was so sure I wore.

I cried for the loss of my parents.

I cried for the loss of my life.

And then I put the cloak back on. Only this time, my bravery was laced with a new emotion. An emotion that I couldn't identify at seven years old but have since come to recognize.

Revenge.

-o-

"Emily Young?" A large man, covered from top to toe in tattoos stares down at my petite frame. He stands over me and shines a flashlight onto my brand spankin' new identification card. His first instinct is to question me, look for fallacies in what he sees with his eyes, but knows better than to believe. He won't find them.

Even in the pair of black stilettos I swiped from a store off of seventh this morning, he still has a full foot of height on me.

"Fuck off." I square my shoulders, kicking my chin up, and stare into his dark brown eyes with my green, daring him to verbally question my legitimacy for a second time.

I learned at an early age that intimidation is a tactic used by the weaker links of society to make themselves feel important. I'm intimidated by no one. If you're gonna play with the big dogs, you've gotta be the one holding the leash.

I've been on the streets for over half of my life now. I've lived more in my eighteen years than most people do in ninety.

I'm not afraid of the devil anymore, because I've seen

hell.

It's a lovely place reserved for people like Vito Adkins, boss of the Adkins mafia crime family.

No, he's not the man I saw murder my parents that day. That man, he was just a soldier. He wasn't a very good one either. He didn't even so much as flinch when I snuck into his small one-bedroom apartment and slit his throat while he slept in the middle of the night a year ago.

It had to be done. An eye for an eye and all that.

Funny, I kind of expected his blood to run black. My entire life I'd imagined that moment. The man that haunted my nightmares dying a slow death, but his blood ran red. Even though it wasn't as I had imagined it, I watched on with a sick joy as it pooled around his lifeless body on his small twin sized bed.

Vito Adkins, he sits at the top, doesn't dirty his hands with peons. But he's the reason I'm here tonight, at his club.

I didn't realize it at the time, not until I was able to fully translate the Latin words of my mother's journal, but my parents were spies for the Italian government, the country's foreign and domestic intelligence services.

They were investigating the Adkins family when their mission assignment was relocated to the United States. According to my mother's journal, she didn't know she was pregnant with me until after they arrived on American soil.

They made the decision to keep my birth a secret because they were worried that if the Italian government found out they would be pulled from their mission. A mission that, according to the words of my mother, they would die to protect.

Which, ultimately, I guess they did, which brings us back here.

"You know what they do with little girls in there?" Spittle flies from the mouth of the giant as he stands his post and threatens to deny me entry.

"Fortunate for me, I'm not little – nor am I a child. But I guess it's a good thing you see me as an innocent, because I'm here for a job and from what I hear…" I cup my mouth with my hand and motion for him to lean down, crooking my finger and pulling my bottom lip into my mouth, between my teeth.

Like the siren that I know that I am, he follows. They all follow. It's a skill I've perfected over the last eleven years.

Lowering his flashlight, he bends his large frame to come closer to my mouth as I wait patiently for him, building the suspense.

When he's close enough to hear me, I whisper the words that I know would gain my entry into this lovely gentlemen's club…"My virginity is a commodity worth more than diamonds…I'm here for Vito." I whisper the name most would never dare utter out loud, slide a business card into his hand that I've held on to for years, and watch the color drain from the face of the giant just before he steps aside and grants my entrance to fulfill my destiny.

As far as I know, the Italian government never came looking for my parents.

My family never sought me out. How could they? They didn't know I existed.

Until Death

I refuse to let their death be in vain.

I'm a figment of the night, an apparition - I'm your worst fucking nightmare.

CHAPTER ONE
ALEX – TWENTY-TWO YEARS OLD

My phone vibrates persistently against the wooden desk as my fingers fly across the keyboard that's hardwired into my main operating system. My eyes remain locked on the six flatscreen monitors that line the wall directly in front of me.

The vibrating won't stop, it's incessant. But the successful completion of my mission tonight is more important.

She demands that I answer, but I'm so close I can taste it. There isn't enough time.

I cut my eyes to the monitor on my far left and glance at her frustrated stance. The way she pops her hip and places her hand there impatiently, she's angry. That's her angry hip pop. I know her body, I've spent hours studying her movements. I watch the slow tap of her foot, and the way she abuses her bottom lip with her teeth as she jams a finger from her free hand onto the screen of her cell phone.

Her ass is on full display. The thin lines of the red thong she wears cut high up on her succulent hips. Tassels and shiny beads that I don't know the correct name for drip from the barely there fabric and brush up against the exposed skin of her lush thighs. Her breasts are pushed up and cupped delicately in a matching diamond studded red bra. She's dressed to perform, and I allow my mind – momentarily – to imagine her fluid movements. Her body bends in ways that don't seem physically possible, and yet she makes it look flawless.

I consider myself a voyeur, for as long as she doesn't know I watch. I don't stalk, I observe. And hell, maybe I touch myself, but damn woman's got curves for days and when she dances…God, when she dances…I am just a man. She sought me out after all, not the other way around.

Movement on the screen to my right snaps my mind back to the task at hand. I'm inside their system, I've hacked their cameras. I see what they see, which means they see her. They watch, and they present an unknown danger to our ability to successfully complete our mission.

My heart kicks into overdrive and races so fast it feels like it might burst from my chest at any moment without warning.

Tonight is the culmination of years of work, of dedicated research and securing funds that were never ours to take then reallocating those funds to achieve a greater goal. I've become a vigilante for a cause that was never mine to fight for, and yet here I am. I fight for her, for her story and for the women and children that come after her. Hundreds of miles separate us, and yet our mission somehow has become one in the same.

The day the man that murdered my mother walked was the day that I decided maybe the judicial system didn't really have a handle on what they were doing.

Reid and I were always supposed to attend the Academy together; we were going to be the good guys. We dreamt of joining the Bureau before we even knew the details of what we needed to do to get there; we were backyard superheroes. That was until I realized the truth, the good guys were bound by laws that I don't hold much faith in anymore. Their hands were tied, and fuck, the only restraints I want to be involved in are in the bedroom.

Why should I waste my time sitting in a classroom when I already had the only weapon I've ever needed at my fingertips? I can make your life a living hell and never step foot out of my living room.

I didn't need school; I've never needed it.

Reid all but slept on my bedroom floor every night our senior year of high school. He would drag me away from my computer each morning, bloodshot eyes, no care for anything outside of what went on behind the four walls of my bedroom. I was running on energy drinks and anger. It was his mission that I graduate, and nothing stops Reid Chapman on a mission - nothing.

After graduation he left for college, and I chose to stay back. I chose my own path and understood when the polar opposite directions our lives took meant that we had to go our separate ways for a while.

I moved into a one-bedroom apartment, far enough from my dad, but still close enough I could keep an eye on him with some well-equipped surveillance cameras. I needed to be able to get to him quickly if he put himself or others in danger, but far enough away that he couldn't drag me down the dark hole of depression with him. My father was already on a path of self-destruction, but he spiraled out of control when my mother died. He slammed full force into rock bottom and has been living there ever since.

I tried to talk to him in the beginning. I did everything I knew to do to fill the gaps my mother left, but I was never enough – no surprise there. I was still a kid, and I was hurting too. I lost my mother, but my father was so selfish that he was blind to the fact that I needed him. His son needed a father.

I lost them both that night. Now I watch on from afar as my father slowly kills himself; I've given up on trying to save him. Instead, I focus on what I can do to vindicate my mother's murder. The official reports sited her death an accident. The driver of the other vehicle involved was well above the legal limit of intoxication. The officer in charge told us as much at the hospital the night she died. Her death was no accident, she was killed. Now her murderer walks free because someone knew someone that played golf with the judge on Sunday afternoons at the country club.

Or well, at least, he thought he did. I haunt him at every turn. Of course, he doesn't realize it's me. Each time his bank account is swiped, or his credit is tanked – I'm there in the shadows. It's become kind of a cute little hobby for me; and he doesn't have a damn clue that each unfortunate event that happens to him is manipulated by yours truly.

I could make it easy, set up an unfortunate event that lands him in jail once again, or worse, takes his life, but that's too easy and I dunno, I just don't think my mother would approve of those methods in this particular situation. So instead, I draw it out slowly, meticulously. It is my pleasure to drive him to the brink of insanity and watch as his life slowly disintegrates.

"Dammit, what is so important?" I let the words fly from my mouth in frustration as I slam my hand down over the green button on my phone, answering the call just to make the vibrating stop.

"Shut it down and get out. Get out now." Her voice is low and serious – a mandate, non-negotiable.

"I can't, we're too close. Five more minutes. I need more time." I speak, but my fingers never stop. My eyes locked onto the set of monitors in front of me.

"Time's up." The line goes dead.

The thin walls of my apartment shake with force as the door to my back is ripped from its hinges. No knock, no further warning. *Time's up.* Her words echo amongst the noise that suddenly fills the room.

"Alexander Straton, you have the right to remain silent. Anything you say can and will be used against you in a court of law…." The metal cuffs cut into the skin on my wrists as I listen to words I always knew would find me and watch as a team of officers begin dismantling hundreds of thousands of dollars of equipment.

My life is torn apart before my eyes…but I can't stop

the sly smile that turns up the corner of my lip as the federal agent jerks my body back towards the door to my apartment that is now laid out on the floor.

I might be going to prison, but hell if I didn't hit send before they got me.

Game on motherfuckers.

-o-

EMILY

"Emily, stage left. Your girl Peaches comes off in five, and Sasha called in sick. My bets on her old man beating the shit out of her again last night, but that's none of my business. Boss man says your fillin' in since twinkle toes back there is still in training." I shove my cell phone back in between my breasts and say a silent prayer that it doesn't fall out during my routine. I don't have anywhere else to put it, and I don't have time to head back to my locker.

I don't dance anymore, not for the patrons of this club anyway. I dance for the boss, and only the boss. But if he says my ass is up on that stage in five, well I guess my ass is up on that stage in five. I'm certain he'll be watching, he's always watching. I'm his prized pony, and yet I lie awake at night and dream of the day it all ends. His life, not mine. I'm a little bit insane, but I'm not suicidal.

So many times, so many times I could have slit his throat, just like I did the soldier in the night years ago. But murder is messy, and I'm trying really fucking hard to keep my hands clean here.

That's why I sought out help, a man I've never even met in real life, Alex Straton…or at least I'm fairly positive that's his real name. It's funny, the people you meet in internet chat rooms on the dark web in the middle of the night when sleep won't come because of the shadows that chase you every time you close your eyes.

He chases shadows too. His might be a little different than mine, but for whatever reason he wants to help me. What started out as a way to anonymously purge our demons has become our joint crusade.

I'm playing the long game. It's been four years since I walked into this club for the first time. So yeah, it's been a hella long game, but tonight – tonight it all changes.

In the beginning, I was so angry, so full of rage that I couldn't see more than two steps ahead of myself. My actions were based on impulse alone; I was reckless.

Two days before my twelfth birthday I laid awake tossing and turning under a stone bridge crossing near Central Park, praying that sleep would take me under, if only for minutes – I could feel the physical pain of the exhaustion through to my bones. The sky was clear, the stars filtered out by the lights of the city. The cold air of the impending winter nipped at my exposed skin and sent a shiver down my spine. That's when I heard the music. I'm not entirely sure where it was coming from, but it carried through the night on the breeze that sneakily threatened to send me into hypothermia in the months to come.

My heart bled for the song that the keys of the piano played. Then the drums cut in and created a low beat that I engulfed my body. I saw color, vivid colors of pink and blue. The more I listened, the brighter they became. I'd heard music before, but never experienced anything like this. Something about this was different. It was the first time I experienced what I now know is synesthesia.

I see music in color. I like to think of it as my reprieve from the darkness I constantly live in. Doctor Google says I was probably born like this, but the genetic variant was repressed until a traumatic event brought it to light. Not that I've ever experienced trauma or anything, wouldn't know anything at all about that.

After that night, it was like the music found me, I couldn't stay away. It became my drug of choice – an addiction. I slept in an alley near a jazz house just to be close enough to see the colors and escape my reality. I listened to the music and danced for hours.

It was late one-night, last call at the jazz house as they prepared to close. I was dancing as the sounds of the saxophone caressed the keys of the piano through the thin walls of the club. I was so lost in my own movements, in the portrait that I was painting in my mind that I didn't realize someone was watching. I had no idea she was standing there until I heard her clear her throat from a few feet away, and I was jarred from my visual illustrations.

She was stunning, the most beautiful woman I'd ever seen. Her white-blonde hair hung in big loose curls down her back, and the red lipstick that she wore made her plump lips pop as she spoke. She promised money, attention and dreams. She handed me a card before she left and told me that if I would be willing to practice and polish my skill, the dancing could bring me a future I'd never dreamt of before. The card read *The Pink Lily*, an invitation.

The Pink Lily. Funny, I was already familiar with the infamous gentleman's club.

I didn't care about money, but I realized in that moment that my ticket to Adkins was through my ability to dance. His clubs are all a front, like most crime families, they all have two things in common – sex and drugs.

Sex sells, and after hours upon hours of refining my skills, I can make a man cum from my routines on the stage alone.

Plenty of women can dance, but the synesthesia allows me to create masterpieces of art with my body. My senses are overtaken, and I become the music.

Four years ago, I walked into the doors of this club with a chip on my shoulder; strapped with a grenade full of revenge and a piss poor attitude.

The face of an innocent, and the body of a siren - a potent combination.

I sacrificed my body to save my soul, and I will never regret that decision.

Vito Adkins thinks he owns me. He's smug with his ability to control everything and everyone in the bubble of evil that surrounds him. He's married, even has a son, a son that – shocker – is even more slimy than he is. Victor Adkins lives halfway across the country with his wannabe trophy wife and three daughters, all the while running the West Coast ring of the Adkins family crime unit through a series of investments and shell companies.

Kind of funny that I'm the same age as his granddaughters…in a sick sort of way.

I sealed my fate the day that I walked in here with my stolen stilettos and took that stage for the first time.

For two years I was the star performer at this club. Now I train the girls that filter through here like water. They never stay for long. They usually overdose, get knocked up or worse…they disappear in the night. I care about my girls, but I don't form attachments, I can't afford to. I'm looking out for me, and if I can cut the head off the snake, then I can look out for them too.

I made a promise to a little girl in a filthy green dumpster years ago. Tonight, I finally fulfill that promise.

My hopes are riding on the ability of a man that I am well aware just sacrificed everything to help a woman he's never met, all in the name of revenge and the hope for a better future. My real-life Robin Hood.

"Emily, you're on!" Beyonce's *Sweet Dreams* filters through the speakers of the club and the colors of the loud music blind me as I step onto the stage for what I hope is the last time.

CHAPTER TWO
ALEX

It's dark outside with the exception of the red, blue and white lights that flicker like the electrical light parade at Disneyland and bring attention from bystanders that have no legal business being outside at this time of night.

My apartment is sufficient. My door has locks, and I'm handy with a gun so I don't much worry about my own safety past that. The general population shy away from men that tower over six feet with tattoos covering most of their visible skin and hair shaved to their scalp. It's a mood – really, I'm unapproachable and I prefer to live my life that way.

The only downside is my inability to get food delivered to this particular area of town. Delivery drivers aren't so keen to shank someone if they try to rough them up. It's unfortunate really, because Chick-Fil-A is the food of the Lord, and a man like me needs all the Jesus he can get without having to leave the comfort of his office chair.

The dwellers of the night outside of my four walls make their money selling contraband that, if these were actual police and not federal investigators, might get their hands slapped. These men aren't here for petty drug crimes though. These men are here because what started as hacking into the accounts of criminals for fun and creatively reallocating their revenue stream to people and organizations that would use it to do some good in the world, turned into hacking the Department of Defense to help a woman. One that somehow, I've formed an unhealthy attachment to.

There, I said it. I've been watching Aemilia Albani for nearly two years. It's cute how she thinks she was so smooth, erasing her former identity and scrubbing her name. Sure, all of her identification says Emily Young, but I found her. Not in a creepy way; but she was asking a lot of someone that was a complete stranger to her at the time. I needed to know who I was working with and the legitimacy of her cause before I agreed to commit myself to it.

I found her, and then I became partial to her. So, I made sure that no one else found her. I had a sneaking suspicion that the people looking for Aemilia weren't wanting to buy girl scout cookies from a little girl.

They look for her, and I block their access at every turn. The Adkins family is corrupt, and the people looking for Aemilia are far more dangerous than the man that got in his pick-up truck on a random weeknight after one too many beers at the local pub and decided it might be a good night to swerve over the line and murder an innocent woman.

Vito Adkins is the boss of a mafia family that spans generations. When the Italian government got too close, they picked up their entire operation and relocated to the United States. Adkins has been at the top of the FBI's most wanted list since the day he stepped onto American soil, but they weren't doing shit about it.

Sure, they watched, they sent some agents in undercover every once in a while, but while they stayed back behind their bureaucratic red tape, Aemilia slid in under the radar with her long, dark brown hair and olive features. She looks innocent enough, but she's a serpent in disguise. She's fearless and willing to sacrifice it all for the mission that her parents died fighting for. The day they died, that battle became hers to win. The day she found me, it became mine too.

"Check in, Reynolds. What's your status?" The man that shoved me not so gently into the back of a black government-issued SUV speaks through an earpiece and ignores my presence to his back as he drives through the night.

"Young is on stage. Premises are secured. Adkins is in the building. The unit is prepared to move." My blood pulses through my veins and runs cold as they verbalize her name and threaten to undo years of planning and work if our timing isn't exact.

"We have Straton." His eyes cut to mine in the mirror of the vehicle and I make sure he sees my smile. Wouldn't want him to think I'm an angry hacker now, would we? "We're moving him to a secured location until we can get a transfer."

"All units are in place. Estimated go time sixty seconds." The words of the man I know to be Special Agent Alan Reynolds echo over the speaker of the SUV as he gives updates to my new friend in the driver's seat.

I glance to my watch as the time ticks down and lean back into the leather of the SUV, allowing it to form to my body as I prepare for what's coming. Five. Four. Three. Two...

Pandemonium.

A series of explosions, carefully timed and spaced carry over the speakers of the vehicle; the loud static threatens to deafen me.

I see the knuckles of my federal chauffer turn white as he grips the steering wheel.

"Reynolds, check-in." Static.

"Reynolds." His voice is a demand, but it doesn't matter. Reynolds can't hear him anyway. Line's dead, whoops.

My lips curve up in a smile, and the agent stares into my eyes instead of watching the dark, deserted highway. He knows, I know, but no one says anything because anything I say and do can be held against me in a court of law...and other shit.

Instead, I focus on the way my heart beats erratically as I think about Emily and worry for her safety, when really, I shouldn't be worried at all. Tonight is the pinnacle of everything that she's trained for, everything that we've worked toward together. This is her moment, but my stomach still twists uncomfortably knowing that I sent her into that battle alone.

Our worlds change tonight. The more I think about

the unknown of what's to come and how that relates to my new reality, which continues to bite into the skin of my wrists annoyingly, the more I realize…I don't think I was quite ready to let her go.

-o-

EMILY

Pink. Purple. Blue. I focus on the kaleidoscope of colors surrounding me and let my body do what I've so meticulously trained it to do. I feel the music in every fiber of my being as I plummet to the ground headfirst. Yet, I seemingly defy gravity, managing to stop myself just before the tip of my head touches the solid timber of the black stage, my hair fanning out dramatically on the floor beneath me.

I don't hear their gasps. I don't see the way they watch me with wide eyes, or the way that they touch themselves in the dark corners of the high back booth seats as they allow their imaginations to wander. These men, they have wives at home, they have daughters, careers, lives beyond the walls of this club. Yet, they continue to come back time and time again because they're addicted to the forbidden fruit, and they see me for what I am – I'm the most forbidden of them all. I am the apple in the Garden of Eden.

My legs are long and lean, my ass is on full display and begs to be touched, but I'm untouchable. My breasts sit perfectly, cupped in the bra that was tailored specifically for me and hand stoned with diamonds; only the best for the property of Vito Adkins. That's exactly what he thinks I am – his property.

My hair hangs in long, loose waves. The dark brown locks border just on the edge of black depending on the way the light hits it. My skin is olive, a gift from my Italian heritage. But my eyes, they're a deep, dark green. My cheekbones protrude just enough, but the dimple that pops on my left cheek gives away my innocence.

I feel his eyes on me. I don't dare look, but I know Vito watches from his grand tower on the second floor of the club. He watches from his side of a two-way mirror. He makes plans for what he will do with his pretty toy tonight, all the while making sure none of the patrons that also watch me get any ideas beyond the small spaces they find their privacy in tonight. Vito is a selfish man, but sometimes he likes to display me. He likes to watch as other men get off on viewing his pretty trophy, and then he punishes me for it. It's a game to him, but it's my sacrifice.

The music plays and the colors flow, but I dance for someone else. I dance for the man that surrendered his freedom for me tonight. For a man that thinks he's so savvy, and well, he is. He thinks I don't know that he watches, but I know. He's been watching me for years, and I dance for him. I always dance for him.

Where I had proximity on my side, Alex had the ability to access a database that should have been impossible to penetrate. I knew from my mother's journal that the FBI was investigating the Adkins family in cooperation with the Italian government. The information I needed would have to be accessed through the Department of Defense database, and I didn't have the skill or the capability to get that information.

I treaded slowly into the recesses of the dark web, and one night happened to stumble into a chat room that would change everything. I lurked in the background and observed as the discussion centered around a man that the group kept referring to as *Robin Hood*. There was a significant bounty out on his head. He was stealing from different upper-level crime groups, gangs, mafia, sex trafficking rings. The money was disappearing from their accounts as if into thin air, untraceable.

They didn't know his name, couldn't track him. He was a shadow of the night – like me.

I made it my mission to find him. Who was this Robin Hood, and how could I locate someone so intelligent that didn't want to be found? I didn't have the education or technical capacity to find someone of such magnitude. Hell, I was working from a stolen laptop off of a bummed Wi-Fi connection.

When I was a little girl, before her murder, my mother would always tell me that sometimes, when something seems impossible, we must believe it to be true, and if it is meant to be, fate will make a way.

Fate, the golden string of hope that ties the possible to the impossible. I believed when I had nothing left to believe in. I hoped when the outcome seemed unattainable. And in the early morning hours as I clicked around on the dark web in places I had no business being, having utterly no clue what the hell I was doing, I found him.

What's more? Somehow I managed to convince him that my cause was worth his time. He was a complete stranger with absolutely no reason to trust me. So why? I still don't know; other than maybe he was bored and looking for a challenge. I can see where hacking the United States Department of Defense would present a challenge to even the most skilled and intelligent hackers. We've developed a friendship, a trust that I have never had with another person. He holds the end to my golden thread, but tonight it snapped. Tonight, he became the one that sacrificed everything for my cause, our cause.

The moment I hear the first explosion detonate behind me…I know we've succeeded.

I continue to dance, even as chaos erupts around me. I don't stop as I feel the heat lick at the skin on my back. I dance and wait for what I know is coming.

A second explosion rocks the stage. The patrons of the club that were at first unsure what was happening now scatter like ants. These men walk around with an air of arrogance as they pretend to be the elite alpha males of society, but in this moment, they run and scream like the little boys they truly are. They run, pushing each other out of the way and jerking their pants back up instead of facing the fear that stares at them now. They're cowards.

Money and status do not make you superior. An alpha is a man that doesn't follow the pack, a man that walks against the grain even if the miles are long and the roads treacherous. The title of alpha, the true leader, is not up for award or purchase but instead is born from the ashes of turmoil and the hunger that is perseverance though the darkness.

Finally, the music cuts out, and my eyes brave a glance at the mirrored windows above me. I can't see through the mirror, but I feel him. I watch as the third and final detonation explodes, and glass rains down around anyone left in the lower vicinity. Fire engulfs the building. It's at that moment that I move.

"Young! Dammit, Young." I can't see him through the smoke and haze, but I hear his voice as he calls for me.

"Reynolds?" I cough out his name as I struggle to breathe through the thick layer of smoke that coats the inside of my lungs as I inhale and threatens to burn me from the inside out. My eyes sting, and I'm blinded as I continue to move toward a voice that I've become familiar with over the last year.

I waited too long, but I needed to see the final explosion. For years I've gone to bed with the devil. I've sacrificed parts of myself that I will never get back, put myself through a hell I may never recover from. This is my vindication. I watched my parents leave this earth all those years ago and tonight they are exonerated as I watch the death of the man that set off a series of events that would change the course of our history. They searched, but they never found me, and yet I was with them all along. Never underestimate a woman with a hardened heart and a pocket full of retribution.

"Young, move your ass. We've got to get out of here. The second story could collapse on us at any minute. We haven't come this far just to die in the damn club, now, have we? I'm sure your parents would come back and haunt my ass if I let you die in here…now move." His large hand wraps around my arm and pulls me from the inferno when I can't force my feet to move.

Maybe the shock that I've lived in for the past fifteen

years is finally wearing off. Maybe this is some sort of delayed post-traumatic stress, or maybe I'm not sure what to do with myself after accomplishing what I set out to do all those years ago.

I'm not naive. This is only the beginning, but our battle has officially begun and tonight we raise our hands as the victors of round one.

We got him. We cut off the head of the snake, and now he will burn in Hell for the evil life that he chose to live here on earth.

Finally.

CHAPTER THREE
EMILY

"Aemilia Albani...so pretty. You look so much like the pictures we have of your mother. We probably would have found you sooner, but word on the street is that cyber-criminal Alex Straton has been blocking us on your behalf in our own damn database." I wear a pair of grey sweatpants and a black Bureau-issued pullover as I sit in a cold interrogation room and stare blankly at absolutely nothing on an empty wall.

I'm not speaking until Reynolds gets his ass in here. He knows better than that. I sure as hell am not speaking to this child-agent wannabe that can barely grow facial hair on his deceitful little baby face. The fact that he's seen my file and knows my birth name weirds me out. He says my name like I'm his favorite flavor of gelato and we're not sitting in a federal interrogation room.

Rationally, I understand that this idiot has no idea that Reynolds and I have been working together for the past year. But I don't have the capacity to deal with this tonight. Not while hours have passed and I'm still covered in the soot from the explosion and fire, we orchestrated to take down one of the most wanted criminals in the world. Really, they should be thanking me. Where's the fucking parade? I swear. Government.

"Don't speak of my mother. You don't have that right." I snap back frustrated and exhausted when I know better than to speak. I've hit my limit tonight, and I swear I just want to sleep for a year. Especially if there's not going to be a damn parade.

"Look, would you prefer me call you Emily? It's been a long night, but we've got to have some answers. Civilians were put in danger tonight, lives were lost. Our entire mission was hacked and rendered irrelevant as you managed to work across the country with one of the most intelligent criminal hackers this division has ever seen to bring down one of the most elusive mafia bosses in the country. How?" I snort through my nose; my failed attempt at holding back my laughter that I manage to turn into some awkward version of Animal Farm. This guy has got to be kidding me right now. The man-boy tips his metal chair backwards and threatens gravity as he leans back on the rear legs and crosses his arms over his chest. What I would give to see gravity retaliate right now.

I don't bother to turn as I hear the large door in the back of the room open, and the man I've been waiting for finally enter. About damn time. "Bennett, sit that chair on the fucking ground and at least pretend to be a grown ass adult. Who gave you clearance to enter this interrogation room, anyway? Just because your father was a respected member of this team, may he rest in peace, does not give you the right to do whatever the hell you want around here. You're a damn intern for God's sake, and this case is well beyond your non-existent pay grade. Go home, and do a better job washing your face in the morning. I think you left a smudge on your chin there."

Reynolds towers over the man-boy that sits across from me so arrogantly and causes his ball sack to shrivel up and retreat back inside of his body. I'd laugh if I could muster the energy, but I can't, not tonight – or this morning – or whatever time it is at this point.

I manage a smirk as lightning-fast Reynolds kicks his foot out and knocks the legs of the chair out from under Bennett before he can regain his balance. His arms flail as he scrambles up out of the chair and tries to save his own ass from hitting the hard concrete floor.

"Out."

He risks one more glance back at a man I've come to respect over the last year before huffing out a breath in frustration like the spoiled little brat I can already tell that he is, and exits through the door Reynolds walked in.

Taking the now abandoned seat across from me, Special Agent Alan Reynolds crosses his arms over his chest, much like Bennett, but far more effective as the muscles in his arms pop and stretch the material of his shirt. He's obviously showered, and clean in a fitted pair of khaki slacks and navy-blue polo. At least someone gets to use the damn shower around here.

Reynolds is handsome for an old guy; I'll give him that. He reminds me of my father, only a little less olive and a lot less tattooed. He's a bit too clean cut for my taste, but he's sexy in an *NCIS Gibbs* sort of way, if that's what you're into.

"We did it, Albani. Your parents would be so proud of you." His smile turns up the corner of his mouth, revealing straight, white teeth as he leans forward and props up casually on his elbows onto the metal table that separates us.

"Cameras?" I question, raising one single eyebrow. My eyes cut to the three cameras I spotted the moment I walked into this room. The only person I completely trust is currently sitting in a maximum-security prison. Reynolds may have proved his worth over the last year, and sure, he's earned my respect, but that doesn't take away from the fact that we still sit in an interrogation room and he's the cop and…hell, I'm a murderer.

"We're clear. You can speak freely here, Emily." He rubs the palm of his hand over his square jawline as he watches me.

I shrug in response, leaning back into my metal chair. By all outward appearances, I look relaxed. My devil-may-care attitude is shining through, but it's all for show; because on the inside, my stomach knots. In a moment that should be a celebration I wonder about my partner in crime. The guilt of knowing I sit here, free, and he is facing years in prison on my behalf begins to gnaw at me from the inside.

"I hope you understand that, regardless of what it took to get here, the sacrifices you made," he gives me a knowing look, but it doesn't hold any of the pity that I expected, instead it's laced with what I think is respect. "It was all worth this moment."

But was it? Is he reading my mind, or am I reading too much into this because I've gone and caught feelings for some guy I've never even met before? For years I've worn blinders, the successful completion of this mission and vindicating the death of my parents was my one goal. Yet, victory seems like a hollow, lonely place now that I've arrived.

Alan Reynolds was my parent's liaison with the FBI when their case was transferred from Italy to the United States. My parents were an anomaly; it's not common to have a husband-and-wife team working alongside each other undercover, and it's definitely not preferred. If anything, you're just painting a giant red target on your backs. Point proven by the fact that they were murdered together, in broad daylight.

My parents kept my birth a secret from everyone, understandably, for my protection. Reynolds didn't know anything about my existence until a little over a year ago when our paths crossed inside of the club that is now in a smoldering pile of rubble.

Bennett was right on one count: I look identical to my mother. When Reynolds was placed undercover as security in my club he took one look at my olive skin, moss green eyes and unique dimple, and began his own investigation.

Lucky for me, I had Alex. The moment he started digging, Alex and I were able to control the information he could and could not access on my background.

If Reynolds was willing to play nice, it's possible we could form a mutually beneficial arrangement.

I was anticipating his move, so it came as no surprise

to me when he slipped me a piece of paper with an address scribbled on it one night after I finished performing that asked me to meet him.

My absence went surprisingly unnoticed that night. I risked everything I'd worked for up until that point to meet with someone that I knew worked for an organization that would surely find me guilty of a slew of crimes I know I've committed over the years. But, instead of allowing my decisions to be driven by fear, I listened to my gut. My gut told me that if my parents trusted Reynolds, so could I, and I was right.

Initially, I gave him very little information, but after months of working together, I slowly brought him into the fold. Reynolds knew that the bureau was desperate, they'd been following the Adkins family for years without a substantial break in the case. I was their big break, and truth be known, I was Reynolds' ticket to a promotion.

According to the background research Alex performed on Reynolds, he found three different applications that were put in over the previous two years for the position of Director; all three times his promotion was denied. Humans are born of sin and inherently selfish as such. In his mind, Reynolds had just as much of a reason to keep my existence a secret as I did.

"Listen, Emily, I just came out of a debriefing on the case, and the Bureau is willing to cut you a deal. While the end result tonight is exactly as you orchestrated it, it's not necessarily how they saw it going down. We both knew that going into this." No, if it had gone exactly as I orchestrated it, Alex would be on a plane to New York and not behind bars in God knows where. But I don't say any of that out loud just yet.

"You proved something to yourself and to this department tonight. This case is far from over. Sure, Vito is dead, but someone else will step in and take his place. We're already seeing an increase in activity in our West coast division. Victor Adkins will be named the succeeding boss. We have to be prepared for that; the wheels are already in motion." The thought that there is a second Adkins out there in the world that is just as dangerous as the first makes my stomach turn.

"You and I both know your involvement with this case isn't squeaky clean. The fact that you commandeered their raid tonight, regardless of the outcome, pissed them the fuck off." I smile at the fact that a young, female dancer off the street and a self-taught genius cyber hacker somehow managed to outsmart an entire division of the FBI.

Using his finger to press on the cold metal of the table that he leans against to drive home his point. The seriousness in Alan's eyes bring me back to reality, wiping the smile from my face. "But, and this is a big ass but…the higher ups are willing to overlook that because of your background and the level of respect that this department had for your parents. They want you on our team."

I'm not sure what I expected to come from my involvement in taking down one of the most dangerous men in the world. I can't say that I ever really gave it much thought. The light at the end of my tunnel always ended with the death of Vito Adkins. On some level, I don't think I ever anticipated living long enough once that goal was accomplished to have a secondary plan. I always saw my mission as a suicide mission; I never once considered that I might actually make it out alive.

I have no formal education other than the online courses I've taken myself over the years. If anything, if I see the good ole' boys in blue I head in the opposite direction. My past is dirty and fraught with hard decisions that usually weren't of the legal variety. I pull my bottom lip into my mouth and gnaw on it while I consider what Alan is asking of me.

"Why me? I know there's a waiting list a mile long of men and women a hell of a lot more qualified than I am to join this department. I'm not qualified. I don't have the training. And hell, as if my security clearance can even get me into *Chuck E. Cheese*." I study Reynolds, looking for holes in his offer, trying to pinpoint exactly what his endgame is.

"You're right, on all counts. But, you have something that none of those other men or women have. Sure, we could probably find someone that has your grit, or your hunger. But, what you have that they don't? Anonymity – you're a ghost." My eyes shoot up to his in understanding.

"You want me to remain under?"

"We want you to maintain your identity as Emily Young. As far as anyone in that club tonight knew, you were dancing when the explosions began. You escaped from a catastrophic event and lived to tell about it. We want to train you, and then we want to transfer you." He looks at me expectantly.

"Transfer me? But where?" I've only ever lived in

New York. My parents were here for a reason. Vito was here, my mission has always been here. I've never had the means nor the inclination to leave.

"You'll go through a series of training courses here. As long as you pass all of the tests, which I'm confident you will, you will be transferred to a city a little smaller than New York. You're headed to the West Coast, just outside of a city called Carlton, there's a nice harbor there. We'll get you an apartment, you'll be paid and, of course, a government retirement plan and all that jazz. What do you say?"

"Do I get a choice?" My voice shakes without my permission.

Everything around me is changing so quickly.

"You take the job, and your records are wiped clean. You get to start fresh. You don't…well, I heard Sally Joe in cell block three likes brunettes." Winking is for wankers, and I'll be damned if Special Agent Alan Reynolds doesn't think he's got jokes as he throws in a wink for good measure at the end of his little sales pitch.

"One condition." I lean forward in my chair and put my elbows on my knees, clasping my hands together in front of me and watching my fingers intertwine.

"This isn't a damn negotiation, Emily. We're offering you a future. Take the offer."

"I said, one condition. Don't act like you don't need me. If you didn't need me, you wouldn't be sitting here dressing up this offer like it's a damn all expenses paid trip to Tahiti; which I mean, if you were curious, I would be all over. Instead, you would already be slapping handcuffs on my wrists." I test the boundaries of our relationship as I push for what I want. The one thing that would allow me to get through the training and the reality that I'm going to have to start my life over…again. I'm tired of reinventing myself…I'm just…tired.

"What is it?"

"Acquit Alexander Straton. I want him out. You know he was just as much a part of getting to Vito Adkins, if not more so than I was. Sure, I had the proximity, but he had access not even you had. If it wasn't for Alex, we'd both still be in that hell hole of a club doing God's know what, praying that somehow we'd get some sort of magical break that we both know damn well doesn't exist."

"I can't do it. I don't have the authority to make those decisions. If my superiors catch wind of either of our involvement with Straton, we're both getting fucked in the ass. You heard Bennett; the rumor mill is already flying. I risked my own reputation to get you this deal. Take it for what it is Emily, please." His voice turns slowly from frustrated to desperate. I get it, truly I do, but I need to do this for Alex. He sacrificed everything for me, and now I risk losing my only opportunity at a future to make sure that I save his.

"Bullshit." I lift my head and lock eyes onto Reynolds. He needs to understand that this isn't negotiable. What he thinks is a negotiation is a demand.

"You're impossible. Just like your mother. You're going to make a damn good agent Aemilia. Look, I'm being honest with you when I tell that I don't have the pull…yet."

My heart warms at the reference to my mother. I don't

know my mother as the ruthless agent that I've heard stories about. Sure, I've read her journal, but that's not the woman that tucked me into bed at night. That's not the same woman that kissed my bloody knee when I decided it was a good idea to try my hand at roller skating on the cement path at the boardwalk. I can dance, but don't try me with wheels on my feet.

"I feel like you're leaving out some imperative information here, Agent Reynolds." I tug on his open-ended words and hope to pull out the truth of what he's trying to say without actually giving life to words I don't think he's ready to speak just yet.

I watch as he shifts uncomfortably in the chair across from me. "It won't be today, it might not be a year from now, but trust my word when I tell you that Straton's story doesn't end behind bars." Sifting through the puzzle pieces of his words, I try to decide whether or not his promises are enough.

Ultimately, I guess they have to be.

Reynolds is the only reason my ass isn't in prison. Alex is already behind bars, and if this is my chance to get him out, I'll take it.

"When do I report?"

CHAPTER FOUR
ALEX

I've been indecently searched, stripped down and handed a standard issue prisoners' uniform. This isn't the first time I've been arrested. I've been cuffed for petty crimes before, back when I was still considered a juvenile and didn't give a shit about the consequences of my actions. This time is different. This is the first time I've been arrested for a federal offense – something serious enough that I know I'm going away for a while. Getting caught wasn't an option I considered, I'm too good for that.

I was caught because I allowed them to catch me. Em needed a diversion. Reynolds was leading an entire unit into that club, and if we could split the resources on the case, they had a better chance of succeeding. I made myself a target for the Bureau's cybercrime division, and then I baited them. I put a target on my back and led them to the shooting range.

If they were tied up raiding a hacker that was penetrating the Federal database and seemingly a threat to our national defense, well, they might not notice when we slipped into the club's online security files and created a series of timed explosions that would take down a mafia boss, and just maybe they might be so concerned with said hacker that I could also plant a bug that would wipe any footage of the event before it was uploaded and backed-up onto their system, protecting both Emily and Reynolds if there was potential for there to be footage that linked the two in a manner that might not be totally above board.

I sacrificed myself for her mission, and I don't regret that. I look hot as fuck in these orange scrubs anyway, if I do say so myself.

"You get one phone call. Don't remember the number, too bad. They don't answer by the third try, so sad. This call will be timed and recorded. The line will cut out when your time is up. Do you understand?" A local yuppie cop with the Jefferson County penitentiary that clearly has little man syndrome or some shit stalks me, barking orders as he hands me a phone.

The county jail is only my temporary home, my lovely new friend from the Bureau dropped me off here for daycare until they could move me to my permanent residence. I'm getting an upgrade just as soon as they can get a transfer lined up for me, which won't be tonight. Their hands are currently tied up, something about a bombing at an elite gentleman's club that had ties to the mafia. I wouldn't know anything about that though. I smirk to myself as I take the phone from the prison guard and dial a number I know by heart. The one person that I know will answer on the first call no matter what time it is.

The phone rings twice before I hear the call connect with a *click*. I clear the nerves that appear out of nowhere from my throat before I speak. "Reid, man, you there?"

"Yeah Alex, I'm here. What the fuck man?" Reid graduated with his degree and pre-admittance to, of all places, the FBI training academy two weeks ago. I couldn't attend his graduation because getting a job with the FBI and being best friends with a cybercriminal don't really go hand-in-hand. I get it. It's been too long since I've spoken to my brother, and I know these aren't necessarily the conditions he wants to hear from me under.

I rub my hand over my face and stare down at the tattoos that cover the skin on both of my arms. In the intensity of this moment, I try to focus on the stories of strength and perseverance that the art on my arms tell, instead of the anger that I can feel radiating through the phone from my best friend.

"They found it. They confiscated everything. Raided my apartment. Shit, I'm in deep." This call is being timed and recorded. I can't risk getting him into trouble, and I don't want to risk digging myself into a hole deeper than the one I'm already in, but this call was a necessary evil for me.

"Dammit, Alex. What did they find? What are you talking about?" Reid's voice is low, like maybe he isn't at home after all, wouldn't surprise me. Reid is a man whore if there ever was one. He can't help it, he came here that way – confident, arrogant and with a body that will make a straight man look twice. The women eat him up like candy, and he's first in line to take them to the candy shop. I don't blame him.

I can't wait to meet the woman that brings him to his knees one day. That'll be a cold day in hell – I'm looking forward to it, I'll even bring my jacket.

Not willing to give Reid details that it's better he doesn't know, I skip right to the point of my call. "I need your help. Anything you can do. I don't think I'm going home anytime soon, Reid. My dad, he'll be alone back at his place. I don't trust him by himself. I've been keeping tabs on him, had him all wired up with surveillance, but hell, I think they took that too. I can't keep eyes on him anymore. Can you check in on him? Just make sure he doesn't hurt himself or some crazy shit." Reid's the only person that understands my fucked-up relationship with my father. He's the only person on this planet I trust enough to make sure that my father isn't dead from his own actions when and if I ever get out of here.

"Yeah, I'll keep an eye on him. How long, you think?" I hear the sound of a vehicle door closing somewhere in the distance as Reid speaks, the exasperation is heavy in his voice.

He loves me, but he doesn't fully understand the choices that I made to get to this point because I haven't been able to tell him. I refuse to put that burden on his shoulders, not when he's meant for so much more. Reid was born a hero; he was meant for a life of greatness. He's disappointed in me and not being able to explain myself makes this conversation that much harder. He wanted me to follow his path; what he doesn't realize is that, even after all these years, we're much more alike than we are different.

The cop stands too close to me, I can hear his heavy breathing in my ear, and his eyes warn me that my time is almost up. He's about four inches shorter than me and is really starting to piss me the fuck off with his shitty attitude.

"Years. I gotta go, Reid. I love you man." I jam my finger over the call ending button on the phone, shoving it in his face and brushing past him, I accidently bump him with my shoulder – whoops – to find my place on the bench in the holding cell that I'll fight to sleep on tonight.

Tomorrow, I face my future. It was never supposed to end like this. I'm too smart to waste my talents rotting away in a prison cell and too skilled to get caught.

For years I watched Reid make stupid ass decisions chasing women and swore that would never be me. Yet here I sit. I gave up everything for long legs and silky, dark brown hair. A body that's so fluid it moves like water through a stream in the middle of the forest and green eyes the color of moss. I bet she smells like fresh flowers. If she were lost in a fairytale, I'm sure little dwarfs and tiny animal creatures would go to war for her attention.

Just like that I'm hard and unable to do a damn thing about it.

I can't help but think about her smart mouth and steely determination to succeed at any cost. She looks like a fairytale, but she's not a princess. She doesn't need someone to swoop in and save her. She's her own damn hero, and I'm the fool that cleared the path to make a way for her, even if she would have eventually made her own way herself.

Instead, I made sure she lived to tell the story. I made sure that she had a future. When she didn't care whether she lived or died, I made sure that she was given a life. Many years ago, her life was stolen from her; her innocence taken without a second thought. It's time for her rebirth, it's her turn. I ate the poisoned apple so that she would have a chance at a future, and now I accept the consequences knowing that it was worth it. I would save her again and again, and it would always be worth it. She came to me a ghost, and for years to come I welcome her haunting my dreams. She's not the nightmare she thinks she is; she's my every fantasy.

-o-
EMILY

It's so cold, I swear my blood is minutes from freezing in my veins. Hypothermia is not the way I'm going out. I stay low, crawling near the ground as the muscles in my thighs beg for a reprieve. It's nearly impossible to see anything through the pitch-black darkness that surrounds me, but I guess that's the point. I fight to maintain my focus and try to hone in on my other senses as I approach my target.

I hunt him like a predator stalking its prey. These are my favorite games to play because if you lose you die, and dead has never really been flattering on anyone, so, I would prefer if it wasn't me. He can't sense how close I am because I'm faster, quieter, and I have an innate ability to anticipate his every move even without my sight.

I stall my approach, patiently waiting for the perfect moment to attack. I'm so close that I can hear his breathing in time with the way I know his heart races on adrenalin. He can't see me, but his body has already accepted his fate. I've been doing this too long. I might not be a trained assassin, but I'm skilled at survival.

I count back from five in my head and then I make my move, giving away my location milliseconds before my knee slams into the back of his leg. His large body crashes to the floor. He's at least a foot taller than me, but size only matters in sex and explosives. Well, that and wine; nobody wants a tiny glass of wine.

I straddle his broad body in the darkness, restraining his arm behind his back but not pulling so hard that the bone snaps. Immediately, I disarm him of his weapon, and slide the blade of my knife until it almost touches the skin of his neck. I finally take a breath. I fill my lungs with the oxygen I was unintentionally depriving them of and make a mental note to work on my breathing techniques. A smile tilts the corner of my lips as I realize how easily I took down my opponent. He knew I was coming for him, but I didn't give him time to react. I won.

"Lights on." Someone in the distance calls out. The training facility is illuminated instantly. I don't move immediately as I work through taking calming breaths and keeping my hands steady.

"Young, get the fuck off of Bennett before your knife slips and you kill someone." Reynolds walks up to where I still hold Bennett down on the floor and smacks my shoulder with a knowing grin. Bennett sucks in air as the blade of my knife inches closer to his throat with my unintentional movement…whoops.

"I like you from this angle, Young." A sneer of disgust replaces the smile on my face as he speaks. The Adam's apple in his throat bobs and touches my blade as he teases me and risks his life. He's lucky that I've come to value the career that I'm building. I kind of like playing with bombs and deadly weapons all day.

The natural instinct of my fingers itch to close the centimeter that separates this life from the next, but I don't. I show self-control and restraint, which is a huge fucking feat if I do say so myself. And I do. I continue to train and perfect my skills because someone else sacrificed their freedom for me to be here. Alex gave me a future, and I refuse to waste it, especially not on a drain on society like Bennett.

I lean forward, careful not to move my knife, but my thighs continue to straddle Bennett. I lay my torso flat over his back making sure that he can feel my breasts press up against his spine until my mouth hovers just over the shell of his ear.

"You're a fucking pussy, Bennett." I whisper the words just before spinning, leaping off of him and harnessing my weapon. I'm careful to make eye contact with Reynolds, who watched the entire exchange, and roll my eyes as I walk away. I don't know what it is about that guy, but I hate him. I've been around enough assholes to know a good egg from a bad one, and Bennett is as slimy as they come.

I've been training for months, and according to Alan Reynolds, who was just named Director of our division of the Bureau, I should be prepared to transfer sooner rather than later. I know Alex was moved to a high-profile prison recently and sentenced to ten years, which honestly, isn't so bad in the grand scheme of things. However, Reynolds has the pull that he needs now to get him out of there, we just have to work out the specifics; easier said than done. Reynolds keeps reminding me that we have to do things above board going forward, and that's been a difficult concept for me to grasp.

The FBI wanted me because of my unique, background, for lack of a better word. A snort escapes from my nose as I chuckle to myself, still in disbelief over the fact that the freaking Federal Bureau of Investigation wanted to hire me.

I am not formally trained, but my lack of fear and unrelenting determination shines through my actions as I continue to master every obstacle that's set out before me. I don't follow a standard set of rules, I make my own. They continue to test me, and with each new challenge I'm presented, I excel. Not because I have brute strength or hyper intelligence. I excel because there is something inside of me that continues to propel me forward at full force.

I refuse to slow down.

I refuse to lose.

Now I have even more of a reason to push myself. I thought I was prepared to lose Alex. My heart is made of stone; black and hardened from a lifetime of trials and disappointments. I don't feel remorse for my actions. I don't feel guilt. I get the job done, and I move on. I don't long for love because my hope for a future died the day I lost my parents. My soul is hollow.

So, when I found out Alex was going to sacrifice himself for our mission, I didn't consider that it might have an adverse effect on me. I understand that our actions have consequences, and those are consequences he was willingly prepared to accept.

Except now I have this ache in my chest that I can't get rid of. I scroll through pages of emails and text message threads that have long since staled.

I vowed the day I stood alone in my parents' bedroom that I would be brave. To me, bravery meant a life of solitude. In my quest for revenge, I unknowingly exposed a part of myself that I wasn't even aware existed.

Alexander Straton didn't just penetrate my fortress of darkness and loneliness; he scaled the walls and snuck inside without warning, and dammit if he wasn't taken from me before I had the opportunity to explore what those feelings might mean.

CHAPTER FIVE
ALEX

I lie comfortably on the luxurious mattress of my master bedroom; also known as the cardboard cot of the prison cell I'm supposed to share with some guy I have yet to meet. Apparently, the man that was in here before me was released just days prior to my transfer, so I'm in between roommates at the moment.

Suits me; it's been nice being able to just have some silence, even if it's only temporary. Prison is uncomfortable, and rightfully so. I hate the judicial system, but I'm not going to say that I don't deserve to be here. I broke the law and then allowed myself to get caught. I'm exactly where I'm supposed to be, technically speaking. It sure as hell isn't an all-inclusive resort. We're herded like cattle, fed sub-par meals – if you can even call it food and spend all of our time unharmoniously together. Don't even get me started on the damn shared shower situation. It's a miserable existence.

I have never been a huge fan of large groups of people, it makes me anxious. I spent most of my time prior to my arrest living alone in my small apartment. My only consistent companions being my computer and a woman that lived halfway across the country. You would think that, over time, my memories would begin to fade, but the solitude and time alone has only increased the frequency and intensity of my thoughts of her.

Not a night passes when I don't fall asleep thinking of the curves of her body; what it might be like to run my hands over her smooth, olive skin. Would she smell like the soft dew in the forest after a rain? Would her eyes be greener in person, brighter? Is she thinking of me the way I'm dreaming of her, or was I just a means to an end?

I can't find it in myself to believe that she was only using me for my ability to hack into a government database undetected. Sure, in the beginning, we had a business agreement. We worked together for a common goal, and we made a damn good team. But the longer we worked together, the more in depth our conversations became. Minutes turned to hours on the phone that turned into late nights and early mornings. Stolen moments between the responsibilities that held her captive.

The way her mind works is incredible. She is an exact match to my level of intelligence. She challenges me, which I never thought possible. Where I know coding and data, she is able to work through problems meticulously as they present themselves without bias. Her thought process is so complex, and the details to her solutions are so intricate. She's hot as hell, but her brain...her brain is sexy as fuck. Like myself, she has no formal training. Her abilities are those that she was either born with or that she taught herself out of survival and necessity.

Emily lost everything as a child. At least I had my mother until I was a teenager. I was almost an adult before my world fell apart. For the most part, I had a semi-normal upbringing. I can't fathom the thought process of a seven-year-old that watched the murder of her parents, the only family that she knew. Then to find out that they were undercover agents with the Italian government. Instead of running scared to the police, she went into hiding and developed a plan to rise above her circumstances. She walked into the face of danger willing to sacrifice everything to avenge the death of her parents.

Emily committed her life to ridding the world of an evil man. Not only did she succeed, but she lived to tell about it. Emily Young is meant for so much more in life, and if my sole purpose on this earth was to be here so that her life was not cut short, I have succeeded.

"Get the fuck off of me!" A man's voice carries from the hallway, interrupting my thoughts. Our cells are unlocked because it's time for grub, but I chose to stay in. It's a fine line for me between peace and starvation.

"What is it, pretty boy? You can't handle the heat? What'd you do? Steal a candy bar from the local gas station? Push your girlfriend a little too hard, and she cried to her daddy?" Initiation. It's a way of establishing a pecking order. They tried that shit on me when I arrived, but I'm nobody's bitch. I knew enough to know to swipe a spoon on my way through the mess hall during my first meal and create something I could defend myself with. You gotta be smarter than what you're working with, and that continues to hold true even inside of these prison walls.

The "welcome crew" assholes. They pushed, I pushed back, and all hell broke loose. It's possible I sent one of their buddies to the infirmary with a gash that required twenty-seven stitches. Maybe that wasn't me, totally up to interpretation, and I'm not pleading guilty to a damn thing.

I pulled the battery backup from the cameras before the fight was shut down, and when they came to question us about weapons…well, even inmates know that snitches get stitches, and by stitches we mean an unmarked pine box.

Because most of these guys are true loners, nobody on the outside cares if they live or die. Their families have long since given up on them. They go all in, a fight to the death; because hell if they have anything left to live for.

I roll off my back and stand up from my bunk, curious enough to want a visual on the new guy and what's about to go down. I'm not typically a violent man. I don't condone hurting innocents for the hell of it. I mean, we're in prison so I guess none of us are really innocent. However, something in the guy's voice makes me think he's not in here for stashing little Cindy Lou's body in the trunk of a Lincoln town car and sinking it in the county lake.

I walk to the entrance of my humble abode and look down the long corridor that is the one entrance and exit to our sleeping-living-hellhole, I mean cell block. Toward the end, near the entrance, it's easy to make out a group of men, probably five or six of them, banding together to create a semi-circle of sorts.

My best guess is that they've got the new guy pinned between them and the wall. It's the exact scenario I was faced with not long ago. Original, this group.

Stepping back into my cell, I grab my makeshift weapon, turn around and follow the voices that continue to escalate with intensity into the hallway. Dammit, I hate confrontation, but something in that guy's voice, I can't let it go. He may be a badass prepared to take down a team of inmates with shitty attitudes, or he may be a guy that was in the wrong place at the wrong time. But now, he's about to get his ass handed to him. Five against one on the playground might get you put in time out, five against one on the prison block will land you in a hospital bed, if you're lucky.

"I don't want trouble. Just leave me the fuck alone."

I walk up quietly behind the group that's currently preoccupied with their childish bullying. I smile to myself; they don't even know I'm behind them right now. And this – this is how these assholes got caught in the first place.

I watch as their captive's eyes dart wildly from one man to the next, and finally land on mine. His ice blue eyes hold an innocence, and a nervousness, that I recognize. He's in here, but he's not like these men. I nod once as he watches me, trying to convey that we're on the same team. I'm going to need him to figure that shit out real quick because I'm about to double his chances of sleeping in a bed tonight and not a hospital room.

I move, finally exposing myself as I jam my makeshift weapon into the rib cage of one of the inmates, and twist it, pulling it out covered in blood that probably has fifteen different diseases in it. But, now is not the time to dwell on spreading infections and hygiene.

My friend surprises me as I watch a familiar rage fill his eyes, and he manages to take down a second attacker with his bare hands, putting him to sleep on the floor next to his bleeding cohort. Chanting from other inmates not involved with the situation brings unwanted attention to us. The remaining crew break away before all of our asses end up in solitary confinement. If I'm being honest, it's not an idea that I'm entirely against.

I turn, quickly, and using the same tactic I had previously, I begin pulling battery backups from the two cameras that I know caught a visual of what just went down. I reset them before closing them back up again.

Not that the guards would say anything either way. I would just prefer there not be visual evidence of the assault I just inflicted. Probably won't bode well when I'm up for parole. I realized after the last time that these officers are well aware of what happens on this block. They are familiar with who are and are not the troublemakers in their group. If one of these assholes ends up sliced up and needs a few stitches, well they probably had that shit coming anyway.

Not saying a word, I slip my weapon into the band of my fancy orange pants that sit low on my hips and pretend to ignore the wetness I feel from the blood of another human that now touches my skin and threatens the reemergence of the minimal contents of my stomach. I will have to figure out a way to get it cleaned up later without drawing attention to myself. I walk back through the entrance of my cell just as the familiar sound of the sliding metal door begins to creak open and the guards file in for damage control.

I swear sometimes they wait it out just to see if we kill each other off before they decide to show up.

"Charles, you get lost or something?" One of the officer's yells at the inmate that I just saved from an inevitable beatdown. He stands partially stunned and mostly misplaced in the middle of the corridor.

"No sir. Block c-three?"

"Get there, before you get lost...again." The officer threatens him with his tone knowingly and turns to address the other inmates that continue to watch on, enraptured in the drama surrounding them. There isn't much entertainment in prison, the slightest disturbance has most of these grown ass men watching on like it's *Days of Our Lives*.

"We might have heard whispers of a disturbance, but my IT guy says he can't confirm or deny anything because the damn battery backups went out again on these cameras." I can't see him directly from where I lay back against the single pillow on my cot, but I can't help it when my lips turn up and a grin spreads across my face. I gotta get my kicks somewhere.

"Bunk up boys, this unit is locked down until dinner. Don't be assholes, and if you kill each other clean up after yourselves. I get tired of having to get the blood cleaned off of the floor every damn day. If you're going to fight, do us all a favor and finish each other off so we can lower our head count." The officer finishes lecturing us just as the man with the blue eyes stops in the doorway to my jail cell.

He's tall, almost as tall as I am, but a little broader where I'm a little bit more lean. His hair is jet black, and his eyes are this iridescent, ice blue color. Kind of reminds of the blue freezer popsicles that we used to eat when we were kids. Ah man, now I want popsicles.

Hard to tell, but he looks a couple of years younger than I am. Despite our obvious differences, we do have one thing in common; though his eyes hold the same pent-up aggression I walk around here with on a daily basis, neither of us look like we really belong here.

"Charles?" I lift my chin slightly in acknowledgement but don't offer to stand from the bottom bunk I'm sitting on. My ass was here first, he can leap like a gazelle onto the top bunk every day. Hell if I'm falling off that bed and catching concrete to the face in the middle of the night.

"No. Do not call me Charles." His blue eyes turn from a dull aggression to a fuel lit fire within seconds. Huh.

Sensing his change in demeanor, I sit up on the bed, throwing my legs to the side, over the edge. I lean forward, placing my elbows on my knees, and I observe him with a mix of curiosity and irritation. I watch as the automatic cell door closes and locks at this back, solidifying the fact that this is officially the man that will watch me shit for the foreseeable future. "Okay, *not Charles*, I just saved your ripe ass out there so calm your estrogen. What name you would prefer I call you?"

"Ryan. My name is Ryan Walsh."

"Alex Straton. Welcome to block c-three. Take the top bunk. Keep it clean, keep it quiet and don't rock the bed when you jack off."

CHAPTER SIX
EMILY
ONE YEAR LATER...

The beat drops, and Julia Michael's raspy voice filters in through the speakers that hide in the walls of this building, singing a song about Issues that is eerily parallel to my own life. I hear her, but the words are all but drowned out as I'm immersed in an array of color from the moment my silver stilettos hit the polished veneer of the stage.

I'm finally dancing again, and this stage, well, it's surprising how much it feels like home. My skin tingles and my senses come alive as the room full of men, and even some women, watch on in dark corners. I use the rhythm of the music and the dazzling display of colors I see to weave a story for them with my body.

My hips rock back and forth smoothly, the bass hits and a burst of green flashes before my eyes. I stretch my body to its limits and slide down the pole that is my partner-in-crime most nights.

The creepy men, the ones that take it too far with their greedy hands and their nasty words, those are the faces I see when I shoot at the range. I've perfected the ability to hit my desired target from multiple distances and angles.

But, the gentlemen that are just here to relax after a taxing day in their high-rise offices, or the upper-crust couples that come in together for a show they can't get at home, I get a high from the way their eyes watch me. I understand what my body does for them in a way that most don't, because I like to watch too.

Men, women, couples, doesn't matter, as long as it's consensual. I don't have a preference either way. Our bodies are works of art. After being in this industry for so long, I've learned to appreciate my own sexuality and that of the men and women I'm surrounded by.

I'm in a different club, in a different state, halfway across the country. But oddly, it feels exactly the same. Well, except for the knife that's strategically hidden behind the seam of my black fishnet tights; or maybe the smoke bomb nestled comfortably between my breasts. They're barely contained tonight, but the black lace corset I wear actually covers up more than most of the dancers in tonight's show.

Oh, and the teensy tiny earbud that's fits snugly in my left ear. It remains silent and free of static, for now. I may be a trained agent, but my team and I have an understanding. I can't focus on the music when they clammer in my ear, so the sound is cut for the three minutes that I dance. During that time of silence, I give myself a moment to think of the man that I still dance for, even today, over a year after I last heard his voice – I dance for him.

I warned him. I told him to get out, but it was too late.

It's not like he would have listened to me anyway. He was never planning to abandon our mission, even if that meant he would spend time in prison. I don't know if I was so consumed with taking out Vito that I didn't see it before, or if the realization has just become clear with the hours I've spent going through our emails and text messages; but as I look back, it's obvious, he was always planning to sacrifice himself for me.

Sure, I issued the warning, but deep down, I was selfish. I was consumed by my need for revenge, I didn't devote the thought I should have to his sacrifice.

I have so many questions that continue to go unanswered as they run through my mind on a constant cycle of repeat. What if we had stopped sooner? What if we hadn't pushed the boundaries so far that night? The Bureau had a unit at the club that night, fully prepared to take Vito down. But, would he have slipped through their hands again, just as he had so many times before?

Was it all worth it? I don't know. I was so sure that it was in the beginning, but the longer the days drag out, and the hours add up, the more I wish I could talk to Alex and ask him those questions. If I could just see him in the flesh and know that he's okay and that he forgives me for my selfishness, I might be able to forgive myself.

Director Reynolds is working in New York while my team and I work undercover here. He assures me that he's finalizing an agreement that will free Alex, but it's taking too long, and I'm getting antsy as fuck.

Until Death

I miss him. How do you miss a man you never met? I don't know the correct answer, but my heart continues to hurt every time his memory crosses my mind, which is far more than I'm emotionally prepared to admit.

The song ends and as the colors clear, I risk one final glance at the packed house of the club. Another employee passes me as she hustles onto the stage to pick up my tips. I'm one of the lead dancers here. Just as Reynolds suspected, my reputation followed me. I don't crawl on the floor to pick up money. Not that it's below me, it's not; even if I am getting a steady paycheck by way of the U.S. Government now. The club doesn't allow dancers to pick up their own tips, it's not the image they want to portray in this fancy establishment. This isn't a strip joint where the patrons shove dollar bills in the thongs of the dancers. No, we dance for the elite, the high rollers, and we're expected to act as such.

I step behind the deep purple, velvet curtain and am abruptly stopped as a large hand wraps around my wrist. My first instinct is always to fight, but instead I inhale quietly, stop in my tracks, and don't move, assessing the situation before I decide if we're talking or killing. It's a skill I'm still trying to perfect. Various scenarios play out in my mind on hyper speed as my lungs are filled with a familiar scent of leather and expensive cologne.

"Sully know you're back here, Riko?" I speak into the darkness, choosing my words carefully.

"I want a dance." His steel cut words aren't a question, they're a demand that is not up for negotiation.

"You know I don't dance for the help. You tryin' to get us both killed?" I snap back at him. His hand remains firmly wrapped around my wrist as my eyes dart to the corners of the darkness that engulfs us. Music filters from the stage as another dancer prepares for her moment in the spotlight.

"Now. Five minutes. The leopard room." With that he releases his hold and turns away from me. He leaves me standing alone behind the thick curtain, questioning what the hell is going down as the speaker in my ear remains silent.

-o-

Five minutes. I take my time as I walk through the dark backstage of the club. The main room is expansive and mostly open. It's quieter than usual back here. Most nights the prep and dressing room is humming with activity; girls gossiping, hair being blown out and styled every which way, and naked women walking around as costume fittings and changes occur right out in the open – there's no modesty in dancing. Private dressing rooms aren't a luxury we're afforded in a place like this.

It's late though, and we're nearing last call. Most of the girls have already been released to go home for the night. I stop at my locker and grab a tube of lipstick, carefully touching up the deep red color that contrasts against my olive skin and solid black attire for the evening, before turning to walk back out down the long hallway that leads to the private rooms.

"Em Cat. Where you headed to this late, beautiful?" His accent is thick, a transplant from Jersey. But tonight his voice is lazy, like he's been sampling the product that runs through this club like water. I feel his approach from behind in the dark corridor and count my blessings when he doesn't immediately try to reach out and touch me. No one calls me Em Cat. I hate pet names, they're cheesy and degrading, especially when they come from someone like Anderson Sullivan.

He runs this club, the *Alley Cat*. Sullivan isn't a boss like Vito Adkins. Vito was old school mafia; he kept his hands heavily involved in every piece of the family business. Keep your friends close and your enemies closer kind of thing. Control was the name of his game, and that's what made him so difficult to nail down. He knew everyone and saw everything. After Vito's death, just as Reynolds predicted, Victor Adkins wasted no time stepping into his role as the new boss of the Adkins crime family. However, Victor is what most would consider a new age boss. Victor grew up in the business, meaning he grew up in the money. He and his family, by extension, are accustomed to a certain lifestyle.

That lifestyle is more about who he can get to do the dirty work for him while he and his family live it up at the country club. Sure, he runs his investment company that's a neat and tidy cover for the money he filters through various family bank accounts. But he's not sitting at the top of the tower physically in the clubs he uses to produce that money. No, that's reserved for men like Anderson Sullivan. The narcissists with hyper inflated egos that think they're family because they're paid well by the boss. Sully isn't top shelf, he's not even the second tier. That doesn't change the fact that he thinks he is. I've been inside these clubs long enough to know that blood is the only family in mafia. Even then it's not always enough.

"Mr. Sullivan, it's a nice evening, no?" I address him professionally, because even though he's told me time and time again that he would prefer if I call him by his street name, Sully, I don't risk pissing him off for insubordination. I've seen other dancers smacked down for doing the same when he wasn't in the right mood, and I tend to get pissy when a man thinks he can put his fist near my face. It's better for my cover and for everyone involved in this mission, really, that I play my part and try to stay out of trouble.

"It's a gorgeous evening from where I'm standing." I've stalled my progress as I stand in the middle of the dimly lit hallway and feel the full height of his body just inches from my back. His breath fans my neck and the distinct scent solidifies my earlier suspicions. He's high, and maybe even a little drunk, which means he's even more dangerous to me than usual. He runs a manicured finger down my arm and goosebumps pop up on my skin, no doubt giving him the wrong message.

"You got time for me tonight, Em Cat?" His inquiry doesn't take me by surprise, I was expecting it. The night is close to over, and before long, the sun will break the horizon. It's not uncommon for the dancers to meet a client in one of the private rooms. They're meant for clientele that want a little more one-on-one attention. Theoretically, we dance for them, and they watch, hands off. Each dancer uses their own discretion though. If the client is willing to pay up, money can buy whatever they want, no limits.

The private rooms are where most of the dancers make their income, and how much money they make is up to them. Cash doesn't directly change hands to the dancers, and Sullivan takes his cut off the top. So, the more we give, the more we make; and the more we make, the fatter his pockets are. If the women in this club choose to sell their bodies to make an extra buck, he doesn't give a damn.

There isn't a square inch of this facility that isn't visible on one of cameras this place is loaded down with. Sullivan wants eyes on every nook and cranny but, lucky for me, I have an IT team in my back pocket that, while they are no Alex Straton, they're good enough they can switch footage for me before Sully gets a peek at it if need be. I dance for my clients at their request, nothing more. I don't want their hands on me. I'm not going to say I haven't been tempted a time or two, I have; but when it comes down to it, they aren't the man I want touching me, so I back out. It's never been an issue.

Right now, though, Sully wants a private dance, and I have somewhere I needed to be two minutes ago. My earpiece remains silent, and that worries me. Two doors down is the leopard room, and I've got someone I need to exchange words with.

"I've got a client scheduled that I'm about to be late for." I answer quickly, short and to the point. I don't have time to play his games right now.

"That's too bad, isn't it? I watched your performance tonight. You were incredible. I really wanted to see more of it, that's why I came looking for you. I want to hear you purr for me." The distinct taste of bile rises in my throat. Pretty sure I just threw up a little in my mouth.

I've danced for Sullivan before, at his request. It's all

part of the job, and I knew that coming into this. He's mid-forties with a wife and kids. He wears suits that stink like cheap Italian cigars, and his greasy black hair is combed back slick to his head with enough oil to crank an engine. I'm positive the man has stock in black hair dye. At his age, it's not possible that his hair is that dark naturally. Not to mention, he's doesn't have one shred of Italian heritage in his genetics. I know, I've looked.

Having a government database at your fingertips does have its perks, even though I'm not quite as efficient with my ability to siphon out information as Alex. I'm fairly certain my access is limited to what they allow me to see, where Alex never allowed measly things like access security points to get in his way.

I'm not one of Sullivan's play toys, he likes them blonde, and thank Jesus for that. But, when he's high or he's had too much to drink, he'll request a dance so he can masturbate as he watches me. I can't blame the guy really, I'm damn good. I will take that over my other options any day. Watching him touch himself is hardly a hardship after dealing with Vito for all those years. Vito had at least twenty years on Sully, and well, things change over time. The mighty fall. By fall, I mean the only way that Rome is going to rise again is in the form of a little blue pill that's taken so often it may as well be a damn daily vitamin.

"Right, but I have a client. It's big money, Mr. Sullivan. You know I will save a dance for you next time though." I pull my innocent act and smile up at him sweetly, hoping that he's just lit enough to let me off the hook this time. I need for him to make a hasty exit back to his suite to request one of his regulars and leave me alone to attend to my own business.

"You know I don't mind sharing Em, especially if it's the *economical* choice, I have options. I wanted you tonight, but I can make a concession. Save me a dance for next time." The fingers that were running down my arm now wrap around my bicep as he squeezes too hard and yanks me towards his body. His free hand runs over my hip and grips the exposed cheek of my ass as he squeezes hard enough that I'll be marked tomorrow. "Go in there and make it worth it Kitty Cat. I want to see the money that you worked for." His words are ground out over his teeth. He uses the hand that grips my bicep to push me forward, propelling me down the hallway as I try to right myself before stumbling to the floor in my heels.

Maintain your cover for the greater good of society.

Someone else sacrificed their freedom so that you could do great things for humanity, which, right this minute, is frankly despicable, but I digress.

I repeat my mantra over and over again in my head as I calm my internal rage and wait for Sullivan to take his leave.

He turns and walks down the hallway, toward the set of spiral steps that lead to his private suite on the upper level of the club, without giving me a second glance. He wants his hit, and he wants it now. The fact I'm unable to give that to him in this moment means he's going to find someone that can.

My stage dancing brings in enough tips that I don't get questioned when my private dances are just that, dances.

Looks like someone is angry that they don't get a turn tonight though, so he's making sure that I know I better make it worth it. That's not going to be easy considering the man I'm dancing for tonight isn't a paying customer at all.

I stop in front of the leopard room and knock twice. My eyes cut up to the camera on my left, and I signal with my opposite hand that it's time to cut over the footage.

I don't wait for him to answer the door, I know he's waiting for me. Instead, I turn the handle on the knob, having given my team enough time to take over the recording, and I step into dark room.

CHAPTER SEVEN
EMILY

I walk slowly into the open room only lit by the LED lighting system that pops rays of color off of the black walls like something out of an early eighties dance movie. In an obvious attempt to keep with the leopard theme, the streams of light reflect a mixture of oranges, yellows and whites. A mashup of generic dance music filters through surround sound speakers and threatens to divert my attention from the purpose of this unscheduled meeting.

What we're doing right now is off script, we're not supposed to meet like this, not here. I'm not so concerned with the threat of danger for us, because we're both trained to defend ourselves. I'm more concerned with what it could mean for our mission if we were to get caught. This meeting holds significance, I just have to find out what it is.

There's a pole in the center of the room that sits on a

wooden platform elevated just off of the ground, creating a makeshift stage for the dancers to perform. Across the room is a small black leather couch meant to give the dancer and client additional room to spread out, if the need arises. A matching leather chair sits directly in front of the stage that is now to my right as I continue my entry.

I see his dark form sitting in the chair as I saunter past him, but I don't acknowledge him yet. Instead, I walk to the stage and gripping the pole with my hand I begin to dance. Not my usual performance, but something slower, something less likely to distract my mind completely.

"I've got to head out, Emily. I've been called out, and I don't know why." He watches me with his eyes, unmoving, as he speaks. He wants me, they all want me, but he doesn't touch because he values his balls.

"What? No, it's too dangerous." I falter, my words a surprised stutter as they leave my mouth.

"Direct orders, I'm out."

I stop my movements abruptly as the reality of what he's saying hits me. In that moment, I make a decision to place our safety and the safety of this mission in the hands of our technical team. If these cameras expose us, somebody might die tonight; bets are it's not me.

"Direct orders? I'm lead on this mission, and I sure as fuck didn't tell you to break your cover and leave half of our team exposed." I walk towards him in the dark, his features becoming more prominent the closer I get.

He's wearing jeans tonight that fit his thick muscular thighs and stretch the material to its limits as he sits in the chair, unphased by my approach. His black button-down shirt is pulled taught over his carved muscles and the sleeves are rolled up to his forearms, exposing his thick veins. He's a machine, his body toned and hardened, ready to go to war at any given moment.

There is only one other person besides the fucking President of the United States that has the authority to pull my lead undercover investigator from this mission.

As if he can read my mind, he finishes my train of thought. "It's Reynolds, got the call this morning. There's already a helicopter waiting for me." I stop directly in front of him, my stilettos almost touching his black combat boots.

"How long?" My words are low and quiet, barely audible over the music that still thumps in the background.

"Didn't say. The rest of the team remains intact." Oh look, a consolation prize. That's shit, and he knows it.

"What am I supposed to tell Sully? You're one his best soldiers, Riko." An arrogant grin shapes his lips at my use of his alias in our private conversation.

I created my own alias many years ago, and it's followed me. But the moment this arrogant schmuck moseyed his conceited ass into a training facility in the middle of a fucking military base and *told* me I would be joining him in the men's locker room, he became Riko – Rico Suave.

Spoiler, I did not join him in the locker room.

"If he starts asking around just tell him that, last you heard, I took too much of the white candy, and for all you know, I'm behind a dumpster down at the harbor somewhere. You'll think of something, you always do." I roll my eyes as he tips his chin up just slightly, his calloused hand brushing down the exposed skin of my thigh.

His touch isn't creepy like Sully's, it's comforting. Reid Chapman became my partner that day in the middle of that training facility. We bonded in a way only agents know how; I kicked his ass for making assumptions about the pretty female amongst a sea of men and then proceeded to laugh every time I saw him limp for the next two weeks.

"I don't know what Reynolds is up to, but this better be the break we're looking for. Sullivan is only a steppingstone to Victor, not to mention his connection with that skeez Sylvester Wilks. We're still building this case; I understand more than anyone that it takes time. Hell, it took me years to take down Vito. Granted, I didn't have the federal government at my back, but some days I don't know if that's truly a benefit or my detriment. I want your pretty boy ass back here in two weeks. Any longer and Sullivan's not going to believe you're strung out on a binge. Not to mention, he's getting a little touchy lately. You're the only person I trust out here to talk me off of the ledge when I'm feeling a little trigger happy."

"Are you worried about your safety, Young? Tell me to stay, and I will tell Reynolds where he can put that helicopter." Reid's large hand tightens around my thigh as his protective instincts kick in, he's got my back. There are three men in my life I have ever fully trusted, one hundred percent – no doubt. One of those men is dead, the second is locked up and the third sits in front of me prepared to go to war on my behalf, damn the consequences. All I have to do is say the word.

"And let you take my shot? Hell no. That man touches me without permission, and it's my bullet that will penetrate his skull. Nah, you just stand there and look pretty, Chapman. That's what you're good for anyway, right?" I tease him knowing I'll get a reaction out of him, he's so easy.

He doesn't disappoint as he quickly removes his hand from my thigh long enough to swing out and smack my bare ass, the sound echoing in the room over the persistent background noise of the music.

"Two weeks. Too much blow. I'm coming back with answers, and we're putting Anderson Sullivan where he belongs. And no, that is not in a pine box, Young. Even the biggest assholes deserve their day in court. You can't blow up every suspect we run across for the hell of it. We're doing this shit legally now. Understand?" My ass stings like fire, but Reid's hand remains, I can feel the heat from his touch on my skin. We're an interesting duo, the two of us.

Reid is devastatingly handsome. He merely looks at a woman and her panties disintegrate into thin air. He's the eternal bachelor, and his arrogance only lends to his charm. He's so pretty that it almost hurts to look at him for too long, but he's not really my type. Now, give me an arrogant, fine ass nerd with a hero complex, and I might be tempted to move a little closer. Reid's my partner and my only friend while Alex remains behind bars.

Reid isn't privy to what went down with Alex. As far as I know, he's never even heard of Alexander Straton. Reid and I went through a large portion of our training together, and Director Reynolds made it clear up front that no one could know of my involvement with Alex and the Adkins case if there was any chance, we would be able to get him pardoned early. So, I've kept my mouth clamped shut. I can keep a secret with the best of them. Just ask the man that murdered my parents. Oh wait, you can't - he's dead. Such an unfortunate ending for him.

I lean down slowly into his space because he loves it when I tease him. My breasts threaten to spill over the tightened corset top I wear as they hover so close to his lips that he could probably lick them if he truly was the asshole he pretends to be most of the time.

Hovering just over the shell of his ear I whisper seductively. "Two weeks. Later, Riko. You sure as hell better pay this tab like I gave you the best fuck of your life." With that, I nip at the lobe of his ear with my teeth before pulling back and sauntering to my spot on the stage. I grip the pole and finish the dance I started earlier. Only this time I let me eyes close, and my mind go to my happy place.

I'm not sure what it says about my mental stability that my happy place is somewhere I've never even actually been before. But in my dreams, it exists. I close my eyes, and I imagine myself on a beach, sugar white sands with crystal clear waves that slide against the shoreline every few seconds. I'm wearing a red string bikini, completely relaxed as I lounge on a large, cushioned chair - one of those big ass couch chairs with the giant oversized cushions. A cabana blocks the sun's rays from overhead, because self-induced skin cancer is for losers. When I go out, it's going to be from something far more exciting than melanoma.

My entire body is totally mellow and, for once, I can just breathe. And fuck if I don't inhale as all six foot five inches of Alexander Straton covers my body as he lowers himself onto my lounge chair, his tattooed hands running over every inch of my exposed skin. Yeah, so maybe I caught a peek at his file on the Bureau's database, sue me. The only picture that I had access to was his mugshot, but dammit if that man didn't make a mugshot look like the cover of a magazine; his predominate Latino heritage, head shaved to the scalp and tattoos that crept up the skin on his neck.

In my imagination, the tattoos cover so much more of his skin; his torso, his toned arms and the muscles that ripple on his back when he stretches, making himself comfortable. I want to study him and memorize each and every line of ink that touches his skin. I want to know his history and the story behind why he became a man that would give up everything for a stranger.

A door closes and jerks me back to reality as I open my eyes to an empty room. One thousand dollars in crisp one-hundred-dollar bills sits in the abandoned chair. The Bureau has pulled my partner, the only other lead on this mission that's actually qualified to do this job. It's obvious Reynolds has more faith in me than I have in myself.

I laugh to myself as I walk towards the money that should be enough to cover my ass tonight. Doesn't matter how many hours I spend in the training facility, or how good of a shot I am, I still feel like a damn imposter.

-o-
ALEX

"You comin' out for food, or you planning on keeping your nose stuck in that book all day?" I smirk as I stand at the entrance to the cell I've shared with Ryan Walsh for a little over a year now.

I was right, he's a couple of years younger than me. Man's in lock up for murdering his own damn father, but the charges were bullshit. Ryan's dad wasn't like my father, he wasn't sick. No, Ryan's dad was full of the evil I've come to recognize easily after being in this place for so long. You can look a man in the eyes and tell pretty quickly how deep their crazy runs. The Charles Ryan Walsh that came before Ryan…his evil ran deep.

I've listened to the story of the events that happened that night and the details of the many nights leading up to that one. I've heard memories screamed out in the dead of night from nightmares that continue to haunt the man that has become more brother to me over the last year than cellmate.

I can say that, without a doubt, in his situation I would have done the same. Hell, I probably would have pulled that trigger a lot sooner. But then again, the devil that sits on my shoulder is a bit more jaded than Ryan's. Yeah, he was the one with blood on his hands left holding the gun, he killed his father to protect himself and his mother, but even with a testimony from his mother, he was still put away for murder. This man was forced to take a life to protect his own and the life of an innocent. Yet the man that killed my mother barely got a damn slap on the wrist.

It only reaffirms what I've been saying for years, the judicial system is fucked.

I can't imagine Ryan having more than a couple more years left in here. With the exception of some minor anger issues, the guy is squeaky clean. He'll be out on parole for good behavior sooner rather than later. He's not wasting his time while he's in here though. Ryan Walsh is one of the most driven human beings I've ever met, he's brilliant. I've listened to the elaborate plans and concepts he has for a company he wants to create and build from the ground up as soon as he gets out. He's got the ideas, and what's more, he's got the intelligence to back it up. We click, he kind of reminds me of another guy that I know. A guy that I hope is out there fighting for the good of the world and accomplishing the dreams that we both had at one time. Maybe he can do enough good to make up for my lack of accomplishments in this hell hole.

Ryan had scholarships for law school before he decided that he needed to put his dreams on hold to stay home and protect his mother. The situation was escalating, and he didn't feel it was safe to leave her alone. It was a decision that would inevitably change his life and land him in this lovely facility. We're kind of the same in that aspect. We both made sacrifices to save the women in our lives that, in the end, stole our freedom.

I haven't seen Emily's face outside of my dreams since I watched her on the screen the last night she danced for me. The night everything went a little sideways. But I have seen Alan Reynolds. Guess he's got a fancy title in front of his name now, *Director*. He visits from time to time, fuck if I know why. Maybe he feels guilty for how it all shook out in the end. Every visit is the same thing, I beg for information on Emily, but he doesn't tell me shit, other than letting me know that she's safe and alive. I guess that's better than nothing. I don't know what I expect from him. Maybe part of me thought she might come here. But honestly, do I want her to see me like this? In here? Wouldn't that be one hell of a first date.

And fuck that, I don't want to date her. We're past that. Maybe it's one-sided of me to assume she feels the same way, but I want to claim her. I'm not wasting the time I do have on pleasantries and breadsticks at the *Olive Garden*. Although, those breadsticks are hella good when they're hot.

For a while, Reynolds would ask me if I needed anything in here. Unless he's busting me out or wiring up my jail cell with some serious WIFI and computer hardware, I'm not interested. Until, one day he offered to hook Walsh up with a program that would allow him to work on his law degree in lockup. Now that was something I could get on board with.

"Go ahead, shove a protein bar or something in your pocket, and bring it back for me if you don't mind." Ryan speaks without ever looking up from his book.

"Straton, someone's here to see you." The words are yelled from the end of the corridor, drawing my attention away. Nothing much going on here except Walsh ignoring me anyway.

"I got you. Later, nerd." I pick at him, but I'm proud of the guy. He's been dealt a crap hand, and yet he's not sitting around complaining about how unfair life has been to him. The man is working his ass off to make the best of his time here and accomplish his goals despite the situation he's in. He made a choice to persevere in the face of adversity, and that's something I can respect the hell out of.

I walk toward the end of the corridor, and my heart beats at an irregular rhythm. I can't help it. I know it's not her. It's never her, but what my head knows my heart chooses to ignore.

In over a year the only visitor I've gotten has been Reynolds. I never hired a lawyer; I don't have the kind of money to do that. Well, I probably could have allocated myself some funds from a few offshore accounts, but somebody took my access to the free world away by way of involuntary incarceration. So instead, I was assigned a public defender – yeah, that was a joke. Cyber criminals don't get internet access in prison, it's a travesty really.

I pass the guard that yelled out my name, and he throws up his fist for me to bump as I walk past. Most of the guards here are cool if you're not an asshole. They pick their battles, and if all hell breaks loose, they know which criminals they want having their backs.

Rounding the corner, I walk through a door and am met by a second guard who pats me down before allowing me access into a room, if you can even call it that. The room is no bigger than a standard walk-in closet with a single chair in the center. On the opposite wall from the door, is a large plexiglass window, which has been my only access to the outside world since being in here.

On the other side of the clear window is a man I've

never seen before, wearing a black polo and a pair of grey slacks. He's probably about my height, maybe an inch or two shorter, hard to tell when he's sitting down. Looks like a prep boy, straight out of the fraternity. The grin that crosses his face when I enter the room solidifies my assessment that he and I probably will not be friends.

I don't acknowledge him as I take my seat in front of the glass and lean back in the chair, spreading my legs and clasping my hands in my lap.

Yep, I'm not here for whatever this discussion is about.

"Alexander Straton, nice to meet you." The smarmy asshole decides to speak. That's awful brave of him.

I nod my head in response but remain silent until I know what he wants with this visit, and what his connection is to me or my case.

"Look, my name is Special Agent Bennett. I'm with the Federal Bureau of Investigation. You familiar?" Am I familiar? With him or the Bureau? Who is this idiot?

I can't help the laugh that sneaks past my lips, breaking my stoic act. I was really trying to be a hard ass, but this guy has got to be kidding.

"Ok, I see how it is. If you won't talk, you can listen. On behalf of the Bureau, I'm here to offer you a deal. We've got a spot for you on our cyber security team. We'll get you out of here, and you'll finish out your sentence working for us." The fuck is this man talking about. Why wouldn't Reynolds come here and ask me about this himself?

I'm listening, but this guy is shifty. I see it in his eyes and read it in his body language. I don't like what I see, and honestly, it's not so bad in here.

"Who sent you?" I finally speak.

"I'm not at liberty to discuss that information. I've got some contracts with me today…"

"Nope. Not happening. Tell me who sent you." I interrupt him, more adamant this time, pushing him for more information. If it wasn't Reynolds…was it Young? I can't imagine Emily working with this frat boy wannabe without shooting him in the leg. Wait, I glance down to his matching leather loafers. Nope, not missing a leg.

"Look, that's none of your business. Just sign the damn papers." Snap. Crackle. Pop.

There it is. It's in his eyes, just as I suspected. Damn, I'm getting good at this.

"Let me tell you something, Special Agent Benny. You can take those papers and shove them up your ass. I'm not signing a damn thing you're in possession of. You can tell your director to come see me himself. Or better yet, you can take your preppy ass right on out of here and go fuck a damn unicorn." I shove back from the metal chair and stand, not sparing him a second glance before I turn and walk back into the hallway.

My mind races, and my adrenaline pumps in a way it hasn't in a long time. What was that about? If he was telling the truth, someone else will be back here, and soon. I need to decide if I'm willing to work with a system that I've spent most of my life fighting against.

CHAPTER EIGHT
EMILY

"Heard you stacked cash over the weekend. You must have a golden pussy to pull those kind of bills." Mel pulls a set of rhinestone studded pasties from the locker next to mine and begins covering her exposed nipples with a body glue stick. The dressing room is bustling again. The night is early, and with every minute that ticks down, it's that much closer to time for my performance.

Rookies go on first, so I've still got an hour or two yet to finish getting ready. The earlier it is in the night, the fewer patrons are out front and the less cash there is to go around. The more those booths fill up, and the longer and heavier the liquor flows, the more freely the money changes hands. That's why I dance later. Save the best for last and all that.

Melanie Davis is the daughter of a preacher and an only child. She grew up in a small town about an hour from here. Her shiny blonde hair falls over her shoulders in long waves of honey that almost appear to be woven with strands of gold when the lights of the stage hit it just right. Her sky-blue eyes and soft pale skin lend to her air of innocence. She has an all-American girl look that easily allows her to steal the souls of even the most righteous gentlemen with the crook of a finger.

Most of the women here, are here out of pure necessity. This is their last resort, they're feeding a drug addiction or they're in a situation that has indebted them to the devil, also known as Anderson Sullivan.

Mel is here by choice, and I think that's why we hit it off so well. Her parents thought that by locking their daughter up in a tower they would preserve her innocence until they bartered with a farm boy for a milking cow or some shit and married her off. They got the shock of their lives the day after she turned eighteen. They woke to find she'd up and left, taking nothing but the clothes on her back and starting a life on her own that most wouldn't consider the American dream at all.

The Davises filed a missing person's report on their daughter, sweet Melanie, within forty-eight hours of her disappearance, but the investigation went stale. Mel was perfectly fine, and a legal adult. She just didn't want to be found. The fancy badge that I leave on my nightstand at home most days might say that I'm a federal investigator now, but it isn't my job to escort grown ass women home to mommy and daddy.

Dancing is Mel's dream, she and I are similar in that aspect. She gets a high from the performance. She thrives on being in control of her body and making her own decisions. Seems like a basic human right to me, but I don't think her parents saw it that way. Who am I to try to convince them otherwise?

It truly is a stroke of bad luck that she chose this club. Her pretty blonde locks put her in danger every time she steps on that stage. While not a rookie anymore, she's still considered fresh meat here. It won't be long until Anderson Sullivan decides to take what she's offering. It's all fun and games until they take without asking. Mel is naïve, that is part of her appeal after all. But she's still a baby in the eyes of the world, and she has yet to come face to face with a wolf in the flesh. I like to toe the line of danger, but Sully – he's the type of wolf that will rip your throat out with his bare teeth and then drink your blood for dessert, only to get his kicks from watching your body decompose until there's nothing left.

It's girls like Mel that need the protection of someone like me. That's not an option I have though. I don't get to just choose one, even if I am kind of partial. I'm here because Sullivan is pushing enough drugs through this club to kill off a small third-world country. Not to mention his suspected involvement with Sylvester Wilks, a man that just recently showed up on our radar as the ringleader of a circle of human trafficking ring we've been following since the late Vito days. Speaking of which, then, of course, all roads lead back to the Adkins family, because that's how the mafia works. Mafia families are nasty little spiders with multiple legs. Just when you think you've got them cornered, the female turns around and devours the male; then we're right back at the beginning of the web.

It's really too bad I couldn't convince Reynolds to let

me do this my way. A few well-placed explosives - Boom. Bang. Boom. Dead. Just like that. But no, everything has to be a damn process. I mean, I get it, to some extent. It does sound easy, kill off the bad guys, and all of a sudden, the world is rainbows and sunshine. It's just not the way reality works and, theoretically speaking, I understand that. Just seems like it would be easier to do it my way, but whatever. I'm an orphan with anger issues. I'm just lucky they let me play on the playground with the other kids instead of locking me up in a padded room somewhere - where I probably belong.

"I don't know about all that, it was a decent night though." I shrug off her comments as I slip an emerald, green thong over my signature black fishnet tights, pulling it up the curve of my thighs until it fits securely on my hips.

Mel's eyes shift around me before she speaks, her voice just above a whisper as she gravitates towards my personal space. "I heard from one of the other girls that Mr. Sullivan has a friend with another club down just off the interstate coming into the city. Said she made ten grand in one week. That's what she got to take home!" My ears perk up, and I lean in, making sure I'm close enough that her words filter through the mic I'm wearing.

Sylvester Wilks, he owns a luxury automotive business. The only legit thing about that business is the name. There's been chatter of some warehouses just off of the interstate that he's using to run women and children down to the docks for trade and market. Reid overheard a conversation when he was working the door about a week ago; it led us to believe he's partnered up with our favorite mafia boss and is using some vacant space there for funneling humans, as well as running some sort of illegal prostitution ring. We've got our cyber team trying to track down the lead as we speak, but they haven't come up with anything solid to speak of.

I suspect that what Mel thinks is a club is in actuality a brothel. We just didn't have a way in or a location until now. "No shit, ten grand in one week. How'd she get in?"

"Invite only. She got an invitation from Mr. Sullivan. Said it was a little different than this club, but that it was worth it. Whatever that means." Oh, I know what that means. I don't elaborate as Mel moves back toward the mirror that lines the inside of her locker and opens a tube of nude lipstick, swiping it over her lips nonchalantly.

She's dressed as a schoolgirl tonight. Her plaid skirt barely covers the cheeks of her plump ass. She wears a white top, unbuttoned and tied just below her breasts. She'll remove her top mid performance, exposing the pasties she so delicately applied earlier. The look fits her personality, and it works like a charm on the men out front. Sick bastards love em' young.

"Sounds sketch. I don't know. It's a lot of money, but it does seem a little too good to be true, don't you think?" I file away the information and try to deter Mel from ideas of hundred-dollar bills under her pillow. I try to use my words to keep her safe, it's the only method I have at my disposal, without putting our entire mission at risk. She's not ready for what I already know is happening down at that warehouse.

"Maybe you're right. Doesn't matter anyway, you have to get an invite into that place. I'm pretty sure Mr.

Sullivan doesn't even know I work in this club." Oh honey, he knows you, it's only a matter of time. He knows all of us, he's just waiting for the perfect moment to make his move.

"Listen Mel, you're a pretty girl, and your dancing is out of this world. You don't have to go about accomplishing your dreams exactly like this. You do realize that, right?" I clasp the rhinestone clip on the front of my bra and turn to her. I place my hand on her arm, look into her eyes and hope that maybe she'll be able to read in my eyes what I can't say with my mouth. I hate that she thinks this is the only way.

"Yeah, I get it Em, but living takes money. It's just me. I don't have anyone else to share the load with. I work extra in those rooms back there to pay for my dance classes during the day. My dream is to own my own studio one day. But the reality is, I will be dancing here until I'm fifty if I don't start making some serious cash. Everybody wants my damn money; my landlord, the lady down at the bank barking about my measly personal loan, the damn supermarket. Seems like maybe, if I could get ahead just once I really could accomplish my dreams. Look, I'm sorry I even brought it up, I'll see you out front." She closes her locker and ducks under my arm, dismissing herself from our conversation.

She's right. She can't accomplish her dreams on the tips of this place alone, but there has to be another way. Or another dream. I don't know the correct answer, but what I do know is that heading out to one of those warehouses with Anderson Sullivan doesn't guarantee her thousands of dollars. It does, however, guarantee that she will likely never recover from the things she experiences out there. Owning her own dance studio and molding future dancers of the world will pale in comparison to the trauma she will endure...if she manages to survive it altogether.

It's not worth it. All the Mel's of the world deserve more. She deserves better opportunities, another way out. I don't know how to get her there though, I'm no role model for accomplishing dreams. My only dream for the majority of my life was ending the life of someone else. That can't be normal.

So instead of letting my worries for Mel overrun my thoughts and take me to a dark place, I can't afford to let my mind wander, I focus on something I do have control over. I need to get myself an invitation to this warehouse, and I think I know exactly what I need to do to get it.

CHAPTER NINE
ALEX

"Alexander Straton, get your shit together, you're moving out." The familiar groan of the automatic door to my cell wakes me as it opens, and a uniformed officer appears in the doorway.

It's middle of the afternoon, and I was trying to catch a nap until I was so rudely interrupted. Sitting up on my bunk I lean my upper body out from under Ryan's bed and place my feet on the floor. I can hear Ryan shifting above me, but he doesn't speak.

"Moving? For what reason?" I question the officer. I recognize the man, we're cool.

My voice is rough with sleep and confusion.

"Consider this your eviction notice. Let's go." He jerks his chin out toward the hallway like he just expects me to hop up and follow him. My sluggish brain is taking too long to connect the dots. Thirty seconds ago, I was on a beach with Emily underneath me, and now I'm awake. My cock is hard as a steal pipe, and an officer is standing in front of me telling me to get my stuff and get out. That's not how this works. That's not how any of this works.

"The fuck, Straton? You didn't tell me you were getting out." Ryan finally speaks from the bunk above me, his voice breaking through the haze of my thoughts.

"The mailman must have forgotten to drop off the Sunday paper because this is breaking news to me too. Wait a minute, I didn't sign those contracts, Officer." The memory of that asshole Bennett whatever his name was flutters through the recesses of my foggy brain. That was what, a week ago? Nobody else ever showed up. I figured that was it, I filed that little altercation away and moved on.

"Look Straton, I don't know what contracts you're talking about. What I do know is when I tell most people that have been in lock up to get their shit together and get out of here, they don't try to pick a fight. Ten for ten they pick their shit up and get out." The officer continues to stand at the entrance of my cell and stares at me with a look of genuine curiosity.

"Yeah, okay, give a man a minute to adapt." I roll out from under the bunk and adjust myself not giving a damn who sees. I grab up all four of my belongings - prison has a way of forcing you into a minimalist lifestyle, I don't hate it.

"Alex, man, don't take this the wrong way, but I'm going to miss the hell out of you." Ryan drops down from his bunk and wraps an arm around me without hesitation.

I get the feeling Ryan Walsh never had many close friends; he didn't have a Reid to lean on growing up. Over the last year we've kind of become that for each other.

"Hell if I know what's happening right now, but if they're letting assholes like me out on the street, you'll be next. I'll make sure of it." I promise myself in that moment that I will do whatever I need to do to make sure Ryan gets out of prison. He needs to achieve his dreams without the stink of this prison sentence following him around like a black cloud. He has the ideas, and I have the means to help him out without him even knowing it. If he stays focused and driven, I will make sure that his business grows beyond his wildest dreams. That's the great thing about the internet. I can create magic with a few strokes of a keyboard, and I can do it all anonymously.

With no other option, and not wanting to draw this out any longer, I turn to the guard that waits impatiently for me at the entrance of the concrete shoebox I've called home for three hundred and sixty-five days too many. I follow him as he leads me down the corridor to the exit for, what I guess, is the last time.

The automatic door at the end of the corridor opens. I follow the officer as we walk through a second door and around a corner until he stops abruptly in front of me. With a sly smile, he grips the handle to a door that leads to my freedom.

"Paperwork has been taken care of. Your ride is outside waiting for you, black SUV."

This is nothing like the damn crime shows we watched growing up. I'm just about to walk the fuck right out of prison, like it's no thing. I feel like I'm on some crazy candid camera show right now, and I'm waiting for the host to jump out and tell me it's all a joke.

When I don't move the officer turns the handle on the door and pushes it open, allowing the bright sunlight to stream in, blinding me.

I always knew I would get out eventually. It's not like I was sentenced to life, but I never expected it to be this soon. I never in my wildest dreams thought I would wake up and they would all but kick my ass out some random side door, no further questions. Naw, come to think of it, my wildest dreams involve a pretty brunette with olive skin and moss green eyes.

"Alexander Wyatt Straton. If I didn't love pussy so much, I would kiss the hell out of your pretty face. I see prison's been good to your physique, spent a lot of time in the gym trying to surpass my level of sexy. I'm sorry to say, you did not achieve your goal, even if you do look damn good if I say so myself." I easily recognize that voice, it's the sound of home.

"Reid fucking Chapman." I turn back to the brick wall behind me that aligns with the door I just walked out of and let my eyes adjust to what my ears have already figured out.

"Ah, you do love me." He presses his hand against his chest in exaggeration, ever the flair for the dramatic. Pushing off the wall in a black pair of combat boots he walks the two steps that separate us. We're roughly the same size, both big guys with tattoos, and I'm still dressed in my prison best. To onlookers I'm sure we make an interesting pair. Not that either of us care. He pulls me to him and wraps his arms around me, embracing me in a hug that only a brother can give.

"How?" My voice threatens to crack. I can't manage to get out more than one single word as he releases me. I run my hand over the bare skin of my scalp and down my neck, allowing a brief moment of emotion to pass before I make a fool of myself. For a guy that doesn't have much in the way of family; Reid standing in front of me in the flesh is a shock to my system.

His lips tip up in a grin I recognize from our childhood as he reaches into the pocket of his jeans. "Check it out, bro." He pulls his hand back out, gripping a shiny piece of metal that he tosses at me. I'm forced to catch it or risk dropping it. Holding it closer to my face I have to read it twice to make sense of the words I'm seeing, FBI – Agent Alexander Straton. It's a badge.

"What the hell, Reid?" I ask as I continue to stare at the badge in confusion. Feels real, looks real, but there is no way in hell this is real.

"Look, twinsies." He pulls out a second badge and flashes it open. This one looks identical to mine with one exception, it says Special Agent Reid Chapman.

A sense of pride washes over me as I read his name. "You did it, man. You really did it." I stare at him in disbelief.

"Nah, we did it." His words echo through my shock riddled brain.

"How did you manage to pull this off?" I run my fingers over the shiny metal of the badge and try to reason how it's possible I went from inmate to agent for the Federal Bureau of Investigation within a period of less than thirty minutes.

"Forged a few signatures, kissed some ass. Just kidding, we both know I don't kiss anyone's ass, well unless she has silk strands of blonde hair and nice tits – then maybe I kiss some ass, but that's neither here nor there. Seems you've got a reputation. I heard the geeks up at the Bureau were drooling over your at-home set up for months after you were arrested. Hell, I'm pretty sure they jack off to your picture in their high-tech breakroom together. They've got a damn espresso machine in there that could probably launch rockets. You're their hero. They worship you, but the problem is, they don't have the skill level we need at the Bureau. Sure, they try, but they're not measuring up. We don't need some fresh out of college, whitewashed MIT-trained nerd. What we need is a damn relentless hacker with street skills and an uncanny ability to break the rules and not get caught doing it. We need you, and Director Reynolds knows that. The entire division knows that. That's why you're standing out here, and not back in there locked up for the next eight to nine years. We both know your smartass wasn't getting out early for good behavior." Holy shit, realization begins to crash down on me as I grasp to the validity of his words.

"Wait, you sent that frat boy Bennett out here?" The thought occurs to me as I start trying to connect pieces of the puzzle that might allow me to accept the reality that's just been thrust into my lap.

"That is a big fat negative. Reynolds sent Agent Bennett out here. I think he expected you to jump at the chance to get out. He underestimated your smart mouth and stubborn streak. For the record, Bennett is a total douche. He is not, nor will he ever be, a member of one of my teams." His distaste for the man seems to mirror my own.

"Glad we can agree on something. He came in here with his leather loafers and entitled arrogance, demanding that I sign papers and contracts that he refused to explain. I'm not down with that. Especially since I've spent the last year listening to Walsh babble on about legal jargon. I wasn't signing shit that guy had."

"Walsh?"

"Ryan Walsh, my cellmate. Reynolds hooked him up with a program that will allow him to finish his law degree in lock up. Dude is a business genius. He caught a stroke of bad luck with his dad. One thing led to another, and he's in for some bullshit murder charge. It's a long story. Back to the main event here, the story of how I'm now standing a free man outside of a penitentiary that I was meant to spend an entire decade in."

"Sign me up, I'm here for the long stories. We're about to spend some quality time together. We have a plane to catch. When I said I forged some signatures, well, I might have expedited the process of getting you out of here. Reynolds came to me and expressed his concern regarding your inability to play nice and our immediate need for your skills on the case I'm currently assigned to." Stepping past me, he motions for me to follow as we cross the street to a black SUV with tinted windows, similar to the one I took a ride in not so long ago on my way in here.

"You see, I've got somewhere I need to be, and you

are more than welcome to tag along. I've watched enough reruns of *Caribbean Life* to know you IT types can work remotely from anywhere. We'll make a pit stop by the office so you can pick up your immediate needs. We can order everything else and have it shipped in. I'm fairly certain the cyber team kept most of your shit from the apartment in a shrine back at headquarters - I mean, a locker as evidence." Reid's chuckle bubbles up from his chest as he laughs at his own joke.

"You won't be a field agent. So, while you don't have to necessarily go through the same program I did, you've still got some training to do. Then there's the onboarding process, I can hook you up with HR. Oh, I might actually can hook you up with my girl Denise. She's in that department, and she might let you get on board, if you know what I mean. Damn, I know it's been a while man." Reid is vibrating with energy as we climb into the SUV, and I'm just trying to keep up.

Everything is changing so quickly. I haven't even ridden in a vehicle in nearly a year, and Reid's already trying to push me into bed with some strange chick that isn't named Emily.

"Will Reynolds be there? I need to speak to him about something." I need to find her, I just want to lay eyes on her and know she's okay, but I don't say any of that because her safety is more important to me than anything. Director Reynolds is the only other person that knows of my connection with Emily Young, and I sure as hell didn't go through the last year for nothing.

"Should be. I will shoot him a text to be sure. We'll fly out within the hour either way. If everything goes as planned, we should be there by dinner. We're in and we're out, don't get any ideas of getting cozy. We need to be back in the air no later than tomorrow morning. If I'm not back on my case within the next forty-eight hours I risk losing my balls, and that's just not a risk I'm willing to take." Reid laughs nervously. I wonder for just a moment who he's working with that has him so intimidated. The man doesn't get intimidated by anyone, but he seems genuinely concerned about the safety of his manhood if we don't make it back to his case on time.

"Heard anything on my dad recently?" The question's been in the back of my mind since the moment I walked out that door and saw Reid. I've been putting off asking because to be honest, I'm not sure I want to know the answer.

Reid stares out the windshield with an intensity that turns my insides over. "Rehab. After you got locked up, I went over there. I was in between cases, and I felt like maybe if he wouldn't listen to you, he might listen to me. He was in shit shape. Honestly, I don't think he would have lived much longer in the conditions he was living in. I had some connections through the Bureau and got him hooked up at a nice facility just outside of the city. They call me and give me a report weekly on his progress. Last week they said they might start letting him go on unsupervised outings soon to allow him to reacclimate to society before he's out completely. He's doing well, Alex. Maybe this time will be better." My lungs expand and contract with pure, unfiltered relief.

I was so sure that my dad would be dead by the time I got out of prison. He's not my favorite person in the world, but that doesn't replace the fact that he's still my father, the only blood family I have left. I'm not as optimistic about the long-term as Reid seems to be, but this is better than finding out he died knowing I was incarcerated.

"I…I can't thank you enough, Reid. I will never be able to repay you for what you've done for my family." I choke on my words for a second time today. I don't consider myself an emotional guy, but damn, getting out of prison gets a guy up in his feelings real quick.

"Thank me? You're *family*. Now, I'm offended. Alex, you are my family. We're brothers. Always have been brothers, always will be. Your responsibilities are my responsibilities. Don't come at me with that garbage again. Family means we do what we have to do to protect each other. Even if that means hauling your asshole of a father to a rehab facility. He only urinated in my car once on the way. You owe me fifty bucks for having the SUV detailed after that shit." His lips turn up into a smile, and everything is set back right again. Reid is a lot of things to a lot of people, but he'll always be my brother.

We turn onto the highway and within minutes we're pulling off again and onto a small stretch of road that leads to a rural airstrip where a lone helicopter sits on the tarmac. "Where's the pilot?" I glance around as we exit the SUV, the place is totally deserted in the middle of the day.

"You're looking at him." Reid smiles before opening the door to the helicopter and hoisting himself in. His hands work quickly, hitting buttons and flicking switches that mean absolutely nothing to me.

"You've got to be kidding me. I thought you said we were boarding a plane?" I take a deep breath as I slide in behind him.

"Plane - Helicopter. Tomato – Tomahto. Go ahead, make yourself comfortable. Oh, and don't forget to buckle up, safety first and all that. You can call me Aladdin, I'll be your tour guide for the evening. It's time to go for a magic carpet ride." He tosses me a headset, his laughter ringing out above the loud noise of the propellor blades as they start up. I say I silent prayer that I didn't get a get out of jail free card just to die at the hands of my best friend from ten thousand feet in the air.

CHAPTER TEN
ALEX

"I still can't figure out why you were in the database for the United States National Defense for over a year. I thought you were strictly some sort of vigilante hacker, steal from the bad guys, re-distribute creatively to the good guys. Off record, I was always down with your operation. If anything, I figured I would be saving your ass one day for stealing from the wrong gangster, not the other way around." I tail behind Reid as he walks through a nearly abandoned apartment near headquarters. We landed about an hour ago, and Reid suggested we swing by his apartment so that I could change clothes before we picked up my gear.

"Eh, I just wanted to see if I could get in. It was surprisingly easy, damn government. Then, once I was in, I got curious. The database was a gold mine for potential targets. I plucked a few of my best hits from your Most Wanted lists. I was never a danger to National Security though, and Reynolds knows that." I purposely leave out the part about hunting down files on a certain mafia boss that would ultimately lead to his murder – eh, accidental death by explosives. Some might call that an accomplice to murder…whatever, technicalities.

One single couch, two twin size beds on opposite ends of the small loft-style apartment, and a television dead in the center of the room – that's it. I step over random pieces of discarded laundry and a few pieces of women's lingerie. A woman's bra hangs from the knob of the bathroom door. "How many women do you have in here, Chapman? And are they always this messy?"

"None, absolutely zero women. I share this apartment with a demon in a thong." Reid huffs as he tosses a pair of panties from a nightstand and grabs a black t-shirt and pair of jeans, handing them to me before walking into an empty kitchen area allowing me space to strip out of the uniform I've worn every single day for the past year.

I nearly groan as I slip into the worn denim and soft cotton of the t-shirt. These may not be my clothes, but they feel like heaven and freedom wrapped up in a comfy synthetic bundle all the same.

"A demon? You got married and didn't even invite me to the damn wedding? What is that about? I mean, I know I was locked up, but hell. I thought we were closer than that, my heart is bleeding." I slip back on my sneakers and follow Reid back out the front door, waiting in the empty hallway as he locks up. Within minutes we're headed right back down the stairs we just walked up.

"No, idiot, I did not get married. I share that apartment with my partner. She might look like a female in all the ways that matter, but she's scary as fuck. That's why we need to wrap up this little meeting and get back in the air. She's sure to kill me if I'm not back within the next twenty-four hours. She'll drag it out too. She won't make my death easy. No, she'll chop my body into tiny pieces one by one and take her time sprinkling me all over North America like some sort of fancy organic human fertilizer. Then, she'll sit back and sip some girly cocktail with her feet propped up while she watches *Pretty Woman* for the one hundredth time, with zero remorse for the life I never got to live." Laughter rumbles deep in my chest at his obvious detriment. I smile because I feel her in his description, Emily. It has to be.

"How long have you two lived together?" It's weird, I guess most men would be pissed if the woman that owned their heart and controlled their every thought was shacking up with their best friend. But, if I'm being honest, the idea is kind of comforting to me.

All this time I've worried about her safety and well-being, and the entire time she was under the protection of my best friend.

"I don't know. It wasn't long after you got locked up. We ended up together in training and were both working specifically with the division of sex and human trafficking. We're both undercover agents, and it's not like we're ever at that apartment anyway. We use it as a landing base, but even if we are there, it's not usually at the same time. Right now, we're working a case undercover. I was pulled out when your ass decided to be stubborn and not take our initial offer. Reynolds felt like I could persuade you, and we needed you now. So, I put my entire team in danger to be here." My stomach drops as we walk out the glass double doors of the apartment building. The sky is a dark grey as the sun sets over the city, and we walk the few blocks over to headquarters.

Realization hits me swiftly in the gut that if Reid is here, no one is protecting Emily there. Wherever there is. Not that she's ever needed protection, but Reid seems to think there's danger. It bothers me to my core that it's my fault he isn't there with her.

"You put your team in danger?" I hedge, needing to confirm details with Reynolds before I out myself to Reid. Reid might be my brother and best friend, but I refuse to put Emily's life at risk for anyone.

"We've been undercover on this case for months already. I'm not worried about giving you details, Alex. I know the minute you get access to a computer you'll know everything I know anyway. I hope you know more, that's the whole reason for bringing you on with us. We're in a club, and I'm currently a soldier – upper level. That means I'm trusted by the owner of the club, Anderson Sullivan, aka Sully. Maybe not totally trusted, but enough that I have the physical access we need. That might all be gone to hell when I get back though, and then I'll have to start rebuilding that relationship all over again. The story is I'm on a bender, too much powder. While not uncommon in their world, the story will only hold up for so long unless I turn up dead. Obviously, I am very much alive, so you see my dilemma. We need to get back or risk the entire mission going to shit." Reid flashes his badge to a guard and nudges me to do the same. It's going to be a while before I get used to this. The guard nods and allows us both the admittance we need to enter the base.

"Director Reynolds is here, he's expecting you. I will take you to meet him, and once you're finished, we can meet back up to get whatever it is that you will need to work with before we head out again." I follow Reid through a building that he's obviously been in many times before until we stop at the entrance of a meeting room. He knocks once and then turns to leave. "Have Reynolds call me when you get done."

Reid disappears around the corner and the door opens in front of me to a man that I've seen on a computer monitor and through a plexiglass window, but never once met face to face. "Director Alan Reynolds, long time no see." I smile, extending my hand to him, something that seems like such a common act, but feels surreal after having had my freedoms revoked for the last year.

"Alexander Wyatt Straton. Or should I say Agent Straton. Get in here kid and sit down, we need to talk." The Director motions me into the room and closes the door behind us. I take my seat in a basic, black chair at a meeting table that looks to seat about ten. We're the only ones here, but the Director sits at the head of the table all the same.

"Where is she, Reynolds?" I don't know why those words are the first to leave my mouth. I hadn't planned to say them, well at least not yet anyway, but they escaped and there was no turning back once they were out there.

A smile tilts the corner of his lips. He proves, for a moment, that he isn't quite as much of a hard ass as he tries to portray. I guess when you're the Director of a division of the Federal Bureau of Investigation, you're expected to have a certain persona; you carry a certain reputation. But the grin the passes his lips when I blurt out the question that's been burning me up for the last twelve hours makes him look at least a decade younger.

"You don't really value your life, do you Straton? Either that, or you have a hell of a set of balls. Either way, that makes you perfect for this job. I need someone that's willing to take risks on this team. We need someone in that cyber unit that's more man than just a computer nerd. Agent Chapman speaks highly of you. We're happy that he was able to persuade you to come around." I know he's referring to my altercation with Agent Bennett, but he can stuff that right on down his pipe and smoke it.

"Reid has his own ways of persuasion, that's for sure." I cross my arms in front of my chest and continue to wait. He knows that he's holding out on me.

"She's safe, Straton. She's been safe the entire time. I've told you time and time again. I've got a soft spot for Aemilia. The Albani's were friends of mine, Alex, we worked closely together. I keep tabs on her, but you know as well as I do that she will not be tamed. Agent Chapman is the best, he was top of his class, and he's been with her since they completed their training. Your contract puts you in our cyber securities division, which typically doesn't fall under my jurisdiction. However, you have been assigned to my case. That means, at least for the time being, you report to me. You've been out of the loop for a while, but I have no doubt that it won't take you long to get caught back up. You already know most of the players in our game, and you're familiar with the way these mafia families work. We need your brain, Straton. So much so that we negotiated a deal that will allow you to complete your sentence a free man so long as you work for us. Understood?" A warning, I get it.

He wants me to play nice. I never signed a contract, but we don't have to get into those specifics today. My mission has been her mission for as long as I can remember at this point if this is her mission, then I'm here for it.

"When can I see her?"

"I'm sorry, did you not hear my question, Straton? Understood?"

"Understood."

"You need to be careful. I'm not saying you can't see her. Two of the best agents I ever knew were married. They worked flawlessly together, but they also died together. Learn from them, Straton. Don't make stupid mistakes. You watch her like a man watches a woman. I watch her like a father. Do not make me put you back in prison. And before you argue with me, trust me when I say that prison is a far better alternative than your other options. Understood?"

"Understood."

"She's undercover. She has no idea you are out. And she and I are the only two people in this entire organization that know the specifics of what happened in the Vito Adkins case. I'm sure you've figured that out by now, though. You've been given clearance to head out with Special Agent Chapman; you can work remotely. Do your damn job, and do not put her in danger. Understood?"

"Understood."

"Good, welcome to the team Agent Straton. We're happy to have you on board."

CHAPTER ELEVEN
EMILY

Well, that's not what that's supposed to do - weird. It's closing in on three in the morning, and I'm trying to check my emails and do the boring-as-hell admin shit I'm expected to do now that the government issues me a paycheck. I can't get access to the secure portal using my login. My legs ache from dancing all night as I sit at my small kitchen table wearing nothing but an oversized t-shirt and thong. I welcome the cold bite of the oak chair on the skin of my ass as I abuse the keyboard of my laptop by banging on it too hard.

I re-type my password three times, knowing with one hundred percent certainty that I'm typing it in correctly and don't have the damn caps lock on, and I'm still locked out.

I don't keep normal working hours, it's impossible in this line of work. But that's okay, the last normal night of sleep I had was nearly two decades ago. So, the fact that the sun will rise within the next two hours and I have yet to fall asleep doesn't bother me in the least. Normalcy is overrated.

I've never needed much sleep anyway. I'll catch a nap before I need to head back to the club for rehearsal later and all will be well. Or most will be well, anyway. Reid's ass hasn't bothered to show back up, to my knowledge. He's dangerously close to the deadline we agreed upon before he left. He knows good and damn well that if we agree on a set time frame, his ass better be back in this time zone before the clock ticks over.

I've got enough unpredictability in my life as it is. I do not need to worry about the safety of my partner or my team any more than I already do. I hate to admit it, but I've kind of developed a soft spot for the conceited jerk.

Dead on my prediction, Sullivan sent a team of his minions out searching for his best soldier after the forty-eight-hour marker. We got damn lucky that one of our younger guys was on that team and was able to convince them that he stumbled upon a strung out Riko down by the docks without further questioning.

Reid's going to catch hell when he gets back, but they won't kill him, he's too valuable to Sully – for now anyway. If his ass will get the hell back here.

Reid and I share an apartment back at headquarters. But here I live in a one-bedroom apartment above a laundromat about a mile away from the club by myself. Suits me, I prefer this to the ghetto frat house Reid lays his head down in every night.

Sullivan likes to keep an eye on his soldiers. They're trained, they know enough information to get themselves killed and are not as easily replaced as his dancers. The majority of them live in a run-down apartment complex that he owns. Being an upper-level soldier means that Reid isn't required to have a roommate. Despite the less than stellar living conditions, the damn place is a freaking fortress to get in and out of.

If soldiers want to fuck the dancers in the club they do so under Sullivan's watchful eye, and at the club – permission to do so not optional. No dancers at the apartment complex, no women for that matter. Like I said, it's a fortress.

Director Reynolds hooked us up with a warehouse building down at the harbor, not too far from the docks that Sullivan uses for transporting his goods. We limit our access to emergency use only. In the rare event that we need to meet privately as an entire team, we've used the location. Most of the time we try to leave it untouched and not draw any unwanted attention to it.

It's currently loaded down with enough artillery to begin a World War, not to mention our armored vehicles and one slick as hell helicopter. Reid likes to pretend that it's his, but we both know it's mine. Sure, he can fly, but we both know who the pilot is and who the co-pilot is in this partnership.

Frustrated, I hold my finger down over the power button on my laptop, attempting to hard reset it. Somewhere in a cold prison cell Alex is cringing; it is what it is. I need this thing to work, and computers are not my area of expertise. I need to update my case notes for the conversation I had with Mel and see if anyone else on the team has gotten any more hits on Wilks's involvement with the warehouses and Anderson Sullivan. We've suspected the two of them are working together for some time. But now that I know they are, and they're doing it right here under our noises doesn't sit well with me.

We already know that Sullivan works under Adkins; and Wilks teaming up with Adkins is a dangerous combination.

My computer restarts, and nothing. It's basically a paperweight, completely useless to me. Lovely. I pick up my cell phone and shoot a 9-1-1 text to one of the geeks in the cyber division to reset my password, but who knows how long that will take. Someone is supposed to be on-call twenty-four hours a day, but with the time difference I'm probably not getting this thing reset before I have to go back into the club.

Giving up for the night, I close my laptop and point my bare toes to the cracked and yellowed linoleum flooring, stretching the muscles in my calves. I lean back into the dining chair and reach my fingers to the ceiling as the bottom of my t-shirt teases my thighs.

Silence.

I'm not bothered by the silence, it's something I've become acutely accustomed to. The absence of noise, the complete opposite to the constant pandemonium of sound that surrounds me as I work in the club. The silence is a different kind of peace, but it's also a stark reminder that I'm alone.

This life is not the life that I dreamed of as a small child, before everything went to hell. For the years that followed, I thrived on the loneliness as a reminder of my bravery. I found comfort in the fact that didn't have to count on anyone but myself.

Then I found Alex, and something changed. I became dependent on the skill set of someone else and learned to leverage that to accomplish my goals. In the beginning that was all that mattered to me, my goals.

The longer we worked together though, the more I wanted to know what made him tick.

Why was he helping me?

Why was he willing to sacrifice everything he worked for, for me? Someone he didn't even really know.

Who was Alexander Straton? I became fascinated with his thought process and the inner workings of his brain.

Flipping from the open, unanswered text message on my phone, I scroll down until I get to the very last conversation I had via text with Alex.

Alex: You ready for tonight?

Emily: Yes and no. It's strange, ya know? I've been waiting for this night to come for years, and now that we're this close, it kind of seems surreal.

Alex: You scared?

Emily: Fuck off, you know I don't get scared.

Alex: Oh right, I forgot, you're bionic.

Emily: Cold as steel. But seriously, I'm just ready. Ready to move on. Ready for this to be done. Just ready.

Alex: I get it. Dreams are like that. They manifest themselves into every fiber of our being, and we become the idea in which we strive to accomplish. We're driven, and sometimes you go so hard that, the moment you're halted at your final destination having arrived at your goal, your brain keeps moving

when physically you've stopped. However, I can't say I imagine many women dream of partnering with a criminal hacker and vigilante federal investigator to end the life of a mafia boss, but...

Emily: About damn time.

Alex: Hey, Em. When this is all over. What happens to us?

Emily: When this is all over, you'll be on a flight out here. Follow the plan, Straton.

Alex: Right, but if I'm not. If something goes wrong. What happens?

Emily: At one time, my every thought was how I would avenge the death of my parents and finish what they set out to do here in America. It's funny how many times I find our conversations infiltrating those thoughts now. Is that weird?

Alex: Not at all. I feel the same way about the death of my mother. Albeit I think we go about it in different ways.

Emily: I mean, we can't all be this badass.

Alex: Dance for me tonight, Emily. When you dance tonight, before that first explosion detonates, think of me.

Emily: Always.

He knew. He was saying goodbye. I was so distracted, so consumed by my own goals, that I couldn't see what was staring me in the face the entire time. His intentions were never to get on that plane.

I know the words by heart. I've re-read the messages over and over again, but it doesn't change anything. I still dance for him. Each and every sway of my hips, every time I step on that stage, it's for him.

Shutting my phone off, I stand from the chair and walk into my bedroom before I finally allow myself to collapse onto the bed and drift off to sleep.

The sun will come quickly, and tonight is the night that I make my move. I need an invitation to those warehouses. I need to see what we're up against.

Alex was right. I always thought that by accomplishing my dreams I would be granted freedom. Freedom from the nightmares, freedom from the insomnia, freedom from the inability to fill my lungs with oxygen and actually breathe.

I accomplished what I set out to do all those years ago, but my brain never shut off. I was never granted the freedom I longed for, because that euphoria – the feeling of accomplishment, it's short lived.

It's replaced quickly by another goal, another dream, another passion. I'm driven, but that drive is my addiction. There is no good enough as long as there are women and children suffering. For as long as old, dirty money filters through the hands of generations of families that carry the blood of innocents on their unwashed hands like a status symbol - I will fight.

There is no freedom for someone like me. My mother was right, I am a warrior.

-o-
ALEX

"Riko. Your alias is Riko? You have got to be kidding me." I pop a piece of popcorn into my mouth as I sit back on Reid's couch in the sparse apartment he currently calls home. The rich taste of butter slides over my tongue, and I nearly groan out loud. It's the little things.

"Nope, not kidding. Could be worse." Reid grunts as he slips a black button-down shirt on over the armored t-shirt that fits snuggly against his skin. The material for the bulletproofing is incredible. To the naked eye, the t-shirt appears identical to a standard undershirt. But up close, the material is like nothing I've ever seen before. The technology behind the production is fascinating. The fabric itself won't fully protect you from a bullet injury, but it is designed to withstand the brunt of the force. The material is designed to keep you alive. You might end up with a broken rib or two, but compared to the alternative, I would take that hit any day.

"Riko – Rico Suave." I chuckle to no one in particular. "I feel like you need to be holding a tumbler with fancy whiskey or bourbon in it or some shit. Sipping the pretentious concoction delicately in your library as the ice clinks against the glass. The name is Bond, James Bond." I'm cracking myself up.

From the look on Reid's face, I'm cracking him up too, he's just too damn stubborn to admit it. Rolling his eyes, he buttons the final button on his shirt and slips a cell phone into his back pocket.

He smiles to himself, but he rolls his eyes because he thinks I don't care. Unfortunately, the problem we have is, I care too much. So much so that I'm just counting down the minutes until he leaves to make my move.

If he so much as catches a hint of my plans for the evening he'll stop me. I can't afford to take that chance, not tonight.

"You planning to work or are you just going to sit there and eat popcorn all night? I hate to break it to you, but that television doesn't have Netflix." Netflix. I nearly choke on a kernel. Amateur.

I lean up and take a look at the coffee table I commandeered the moment we walked in the door. On the flight in I was able to hack the security on this apartment complex remotely. According to the files we have, this location is heavily secured and monitored, sending video footage on a timed rotation back to a central server.

Nobody in, nobody out.

Unless you work for Anderson Sullivan that is. Or well, you're me.

Sullivan is a next level control freak; he's got his soldiers on lock. It's curious to me that he is so concerned with the whereabouts of these men, and yet the women of the club roam freely with little to no security.

I've scoured his personality profile on the federal database. His fatal flaw: Sullivan doesn't value women. They're a fixture in his front; standard issue carbon copies that allow the club to function. But they're all the same to him, easily replaceable.

He doesn't see the dancers in his club as a threat. His mental capacity literally cannot fathom that they would be capable of anything more than performing the job in which he employs them to do. That is exactly why Emily was the ideal candidate to take the lead on this case.

At the *Pink Lily*, Emily held clout, she was the lead dancer. She was heavily respected, and everyone knew that she belonged to Vito. The waters parted when she entered a room. While her reputation for dancing and an ability to siphon cash from unsuspecting patrons followed her here, the way Sullivan operates his club is different than Vito's.

Vito saw women as possessions and, often times, a means of currency. He treasured them as collectibles, and as such he watched them like a hawk. Sully uses and discards the women of this club without thought.

Emily is easily the best dancer in that club, but she's able to stay under the radar because of Sullivan's complete disregard for the female population. That might make him a total douche, but we already knew that. Honestly, it's a character trait that our team can use to its' advantage.

Both men are evil, their demons are just of a different variety.

I've been inside his systems from the moment I gained access. I'm confident angels sang the instant my ability to access WIFI was granted, and I was given the greenlight to hack, I mean log, into the Department of Defense database and search it to my heart's desire. My fingers were itching for the technology; for the ability to see things that others dismiss so easily.

I swapped a few images around through some public domain satellite streams and got Reid and I into the apartment complex undetected. Reynolds and I agree on one thing for certain, my presence needs to remain a mystery. As long as I am working on this case, I need to remain invisible. My ability to move around without detection is our wildcard. Lucky for everyone involved, no one knows who the fuck Alexander Wyatt Straton is.

"I am working. I happen to know that your partner researched various scalpels and blades last night during one of her numerous internet searches. Better watch your back. I've heard lack of communication can be fatal." Reid might pretend to ignore me, but he can't hide the flash of fear in his eyes. He's terrified of the pretty dancer, and I am living for it.

Emily didn't research anything last night because I locked her out of her computer, but Reid doesn't have to know that. I hacked the camera on her laptop and changed her passwords. Temporarily, of course. I just needed to see her.

Security footage tracked her leaving the club around two in the morning and arriving at her tiny apartment about twenty minutes later. The Bureau doesn't have access inside of her apartment, which is utter bullshit if you ask me, so I had to garner my own. Without stepping foot inside uninvited - I'm not a total stalker - the only way I could hack the stream was through remote access from her government-issued laptop.

The moment she walked in the door she stripped out of a large black pullover and tossed it to the small couch that sat against the wall of her even smaller common space. Underneath she wore a basic black sports bra, a complete contrast from the flashy lingerie she wears at the club. Her raw, natural beauty in that moment was overwhelming. She doesn't need the glitz and the flash, she's perfect without all of the extras.

Gripping the underside of the bra she pulled it up over her head and threw it down on top of her discarded sweatshirt. Her breasts are full, more than a handful;

because of her dark olive skin tone, her nipples are a deep, rich burgundy. I want to feel the weight of her breasts in the palm of my hands. What I would give to pull them into my mouth one at a time until they're hardened to stiff peaks.

My thoughts were an avalanche of unleashed desire. I watched her from the darkness of Reid's couch as he slept just a few feet away from me on a small twin-sized bed. He crashed out the minute we walked into the apartment, needing to catch some sleep before he prepared to head back into the club for the night.

Slipping my hand under the band of a pair of sweatpants I swiped from Reid's clean laundry, I gripped my rock-solid cock. At this point I don't even know what my initial intentions were. Hell, I never expected her to strip the moment she walked in the door, I just wanted to see her in her home and know she was okay.

I should have shut it down, I should have stopped, but I couldn't. The desperation that I felt flowed through my veins and infected every ending of every nerve in my body. It stole the air from my lungs as the blood from my brain throbbed in my cock, leaving me unable to form coherent thoughts.

Having eyes on her, seeing her exotic beauty and knowing she was so close caused my cock to pulse in my hand with need. My inability to get to her only made me want her that much more.

I watched her kick off a pair of sneakers, not even bothering to untie them first. She walked the short distance from the living room to the kitchen where her laptop sat open, the screen totally black and unused, except for the lens of one tiny camera.

Standing on her toes, elongating her lean frame, she grabbed a glass from a cabinet above the sink and filled it with water. The muscles in her throat bobbed up and down as she hurriedly drank the liquid. I wondered how she might look on her knees, between my thighs, sucking my erection down that same narrow column of her throat. Would she be able to swallow all of me, or would she need to use her hand as a grip?

Abandoning any pretense of chivalry, I gave into my need as I pulled my cock from the top of my sweatpants. I spit in my hand for lubrication as my erection twitched angrily against the crevices of the abdominal muscles of my chest.

Her breasts bounced in time with her steps as she walked past the kitchen table to the door of what I'm assuming is the single bedroom in the small apartment. Cum leaked from the tip of my cock onto my chest as my desperation for her accelerated, and I ran my palm up and down the length of my cock.

Stopping in the doorway, she gripped the band of the pair of black leggings she was wearing and slowly pulled them down her hips, exposing the smooth skin of her ass.

Fuck, that ass. How many times have I cum to the memory of that ass straddling the pole as she danced?

Gripping my cock harder, I thrust my hips forward into my hand as I fucked myself watching her undress. She doesn't realize she's putting on a show, but she may as well be on Broadway. Her movements are flawless. I want to see her dance for me. I want to watch as she strips naked and moves in such a way that she creates a masterpiece that is only mine.

Harder.

Deeper.

The outline of her pussy was visible as she leaned over the bed to grab a t-shirt in only a thong. I ran my hand over the head of my sensitive cock, imagining it was her wet pussy I was sliding into. I squeezed the palm of my hand over the bulging veins as they popped irritably through my skin, knowing just how tight of a fit it will be when I finally slide inside of her.

Reid lays just a few feet away from me, dead to the world. He could watch for all I care; I just need her. I need to touch her, to fuck her, I need to mark her as mine. The thought of being watched as I fuck her, of someone else seeing me take her pleasure as my own pushed me to the edge.

My orgasm barreled forward, and I lost all sense of control as I thrust my hips harder into the grip of my own hand. Dropping the phone to the couch, I allowed the need to pull me into the infinite depth of pleasure. My brain short circuited and cum exploded from my cock, covering my chest. I came harder than I have in over a year, but it still wasn't enough.

God, I want to fill her up. I want my cum to drip from her pussy. *Mine.* Aemilia Albani is mine. Emily Young is mine. One day, she'll have another name to add to her unique collection if I have anything to do with it.

A low grunt escaped from my chest as I slowly came down from my high and picked the phone back up just in time to see her slam the top down on her open laptop; angry as hell at her inability to login, no doubt.

Until Death

Within minutes my phone buzzed with a new text, a 9-1-1 about a password reset. The corner of my lips turned up into a slick smile.

Someone should probably look into that.

CHAPTER TWELVE
ALEX

It's nearing midnight. Reid left hours ago, reporting back to the club for the first time in two weeks. I maintained his visual cover as he left the building, allowing him the ability to preserve the alibi that he's been out at the docks on a bender for the last two weeks.

It was in Reid's best interest, and the best interest of the case, that Anderson Sullivan was taken by Riko's surprise return from his two-week hiatus. Lucky for him, it's not uncommon for soldiers to go missing for periods of time. Unlucky for us, that usually means some sort of retaliation on the return end.

I'm watching, and I have access to all of the players involved, ours and theirs. I have eyes everywhere. I'm inside of Sullivan's systems, and his people have no idea. I'm not even a blip on their radar.

I saw Emily arrive at the club for rehearsals with some of the greener dancers and then watched as she dressed for her evening performance.

Just as we suspected, Riko's return did not go unnoticed. Reid was moved from his spot in Sully's inner circle to counting inventory down at the warehouses at the docks, punishment for laying out for the previous two weeks. It's better than the alternative, cement shoes in the harbor. But, it's still not ideal for our case, and I can't help but remember that it's my fault he was pulled off to begin with.

While the move means that he's been knocked down a rung or two in the pecking order, it also means that my mission tonight was just made infinitely easier.

Reid and Reynolds knew the sacrifice the moment they pulled him, but they also recognized the reward. I don't live my arrogance out loud like Reid does, but I'm confident in my abilities and the fact that I'm skilled far past anyone else that the Bureau currently has on their roster.

With my addition, our team is stacked, and we're preparing for battle. I'm already flying through the data, building spreadsheets and organizing facts into files that will lead us in the right direction.

Field agents are invaluable, and while I don't discredit the work Emily and Reid as well as the rest of their team do, I also know that this is the age of technology. Everything we do is traceable if you know where and how to look.

There's a reason these crime families have been around for decades. There's a reason they remain untouchable. It's going to take all of our skills in order to succeed.

Pulling a baseball cap down low over my eyes and the black hood of my sweatshirt up over my head, I step up to an unmarked entrance in a seemingly ordinary alleyway.

Cold metal bites at the skin on my back, but the knowledge that it's there, should I need it, is comforting. I swiped a pistol from Reid's stash, not so cleverly hidden inside a slit in the side of his mattress. It's where he used to hide his dirty magazines when we were growing up – some things never change. I need to remember to order some microscopic tracking devices for these weapons. Having the ability to track the weapons of the agents on my team might come in handy in the future, and that fancy black credit card the FBI gave me is burning a hole in my damn pocket.

I've been glued to both databases for the past twenty-four hours. I've downloaded everything I would need for tonight onto my cell phone. Technically speaking, I might be required to wear a wire that I may or may not have left back at the apartment. Eh, whatever. It clashed with my vibe for the evening, whoops.

My steps are certain, I don't hesitate. It's time.

One final step and I make a move that I should have made over a year ago but never had the opportunity.

"I'm gonna need to see some ID." A man steps up to me like maybe he thinks I will back down just because he says so, but we're the same size. He's got some width on me, but that just means he's slower than I am. He's a soldier, dressed similar to Reid. He shines his flashlight in my face, but instead of backing down, I meet him at the door. Sliding my hand from the pocket of my sweatshirt his eyes watch my every move as I pull out my standard issued identification. Not this state, but it reads Alexander Straton. It's legit, because why not. Not like I'm walking around flashing my badge, which still feels weird as it presses up against the waistline of the jeans I'm wearing.

My name may as well be John Doe. I'm unknown to them. The soldier nods once, takes my cash and ushers me through the doors. I'm underdressed for a club of this caliber, but it was obvious after a few minutes of standing toe to toe that the oversized gatekeeper out front wasn't down for a confrontation tonight. The night is almost over, as long as he doesn't perceive me as trouble and I have cash, we're good. Actually, I've got something even better than cash, I came prepared – proper planning and all that.

The walls of the club are lined with a deep purple velvet, giving the vast room a warm, expensive feel. Women dance in elaborate cages in the darkness throughout the room, but front and center there's a stage with one single pole and a spotlight. Streams of fabric dust the floor from the ceiling, hanging by silver rings.

Closer to the stage, ropes separate the common from the elite. Lush, high-back booths line the front two rows – access that I don't currently have, nor do I need. Not for my mission tonight.

I granted myself access to the blueprints of this club earlier this evening and wasted no time memorizing its layout.

Up a small set of stairs to the right of the stage is a hallway that leads to six private rooms. Each of those rooms is themed differently but set up exactly the same. One couch, one chair, one stage with a single pole in the center.

A spiral staircase in that hallway leads to the second floor of this building. The second floor houses the office of Anderson Sullivan, who I know looks down at the activity in his club now from his perch above. It also houses a luxury apartment, a gym, a meeting room for business transactions and a private safe room. The walls of the safe room are bulletproof and fully lined with weapons and artillery.

Everything else is kept in offsite warehouses, near the harbor. The harbor gives them water access to funnel drugs and people. The downside is their inability to transport goods undetected. In my review of the case files earlier, Emily had some notes about possible warehouses near the main interstate – location currently unknown.

I need more time to research. The warehouses would allow easier transits to the docks if they have interstate access, but moving product by truck is still a tricky endeavor. Then there's Sylvester Wilks, guy owns a luxury automotive business. But, Em's notes indicate he may be involved in transporting more than vehicles. I flagged the information to follow-up, but that's not my priority tonight.

Behind the stage is an open backstage area that leads to the dressing room for the dancers. Their prep space is completely open, no privacy. The women strip for the men of this club, they strip in front of Sullivan's cameras and they strip in front of each other. They're treated like animals and herded through here as such. Honestly, I'm shocked Emily hasn't killed anyone for the complete disregard of the entire female population in this place.

She really is becoming the kick ass agent I always knew she would be, and that's hot as hell. Her strength is the only aphrodisiac I need.

I prop myself up at the back of the club, the bar to my right, as the music changes and a low beat vibrates through the open room. The music is so loud that I can feel it in my bones and the floor moves beneath my feet. Lights shine down onto the stage, and the room goes silent in anticipation.

Then, darkness. The room is cast into a pitch-black abyss. When the lights come back up, she's there, dangling from the ceiling. Her hair fans out below her like a halo, but she's no angel.

Time stops. Every noise, every light, every movement around me ceases to exist with the exception of the woman that falls from the sky and plummets to the floor, only to come to an abrupt stop seconds before her skull kisses the lit stage.

She defies gravity as she dances in perfect harmony with every beat of the music. I watch her, completely enraptured by her every move. I'm not the only one, every person in this room watches her in awe. She's a magician of her own body, and while she appears to be totally in control, I pay attention to her eyes. While the men and women in this room are distracted by her body, I see the way she doesn't see them. She's not of this place, this time, she's not here in this moment. For as long as the music plays, she sees the colors of her masterpiece and creates artwork with her body that only she is privy to in her mind.

This is her job, her cover, but she dances for herself.

Or is it possible that she still dances for me?

It's been so long.

My eyes track every movement of her body. I memorize every curve as I pull myself away and walk from the back of the room to the far corner where a second soldier stands guard in front of a single door.

"You lost?" His voice booms over the music, a threat and a question tied up in a pretty bow. I spent the last year of my life in lockup with his carbon copies, if this man thinks he can intimidate me, he's wrong.

"Bond, check the list." I tilt my head to the side, looking him in the eyes from under my baseball cap and hiding the smirk I so badly want to release. James fucking Bond. Reid is going to kick my ass when he finds out about this. My only hope is that I get Emily on my side before that happens.

"Come again?" He holds a tablet as he leans closer to me, the stink of his stale breath fanning over my skin.

"James Bond, check the list." He eyes my black sweatshirt and faded denim suspiciously. It costs a pretty penny to book a private room with any of the girls here, let alone their star performer, who is currently finishing up her performance as this man continues to question me. Not that I blame him. James Bond, I cough to stifle the chuckle that escapes from under my breath.

"I do not believe this shit." The soldier finds my name, I knew it was there the whole time. Put it there myself a couple of hours ago. He shakes his head as he leans over to a petite girl wearing a piece of leather over her ass that one might be inclined to call a skirt and a matching rhinestone black bra. She barely looks a day over legal, at least I hope to God she's legal. Waves of blonde hair flow smoothly over her shoulders. An innocent, she looks too young to be in a place like this, that's for damn sure.

I can't hear what he's saying to her over the music of the club, but she nods and takes my hand in hers with a sweet, naive smile before leading me to the door that separates my past from my future.

Maybe there are about two hundred and fifty-seven safer ways to have gone about doing this.

Maybe I'm walking into my own suicide mission. It's arrogant as fuck for me to think she won't shoot me on the spot for putting her team in danger for my own selfishness. But dammit if I didn't earn this moment every minute of the last year.

I've waited too damn long for this night – I've sacrificed everything.

Tonight, I'm selfish. Tonight, I claim what has always been mine.

Tomorrow I will answer for the consequences.

It's time to shake things the fuck up.

-o-
EMILY

"Emily, hey, Young." A loud voice yells over the music as I step from the stage after my last performance in the club for the night.

I groan to myself and turn towards the voice I recognize as one of Sully's guard dogs. I'm on a mission tonight, I don't have time for petty distractions. I have somewhere I need to be.

"Yeah, what's up?" Sweat glistens from the crevice between my breasts as I catch my breath. I left everything I had out on the stage tonight. It's funny, this is my job, and some days the details of that are really shitty, but the dancing, my ability to move and create with the music, it doesn't get old. I love it.

"Island Oasis. You've got a private room booked. Didn't recognize the guy, and he gave me a phony ass name, but he paid up front. Five grand, wire transfer. No cash. Gia cleared it up front. Money is clean."

"Five grand?" I question him because a good night for a private session is a grand cash money. Especially considering I don't lay down with the stray dogs that roam through here, no matter how thick their wallets are. What the fuck is this man expecting for five thousand dollars? And who wire transfers money to a damn strip club? We're high class, but this isn't the Vegas strip. I didn't even realize Sullivan had the capabilities for that type of transaction in this place. Where is our damn IT unit when I need them?

"You heard me. Five thousand dollars for the rest of the night. Better get your ass in there and do it up right. You screw this up and you'll have to answer to Sully."

Ugh, Sullivan, that's where I was headed tonight. I'm still trying to secure an invitation to those warehouses, and currently my only access is through my good buddy Anderson Sullivan.

Mel's working tonight, I saw her dance earlier. She was driving every man in here wild with the contrast of her black leather against her blonde locks and innocent eyes. I know Sullivan is watching her. I know, if given the opportunity, she's going to jump at taking the money with or without my subtle warnings. She has no reason to trust me, no reason to think that I'm not just trying to take the money for myself.

My plan was to intercept him, distract him long enough to figure out what's going on down there before he can get to Mel. I don't know if it's the masked innocence I see behind her eyes despite her chosen career path and her attempts to disguise it; or maybe it's her streak of rebellion a mile wide that reminds me a little of myself. Whatever it is, I'm partial to her when I've watched so many before her make the ultimate sacrifice.

If she heads out to those warehouses, she might not come back. Maybe she does return, but the repercussions of what's happening inside of those walls will forever change her. Without a doubt, she will not return with the same light in her eyes that I see every day. I know what happens in those brothels, I've seen it firsthand – lived it; it isn't something a person ever truly recovers from.

"Give me two minutes to touch up, and I'll be there."

Five thousand dollars, I still can't fathom it.

"Two minutes. Get it together, Young. He's already waiting. I wouldn't keep him waiting much longer." The no name guard dog grunts as he drops his notice and walks away, back in the opposite direction toward the front of the club as I head to my locker to touch up.

"Girl, you hit the damn jackpot tonight. Island boy is fine as hell." Mel swings in beside me as I swipe on my lipstick and check my mascara for smudging. I'm sweaty, but it is what it is. Two minutes doesn't give me a lot of wiggle room to work with.

"Island boy?" I question her, knowing she has to be referring to my private booking.

"I just walked him to the room. I would be lying if I said I wasn't a little bit jealous of you right now, girl. Dude isn't one of the old skeeves that always pay out fat cash for the dances. This guy is poppin'. I tried to get him to touch, but he was so damn serious. He literally just sat there, didn't say a single word. Hell, I was offering mine up for free, just trying to get him warmed up for you, but whatever. He wasn't into it." Who pays five grand for a stripper to dance for them, and then turns down some free entertainment while they wait?

I focus on Mel, all the while my brain works in overtime trying to work out who could possibly be in that room, and what danger they might present to me or this case.

Something about this doesn't feel right, something is off. The pit of my stomach swirls with the sickening anticipation of the unknown.

I know Reid made it back from his meeting with Reynolds. We haven't had a chance to catch up, so I'm still not sure what that was about. I might not ever know, just the nature of the job. Some things are better left undisclosed.

He checked in through my speaker hours ago, but he's not in this building tonight. He was moved down to the docks for inventory.

The chatter in my ear tonight has been minimal. Our cyber team eerily quiet, except for a notification I received that my damn password had been reset. Thanks a lot for that. Now if you could just do your damn job and let me know what I'm dealing with here, that would be nice. But, no, apparently that's too much to ask.

I glance over at Mel who should be wrapping up for the night, but instead is swiping on an extra layer of lipstick and pulls nervously at the leather of her skirt.

"You dancing tonight too?" I ask as I stare at her curiously.

"Mr. Sullivan wants to see me upstairs." Her lips tip up into a smirk that threatens to smudge the work she's putting into touching up her lips.

"No option?" I question, already knowing that if he requested her specifically, she doesn't get the luxury of saying no. Turning down a request from Anderson Sullivan ensures you don't step foot in this club again. The uneasy feeling in my stomach only grows at the reminder that sometimes we're just not fast enough.

What I want and what I'm capable of accomplishing, given my resources and restraints, are two totally different things. Doesn't matter how much I want or wish for something. Time is a bitch that waits for no one. No matter how hard I try, it still may be too late for her.

"Nah, but it's all good. You know I could use the extra cash. You worry too much Emily, it's gonna give you wrinkles, you know that right? Big ugly ones on your forehead. What you should really be worried about is getting in there to the man that just paid five grand to watch you shake that ass. Five freakin' grand for one dance. Let's go slut, the music is calling, and we must answer." She giggles to herself as she slams her locker closed and reaches down to grab my hand. She pulls me behind her toward the narrow hallway that leads to our two totally separate destinations.

Two doors.

One is a mystery.

The other a certain detriment.

CHAPTER THIRTEEN
EMILY

One breath. Two. In and out.

Mel's high heels echo from behind me as she walks the spiral staircase to the lion's den, oblivious to the potential danger that awaits her. For one split second, a fraction of time, I make the mistake of allowing myself to question my decisions.

I could stop her. I could yank her out of this club, and we could run far away from here, someplace where we could both start new. I'm an expert at disappearing, I've reinvented myself more times that I can remember.

But instead, my hand rests on the handle to a door that is a complete mystery to me.

Guilt is a luxury afforded to those weaker than their circumstances.

You were born with the bravery of a thousand warriors, Aemilia.

My mother's words ricochet against the doubt that plagues my mind.

Who is the person on the other side of this door, and why me? Why this night? Where did the money come from? The transaction itself is unusual. The fact that Reid isn't here tonight and the speaker in my ear remains totally useless to me is intriguing.

I can handle myself, I'm not dependent on anyone, but I've become comfortable in knowing someone else has my back if things start going south. Not to mention, the Bureau frowns on what the legal system likes to refer to as…homicide. If something goes wrong in this room and I'm forced to make a hard decision between this man's life or mine, well, you can wrap him up and stick a bow on him – he's dead.

A dead body would no doubt throw a hiccup in my cover and our case.

Some things were easier when it was just me and there were no rules to abide by.

I understand more than anyone at this point in my life that each of my actions has a direct consequence. I will never again allow my goals to blind me to the sacrifices of those around me. Now, I consider the lives of other people in each and every decision I make. Sounds sweet and fluffy, but dammit if it doesn't make things trickier on my end.

I take a third and final breath and turn the handle.

I make the choice that I've always made. The choice that I know my parents made, and I will continue to make again and again. I choose not to run from my commitments. I refuse to turn my back on my team, even if that means making a sacrifice. I choose to maintain my cover and move forward, even if at times that just means taking one single step into a room that feels like it might change my life.

The air shifts as I cross the threshold, and my lungs contract. I elongate my spine and square my shoulders. A chill skates across my skin. All of a sudden, the uneasy feeling in the pit of my stomach turns to something else that I can't quite put my finger on.

I feel his presence as he sits in the lone chair in the center of the room. His eyes burn my skin as I close the door behind me, secluding us from the outside world.

I know he watches me, but I don't dare look at him, not yet.

The room is dark except for the lights of green, blue, and white that flash around the stage on a rotation.

It's déjà vu, but this is a different room and a very different man. I can feel it in my bones. The universe has shifted and the electricity is in the very air that I breathe.

He doesn't speak, and I don't stop until my hands touch the pole in the center of the stage. The music pulses around us, but my blood pumps to a different rhythm. My heart races, but I'm not scared.

Fear is an interesting concept. On a basic level it is merely the perception of danger. In reality, fear is much darker than that, it runs deep into the depths of our soul. A life of fear is a life stolen by the devil himself – a life lost. I've seen the depths of hell, lived through unimaginable evil. But, I refuse to give into the fear that threatens me when the darkness seeps into the deep recesses of my thoughts. I refuse to lose.

My heart races, but I allow the fear to fuel my actions instead of steal them.

Fight or flight – I will always fight. Even if the battle is within me.

My chest presses against the cold metal, but my back remains to him. Closing my eyes, I breathe in the music; I swallow it down and allow it to wash away my trepidation. Pulling my leg up and over my shoulder I dip to the floor with my right hand, and I dance.

-o-

ALEX

Ecstasy.

I sit in the darkness in the single chair in the room facing a stage lit by various lights. Music thumps to a heavy beat in the background, but my focus remains solely on the woman in front of me.

She didn't change clothes; she's dressed in the exact outfit I saw her in on the main stage just moments ago. One single red stiletto reaches up and over her head as she wraps her thigh around the pole in the center of the room. I follow the weaving of the black fishnet tights over the curve of her muscular legs until my eyes reach the juncture of her thighs. Using the remarkable strength of her core she pulls her body onto the pole as she dances to a rhythm all her own.

Her hair looks nearly black as it falls in loose waves, brushing the skin of her bare shoulders and floating effortlessly around her as she moves. She dances, creating art that is all her own. Her moss green eyes don't see me, not yet.

Instantly hard, my cock presses painfully against the zipper of the denim jeans I wear. As much as I've yearned to watch her dance for me, it takes every ounce of restraint in my body to remain seated in this chair. She's so close, it would just take two steps, maybe three, and she would finally be in my arms.

What would she do if I grabbed her and hoisted her over my shoulder?

She would probably kill me. That's exactly what she would do. The thought of dying before I could taste her is enough to keep me planted.

Having waited this long, I force my ass to remain seated and watch a performance that I hope to replay in my mind for a lifetime.

Dance for me, Emily. Always for me.

In need of relief, I lean forward placing my elbows on my knees, putting the pressure of my body onto my relentless erection. We're just getting started, and my body is already begging for a release – I didn't consider how hard up I would be for her. Or maybe I did, but I didn't anticipate nearly coming in my pants before she even touched me.

The black hood of my sweatshirt remains over my head, casting me further into darkness.

I'm not sure how long she dances on the stage, or how long I'm mesmerized by her every movement. At some point the music changes and my heart rate kicks up a notch or twenty as I watch her extract her longs limbs from the pole.

One step.

Two steps. She's off the stage, slowly sauntering

towards me.

She's a seductress. Reid was wrong when he said she was a demon. She's not a demon, she's an enchantress, a siren that is sure to lead me down a path to hell. I'm hypnotized by the sway of her hips. I know for absolute certainty I would sell my soul to the devil himself for one single touch.

Men have fallen for much less.

I observe her every nuance and I know in that moment that I would willingly hit the floor at her feet and beg if that's what it took.

But it's not. As she steps into me, I lift my eyes to hers and see the flicker of recognition, the utter disbelief, and she falters.

She claimed to be bionic, but I feel the physical crack in her armor as her eyes catch mine for the first time. I study the story of emotion that passes them as she stares at me.

"Dance for me, Aemilia." My words are a whisper. A forbidden name spoken into the darkness.

"Oh God, it finally happened. I've lost my fucking mind. There's no way." She stills, her body straddling my thighs, with one leg on either side as she fumbles through words and curses like a sailor.

Leaning back, I place one hand hesitantly on her thigh, needing to know that I have a hold of her in case she decides to run. Also, because I can't not touch her with her this close. Using my opposite hand, I reach up and pull the black hood from my head, leaving me in a black baseball cap but exposing my features.

The music continues to play, but in this moment she

doesn't dance. She merely stares at me and tries to make sense of what's happening.

"Look at me, Aemilia. What do you see?" My hand lightly squeezes her thigh, and I wonder if her heart beats as fast as mine. My adrenaline pumps so hard through my veins that it's nearly impossible to breathe.

This is our moment. This moment solidifies our destiny.

"*Robin Hood.*" Finally, she speaks. My lips tilt at her use of a nickname I haven't thought about in a long time.

"Yours." I slide my opposite hand to her other thigh, now holding her securely with both hands as she hovers over my lap.

"Alex, Jesus. I don't understand. How?" Finally moving, she reaches with her hand and grips the hat I wear on my head, tossing it to the ground and fully exposing my identity.

"Agent Alexander Straton, in the flesh." I don't bother to grab my badge, there will be time for that later.

"Agent? You're working for the Bureau? I swear on my life you were just in prison two or three days ago. I know for a damn fact. I checked." There's my girl.

I welcome her feisty attitude as I watch the doubt fade away and the fire return to her eyes. Crossing her arms in front of her body, she questions me with the intensity of a federal agent and a woman jaded by a lifetime of disappointment.

I expected this. Actually, this is going a hell of a lot better than I expected to be honest. I'm not dead, and there haven't been any gunshots. I'm living the high life right now with the woman of my dreams on my lap and no current threat of bodily injury for potentially fucking with her case.

"You checking in on me, Young? That's cute." I tip my chin up towards her as her body floats over mine. I fight the urge to yank her down against me. My smile expands, ignoring the hint of irritation I hear in her inquiry, as I realize maybe she's been just as strung out as I have. "It was Reynolds."

"Motherfucker finally came through. He couldn't just get you out though. Oh no, he had to go and hire you too? What am I saying, of course he hired you, the man's not an idiot. He could have issued a damn warning, a memo, company email...something. Wait, did you lock me out of my computer? How long have you been here?" Her words start coming, and they don't stop.

Her complete lack of finesse makes her all the more alluring. She's not fancy, she doesn't try to put on a show to impress me. Why should she? Hell, I'm a damn convicted felon. There is no false pretense between us. She is exactly who she says she is, well – except when she's not, but that's not for me.

"Em, can we save story time for later? Right now, I need you to dance for me." I'm becoming increasingly impatient. I rock my hips up and into her thighs that still straddle me in the chair, allowing her to feel what she's doing to me. Her breasts sit on a shelf, displayed in front of me like a damn all you can eat buffet, and I'm fucking starved. Her body is taunting me, and my limits are being stretched beyond what I ever imagined I could withstand.

"The cameras, Alex." She hesitates, searching the room for cameras that were overridden the moment I stepped foot into this room.

"Really, Emily?" I raise my eyebrow at her and grip her hips tighter. I finally give in and pull her down onto my lap until she's sitting flush against the zipper of the pants that are currently torturing me. I can feel her heat through the thick fabric that separates us, and it's driving me wild with need.

"This is dangerous, Straton. You fuck up my case, and I swear to God Alex, I will cut you. I won't kill you because I might like you, a little – don't let that go to your head."

Her small hand reaches up and brushes the scruff of hair on my cheek, the tenderness of the action taking me by surprise until she opens her mouth again and all is set back right in the world. "But I will fuck you up. I had somewhere else I needed to be tonight, but I'm giving you a pass because you couldn't have known that. Well, you might have, had you not locked me out of my laptop and allowed me to update my case notes. Dammit Straton, we're going to have to learn some boundaries." Her rambling would be cute if it wasn't cutting into my dance. The dance I paid five grand for, Sullivan's own money, of course. He didn't even realize it was missing, but I stole from him and then wired it right back into the club's account. Damn criminals are a bunch of idiots.

"Emily. Hush, woman." Her mouth snaps shut. Her spine stiffens as she looks at me and no doubt debates pulling the knife from under her corset.

Most people would take one look at the woman sitting on my lap and think there is no way she has anywhere to even put a weapon, let alone more than one. Most people would be wrong. In fact, I would bet my ass she has at least two weapons on her person minimum.

Slowly, so slowly, I rock my hips into her again, this time I feel her body as it relaxes into mine and we begin to move together.

"Tell me that you imagined this. Tell me that I wasn't alone all those nights I touched myself watching you dance. Tell me you felt it too. I feel your heat, Emily. I know you feel it. I want to hear you say it. Tell me."

CHAPTER FOURTEEN
EMILY

"I knew you were watching me. I've known since the beginning. Before I knew your face, I knew your heart. Before I knew your heart, I knew your mind. And before that, I think fate knew that your soul was tethered to mine by an unbreakable thread. I dance for myself, it feeds the depth of my creativity. But my soul recognizes yours on a level beyond that of human comprehension. You and I – we're linked together from another time, another dimension. Every time I step on that stage, I feel you. Every time I close my eyes and allow the colors to immerse my thoughts, I see you."

What I now recognize as anticipation and a hell of a lot of lust builds in the pit of my stomach. My skin tingles and alights as Alex runs his large hands over the muscles of my thighs, taking his time with his torturous ascent.

My history is just that, mine – my choices. I've made decisions in my past that the world might view as less than pure, something I should be ashamed of.

I'm not.

Anyone that wants to judge my actions can go fuck themselves. The decisions that I made are what made me the person that I am today. Those actions and the consequences of such are the very reason I currently stand in front of a man that has no idea what he's doing to my cold heart. A man that is seemingly oblivious to the way my stomach nosedives like the highest plummet on a damn roller coaster with every pass of his fingers.

I've had plenty of sex in my line of work, especially before joining forces with the FBI. I did what I had to do; I made the sacrifices that had to be made. Sex was, and always has been, a means to an end for me. The action mechanical and unfeeling.

This is different. With Alex, it isn't sex – it's something else entirely. That point is only driven home by the unfamiliar feeling of wet warmth that seeps from the material of my thong and coats my inner thighs as my hips demand that they follow the slow motion of his.

His fingers drift over the exposed skin of my ass, lightly squeezing until he reaches the visible skin between the top of my thong and the silk strings of my corset.

His eyes watch mine, but his fingers move with deft skill as he pulls on the lose string at the bottom of my corset and the material loosens. "I've been waiting for you, Alex."

With one hand on his shoulder, I brush the other over his exposed scalp, and let the barely there prickles of hair run over the sensitive skin of my palm. I study the ink that covers the skin on his neck and wonder what it all means.

I grind my hips down over his erection that presses into my clit through the material of his jeans and lift my arms for him. He grunts instead of using his words, having loosened the corset enough to pull it over my head.

Good decision?

Bad decision?

On the one hand, this is dangerous as fuck. I trust that Alex handled the security situation, but we're still in the club of a known FBI target and are both employed agents of the Federal Bureau of Investigation. There has to be a damn policy somewhere about what is happening right now. I'm certain we're breaking every rule in the employee handbook, plus some laws I should probably be privy to. I paid more attention to survival skills than pesky laws and rules when I went through my training.

On the other hand, the man paid five grand for a dance, and in this business five grand means it's perfectly acceptable for me to strip down and fuck him like I may not live to see tomorrow. I've never been one for rules anyway, or laws for that matter, and really – we may not live to see tomorrow.

Decision made.

"Shit Em, they're even better in person." Tossing my corset to the floor, Alex wastes no time running his hands over my exposed breasts. My nipples immediately harden under his touch.

"In person?" I question him. I know he's a cyber genius. I realize that he watches me, but I still question him because it's fun. I'm doing everything I can to drag this out and enjoy it. We've barely just begun, and I'm already dreading the moment it's over.

I internally battle my brain's inability to live in the moment.

His thumbs swirl over the peaks of my nipples. My breasts continue to swell in his hands as a boyish grin tilts the corner of his lips. "Last night, that's why I locked you out of your computer. I was checking in on you, but you up and decided to strip the moment you walked in the door, and hell if I couldn't help but touch myself."

He's truthful. He doesn't hold back, and I can appreciate that. Any other man and they'd probably be dead by now, bleeding out onto the floor while I called Reid for backup. Not Alex.

Leaning back, I grip the underside of his black sweatshirt and pull it over his head. Immediately I notice two distinct objects. First, I see his badge, pressed up flush against the ridges of his lower abdomen. Then my eyes catch the glint of a pistol holstered in a belt around his waistline, but I don't bother with it yet. There's something sexy about a man with a gun.

The tattoos on his neck cover his shoulder and upper torso, but his lower abdomen is bare except for the light dusting of hair that leads to what I hope to God is in my near future. The contrast only makes his abdominal muscles stand out that much more.

Leaning my body into his, I brush my lips over the shell of his ear. "Did you make yourself cum while you watched me last night?"

"Jesus, Emily." I watch on in rapt fascination as goosebumps cover his exposed skin, and relish in the fact that I have that control over him.

"I watched your breasts bounce. The perfect shape and color of your nipples." Leaning forward he swipes his warm tongue over one nipple and then the other before groaning out loud and pulling back again.

"I watched as you bent over your bed in that thong. The outline of your pussy torturing me." Using his hand, he brushes his thumb over my clit through the material of my black thong and sends more warmth from my already dripping heat.

"I came all over my chest. I came so hard for you, baby. You've been the center of my every orgasm for years. Tonight, I'm going to come inside of you. Please, Em, tell me that's what you want."

The open end of his statement takes me by surprise. He looks so hard, and his attitude is so demanding, but he's giving me an out when, judging from the rock-hard erection threatening to burst the material of his jeans right now, he really doesn't want to. He's letting me make decisions for my body.

"I'm on the pill. I want you to fuck me, Alex. Then I want you to come inside of me so hard that you fill me up."

"Thank fuck." He exhales an exaggerated breath and pulls me further to him as he removes every remaining centimeter of space between us. His mouth devours mine as he lifts us from the chair, and I wrap my legs around his torso.

The cold metal of his pistol hits my calf, but I don't pause. His tongue fights mine for real estate in my mouth as he walks us across the room to the small couch and lowers me down, pulling away from me and stealing my air with him as he goes.

"I think I know, but I need you to tell me with your words, Em. Do you need me to be easy? Slow? Or do you want me to fuck you hard? What are the limits?" His eyes scour my body as he stands above me. His restraint is evident in the hard set of his jaw and the way his hands flex open and closed at his sides.

"No limits. But listen to me. Pay attention to my body. Your body already knows mine. You'll know what to do." I sit up, my back flush against the back of the couch, and spread open my legs, giving him a view of what's to come.

"I've been waiting for you, Alex." I repeat words I spoke earlier.

His nod of understanding tells me everything I need to know; I can see it in his eyes. I can feel it in the restraint he's so tightly held up until this point. Slowly, he kneels to the ground beside the couch and grips my fishnet tights and thong, peeling them from my body. Reaching around my back I unclasp the knife that was secured beneath the corset I no longer wear while Alex pulls my second weapon from the back of my calf.

The lights and the music around us are forgotten as he pushes me back on the couch and places his hands on my knees, spreading my legs open even further. Moisture glistens from my thighs and pools at the entrance to my opening.

"Emily, baby, you're soaked." He leans forward, hovering over my bare pussy on the couch. His nose is not even an inch from touching my skin as he takes his time breathing me in. "God, you smell delicious, woman.

Like the first rain of spring on a cool, sunny day."

A low groan escapes from his throat as he runs his tongue from my entrance to the top of my clit. The action causes an immediate reaction from me as my body is jolted from the couch from the sensation. The intensity is almost too much, the build up nearly sending me into my orgasm. Using his hand, he presses down on my lower abdomen, holding me into place as he spreads the lips of my pussy with his opposite hand and goes to work devouring me.

"You taste like fucking rainbows and sunflowers or some shit. It's not enough; I can't get enough of you." The ridiculousness of his words make me giggle, but that quickly turns into a moan as he sucks my clit into his mouth and lightly bites down until I buck my hips forward in rebellion under his grip.

"I'm going to come Alex. I don't want to come yet. Not like this." I try to breathe, try to hold off on my imminent orgasm, but I could feel it taking over without my consent. I'm on the edge of a cliff and the weight's leaning further and further towards the bottomless ravine.

"Not like this? This isn't the county fair, Em. You can win more than one prize. Do you trust me?" Trust. Can he know that he's one of the only living humans that I do trust? I trust him with my life, but what's more than that…I trust him with my heart.

"All you have to do is say the word. Understand? Tell me to stop and I will." His voice is so serious. Maybe I should consider that a warning, but I can't find it in me to care. I'm so close to reaching my nirvana that I'd probably agree to anything at this point.

"Alex, please." My hips rock forward on their own as I watch him pull the slick, shiny pistol from his belt.

My heart races as I watch him unload the firearm. I watch as he unloads the magazine, rendering the weapon seemingly useless.

Then his mouth is on me again. He bites with his teeth, and then soothes with his tongue. He takes what he wants, and then when that's not enough, he takes more.

I feel the cold metal as he slides it over my clit, and then I feel the barrel as he glides it into my pussy.

"Alex?" I question him. But honestly, I don't know what this question is. I'm not expecting an answer, and if he stops somebody really might get shot.

"Say the word, Em." Not that word.

"Fuck me." My voice is thick and raspy, the words barely audible in the madness of our frantic movements.

Holding the grip of the firearm he slides the metal out of me, and then back in. He fucks me with the barrel of the pistol as he works my clit with his tongue. My hips press up into his hand harder, my movements jerky and erratic as I finally give in and allow myself to trip over the edge into the ravine.

"Harder Alex, fuck me harder." Slamming my hips into the metal once more, I grasp for the final hit I need. Every muscle in my body freezes as my pussy begins to contract around the foreign object. Alex doesn't let up his assault on my clit, pulling every single pulse of my orgasm from inside of me and drinking down every last drop of moisture that my body is willing to give him.

Finally, after what seems like hours and only seconds at once, my heart rate begins to stabilize. But, it's short lived as Alex extracts the metal from inside of me and places it carefully on the floor beside us.

Forcing movement into dormant limbs, when really my arms and legs feel like jelly from the intensity of my orgasm, I sit up on the couch pulling him towards me by the loops of the jeans he's still wearing.

He flicks the button with one hand and pulls the zipper as I yank the fabric down over his muscular thighs.

"Commando? Really?" I lick my lips as his cock drips pre-cum from the tip bobbing between us.

"No time to shop…aghh.." his words turn inaudible as I lean forward and swipe my tongue out quickly claiming what's mine – waste not, want not. Wouldn't want to waste any of that liquid gold now, would we?

"Fuck, I didn't think this through. Em. Shit. This is going to be fast." If it wasn't so damn dark in here, I could swear there's a tint of blush to this man's cheeks.

A grown ass felon, covered in tattoos, stands before me blushing. Stranger things have happened. This is the life I live, no surprises.

"It's okay, we can do it again. Practice makes perfect and all that." Unwilling to wait any longer, I pull his body down onto the couch. Using my leverage, I flip myself around until I'm straddling his thighs. His cock sits flush against my swollen pussy and immediately my body is ready to go again. I've never come like this, not with a man.

I've never had time for a relationship, never wanted one. It's hard enough keeping myself alive. The men I've slept with were all for work, not play. Straton's right about something, technology is fascinating and the internet and a toy or two work wonders when I'm in a pinch.

I've been with my share of women for funsies. What can I say? I'm partial to caramel skin, full breasts and a plump ass. In my line of work, love is love. Taboo is the standard, and if you're vanilla, you may as well name yourself snowflake because rainbow is the norm. Well, my previous line of work; back in my *vigilante* days, as Reid so lovingly refers to my past. I can't say for sure what the FBI's stance on *rainbow ice cream* is. Should have read that damn handbook.

Anyway, yeah, that was a good time, but this is a whole other level.

What Alex just did? That was a life altering experience. I have never had an orgasm so intense, and I sure as fuck have never had multiple in one night. The slow pulse I feel already building inside of me again tells me that Alex is about to change that for me too.

"Again?" His eyes search mine in the darkness.

"After this, yeah, but not here. We make it out unscathed tonight, and we'll do it again when we get home." Whoops, that didn't come out exactly right, but it's out there now.

"Home?" The question barely makes it out of his mouth before his words become inaudible again. Gripping his cock with my small hands, I lift to my knees, running his length against my wet pussy to distract him from my verbal word vomit.

Ignoring his question entirely, I adjust my body until

his cock is lined up perfectly with my entrance. Slowly, I slip the tip of his cock inside of me, using the muscles in my legs to maintain my body weight.

"Ahhhhhh...fucking hell...Em. Shit, woman." His hands shoot up to grip my hips, an attempt to maintain some sense of control as I slowly begin to lower myself onto his thick length. His girth stretches me almost painfully as my hips finally sit flush against his. Skin kissing skin, and yet somehow, I still crave more.

"Damn geeks packing heat. I feel so full Alex." I tease him to lighten the intensity of what we both know is happening between us.

"You're so tight. Your pussy feels like an inferno, Emily. Jesus, woman." He's still beneath me; he doesn't dare move. Lucky for both of us, I'm in control of this show.

Smiling, I begin a slow rhythm as I rock my hips forward and then swirl them around in a circular motion. The tip of his cock touches a spot deep inside of me that threatens to send me over the edge again, but I focus on his pleasure, not mine.

"Aemilia. Give me what you've given no one else. I don't just want your body. I want your heart. I want your mind. I want all of you Aemilia Albani." Unexpectedly tears sting my eyes at his use of my real name. I haven't cried since the day I left my parents' bedroom in shambles. But now, tears fall from my eyes down onto my cheeks and splash against the sweat glistening on Alex's chest.

"Alex." I whisper his name through the emotion, and he takes over our movements. Never removing himself from inside of me he manages to flip us until my back touches the couch again and he regains the control.

Alex uses his lips to catch my tears as they fall. He moves in and out of me at a steady rhythm. There are no words, just feeling. Raw emotion.

My hips rise to meet his over and over again. "Now, Aemilia. Come for me, baby." And just like that my body releases me. I feel my heart contract in sync with my pussy as I begin to pulse around him, pulling him deeper inside of me until he slams into me a final time and his body stills.

I hear his labored breathing as he drops his forehead to mine and closes his eyes. "I'm yours. Fuck, you own me Aemilia Albani." His words are a desperate plea. I feel the intensity in them and understand what he means as the contractions of my orgasm drain even last drop of his cum.

I was surviving.

I missed the complexity of his mind.

I never had to miss his heart. You can't miss something that beats inside of you with each and every breath you take. Even before we knew, our souls knew.

But now that I've had all of him, now that I've visited the depths of nirvana, death would be sweeter than an existence in this world without him.

It's not that my presence of life has become irrelevant.

No. It's that what we've formed together is irreplicable. In this moment, I feel an overwhelming peace. I understand now why my parents continued to work as a team, even when the risk seemed too high. Their sacrifice was tragic, but their death was not the end.

Until Death

Death is not a barrier for love, it's merely a bridge to an eternity together.

CHAPTER FIFTEEN
ALEX

My forehead rests flush against hers. I breathe in through my nose and out my mouth, allowing my mind to reinhabit my body after it's departure and return to and from another stratosphere.

Emily runs the palm of her hand over my exposed hip and gasps quietly as I realize it's likely I'm suffocating her. Our bodies are glistening in a heavy sheen of sweat. There isn't much space to move on this small couch. I don't allow my eyes to leave hers as I fight to regain my ability to move and lean up on my arms. I force myself to pull back just far enough to allow her lungs to refill with oxygen.

My cock has made its home inside of her and screams in protest as I slowly remove it from the warm cocoon of ecstasy. I take my time; I hover over her until I'm back on my knees between her legs. Spreading them even further apart with my hands, I watch my cum as it drips from her swollen pussy.

There's something primal in seeing her exposed this way. In seeing the mark I've left on her, inside of her. *Mine.*

She surprises me as she reaches her hand between her legs. With two fingers she runs through our combined orgasms, spreading the fluid over her warmth. She pulls her fingers back up to her mouth and sucks them clean as a knowing smile pulls at the corner of her lips.

My cock jumps from semi-hard to ready to go again in an instant. Fuck if I'm ever going to get my fill of this woman. I lean down between her legs needing to taste for myself.

Running my nose up the length of her thigh, I allow the smell of our sex to intoxicate me the closer I get to her dripping pussy. Emily's small hands grip my head impatiently as she pulls me closer and tries to place me exactly where she wants me.

"You want me to taste, Em? You want me to lick my cum from your pussy?" My lips brush her clit and vibrate against her oversensitive slit as I speak.

"Dammit, Alex. Yes, I want to feel your tongue inside of me. I want you to taste how good we are together." Her hands tug at my head again. But, agent or no agent, her strength isn't a match for mine.

"You like it dirty, don't you Em? You want to be my dirty girl?" I feel the heat and moisture pulse from her pussy with every word I speak. Just how dirty are you, Emily Young?

"Fuck. Yes, I want to be your dirty girl. Please." Lifting her feet from the couch she crosses her ankles at my back and uses the strength of her thighs to pull my face the remainder of the way to her. Her hips fit perfectly in my hands as I lift her to reach underneath her body, running my tongue over the entrance to her curvy ass. I swipe up until my tongue hits the entrance of her pussy. I swallow down every last drop of the intoxicating combination of our elixir.

I work my tongue in her pussy as she rocks her hips forward and pulls me down, using the force of her entire body to take what she wants. I'm buried inside of her, and hell if this isn't the eighth wonder of the world.

Moving my hand, I manage to slip two fingers inside of her as I drag my mouth up to her clit. Her movements are feverish. I know what she needs to get there for a third time. She's already so close.

"Fuck my mouth, Emily. Show me how you like it, baby." I pump my fingers in and out, adding a third to stretch her further.

"Agh, Alex." Her words are a demand for more as her hips rock faster, her movements jerky and desperate.

Curling my finger inside of her, I touch the one spot I know will push her over the edge. "Come for me now, Em. Come on my face." I suck her clit into my mouth and feel her explode. I feel the pulse of her pussy around my hand, and the warm fluid the gushes from inside of her.

He legs drop back open, and I slowly remove my hand. She's exhausted.

I pepper kisses over her thighs as I pull away from her again. Moisture coats the thick overgrowth of stubble on my jawline, and I wear it like a damn trophy.

Her eyes flutter with the need for rest. She fights against the exhaustion as she sits up on the couch, running her fingers delicately over my hardened length.

"Em, baby, it's late, and we've overstayed our welcome. Even with the five grand that I stole from Sullivan." I speak words that contrast every need and feeling that flows through my veins in this moment. I deny myself, because I see the fatigue in her eyes. We've put our entire team at risk tonight. It's not enough, but for tonight, it has to be.

"The five grand you stole?" An accusation, not a question. Her eyebrows pop up, and the adorable dimple on her cheek that maintains her innocence, pops out. She knows better than to be surprised. The underlying sass in the tone of her voice says as much.

"Borrowed. Technicalities. Whatever. I gave it back, obviously." I shrug my shoulders in response. It's all the same in my world. Give and take. Plus and minus. She knows this about me.

I reach to the floor, grab my jeans and pull them up my thighs. I wish I had a t-shirt or something for Em. I don't like the idea of her walking out of this room in her lingerie. Sure, it was fine when she walked in, but things have changed now. The world has shifted.

I know dancing is a part of what makes her who she is. I love that about her, but I want to hold on to this time between us for a little longer. I'm not ready to give her back yet, and the moment she walks out of this room wearing nothing at all is the moment I have to reconcile what I so desperately want with the reality of what I can have.

She pulls on her fishnet tights, and I reload my pistol, clipping it back into the belt at my waist. I take a sick joy in knowing that I do not plan to clean her juices from Reid's weapon before returning it. If I return it. I'm feeling a little partial to the firearm now.

"Wanna wear my sweatshirt? I don't need it. I can walk out of here shirtless." I walk over to the lone chair in the room and grab my hat and the black hooded sweatshirt I wore tonight.

"The fuck, Straton? This isn't Chippendales Male Revue. That won't look suspicious at all." She stands from the couch in nothing but her red stilettos, fishnets and the black thong that I know is still soaked with the consequences of our actions tonight. I question every decision I made about needing to leave this room.

Her hair is a mess, and what's left of her makeup is smeared. A tear runs the length of her tights from her ankle to her thigh on her left leg. She looks thoroughly fucked, and I smile to myself with pride. I did that.

"Stop looking at me like that, weirdo." She saunters her sexy ass right on by me, bending over mere inches from where I stand to pick up her corset. Is everything this woman does seductive? I swear she's trying to drive me insane.

"Like what?" I walk up behind her and take the strings of her corset from her capable hands, re-lacing them and concealing as much exposed skin as possible as I go.

"Like you wanna get shot. I am not a conquest, Straton. Don't go all caveman on me now, you're smarter than that. Remember, super genius. I like my thug with a side of data analytics and code interpretation. It would behoove you to remember that." She spins around out of my hands as soon as I tie the final string, pushing me down in the chair.

She towers over me now, and I brace myself for what's to come.

"I've missed the hell out of you Alex. So much that my heart physically ached every single time I stepped on that stage to dance. For whatever reason, I think my heart might lo…um…like yours a little. I guess you've been assigned to my case, emphasis on the MY. This is my team, and I will fight like hell to protect them. We've got work to do, and that will always be priority one. I can protect myself. I do not need a bodyguard. What I need is someone that can damn well do their job and not get themselves killed in the process. Understood?" Her hands grip her hips tightly. Her voice is firm.

This woman is my queen.

Leaning forward in the chair, I clasp my hands together in front of me. I like to play, but she needs to understand that I'm serious about her protection. I'm serious about her mission and the protection of this team. "Your mission is my mission, Em. It has been for a long time. I might have a badge now, but I still fight for you. Always."

A smile creeps up the corner of her lip, despite her best attempts at maintaining a serious face. "Welcome to the team, geek. Now, let's go."

Leaving me in the chair, she turns and heads to the door. She's dismissing me.

Bump that noise.

I speak seconds before she can turn the handle to

leave, forcing her to pause her quick exit. "Home? You said we could practice more at home. I'm wondering if you meant that in the present tense or if that was just a theoretical statement made in the heat of the moment." I lean back in the chair like I have all the time in the world and cross one leg over the other. My hat and the hood of my sweatshirt shroud the arrogant smile that teases my lips.

"Get your ass up, Straton, and walk out the front door of this fine establishment like you just had the best lay of your life. You know how to contact me." Her voice remains hard, but the smile in her eyes and the extra sway in her step when she turns the handle and walks back through the door tell me she's not unaffected by what just happened between us. Quite the opposite.

She's stubborn as hell, and I don't give a damn if she chooses to live inside of a fortress. I scaled the gates a long time ago. Maybe she realizes it, maybe she doesn't – doesn't matter. She found me. I was doing just fine on my own, but she searched me out, and I don't come with a return policy. We're in this battle together.

Standing from the chair, I follow her path out the door, but where she turned left, I turn right.

I keep my hood up and my head down. This club was open to the public when I walked in tonight, but as I walk out, it gives off a very different vibe.

The front door is locked and guarded by two soldiers, one of which I recognize as my friend from earlier. The lights are up, enough to cast the room in a low glow.

Various drugs are tested, weighed and cut on a table near the bar. The young, female bartender that verified my transaction earlier now counts cash as another soldier stands behind her and watches her every move.

I observe as I pass, but I'm not a field agent. I investigate data. I know what's happening here is illegal, but it's just part of the world I now find myself engulfed in. I move along and don't stop until the man that questioned me earlier opens the door and grants my exit without further protest.

Tonight, or I guess this morning, I head back to Reid's apartment under the cover of darkness. I've had a taste of the forbidden fruit, and now I'm addicted, it's that simple.

Em was right earlier; she isn't a conquest. This isn't some rare, once in a lifetime event. No, she is my commitment for a lifetime. She's intelligent, wild and free. I just want her to allow me to continue to live in her presence. I don't want to own her; I want to be on her team.

The kind of team that shares a last name. Forever.

CHAPTER SIXTEEN
EMILY

My stomach flips and my cheeks hurt from the cheese whiz smile that I can't shake as I walk into my apartment just before three in the morning. I am not a cheek-hurt kind of smiler, that's reserved for girls with dreams of big white dresses and overpriced cakes. But I can't help it, I smile anyway.

My entire adult life I've carried the weight of the world on my shoulders. I'm constantly compiling and compartmentalizing. Years before I was ready, I was forced to grow the hell up, and fast. Tonight though, I feel young. I'm sore in all the right places, not to mention some other places I didn't even realize I had muscles in. I will take that workout any day of the week.

I should be exhausted, but I'm exhilarated. The endorphins that pump through my system at a steady pace serve as a reminder that sleep won't come tonight.

Alex.

I knew it. I knew something was different the moment I walked into that room. My world was tilting. Hell, it didn't just tilt, it flipped right on over.

The door closes at my back. I'm careful to lock it, this neighborhood leaves a bit to be desired, albeit much fancier than a dumpster.

I drop my bag onto the couch, kicking off my sneakers as I go. I walk to the kitchen table where I closed my laptop in a fit of frustration what seems like months ago but was really only hours and open it back up, not bothering to turn it on. He doesn't need me for that piece. He sees me, I can feel him.

The phone in my back pocket dings with an alert that my password has been reset. Impeccable timing, really.

"*Robin Hood*?" I speak out loud to an empty room, but I'm not alone.

"Robin Hood? The fuck kind of alias is that." Reid's voice surprises me as it filters through my earpiece. While it's not the voice I anticipated, it's familiar and comforting. I'm glad he's back.

"It's a hell of a lot cooler than Riko. You still at the docks? I'm tracking you. What's your ETA?" There's the voice I was expecting. Only, he's not talking to me.

I hear a brief rustling through my earpiece, and I cringe at the unwanted intrusion of noise. It is too late for that level of racket in my head.

When Reid speaks again his voice is lower, but his words come through loud and clear. "Hell yeah I am, asshole. We're counting in an illegal shipment of firearms. Sullivan's got me down here with some damn strung-out street soldiers that are working for their next hit. Most of them are crashing, so you can imagine it's a party. I'm taking my punishment on the chin for your ass, so you damn well better not be in my bed when I get back. Don't even look at it. Memory foam is only reserved for the elite, keep your ass on the couch." Wait, what? His bed? Alex snickers through my earpiece not even remotely offended by Reid's ranting.

"Hold the damn phone, you two know each other?"

"Since before birth. You should know by now I only associate with the most badass people on the block. Alex is my best friend, Emily. He's also the newest agent assigned to our case, cyber security and IT specialist. Reynolds should have sent something over to you. Wait, how do you two know each other?"

What is my life? I swear. What are the fucking chances my boyfriend and my partner have been best friends since birth?

Whoa there Betsy…my boyfriend? That tastes weird in my mouth.

I walk back to the living space from the kitchen and collapse onto my tiny sofa. I rub my temples with my fingertips and try to think of a good lie. Generally speaking, I consider myself pretty quick witted, but right now my brain is totally stalled out.

"Um…" My words have gone on a temporary strike. Why did Reynolds not send a memo about this? Communication people, communication. It's like I work with a bunch of damn men or something. Wait, maybe he did send a memo that I didn't get because I literally just got my password reset. Damn super genius criminal hacker.

"Currently, all of your IT requests are being filtered through to me. I received a text notification about twenty-four hours ago to reset the password on Agent Young's computer. Instead of delegating the task, I took the opportunity to introduce myself. Emily was so overcome with gratitude for my willingness to assist her in such a dire time of need that she so graciously awarded me an alias of my own...Robin Hood. Fitting, no?" The lie rolls off of his tongue effortlessly, hand dipped in overexaggerated sarcasm. But, why the secrets? I guess this isn't the time or place to let my partner know that I'm in love with his childhood best friend.

Love. Jesus, the hits just keep coming tonight, don't they? This conversation has been more productive than therapy.

"So, overcome with gratitude? Graciously? Young, I told you to stay away from the damn white powder. It is not fun dip. How many times do we have to go over this?" Reid's sarcastic response proves just how close these two must be, huh.

Their bantering does something to finally kickstart my brain, and I waste no time getting in on their little game. "Ah, it all makes sense now. Two pretty boys. Overcompensation of arrogance. The girly hair products you leave all over the bathroom counter back at our apartment. You're sharing a bed. Is there something you need to tell me, Chapman? It's cool, really. Love is love, I'm down with anything. Hell, I play on my own playground too sometimes. This is a judgement free zone as far as I'm concerned."

"Shhhiiiiittt..." They react in unison. I bite down in

my knuckles to hold in my laughter. This is going to be fun.

"Um…uh…Young. Clarify." Alex stumbles over his words, clearly having been transported back to his prepubescent years.

"You heard me. Men…women…I'm here for a good time." Releasing my abused knuckle from my teeth, I smile slyly to myself. It's not a lie if it's the truth.

My laptop remains open in the kitchen just a few feet away from me. I know he's watching me, so I put my phone on the table beside me and pull my sweatshirt over my head, careful not to bump my earpiece.

"And that's all I need to hear about that tonight. I'm out. I've got to get back out on the floor, or I really won't make it back to my bed until sunup. I'm muting my speaker, you know what to do if there's an emergency, Em. *Hood* over there is tracking me. I'm glad you two are hitting it off, it's going to make working together easier. Don't let her lure you into a false sense of security though, Alex. Em's the most dangerous of us all."

I hear a soft click through my earpiece as Reid mutes his side of the conversation, and then nothing – silence.

-o-

ALEX

The most dangerous of us all.

Reid's parting words ricochet in my mind as I sit on the couch in his small apartment and watch Emily on the other side of a monitor I have set up on the coffee table.

If he only knew.

She's silent, but she doesn't remove her earpiece.

Instead, she stands from the couch and pulls a pair of dark washed jeans down her thighs, slowly. Thighs that were just wrapped around my back. She knows exactly what she's doing. It's barely been an hour since I was holding her, and yet I feel incomplete without her here. Her body is angled towards her laptop, that still sits in the same spot I watched her from last night.

Stripped down to her sports bra and thong, she lays back on the couch and runs her fingers through her long, dark hair. She's effortlessly sexy. "Hey, Alex." Her voice is soft when she finally speaks.

"Yeah, Em." I lean back into Reid's couch and get comfortable. I see Reid's location on a second monitor, as well as two more soldiers we currently have undercover back at the club that have yet to return to the apartment complex.

"Why'd you do it?" The blunt delivery of her question momentarily takes me by surprise.

"Do what?" I know what she's asking, but I'm not sure she's ready for my answer.

"We had a plan. It didn't have to go down like that. Hell, it didn't even have to go down at all that night. I warned you. I told you to shut it down. We could have pushed it off. We would have figured something else out." Her movements still, her hand tangled in the disarray of her hair in frustration. She stares directly into the lens of the camera on her laptop and waits for me to speak.

"The answer doesn't have to be complicated." My sigh is audible. I wish she could see my face. I wish I could touch her.

"Just like I told you back at the Club, Em. Your mission is my mission. When my mom died, I was pissed at the world, but most of all I was mad at myself. I was angry because I felt like it was my fault she was on the road that night at that exact moment. If I hadn't called her to come home, she would have still been at practice. She would have come home later, and maybe that asshole would have just landed himself in a ditch somewhere. I was angry at my dad because his sickness, his inability to win his battle against his depression and the coping mechanisms that he chose to deal with it put me in that position to begin with. I just had so much damn anger.

"Then, I discovered that, through technology, I could channel that anger into something positive. I took revenge on the bad guys of the world in the only way I knew how. They couldn't catch me because I was too damn good, too smart. I lost my best friend; I lost my future. I was so consumed with the anger and the revenge that I lost everything. Reid was off becoming a hero the legal way, and I was alone. Then I met you, and I saw the same fire, the same need to vindicate a wrong burning inside of you. But I saw something else too. I saw a strong, intelligent woman. A woman with the strength of an army of men, a strength that I didn't have. I saw a warrior. I wanted to be a part of that. A switch inside of me turned on that had been dormant for a long time." She stares at me through the camera, and I watch her.

She's listening, and I focus on that knowledge and on the fact that for as long as she doesn't interrupt maybe I can purge some of these demons inside of me. Maybe I can get the words out that need to be said. Words that I practiced over and over again in my mind as I laid awake at night for hours in that damn prison cell.

"We were so close. I felt it, you felt it. The air surrounding our mission was pulsing with energy. I could see them closing in on me. I was monitoring the situation, but you'd worked too hard. We'd come so far. It was my sacrifice to make. My decision. And I chose you. If I had it to do over again, I would make the exact same call every single time. Always you." I can hear the beat of my heart as it pounds in my chest and I lay out my truths in front of her. She holds the power here. The thought that the sacrifices I've made up until this point could be in vain scares the shit out of me.

Her hand covers her mouth. "Loyal to a fault. That's your fatal flaw. As a human race, our creation is that of imperfection. Your loyalty, while admirable, is also your greatest weakness." She stands from the couch and walks to the laptop, sitting down at the table and running her fingers carefully over the keys.

"Tell me how you really feel, Aemilia." A laugh of self-deprecation bubbles up from my chest.

"No, listen. Just listen to me. I am fiercely independent, I refuse reliance. I am physically and mentally incapable of admitting defeat. My fatal flaw. All things in the universe are governed by opposing, yet interdependent forces." The more she speaks that faster her words come. It's like she thinks if she doesn't get it all out in the open, she might lose it forever. I listen to her words and begin to understand where she's going with her train of thought. This woman's intelligence never ceases to amaze me.

"The theory of yin-yang." I finish for her.

"Exactly. You're my yin. My balance. Apart, we are flawed. But together, our imperfect qualities form perfection." God, this woman. I physically ache to be near her.

I start to speak again, but she interrupts before I can say the words that sit on the tip of my tongue.

"Wait, hold on. Dammit." Em's words come out urgent, rushed. Her moss green eyes turn stormy as I watch her push back from the chair at her kitchen table, knocking it over to the floor. I see something flashing in the corner of the video feed as she snatches it up form the table.

Wait? Surely not. Does she have a beeper?

"What is it, Em? What's wrong? What's in your hand?" I scan my monitors looking for something out of place, anything, but everything appears normal. Everything with the exception of Emily running around her apartment grabbing up articles of clothing in a panic like a crazy person.

"Code red. Reid used the code. Pick me up, Straton, we've got somewhere we need to be."

CHAPTER SEVENTEEN
EMILY

I shove my hands into the pockets of my oversized sweatshirt as I wait impatiently for Alex to arrive in the dark recesses of the alley adjacent to the laundromat below my apartment. Does he even have a means of transportation? I didn't consider that when I told him to pick me up, I just kind of assumed he would. But, come to think of it, I really have no idea.

I swear, that's all I need. Alex rolling up on a bicycle. I giggle as my mind runs away with itself. I imagine Alex, all big and bad and covered in tattoos pulling up to the curb on a little girl's bicycle.

Surely, he would have called me back if he didn't have a way to get here. How long has it been since I hung up on him? Feels like forty forevers. My earpiece is on, but he's quiet. Reid is silent, except for the damn flashing of the twenty-year-old beeper that I hold in my hand. Bet Alex got a kick out of that.

Reid and I have been working together for a while now. We made the decision at the beginning of this mission that we needed a way to communicate that wouldn't be monitored. Not even by the most savvy, intelligent computer geniuses that the FBI may or may not employ. Reid purchased a set of old beepers off of some black-market website. We only use them for code red, meaning we need to meet at the warehouse location privately, or someone is dead. The beeper literally flashes red over and over again when the call goes out until the original sender cancels it. It's alphanumeric, so it also reads 9-1-1 across the screen. Don't ask me the specifics of how it works though, that was all Reid. He might not be a technology expert, but I'll give it to him, the man knows a thing or two. Just don't let him hear you say that. His head is big enough without the added compliments. It would be unfair to the entire female population to continue to pad his ego.

I hear him before I see him. The engine of a motorcycle roars through the quiet of the night until it comes to a stall on the sidewalk in front of where I stand. Lifting the shield on a black helmet that matches the sleek black motorcycle he seemingly manifested out of thin air, Alex smiles like a little boy with a new Tonka truck as he speaks.

"Care to explain what's on fire? Or was this a ploy to get me back in your bed, Em? Because honestly, all you had to do was ask. I don't have any possessions to speak of besides my equipment. I'm happy to move in. I will even buy us a sweet little 'welcome to our humble home' doormat for the entrance." Oh God, twenty-four hours and Reid's arrogance is already rubbing off on him.

"Did you steal this, Straton? Did you not learn anything from your time in prison?" I stalk towards him as I tease him. It's fun and he's hot as hell sitting on a motorcycle that could be stolen property. I've got a thing for bad boys, sue me.

Well, that and, for some reason, I'm feeling a little nervous. Humor seems to be my newfound crutch in these situations that are still very foreign to me. It's probably best that I not get stuck thinking about that too heavily for the time being.

We don't have time to waste. Without further hesitation, I slide in behind him, spreading my legs around his and letting the purring vibration of the engine massage the soreness that remains there from earlier.

"It's Reid's." He turns his body slightly and pulls the helmet from his head, plopping it down over mine. I open my mouth to protest, to question, but he doesn't give me the chance. He turns right back around and presses the gas full speed ahead. The low purr between my legs turns into an angry roar within an instant. My arms fly around his torso, not wanting to risk death by cement to the face, and I hold on for dear life.

How does he know where we're going? Did he not just ask me about the fire? Now we're flying through the night with no way for me to tell him where to go.

I try to focus on the possible cause for Reid's 9-1-1, really, I do, but my body betrays me as I feel a familiar tingling low in my abdomen. My body presses even closer to Alex's. I lock the muscles of my thighs around his and allow my hands the freedom to wander over his torso. He didn't bother to put the sweatshirt he had on earlier back on, he's just in a t-shirt. My hands run over the ridges and concaves of his carved abdomen as we fly through the dead of night at a rate of speed that an actual officer of the law might take offense to. Good thing there aren't any of those around right now.

The steady vibration against my still sensitive clit reignites the fire that was never fully dormant. My hips rock forward on their own, and I am not ashamed in the least bit as I dry hump this man from behind. If I was a betting woman, I would place all my money down on Alex being hard as a steel pipe. I slide my hands down over his chest again, and yep, there it is. Winner, winner.

I've lost track of time and space. I barely realize that we've slowed until Alex kicks out the kickstand on the motorcycle and turns to look at me, that boyish smile still there from earlier. His eyes dance as he looks to my hands that are still very much on his hardened length.

Caught. Dammit. I jerk my hands back quickly, placing them on my own thighs instead.

He chuckles to himself. I feel my cheeks pink for what's surely the first time in my life, which is exactly why I leave the helmet securely on my head. Blushing is not for badass FBI agents.

"Wanna finish this little game you started, or do we have somewhere we need to be?" Alex's voice echoes through the earpiece inside of my helmet and reminds me exactly why we are on this motorcycle. Get your shit together, Albani. This isn't a fucking joy ride.

My eyes dart through the darkness, and I recognize the alley we're parked in as one near the harbor.

We're close to our secure location, but these particular warehouses are owned by an older gentleman. Retherford. I think I remember seeing the name in a file somewhere. He owns a farm out in the country, but his health is declining so these warehouses remain unused and vacant. Or did he recently die and leave them to a son? Grandson? Hell, I don't remember. He can do whatever he wants with them as long as he's not involved in my case.

Thankful that my mind was distracted long enough to hopefully return my face to its natural color, I pull my helmet off and hand it to Alex, who leaves it on the motorcycle as he steps off and extends his hand for mine. Well, would you look at who's a gentleman.

"How did you know?" It's the only thing I can manage to say in my current predicament. My brain and my body can't figure out how the hell to work together. I have fifty questions that are pertinent to our mission, but the words I really want to say involve asking him to throw me up against the brick wall to our backs. That's not an option right this minute.

"Educated guess. Meeting location is in the files. You said code red. I could still track Reid's location, so I made a decision based on the known variables, and here we are. As for the charges I see you trying to pin on me in the recesses of your mind for grand theft auto, despite my earlier statement, Reid keeps this beauty stashed in the overgrown shrubbery at the run-down park just off of the property adjacent to the apartments.

Close enough for easy access, but far enough outside of Sullivan's extra eyes. Reid's a horny son of a bitch. My best guess is this is his ride when he needs to find a release and doesn't want the Bureau knowing about it." He shrugs like it's no thing that my partner feels the need to keep secrets from me. Rude.

"I just took a ride on Chapman's sex motorcycle?" I eye the clean lines of the gorgeous piece of machinery and try my best to look disgusted. But really, it is sexy. Maybe I'm a little jealous. And okay, a hella lot horny, so I guess it's doing its job.

"Neh, this thing is just an overpriced piece of machinery. That feeling I know you feel right now because I see it in your eyes, that wasn't because of this motorcycle. This thing might be in Reid's name, but your panties are wet right this minute. Aren't they, Em? I did that. That was all me. Remember that." Tugging at my hand, he pulls me to him and smacks a kiss on my lips before turning down the dark alley. He drags me behind him toward a location that I know well, but have had to use very few times before.

Through the swarm of butterflies and the bucket full of *feelings* that float around in my stomach, something else gnaws at me. An uneasy feeling that I can't shake. I unknowingly made a selfish decision tonight and, in doing so, put someone else's life in danger. Mel walked up those steps to Sully's office, and I can't help but wonder if this has something to do with her.

But Reid doesn't even know about Mel's history, or does he? I started, but I haven't had time to finish updating my case notes yet. But, what else could it be about?

"Twenty-four hours and you're already replacing me?

I'm wounded." Alex drops my hand as we enter the dimly lit warehouse and Reid saunters towards us with his hand pressed dramatically against his chest.

"Shove it, Riko. I just took a ride on your secret sex toy. You've been keeping secrets. I don't want to hear your pouting." I toss my beeper at him and try to remain unaffected by the way Alex distances himself from me in front of Reid. It might be necessary, but I don't like it. Not even a little bit.

"You stole my Ducati, Straton?" Reid's eyes whip from mine to Alex's.

"Stole, borrowed. Remember what your sweet mother always said about the sharing." Alex stops a few feet to my right.

"I do not share the Ducati." Reid doesn't yield his approach until he's toe to toe with Alex. The two look like they might throw down right here in the warehouse.

Alex leans against an exposed support column and crosses one foot over the other, not a care in the world for the man that looks like he's prepared to put a bullet in his leg. "You see, Em, Reid here never has been good with the sharing." He smirks, and I swear I see steam legit blow from Reid's ears as I try to hide my smile.

Reid huffs like a child and holds his hand out in the space between he and Alex. "Give me the keys, Straton."

"Can't, I left them in it." Oh, for the love of God.

Alex's smile continues to grow as Reid steps into him, but I move before either of them can react. Pulling my weapon, I discharge one single round into the air. The echo rings out in the silence of the night as it blasts through the metal roof of the warehouse. I'm fairly certain both men nearly wet their pants.

Extreme yet effective.

"Bloody fucking hell, Young." A slew of curse words fly from Reid's mouth as he turns abruptly towards me. Alex doesn't move, but he stares at me offended like I physically shot at him and didn't just issue a teeny tiny warning.

"Bloody? Did I scare you British, Chapman? That's a new one for me." I laugh now that I've gotten their attention and re-holster my weapon.

"Speak. Now. What's with the 9-1-1, Reid? One minute you were in my ear counting in stock a few blocks from here. The next minute my beeper is flashing a code red and I'm thinking maybe you're dead." I place my hands on my hips and prepare myself for his answer.

"Dead? You sure as hell didn't get in a hurry. I could have taken a nap, commandeered a prostitute and gotten in a quickie in the time it took you to get here. Shows how much I mean to you, Young. We've got to work on your response time." His stance obviously relaxes as he steps out of Alex's personal space.

I roll my eyes and shrug my shoulders. If this were a true emergency, he wouldn't be standing here shooting the shit, more worried about the state of his precious motorcycle than the mission. I allow myself a second to breathe and my muscles to relax. Or relax as much as my body will allow with Alex standing just a few feet away making my blood hum.

"Eh, we both know you're like a cat. You've got…what? At the very minimum nine lives. As far as I'm aware, you've only used up five or six, if that."

Reid nods and his face turns serious before he speaks again. "One of the newbies got a call as I was walking back out onto the warehouse floor. Sullivan had one of his other guys call out for product testers. Guns weren't the only thing that came in on the shipment that arrived last night."

"Yeah, well, that's not uncommon. He'll be dead by daylight, and his body will just be one more we add to the file." My face hardens. My thoughts immediately start categorizing facts that might be pertinent to our case.

"Right, except this product wasn't just the typical. Powder wasn't the only drug in this shipment. They also had a ketamine knockoff coming in from overseas. Not the FDA approved shit if you get my drift."

"So, we're not just talking a sedative, date rape. We're talking date rape on steroids. Human trafficking. Potential for long distance transport. Total blackouts and memory loss. Hell, that's just wishful thinking. Unknown side effects, including but not limited to death." The butterflies in my stomach die a quick death. My gut churns with a familiar anxiety that quickly turns to adrenalin.

"Bingo. I overheard bits and pieces. My guy was repeating a location back through on the call and it wasn't the club. I wasn't able to make out his exact words." His eyes lock onto mine. We're closer to sunrise than we are to sunset and none of us have slept yet. Reid and I will both be expected in the club later to work. So, instead of getting tired, I straighten my shoulders and prepare for a long ass day.

"He's headed to the location we suspect to be out on

the interstate?" My question is more of a statement of fact as we work through what we know.

"Wilks and Sullivan." Reid replies knowingly.

"We very well can't go into those warehouses guns blazing. We don't even have verified location coordinates. You know as well as I do that's a recipe for disaster. Not to mention, Reynolds will have all of our asses." Mel, why do you have to make stupid decisions? We need more time. Please don't be out there tonight.

"Mel? Who's Mel?" Alex speaks, and I realize too late that I was thinking out loud.

"Mel. Melanie Davis. The dancer?" Reid asks.

"Yes. Look, I haven't been able to update the file. I got some information while you were back at headquarters on the suspected interstate warehouse location. Sullivan has been taking some of the dancers out to those warehouses to *earn* some extra money. I have reason to believe that it's a brothel disguised as a reward; sickening really. God knows what is going on out there, but the money is enticing to these young girls that barely make enough to live off of. It's still really quiet at the club; rumor has it that it's invitation only. He's glamorizing it right now to build the suspense, but it's only a matter of time before something goes sideways and somebody dies. One wrong move and we've got a blood bath on our hands. Or worse, we lose the operation entirely, and are back at square one.

"My plan tonight was to meet with Sullivan at close and persuade him to give me an invitation. However, I got tied up with a client, and Mel was called up to Sullivan's office instead. She's too young, too innocent.

She won't last twenty-four hours in one of those brothels. Heaven forbid they drug her. She'll never be the same again. She has dreams, she wants a future." My words are coming so quickly that I can barely catch my breath.

"Whoa, whoa, whoa. Slow the damn train down. You were planning on heading out to the warehouses tonight? Warehouses that we know next to nothing about, to investigate a brothel without any backup whatsoever. No prior approval? Not even a damn note in the file? You didn't even realize I was back in the state, did you? What the fuck, Em? You're my partner, your life is my responsibility. You said yourself that we can't just go in there guns blazing." Uh oh. Reid's pissed.

I don't know why I look to Alex for support, but I do. My brain immediately thinks he'll have my back, instead, all I get is a face carved of stone. He begins to pace the length of the warehouse, back and forth, but he doesn't acknowledge me.

It's in that moment that I realize that I've just admitted to using my body to persuade a known criminal to invite me into a brothel. Logically, I can see why the man that holds my heart is angry. Now both of the men in my life are pissed. Lovely.

I turn back to Reid because my discussion with Alex is for later, and in private. I speak directly to Reid, but hope that on some level my words register with Alex. I have to count on him not being mad enough to block me out completely. I just got him back. I sure as hell am not going to lose him now. Not over something like this.

"This is my job. I don't know any other way to do it, Chapman. I take risks, especially when they involve something or someone that I'm passionate about. You know this about me. I give one hundred and ten percent all of the damn time because I'm never satisfied with just enough. Good enough is for fucking fairytales. If I'm satisfied, if I become complacent, I'm dead. I was here and you weren't. Decisions had to be made. For years it was just me. I can damn well take care of myself. I did make an attempt at updating the file. I knew you would be back. I considered risk versus reward, and well, per usual, I just couldn't find it in me to care about the risk when the reward was saving the lives of innocents. I listened to my gut. I won't apologize for taking a chance that could have given us the break we've been waiting for in this case."

CHAPTER EIGHTEEN
ALEX

My feet move on their own as I try to categorize my thoughts.

Respond, do not react.

It's a mantra I heard my mother repeat over and over again as I was growing up. My mother was and still is the most patient human being I've ever encountered. It's how she dealt with my father's illness. It's how she kept our family together.

Instead of reacting immediately in a stressful or overwhelming situation, she would close her eyes, take a deep breath and repeat those words to herself.

I don't say the words out loud, even though I hear her voice repeating them loud and clear in my head. Instead, I pace. It's how I process. My feet move and they take me with them. I focus on the facts of the situation. Instead of acting out of emotion, I allow my mind time to form an appropriate and well thought out response.

Most of the time. Okay, half the time.

I am only human.

My gut turns, but not for the reasons that I'm sure are running through Emily's mind right now. She thinks I'm angry. She thinks I'm pissed that she would sacrifice herself. She couldn't be more wrong.

We were almost too late, and if fate deemed it true, it wouldn't have mattered. None of it would have. If I hadn't walked into that club tonight and intercepted her, she might be at that brothel right now without the support of our team. This job isn't for the faint of heart. Emily is one of the toughest, bravest agents I know. She's also one of the most reckless. It's what makes her good at what she does, but it's also dangerous as fuck.

My heart seizes in my chest. I question for a moment whether or not I will survive a life with this woman and her inability to stay away from danger.

It's like what happened to my mother. You see, after the anger faded away. At some point, maybe when I was laid up in a prison cell with nothing to do but contemplate my decisions in life, I realized something.

Fate is inevitable. Your ability to change it is the same as your ability to force the sun to rise in the morning or the moon to shine in the night sky. You can't.

Every single day we make decisions, most without even thinking. Time continues forward. There is no rewind button for life. We can't go back, and so what if we could? The outcome wouldn't change because of one single thing…fate. Respond to the circumstances you're handed and continue forward, don't dwell.

"You weren't meant to be there tonight, Em. Sure,

you might have planned it, but the fact that it didn't happen means that it was never meant to happen at all." My words are certain as I finally respond to words that were never meant for me to begin with. Her body faces Reid. She's not speaking to me, she's not even looking at me, but she pauses when my voice echoes through the warehouse.

An arsenal of weapons, cases of ammunition, explosives, two pristine identical black SUVs and one completely badass helicopter fill the space surrounding us. I don't focus on those things though; I focus on the way her body freezes when I open my mouth. I listen for her breathing. Even though I can't hear it from where I stand, I physically feel her as she takes a deep breath and it filters through her lungs.

"This isn't the time, Agent Straton." Funny. I've respected the wishes of the Director. Well, mostly. He asked me not to tell anyone how Em and I were connected. But just as I can't force the new moon to shine in the night sky, I can't hide what's happening between us from my best friend, my brother.

"Really? Then when, Em? Because what if fate said something different last night? What if fate ended with you at that warehouse out on the interstate with no backup? What if we didn't get back in time?" I drop my tiny bombs of truth as I walk toward her and don't stop until I'm well within her personal space. I push her because I know she can handle it. She's already discharged her weapon once tonight, but I risk my life and place a hand on her hip. I come to a stop, looking down into her muddied, green eyes.

She's conflicted. She doesn't know if she's wants to hit me or kiss me. It's cool. I'm down for either, as long as she's mine.

Her eyes remain locked on mine as she speaks through gritted teeth. "Is this warehouse secure, Reid?"

"Yes."

"This is your code red, it's your call tonight. Are we moving in or waiting?"

"The sun will be up within two hours. What's done is done. We report to the club per usual. Speak to Mel, find out what she knows. We'll go from there." I guess we're all gonna assume this Mel person is alive; half glass full, I like it.

She nods and takes another deep breath, this one shakier than the first, but she doesn't step out of my hold. My hand remains on her hip, my eyes fixated on hers.

What are you scared of Em?

"So, I'm just going to go out on a limb here and say that I feel like there's something I'm missing." I feel Reid's glare as he stares at us.

"Way to read the room, Chapman." Em smarts as she pulls her bottom lip into her mouth between her teeth and begins abusing it. She's thinking, determining her next move. I give her a minute. I try to remain patient and let her make the decision here.

Reid might be her partner, but he's my best friend. He's no idiot. He sees me. He sees the way my hand holds her hip. He notices the way she leans into me, even though she's trying to act unaffected.

Life is short. Only fate knows if today will be our last. It's important to our case and our safety to keep what's happening between Emily and I on the low, but we can't keep hiding it from Reid. It's impossible. If anything, he needs to know so that we can all maintain our safety on this mission together. So, I make a decision, I choose. And I hope that my fate isn't getting murdered by the woman that I love, and my body dumped into the harbor.

"What if it wasn't me in that room with you tonight, Em?" I hold her gaze, even as Reid interrupts.

"Wait. In that room? Em, your client? Alex, I left you in my apartment tonight. Your ass was literally sitting on my couch shoving popcorn in your mouth when I walked out." I feel his eyes dart between us as he searches for the truth.

I finally break eye contact with her as I cut my eyes over to Reid. "I watched you check in at the club, and then I watched as you were reassigned to the docks. Then, maybe, I took a little field trip." I can't help the goofy smile that sneaks up the side of my mouth as I let my arrogance show for a second. This sexy, independent, totally badass woman is mine.

"You spent months with sweet little Julie Campbell in the library, sniffing her hair and pretending to be an idiot, and never once did you make a move on her. You meet my partner one single time, and now you're taking field trips to a gentleman's club to watch her dance? Damn, Straton. What happened to you in prison, man?"

"Are you going to tell him, Em, or do you want me to?" Her eyes remain on me. I see her brain working as I squeeze her hip with my fingers and pull her closer, flush to my side.

"I'm the reason Alex went to prison. He spent the last

year locked up because of me."

Not exactly the confession I was expecting.

"Nope, you do not get to blame yourself for that, woman. I was the reason I went to prison. I allowed myself to get caught. There's a difference." Her forehead lands on my chest as she exhales. I allow my lips to brush over the top of her head. I breath in the scent of fresh rain and sunflowers from her hair and allow it to fill my lungs, giving me a renewed strength.

"I've seen your file, Alex. You went to prison for hacking the database of the Department of Defense. We've discussed this." Reid continues to question us, clearly puzzled by what he thinks he already knows and what he sees in front of him.

"And that's all true. I was inside of the Department of Defense. Specifically, I was inside of your files. This case before it was this exact case. Before Em was ever your partner. Before she was employed by the US Government, she was mine. She needed information, and I had the means to get it for her."

"More like you were mine, Straton. My *Robin Hood*." Emily finally speaks, leaning her head back and looking up at me.

"Yours. Always yours." A let my lips tilt into a grin.

"Wait. You two? You're together? Does Reynolds know about all of this? How in the hell did this even happen?"

"Together. Yes. We met in a chat room on the dark web, it's all very romantic." Em snickers to herself as the gravity of our secret is lifted from her shoulders and she sums up years of correspondence and co-dependance in one over-simplified sentence.

"I guess we've always kind of been together. It just took us a while to find each other. As for Reynolds, the answer is need to know. But yes, he is aware of the circumstances." I feel her body stretch under my hold as she reaches up on her toes and grips my neck with her small hands. She pulls me down to her level and slides her tongue in my mouth without hesitation.

Turning into her body, I grip her hips with both hands and take as much as she's willing to give. Her tongue swipes over my teeth, and I'm hungry for more of her instantly. My grip tightens as I momentarily lose myself in the way her soft hands tug on my neck; a demand for more and a complete contradiction to the tough persona she portrays to the outside world. Her body grinds into mine. I'm about two seconds from laying her down right here on this concrete, audience and all, until Reid's obnoxious chuckle breaks through our haze of lust.

"Huh, I can't get over it."

I pull back reluctantly as he speaks. Glancing over to him, it's easy to see that he's just as affected by our little show as I was. He doesn't even try to adjust his obvious erection.

"Get over what? The fact that your best friend is in love with you partner or the fact that you're surprised that you think it's hot?" Emily's words come out in a pant as she tries to catch her breath. I haven't said those words to her. Not fully, not yet. Not in the way that they need to be said, but she knows anyway. The heart knows what it knows.

"No. The fact that all this time I've watched you

prance around half naked. I've seen you dance for a room full of men. I've even jacked off while I watched you shower. I've slept in a room with you more than I've ever slept with another woman. This entire time I was convinced that you were a lesbian."

Emily's laughter rings out loudly through the warehouse. She's nearly hysterical as she heaves, bending over at the waist, falling out of my grip. Piggy snorts come from her nose, and it makes her all the more adorable. This hard-as-hell chick snorting, there's just something cute about it. Innocence when she's far from innocent.

"The fuck, Chapman? A lesbian?" I try to keep Emily upright in her fit of giggles. I raise my eyebrow at my best friend and try not to imagine him touching himself while watching my woman naked in the shower.

"Slow your testosterone, both of you." Emily finally begins to catch her breath as she throws her arm out in front of me. Is she protecting Reid, or is she protecting me? Who knows, really. What she doesn't realize is that neither one of us need protection. We might kid around, but we've always been on the same team. That doesn't change now that there are three of us instead of two.

"What? Don't look at me like I'm the crazy one. She literally just said she likes to play on her own playground. I have seen her tongue down another woman's throat before with my own eyes. I've never seen her with a man that didn't pay up front in cash. What am I supposed to think?"

My eyes cut to Emily. Damn, I want to see her mouth on another woman, but I don't say that right now.

"All facts, I'll give you that, Reid. The only man I

wanted was locked up. Why bother with a half assed attempt at a substitute?" She shrugs as she straightens back up and looks up at me before speaking again.

She pretends like she's telling me a secret, but she makes for damn sure she speaks loud enough for Reid to hear. "He's just salty that I never came onto him. His big ass ego just took a hit, and he doesn't know what to do with himself." Now it's my turn to snort. I laugh at her obvious burn.

"Karma. You thought I didn't know about Julie Campbell. Not that I cared at the time, but I feel like this is somehow karma biting you in the ass for taking her to Winter Formal." I run my hand over Em's hip until it rests in that perfect nook of her back, just above her ass.

"Wasn't the only thing I took." I can hear the smirk on Reid's arrogant face as he speaks without even looking at him. Really, I don't give a damn. Maybe he slept with Julie Campbell, maybe he took her virginity, I couldn't care less. I wasn't in the right mind space at the time. If you really think about it, it always comes back to fate anyway. I was never meant to sleep with Julie Campbell, my heart was never hers to take.

"Oh, for fuck's sake. Is it always going to be a pissing match between you two?" Em smiles into my chest as she rolls her eyes.

"Yes, yes, it is. Better hop on board now, Young." I remove my hand for just a second before swatting her plump, denim clad ass. Reid's laughter mixes with mine as we both hear her surprised squeal turn to a soft moan. Her body folds into mine completely. I encase her body with mine, planting soft kisses over the top of her hair.

This is going to be fun…if we all make it out alive.

What am I saying? We have to make it out of here alive, there is no other option. Em isn't the only one that needs to get on board, fate better get its ass on board too.

CHAPTER NINETEEN
EMILY

"How are you getting in and out of Sullivan's fortress over there?" I ask as Alex's hand rests on my lower back and hovers just above my ass. My skin still stings from where his palm landed just a few minutes ago. If he would just slide his hand down a hair...

"I've been blocking the footage. Covering the seconds it takes me to get in and out of the property with a time lapse. It's nothing really. The glitch that my presence creates in their system is non-existent. They don't have a clue I'm in there, and they're not smart enough to find me even if they knew."

The longer we stand in the warehouse, the heavier my eyes feel. I'm exhausted. The threat of danger is what it is tonight. It's not time; we have to be patient. If the years I spent in the *Pink Lily* taught me anything positive, it was the value of patience. Even if I don't always like it.

The last twenty-four hours feel like twenty-four hundred, and it's only a few hours yet before I need to be back in the club.

I cover the yawn that tries and succeeds to escape my mouth as I speak through my hand. "Oh, so I guess you're fine with staying there, then? No biggie."

I shrug as if I could care less where Alex lays his head at night. Like I'm not already certain that he's coming back to my apartment with me. It only makes sense, really. No cameras, no security, no control freak narcissistic mafia ringleader ready to put a bullet in your brain if he finds you.

Plus, at this point, I just really wanna snuggle.

Alex's hand slides the rest of the way down and over the curve of my ass, and I smile. Oh yeah, he's coming home with me. "Oh, hell no, woman. You heard the man earlier. He doesn't let me get anywhere near the memory foam. You made promises last night, Young. Maybe those promises were made in the heat of the moment, maybe they weren't. Don't care. We had a verbal contract. I've got an almost attorney friend that I'm certain would be willing to argue my defense. Once he gets out of prison that is."

I turn back to Reid as Alex continues to babble on, arguing his point for no reason. You don't hear me arguing back. "Chapman, we're taking the Ducati home. I will see you at the club in a few hours." I angle my body like maybe we're going to make a grab for the motorcycle, we're not. I'm crazy, but I'm not crazy enough to try to steal Reid's toy for a second time in one night. Every man has his limits, and I'm pretty sure Reid is at his tonight.

"Like hell you are, don't make me shoot you both. I'm feeling trigger happy. I need to warn you Young, I'm partial to Straton, so it's likely you'll die first. Bros before hoes and all that." Bros before hoes, he's full of shit. That man chooses pussy first every damn time. He knows it, I know it, I'm pretty sure the majority of the female population in half the country know it.

"How are we supposed to get home, then?" He's lost the plot if he thinks we're taking public transportation at four in the morning.

"Keep calling it home, woman. My cock is hard just hearing you say that word." Alex groans from behind me and sends the butterflies in my stomach swarming again.

Reid jerks his chin toward the fleet of vehicles we keep in the warehouse. "Take one of the SUVs. Alex can bring it back tomorrow night. You can park it in the garage two blocks behind the laundromat. There are cameras on that lot."

"If there's a camera, I can hack it. We'll be able to control the footage. We're good." I turn toward one of the vehicles. Alex follows, not removing his hand until we've approached the driver's side door of the vehicle.

"I fully expect you two to sleep at some point today." Reid speaks, sounding more like a father scolding his teenage children for staying up past bedtime than an FBI agent.

He huffs when neither one of us respond immediately and runs his hand through his jet-black hair. "I swear, how did we go from a prime-time crime show to a freakin' daytime drama within a matter of hours?" Reid turns to walk in the opposite direction, toward the entrance of the warehouse. We're less than an hour from sunrise. We need to move out sooner rather than later. The cover of darkness is our friend.

"Your hang up, not mine. We're going to sleep. After I watch Em shower." Alex reaches around my body and opens the driver's side door. Again with the chivalry. This man is a walking contradiction.

"Enough with the pissing. Get in, Straton, we're going home." I emphasize the last word, knowing what it's doing to him. My attitude might be snappy due to lack of sleep, but I've got a soft spot for the tall, dark and handsome nerd that just brushed my arm with his and sent tingles running down my spine.

"I'm driving. Don't touch the fancy screen. My vehicle, my technology. When we get home, I'm going to bed. You can masturbate while I shower after I get some sleep." I point a finger between both of the insanely hot men that stand before me. "You two are going to be the death of me." Alex rolls his eyes as he closes the door, and I start the vehicle.

I hear Reid through the door. I strain to make out the words he's saying to Alex while he thinks I'm out of earshot. Something about taking care of me. Pssttt…like I need someone to take care of me. Yeah, right. These two and their caveman complexes.

I watch through the tinted window as Alex pulls the keys to the Ducati from his pocket and tosses them to Reid before walking to the passenger side door and sliding in next to me.

"Take me home, Albani." Alex's use of my real name warms me up from the inside out. I feel my dimple pop and that damn blush creeping up my neck for a second time tonight. This can't become a thing.

Pressing a button on the screen in front of me, a door to the warehouse opens. I hit the gas, flying past Reid as Alex and I head back to the apartment. At one time, it was just a place for me to lay my head, but I dunno, now that Alex is here, it really might feel a little like home.

-o-

ALEX

"So that's a no on the shower, then?" I grab the hem of my t-shirt and pull it up and over my head as I follow Emily into her apartment for the first time.

One single flight of metal stairs on the outside of a cinder block building that probably saw Alice from the Brady Bunch at some point lead up to the apartment. There are no other apartments up here, just this one. It's possible that the owners of the laundromat once called this home, but it was long since abandoned by any type of business owner. Now it serves one purpose and one purpose only. Low budget rental. My best guess is cash under the table. If Em is paying at all. It's equally as likely she is squatting in the property. Depending on the laws of this good state, if we squat long enough, we might just own a new laundromat when this is all over with. Maybe I need to get Walsh to look into the legalities of that.

Paint peels off in chunks from the outside of the door. What was once a plush orange shag carpet is now worn through to the padding beneath it.

She doesn't even turn to look at me stripping in her living room as she walks the apartment looking for who or what, I don't know. Danger, I guess, it's just part of who she is. Don't get me wrong, I'm thankful she's capable enough to protect herself, but I don't want her to have to look in the shadows for danger everywhere she goes.

One day. Maybe not today, but one day, I will provide this woman a safe place. A place where I can watch for the evil of the night, and she can finally breathe. I want to give that to her. I want her to have a place where she can find peace.

The yellow linoleum in the kitchen isn't fairing much better than the carpet, but something about it is oddly cozy. It's lightyears nicer than a prison cell, so I'm not here to complain.

"No shower, but I'm about to strip naked and lay in that bed right there. I won't slide under the covers if you wanna check me out for a minute while I sleep." Satisfied with her walkthrough, she finally turns back to look at me as I stand barefoot in only a pair of jeans in her living room.

"I'm really glad you turned out to be sexy. This could have gone either way, honestly. I mean, don't get me wrong, I'm not shallow. But I'd kind of built you up in my head for a while there. I had this image of what you looked like, and this, well this was a definite upgrade, even from that."

"Yeah, tell me, Aemilia. What exactly did you imagine?" I walk towards her, meeting her in the doorway to her tiny bedroom. The same doorway I watched her in that first night. The room is even smaller in person. The bed touches nearly all four corners of the walls. You have to climb over the mattress to get to what I'm assuming is a washroom.

I know she's tired. I know she needs to rest. Lack of sleep means a slower response time, dulled senses and an inability to form appropriate reactions. I will not be the reason she's in danger at the club later tonight. So instead, I stop in front of her and grabbing her sweatshirt I pull it up over her head, careful not to snag it on her long hair.

Her head tilts to the side as she thinks. "In my mind I always imagined you were tall, but then again, usually you sat at a computer, so it wasn't super evident. You wore glasses, which really were a turn on. Do you wear contacts?" Her green eyes snap to mine as I kneel down in front of her and pull her shoes off one at the time. Like, she just realized that I do not, in fact, wear glasses.

"Well, first of all, I am tall. My vision is 20/20, but I can order up some blue light glasses in a minute. Don't let that be a deal breaker here." I smile at her stereotyping and continue to undress her.

"Oh, I've actually heard there are a lot of benefits to wearing blue light glasses." She shimmies as I pull her jeans down her thighs.

"Sure you have. What else did you imagine?" I stand up leaving her in only a thong and sports bra.

I turn her body toward the bed and press gently on her shoulders, nudging her to sit on the edge. Due to the tight space, I'm forced to crawl over her in search of what I'm sure is in her bathroom, if this door does lead to her bathroom that is.

"Don't take this the wrong way, but you totally had hair." She does that adorable piggy snort thing again. I look back over my shoulder at her and shake my head at her complete and utter honesty.

"But I am all about a bald man. Trust me when I say that your hair, or lack of, is capital S sexy. The feeling of those tiny little hairs rubbing the sensitive skin between my thighs, sign me up, I am here for it." She stumbles over her words when she thinks maybe she offended me.

Shaving my hair off was one of the first things I did after my mom died. I didn't have time to deal with it, and scheduling an appointment to get it cut just wasn't a priority for me. That was something my mom did, I just couldn't bring myself to fool with it. Still can't.

I open the door to what is, in fact, the bathroom. Laying on the bathroom counter is exactly what I was looking for. A hairbrush. She couldn't have known that's what I was in search of, but the look on her face is priceless when I turn back with it in my hand.

"Shut up. Do not pull a toupee out of your pocket, Straton." I pause, staring at her in disbelief.

"So, the toupee is going to be the deal breaker then?" I sit on her bed on my knees facing her as she sits on the opposite side.

"Wow. I feel like we're at an impasse." Her face is like stone. No emotion.

"Dammit. Oh well, at least the sex was only subpar." I drop the hairbrush on the bed between us as I fight against my instincts to maintain the serious tone of my voice.

"Subpar. Subpar my ass." In hindsight, I shouldn't have given her a weapon. Grabbing up the hairbrush, she lunges toward me, wielding it like a medieval mallet.

Lucky for me, weapon or not, I'm fast and twice her size. We're working with a limited amount of space, and for every move she makes, I make two. I flip her easily, pinning her hands above her head with one of my hands as I let my other hand drift down over her exposed ribcage.

My fingers move, and she loses her mind. She screams at the top of her lungs and her body convulses into a fit of giggles.

"Ah! Ah! Stop it, Alex! Stop it right now!" She fights against my hold, kicking and screaming through her laughter. If there were other apartments up here, we would be waking everyone in the damn place up.

I should let her go, but I can't. The sound of her laughter is doing something funny to my insides. I feel unfiltered happiness as her joy radiates beneath me in between her threats of imminent death.

"A toupee, Em? Do I look like a carry around a spare toupee in my back pocket?" I give her a second of temporary relief because I know I will fall asleep next to this woman at some point tonight. I would like to build a life with her and put my babies in her belly before she murders me in my sleep.

"I don't know the habits of bald men. Maybe you all carry around a spare toupee. You stole my hairbrush! What was I supposed to think?" Her words fade to laughter as I continue my attack, until finally, I think she's probably had enough.

"Sit your ass down and stop insulting me. Maybe I will show you what exactly I was planning to do with your hairbrush. A toupee, I swear, woman." I release her hands reluctantly and sit back on her bed, leaning against the wall and yanking her body in between my spread legs before she can run from me.

Her movements cease as I pick up the discarded hairbrush from the bed and slowly begin brushing her long, dark locks.

"My mom had long hair. When I was a little boy, I don't know, maybe seven or eight, she would sit on her bed and cry on the bad nights. The hard nights. The nights when my dad wasn't the man she married. Or the nights that he wasn't at home at all because he was in another rehab program. Or worse, he was out at a bar. She would sit on the bed and cry, and I was a scared little shit. I didn't want to be in my room by myself, so I was in there with her. I hated seeing her sad. So one night, I saw her hairbrush sitting on the nightstand, and I grabbed it. I don't know what compelled me to do it, but I felt helpless. Even at seven years old, I felt like I needed a way to fix what was wrong. I sat on my knees behind her and started brushing her hair. I'm not sure what happened in that moment, but she stopped crying." I watch the shine return to Em's hair as I pull the brush through again and again.

"I feel your stress, Em. I know you carry the weight of the world, and if anyone can handle that load, it's you. No doubt. But, if I can take just a portion of it, if you would share some of that load with me, I'll carry it for you. I know you're independent, and I'm not trying to take over or be some sort of knight in shining armor. I just want you to trust me enough to share the burden. I want to hold it up for you long enough to give you a break. Let me be that person for you." She doesn't turn, but I see her shoulders bounce with emotion. I don't push her; I won't try to force her to address the feelings that are obviously overwhelming her right now. Instead, I rhythmically continue to brush her hair.

I brush her hair until her shoulders stop bouncing and her body slowly relaxes back into mine. We're sitting on top of her comforter. I'm still wearing the jeans I arrived in, jeans that don't even belong to me to begin with, but I don't dare move. I let her body cocoon into mine. Setting the hairbrush down gently on the bed beside us, I reach for a blanket near the foot of the bed, careful not to disturb her peace, and drape it over her exposed skin. I wrap my arms around her and lean my head back against the wall behind me, finally allowing myself a moment to close my eyes.

Today is a new day. Right now, we sleep, but soon we work. Wheels beyond our control are already in motion, and we've got to catch up or risk losing our lead entirely. That's the thing about working an active investigation, it involves real people. This isn't a crime show, as Reid so easily joked about earlier. This is the real world, and in the real world, people die.

Follow the data.

For years, investigations were about following anonymous tips, word of mouth, suspect interrogations. Those things still serve a purpose, but in today's world, they're all secondary. Let the data guide you to the answers you seek and everything else will follow. Data doesn't lie if you know how to interpret it's meaning.

I need to work toward uncovering what's happening

down at those warehouses and how these men are all tied to a mafia family that we tried to eradicate over a year ago.

I need to work toward finding a solution to this investigation that doesn't involve my woman sacrificing her body and ending up in a brothel.

There's no margin of error when the results of my work will determine the fate of my best friend and the woman that holds my heart.

CHAPTER TWENTY
EMILY

"Would you look what the cat drug in. Please, please, please tell me every dirty detail about your encounter with the mystery man last night. Did you let him touch? I mean, you did, right? It was five freaking grand. He did want to touch, right? Oh God, he was a biter, wasn't he? He looked like the broody, biting type." I suffocate on air as the distinct sound of Mel's voice comes from over my shoulder as I stand in front of my locker and dress for the night.

I've been here for hours already and, notably, Mel has not. I try to not let the obvious relief that I'm currently feeling flicker across my features. Instead, I focus on perfecting my mascara in the mirror as I sneakily search for her reflection.

I woke up snuggled in the thickest, comfiest, heaviest blanket I've ever slept beneath. I fought the good fight against my conscious that continually reminded me somewhere in the recesses of my brain that I had a job to do today, a mission to forge forward on. When in reality, I just wanted to stay snuggled up for an hour or ten longer.

There's something to be said for waking up with a man's hand inside of your sports bra. Especially if said hand is covered in ink, attached to the arm that's attached to a body that houses the heart of a man I kind of want holding my tit every morning.

Monogamy isn't a topic I've had reason to spend much time thinking about over the years. But now that I've dropped the hypothetical drawbridge on my castle and allowed this man inside, er – quite literally, I'm feeling like I need to spend some more time considering it.

He brushed my hair. The last person to brush my hair was my mother. It sounds weird, but something in the act was surprisingly intimate. The words he spoke, sharing that part of himself with me. He trusted me with a memory that was obviously important to him. I couldn't find the right words to respond with. So, instead of babbling, I didn't say anything. I listened as I purged emotions of my own. I offloaded them into the universe and allowed Alex to be the support he swears he wants to be. For the first time in my life, I allowed someone in.

"Dude was a total dud. Dropped five grand to watch me dance when, if he'd have arrived just a few minutes earlier, he could have seen me up on stage for the cover alone." I lie.

"He didn't touch you at all? You're kidding." My eyes finally find hers in my peripheral as she sidles up beside me and opens her locker. I glance over her exposed skin and make note of the lack of bruising or obvious harm. Good.

"Nope. He watched, I danced, and when it was over, he walked out without a single word." I don't typically condone lying to someone's face. Especially if said someone is a person I respect. Maybe Mel isn't my friend, because I don't believe in friends, but I don't want to see her die, so there's that.

"Strange. You don't think he's a stalker or something do you?" She lowers her tone to a whisper, but I still hear the thread of panic woven in her voice.

"Doubt it. I didn't recognize him. It was difficult getting a good look at him under the hat and the hood and whatnot, but he looked young. Probably just had some of daddy's money burning a hole in his pocket and figured this was the place to use it. Wanted to brag to his frat boy friends that he got a dance in one of our privates." Stop asking questions about things you don't need to know anything about, Mel. It's called self-preservation; get some, woman.

"I still think it seems odd, Emily. Maybe you should tell Mr. Sullivan or…"

"No. Absolutely not." I slam my locker closed a little more briskly than the situation warrants.

I turn, leaning my back against the cold metal and cross my arms in front of my body as I stare into Mel's eyes. I stare just long enough to remind her who the rookie here is and who's not. Anderson Sullivan does not have a place in this conversation, period.

"Whoa, ok, we're cool. I was just suggesting." As expected, she backtracks when she notices my change in demeanor. We're done with this topic of conversation for now. I have questions of my own that need answers.

"I didn't ask for your suggestion. But speaking of Mr. Sullivan, what happened last night? You get an invitation out to those warehouses you were talking about?" Oh God, she smiles shyly, and the action turns my stomach.

"Oh ummm...yeah, no, not yet. But he did tell me that if I was really good and my dancing keeps bringing in the kind of money that it's been netting lately, he will have me out there in a week or two. He's noticing me, and that's more than I had last week." She tries to act nonchalant about it, but her poker face is shit.

"That was it? You just went up to talk?" I'm pushing my luck. Most dancers are private about what happens behind closed doors. It's the nature of the industry we work in. Loose lips are a dangerous attribute to have.

"Well, yeah. He wanted to see my schoolgirl routine. The one I did last week. I was still wearing my leather, but it's not like I had it on for long anyway. I'm actually performing that routine again tonight on stage. Apparently, it's a crowd favorite." Or a pervy old man favorite, but I keep that comment to myself.

"Em. Mel. Either of you seen Laura?" Reid's back in the club, or should I say Riko, and he's on the door to the private's tonight. His eyes dart from mine to Mel's and then back to mine again as he questions us.

"Nope." We answer in unison. Maybe one of us know. Maybe not. Either way, we follow our own set of rules, our unspoken girl code. We cover for our fellow dancer when one of Sully's soldiers start asking around about her.

"Well, she's on in five and she's MIA." Riko runs his hand through his hair. The pointed look he gives with his blue eyes, tells me everything I need to know. My eyes track from Reid's and over to Mel's, I read the brief flicker of anxiety as it flashes in her eyes.

She knows something she shouldn't.

"I've got it, Riko. If Sasha is ready, go ahead and put her on. I will be ready to fill her spot when she comes off." I nod in his direction and hope he takes a hint.

"Yeah, ok. Be ready in ten. I don't want to have to come back here and look for you again, Young. I'm on the side door tonight. I swear, you women can't get your shit together enough for me to do my damn job." Oh Reid, actually, you are too damn good at your job. Ass.

Turning back to her station immediately, Mel fidgets with her hair, curling and re-curling the same piece of hair three times before pushing it to the side and picking up another piece.

"You know anything about that? Come to think of it, it's been a couple nights since I saw Laura. She wasn't even on the schedule last night, was she?" I re-open my locker and pull out my stilettos. I'm ready to go on.

Other than some tips that I probably would have gotten later in the night, I'm not losing anything by dancing early. I don't survive on tips anymore. In a world that looks dark most of the time, that's a little glimmer of light to be thankful for.

"Maybe. I dunno. I shouldn't be talking about things that don't involve me, especially not here." Her eyes dart around the room like maybe Sullivan is standing behind her. He's not. Not physically anyway, but his eyes, they're everywhere.

Doesn't much matter to me though.

Mel's not the only one with secrets tonight.

Alex is in my ear. He's been there since we walked out of my apartment earlier and went our separate ways. The majority of his equipment was still at Reid's, and he needed to get the SUV back where it belonged safely. I fully expect him to be waiting in my bed when I make it home tonight. We didn't discuss it, but I'd really hate to have to go looking for him in the middle on the night.

Just knowing that he's with me, without actually being with me, brings back a comfort that I never realized I was missing until it was gone. I feel his presence just as sure as if he were standing here. Something I'd gotten used to back when I danced for Vito. Even though he thought he was being sneaky, I could always feel his presence. I knew he was watching.

He's checked in, and I know he's listening to every word that leaves my mouth. He watches through Sullivan's system. He sees my every move. He's monitoring what can and cannot be relayed and intercepting conversations to play them to our advantage. He's doing his job, which is more than can be said for those that came before him. Maybe that has less to do with his ability and more to do with the fact that he's got something to lose.

He couldn't care less about his job, the money or even serving out his sentence working for the FBI. For a man that has so little left in this world to live for, he could lose everything he has left with one misstep.

Okay, and who am I kidding, he's a genius. The nerds

that came before him aren't even remotely close to playing on the same field.

But I know that feeling of having something to lose.

I feel it every day, it's always in the pit of my stomach, haunting me. Because once upon a time, I did lose everything. I was completely and totally alone in the world. Now I have Alex and Reid, and hundreds of thousands of women and children and their lives all depend on me.

Alex said it best when he said I carry the weight of the world. It's there because I put it there. I put the burden on myself because the thought of not fighting when there's so much to fight for is worse than the thought of never entering the ring. I refuse to allow myself to become paralyzed by the darkness that exists in this world. I have embraced the notion that I'm still here for a reason. That some higher being has deemed my life valuable to this world. I won't take that for granted.

"Yeah, okay. I get it. I would just hate for something to have happened to her. You know she has a kid back at home? She's been working to get custody back from her parents. A little boy." I feel zero guilt using Mel's empathetic nature to get information. The truth of the matter is, Laura truly is missing and that doesn't look good for the home team. I need her to give me something to work with here, I need her to let me protect her.

"A little boy? No, I didn't realize that." She drops another curl and picks up a new section of hair, refusing to meet my gaze in the reflection of the mirror.

"Yeah, she told me about him once, he's into racecars right now. I think he's five or six." He's five. Laura lost custody of her newborn at birth when he was born addicted to heroin. She hit rock bottom and has been working towards getting cleaned up since then. Unfortunately, she owes Anderson Sullivan quite a bit of money. Local police records show she was roughed up a couple of times. Now, as if by magic, she's here. I guess she decided dancing was the only way she could pay off that debt, unless she was willing to pay with her life, which, I dunno, kind of looks like maybe she did anyway.

Mel drops another curl over her shoulder before abruptly grabbing my hand and turning toward the far exit. I try to not draw suspicion to either of us as I hurry to follow behind her. I stay close to her body, follow her past other dancers and through the heavy metal door that leads to the parking lot some of the employees and dancers of the club use; the ones that can afford a vehicle. She thinks she's safe out here to speak. She's not. But I have no doubt Alex will make it safe for her, for now anyway.

"Look, I don't know this for certain. I didn't see it with my own eyes or anything, but I heard Laura went out with Mr. Sullivan a couple nights ago. Then, he got a call last night. I only heard bits and pieces of a one-sided conversation." She stutters over her words, trying to get them out, but unable to circle back around and make a clear point.

"Who got a call? Sullivan?"

I watch as she fidgets with the hem of her shirt nervously. "Yeah, I was...well...I was sucking him off and he answered his cell phone. I was literally right there, and he was talking on the phone with my hair wrapped around his hand like the person on the other end of the phone couldn't care less whether or not I was gagging." That's not as surprising to me as it is to Mel. We'll just add that to the list of reasons I should be concerned for her safety. Just goes to show how inexperienced Mel is in this world that she's chosen to make her own.

"Okay, and? What exactly did you hear?" I prod.

"He said someone's name. Sylv I think is what he called the guy. Yeah, Sylv. I remember thinking about what a strange name that was. Anyway, it was some sort of transaction, but it wasn't drugs. I've overheard enough of those conversations in this place to know what they sound like. No, I think Laura might have been out there last night with this Sylv guy. Now she's not here, and I'm wondering what sort of transaction I really heard go down last night now that I'm thinking about it."

"It's okay. It's probably nothing. She's probably sick or something. I mean, it's not like you weren't preoccupied. You could have misheard, right?" I soothe her because there's no reason for her to panic. If anything, keeping her calm is vital to her safety.

She can't do anything about the situation now, but I can. There is no doubt in my mind that Alex is already looking for Laura.

"Yeah, maybe." Her eyes scour the cracked asphalt of the parking lot, not looking up to make contact with mine as I rest my hand on her forearm.

"Look, there is no reason to let it mess with your mojo tonight. Mr. Sullivan said your dances have been killing it lately, right? So, let's go back in there and show the newbies how it's done. Riko is an okay dude from what I can tell. He was looking for her, and you know how Mr. Sullivan's soldiers are when they're on a mission. He'll find her." We've been out here in this vacant parking lot long enough. It's not a safe place for either of us in the dark. I don't know how much time has passed, but my best guess is they're already looking for me backstage.

"Right, yeah, you're totally right." I see her visibly swallow as she nods her head, willing to agree with me even when she isn't entirely sure. She's right to feel nervous about what she overheard. Her mind is telling her to trust me, but her gut is spot on. If it smells like fish, it's probably fishy.

"Look, Mel. Just do me a favor. I know you want the money. I know you need it, I get it, truly I do. But do me a favor and lay low for a bit. Friends?" I all but beg her to play it safe. I offer her something I don't even think I have to give anyone, but I do it anyway because that's her language. Unlike myself, Mel functions off of emotion and feelings. It's a dangerous way to live, but it's how most people in the world operate.

"You know friends don't exist here." Well shock me silly. Maybe she understands more than I give her credit for. She finally lifts her eyes from the concrete and smiles the deceivingly innocent smile that gets her too much attention for her own good.

"Yeah, but close enough." I shrug and this time I grab her hand, pulling her behind me back to the metal door at the back entrance of the club.

"Close enough." She agrees as we step back into the chaos of the changing room.

"I'm not making any promises Emily, but I will be

careful. I know I've got the innocent girl routine down pat, but I can take care of myself." The never ceasing tension that constantly pulls at my chest eases just slightly. It's barely noticeable, but my lungs expand for just a second. I try to trust her words. I try, but there's still something there bothering me. Something I can't put my finger on. Where's Laura? Why was Sullivan on the phone with Sylv last night? What was that call about?

"I gotta go or else Riko will have my ass. I'm sure Sasha is getting ready to come off the stage any minute." I don't stop until we're both standing back in front of our lockers again. I can hear Sasha's music as it filters through the speakers. It's definitely closer to the end of her performance than the beginning. I should already be behind that curtain ready to go on and not still standing back here in the middle of the dressing room. Leaving Mel at our station, I turn and head backstage.

"Riko could get my ass if he wanted it, just sayin'. That man is finnnnnneeee." I turn back to see Mel's smiling face as she shouts over the ruckus surrounding us through her laughter, and I let myself smile too. She looks so carefree, and I wonder for a second what it might be like to actually have friends. To have a female relationship with another woman, even a platonic relationship. Alex and Reid have each other, and well, I have Alex and Reid, I guess. But maybe it would be cool to have another girl friend to talk to.

"Keep it in your pants, Mel." I cup my hand over my mouth and laugh as I shout back and step behind the curtain.

The truth of the matter, though? I'm not kidding

anyone but myself.

I can't have friends.

The music blasts through the speakers to my right, and my senses are jarred back to my reality. I see Sasha as she hits her final decent from the pole, and I take a deep breath. It's time to dance.

CHAPTER TWENTY-ONE
ALEX

Three screens.

One twenty-year-old, probably not solid oak, dining table.

One lumpy as hell loveseat with a hole in the cushion that, oddly, resembles the state of Texas.

I sit in the tiny living room of Emily's apartment, and I work. Her small kitchen table has now become my desk, hope she doesn't mind. I picked it up and moved it two feet from its previous home to its new location in her living room.

It took me fifteen minutes to pull my equipment from Reid's and load it into the SUV. Using a digital time lapse on Sullivan's cameras, I easily replaced footage, allowing me to get in and out of the building unnoticed. It's safer for me to work from Emily's apartment, and something about the way she told me she would see me at home when we parted ways earlier told me she wouldn't be opposed to the idea.

Subtlety isn't her strong suit.

I took it upon myself to make a quick stop at a local box store for a few t-shirts, a pair of jeans and a sweatshirt before returning the SUV to the warehouse down at the docks this morning and locking everything down, covering my tracks in the process.

Now, my fingers move and my eyes scan as I watch Em in my periphery. She stands behind a thick velvet curtain, hands clutched at her sides as she waits for her turn to go on. She was pulled to dance earlier than usual tonight, which may actually work out for us. I hear the redundant inhale and exhale of her steady breathing through the earpiece that I am now married to. If she's breathing, her heart is beating, and if her heart is beating, mine is too.

On a second monitor I follow Sullivan's cameras as they flash through a series of timed rotations. I see Reid at his post by the entrance to the private rooms. The same entrance I walked through just twenty-four hours ago. I feel like I've aged forty years in that same span of time.

I see Emily's friend Mel standing backstage at her locker, putting the final touches on her makeup.

I see the patrons of the club as they sit in what they naively believe is the privacy of dimly lit booths and prepare to watch my girl dance for them. Except, she's not dancing for them at all, she's dancing for me.

And on the third screen, I search.

Laura.

I scan through hours of security footage. I was listening to Emily when she said that Laura wasn't on the schedule last night, but I search the club anyway. I leave no stone unturned because assumption is the gateway to failure.

We still aren't certain of the exact location of the warehouses that Sylv and Sullivan are reportedly operating out of.

We're close and our search radius isn't that large. I'm looking through hours and hours of footage from various vantage points in the vicinity we currently suspect in an attempt to nail down the exact coordinates.

I'm searching real estate records and diving into the sordid financials of Wilks Luxury Auto. If the IRS ever needed to send a forensic accountant in to audit a business, it is this one. The numbers are so obviously erroneous, even your basic IT guy can see it's fraudulent. Maybe I should send in an anonymous tip. Neh, who am I kidding. I don't need that kind of bad juju in my life. Let them figure it out on their own. I might work for the FBI, but that doesn't mean I'm willing to partner up with the IRS. Fun suckers.

It's there, I know it is. I just have to find it.

In the meantime, I run a parallel search for information on Laura, our missing person.

According to her credit card statements, she doesn't stay in one place for very long, which, by itself, isn't surprising given what we know about her background. She's been staying at a pay-by-the-night motel two miles from the club for the past two months. The records I was able to access from the motel database show that when payment wasn't received forty-eight hours ago, they automatically checked her out. No questions asked, she could be dead in the bathroom. This is the kind of place that would just dispose of the body out back and spray the floor down with a water hose.

I look at her cell phone records. She has a standard prepaid phone but, lucky for us, it's not a burner. That makes it harder to hack, but not impossible. Even if it's been turned off or destroyed, I might be able to pull down some history using the cellular towers in the area. Most of those prepaid phones use either one of two networks here. It's still a lot of data to sort through, but if it gets us closer to finding her location, it will be worth it.

If we find Sylv's location, we potentially find Laura. We find Laura, we have our location. It's a win, win. Unless she's dead already. Even then, we do what we have to do to make her fight worth it.

The thing we don't have is time. We desperately need more time. We're not sure how long Laura has been missing. At this point, we're pushing forty-eight hours, best case scenario. We're not even certain that what Mel overheard was totally accurate.

We're swimming upstream, and every minute that passes is another life that we could potentially lose.

My fingers continue to move, but I allow my eyes to drift. I hear her breathing as it accelerates and watch the confidence that elongates her neck and broadens her shoulders as she steps onto the stage. She never once looks at the audience that gathers to watch her performance. Instead, she walks to the center of the stage. The spotlight that follows her cuts out as she pauses at her destination, and the room goes dark.

The music changes, her breathing takes on a totally different rhythm, and the lights come up. In that moment, she's transported to her own world. Her movements are fluid, and every person that watches her tonight sees what I see. They're not just watching an exotic dancer put on a practiced routine. They're experiencing something special; they feel it. It's just as real to them as it is to me. She's taking each and every person in that room with her on her magical journey.

"Hood, what you got?" Reid's voice cuts in on my feed, interrupting the euphoric experience that I don't think I will ever tire of.

"Dammit, Riko. Really? You know I'm preoccupied." His low chuckle tells me that he knows exactly what he's doing. He could have waited until she was done dancing, but no, he knew I was watching her. That's an asshole move if I've ever seen one.

"Preoccupied with your hand. You found her yet?" I wish. On both counts.

"Go fuck yourself. I'm close. I've been scanning this security footage for hours. I've been picking up some suspicious activity at an exit off of the interstate about ten miles north of the club. Not far from Sully's place, but close enough for easy transport down to the docks."

I tear my eyes away from Emily as my computer alerts on one of the call logs I'm running in the background.

"What else you know?" He chooses his words wisely. I see him, there's no one else in his immediate vicinity, but if I can hear him, there's always a chance someone else can too.

"I just got an alert on a call log from a prepaid phone.

Phone was shut off yesterday evening, hour or two before midnight, but my database cross referenced the last location that the phone was pinged. It fits within a three-mile cross-section of the exit I was looking at. I'm about to reference that location with possible real estate purchases in the area within the last six months and see if I get a hit." I speak as I continue to work.

"Aight. Listen, Young is about to come off. Word is upstairs is going to pull her in for a private dance. Keep it cool. Keep it quiet. But keep your damn eyes on her. Understood?" My hands freeze. I focus on my own breathing in an attempt to control my immediate reaction, which may or may not be to blow the building up.

"Respond, do not react." I pinch the bridge of my nose with my hand and try to force my brain to focus.

"Are you pacing, Hood?" Well, no, but now that you mention it, my feet do feel a little tingly...

"I'm cool. It's cool." I lean back into the couch and stare at the ceiling. I count the nasty yellowed tiles, making note of which look like they might fall through first. I should fix those for Em. Well, unless she's squatting on the property. In that case, we probably shouldn't touch anything...

"So, I understand that you are not, in fact, cool." Something in the tenor of Reid's voice settles me. It reminds me of our brotherhood, our childhood, of the goals that we made for ourselves all those years ago – goals that we're now getting the opportunity to live out. Which reminds me why we're here, in this moment.

Our mission is greater than our individual wants and

desires. It's bigger than any of us.

I signed up for this.

"It's her job. It's always been her job. This is her heart, her mission. I understand that. It's my job to protect her." I breathe the words into the atmosphere and will the universe to make them true.

"That's where you're wrong, Hood. It's my job to protect her. It's your job to protect us all. Remember Jackson Rogers?"

I grunt in response, not sure how this memory will make me feel any better about my current situation.

"Dammit, Hood. Do you remember Jackson Rogers?" Reid's voice is low, but adamant.

"Yes, fuck. I remember getting my ass kicked on the playground when I was eight years old and needing you to come to the rescue."

He lowers his voice to a whisper, so low that I have to press my earpiece into my ear with my hand to hear the words he's saying under his breath. "Wrong. We both got our asses kicked that day. Why? Because we're brothers for life. It's my job to protect her, it's her job to protect me, it's your job to protect us all. This is the damn Titanic, and there is one lifeboat. We get on that lifeboat together, or we go down with the ship together. I don't know about you, but I'm not okay with sitting around on the deck listening to the fucking violins. Let's get on the lifeboat. I'm out." I allow Reid's words to renew my drive. I watch as Emily steps off the stage and see her nod as a second soldier, one that I don't recognize speaks to her.

I hear the orders that he lays out, and then I watch her

nod again in understanding.

It's my job to protect them all. I pick the burden up and I place it squarely on my shoulders. I accept my mission and I get on that damn lifeboat.

Ding. My computer alerts.

A bright blue line flashes on the screen to my right demanding my attention.

Exit 49A.

CHAPTER TWENTY-TWO
EMILY

"Young."

I step from the bright lights of the stage back into the shadows of the curtains. I try to shake off the colors that cloud my mind as I hear my name being called for a second time.

"Young."

"Yeah, what's up?" It's one of Sullivan's soldiers. I've seen him around, know a little background on him, but there's nothing special about the guy that I can put my finger on.

"Got a call from Sully. He wants to see you upstairs. You got ten minutes to prep." Finally, this is the moment I've been waiting for. I nod toward the soldier before brushing past him and heading back toward the dressing room.

"Hood, check-in. You got me." I don't know why, but for the first time, I feel little pin pricks of nerves as I speak to Alex through my earpiece. I walk slowly, hoping I don't run into any of the other girls before I'm thrust back into the chaos of the dressing room.

Maybe this whole relationship thing is new to me, but Alex and I are anything but. He's seen me at some of my worst points, and he's held me at my best. But, for some reason, now that this nonexistent label floats dauntingly over my head, I feel like I need his blessing or something.

I've never needed to ask permission to risk my life before. Never felt guilty dancing for one man when I was thinking about another. I don't want to feel guilty for doing my job. Dammit.

"Always, Em. Don't waste your breath on stupid questions that don't even warrant an answer. Who do you dance for, Emily?" I don't know how he does it, but Alex says the exact words I need to hear in that moment. I can't help but smile as I imagine him watching me right now, because I know he's watching.

"I dance for me, Alex. But I love you." I say the words because it is what it is. He and I both know I could walk up those stairs and never walk back down them again. It's not romantic because what we have together is not about hearts and flowers. Our love is beyond average simplicities, it has to be. Our love is about loyalty, commitment and a willingness to die for a cause greater than the future that I know we both want to build together.

I don't know what that future looks like. But last night, when I leaned my head back on Alex's chest and heard his heart beating in sync with my own, I imagined cute little bald babies with tan skin and green eyes. I can say without a shadow of a doubt, I've never had dreams like that before.

"Alex, shit, you gonna say it back or what? That's not how this is supposed to go down. I say it then you reciprocate." His prolonged silence irks me, and for just a second, I doubt myself.

"Give a man a minute to finish downloading the audio of the first time his woman tells him that she loves him. Got myself a new ring tone." Oh God, how I love this man. Dork.

"I love you, Em. I love you so damn much that I'll watch you walk into a room with the devil and trust you to take care of business one hundred times over. I love you so damn much that I will watch you dance for him, all the while knowing your heart belongs to me. We are on the same team. We're fighting the same fight. So yeah, I've got your back tonight. I will always have your back. I've loved you since the day you trusted a total stranger with a mission that you'd been building your entire life. You put your heart in my hands, and I will always guard it with my life." I hear his words through the speaker of my earbud loud and clear. My eyes do this weird itchy thing, and I have to look up at the ceiling to keep the mysterious water that threatens my mascara from ruining my well applied makeup.

"You sitting in my bed?" I ask, the words nearly breaking before I can get the sentence out.

"Neh, not yet. Imma keep the couch warm until you get home."

"Home." I repeat the word. It's meaning resonating somewhere deep within my chest. Some place I haven't felt anything other than a cold emptiness for so long.

I've never really had a home. Alex is giving that to me.

"You're my home, Em."

"You're my home, Alex."

"Good. Now, go dance for me woman. Then come home and finish what you started." I hear the smile in his voice and know exactly what he's talking about without him even needing to say it.

"I want you in my bed by then." I'll finish what I started alright…and then we can finish again and again…

"The couch, the bed, doesn't much matter…" I let his words trail off as I enter the dressing room again.

Only, my night isn't over. Quite the contrary, it's just barely getting started.

-o-

"Em Cat, my sweet and seductive kitty. I finally get my turn with the infamous dancer." Anderson Sullivan sits in a high-back leather chair behind a wide, elaborate black desk as I enter the room.

I pause in the doorway and allow the soldier that stands guard to my left to shut the door at my back. There are two other soldiers in the room. One is directly behind Sullivan and the other stands in the shadows of a far corner. He thinks he's hidden, but I see him.

Music from downstairs plays through the surround sound speakers in the office. To my right is a smaller replica stage, almost identical to the one I performed on just minutes ago downstairs. Glass privacy windows line the walls, allowing Sully the ability to watch the dancers and patrons below, but they are impenetrable from the opposite side.

Alex wasn't too far off when he said I was willing to enter a room with the devil. More often than not, religion paints the devil as a distinct being, one person that rules eternity in Hell. The truth of the matter is, the world is full of sin because humans are innately born of it. For those that do not choose the path of righteousness and grace, the devil is omnipresent, shifting and morphing into cracks and cervices of any and everything here on earth.

Vito chose a path to hell, and his soul reflected such. Anderson Sullivan is no different, his soul is inky black like the night, and his eyes…his eyes burn the fire of a thousand innocent deaths in their depths.

"Good evening, sir." I speak, but I don't look at him. My eyes search the floor as I study the large white fur rug that covers most of the space between where I stand and the man that has the authority to lead me to a break in this case, but that also has enough fire power in this room to end my life with a single shot and nod of the head, without ever lifting a finger himself. Sure, I'm armed, but this corset and thong aren't bullet proof.

"You show respect to your superior. I like it. You understand your place here, and it shows. It's why you've been so successful in this club. If I had to place bets, I would wager that it's probably why you were Vito's play pretty as well." I was, and he lost his life as a result. So will you. I might not kill you myself, and maybe you only lose your life hypothetically speaking when we cuff you, but either way – I will win. I speak the words in my mind, but I don't say any of them out loud. That's not my part to play tonight.

"Did you need me, Mr. Sullivan?" I ask shyly, my words barely audible over the music that plays throughout the room.

"You're one of my best dancers. Personally, you're not my type. I prefer my women blonde, and a little less curvy." I feel his distaste as he eyes me possessively, as if I'm a piece of meat and not a living, breathing human. "You could do with a few less cheeseburgers if you ask me, but the men down there seem to love you. It got me thinking. I had one of the other girls up here the other night. While I enjoyed the show she put on, an idea came to me. What if I combine the best of both worlds?" I cut my eyes up to his, just briefly. Just long enough to see him lean forward, placing his elbows onto the desk and steepling his manicured fingers together in front of his slimy face.

A little less curvy. A few less cheeseburgers. He's got a death wish; the man very clearly has a wish to meet the devil in the flesh.

You know, I really was planning to do this the legal way. I was pumped up to handle this the way I've been trained. I was going to allow Anderson Sullivan to live out his days in a fancy-smancy white collar prison. But you know what, nah, I'm over that idea. Let me get the information I need. Let me crack this case. After that, this man can go play with his friend Vito in hell for all I care. They sure as fuck won't have cheeseburgers there.

"Sir?" I question his open-ended statement and allow my eyes to drift back to the fluffy rug. I demand my adrenalin fueled heart to calm down. This time, I divert my eyes, not out of playful innocence, but out of self-preservation. I'm afraid if he looks into them now, he will see the raging fire that pulses through my veins.

Before he can answer, a knock comes from the door behind me.

Taking two steps to my right, I allow enough space for the soldier to open the door again.

My eyes drift from the rug over to a pair of black stilettos, up white stockings that hit just above the knee and then over creamy thighs. Thighs that are notably thinner than mine, if we're comparing, which, hell, I guess we are tonight. My eyes catch a distinct freckle just on the inside of one thigh that I easily recognize, and then up to a pleated plaid skirt.

"Mel, you know Em Cat." Sullivan speaks as she takes the two steps into the room next to me. The material of her skirt brushes the skin of my thigh as I stand in my red, faux diamond studded thong and black fishnet tights.

"Yes, Mr. Sullivan. Our lockers are beside each other downstairs, and…"

"Enough. You speak too much for your own good." Sully snaps at Mel as he pushes back from his desk and stands from his chair before slowly making his way towards us. At least he and I can both agree on something.

"Sorry, sir." She apologizes quickly. I watch from my peripheral as Mel's hands fidget nervously with her skirt. I wonder where he's going with this.

Why are we both here?

"The best of both worlds." He repeats, seemingly to himself as he continues to walk.

"You are such a pretty girl, Mel. An angel with the tongue of the devil." He doesn't stop until he's standing in front of her. He grabs a lock of her hair that she so meticulously curled just a couple of hours ago and runs it between his fingers as she stands next to me, unmoving.

"And you, well your dancing is unmatched by even the most trained dancers we have in this club. There's something mysterious about you that the men out there cannot get enough of. You are the embodiment of the darkness, Emily." I don't react as he moves over just enough so that he now stands directly in front of both of us and brushes my hip with his opposite hand.

"I'm to assume you have both heard the rumors?" His stale breath feathers over my face. It takes everything in me to keep the contents of my stomach where they belong. It's really too bad, he deserves regurgitated cheeseburger on his fancy, overpriced black and white suit.

"No sir." We speak in unison. Deny. Deny. Deny. That's the name of the game.

"Right. Well, I would like to offer you both something very special. Something I'm only willing to offer my best dancers." An offer. He's going to extend the invitation. This is it – our break.

"The light and the dark." He grabs Mel's hand and then mine, pulling us away from the door, toward the stage in front of the mirrored windows.

"I want you both. Together." Stopping at the stage, he pulls our hands from his and places my palm in Mel's.

Together – and all of a sudden it becomes glaringly obvious why we're both here.

I feel the shake in Mel's palm, she's nervous. I squeeze her hand just slightly in reassurance. It's okay, we're going to be okay. If she'll just let me take the lead, I will get us out of here.

"The light and the dark, girls. You're every man's dream and nightmare in one very profitable duo. I want to see you perform together. Then, I will make my decision." Turning his back to us, he walks until he reaches a small sofa that sits just in front of the stage. He snaps his fingers and the music from downstairs is drowned out by a new playlist, one of his own choosing. I can't allow my mind to lose focus. I fight against the colors that my vision demands I see. I focus on ignoring the outside factors that threaten to derail the opportunity that I've been waiting for.

This is my chance. No distractions.

Making himself comfortable, he leans back on the couch and unzips his black dress slacks, pulling his flaccid cock out and holding it in his hand. He's waiting for us, and Mel is frozen. I feel her uneasiness as it radiates from her in waves.

It's go time. One way or another, I have to find a way to make her trust me. I turn into her body and walk her backwards towards the pole until her back presses flat against it. I look into her eyes, and nod slowly, she's got to break this trance.

I need her to dance with me.

I grip the material of her skirt with my hand and press my body flush against hers. My mouth hovers just over hers and I wait. I wait for her to finally react. To give me something, anything. Then, when I don't think she's going to play along at all, her tongue finally swipes out and into my mouth.

From off in the distance, I hear Sullivan's disgusting labored breathing, the result of one too many cigars, and I know, we've got him.

CHAPTER TWENTY-THREE
ALEX

I watch Emily as her hand moves from the cloth material of Mel's skirt down her upper thigh until she finds purchase on the patch of silk skin that remains exposed above her knee. She runs her hand seductively up and under the material. Her fingers brush the lace fabric that barely covers Mel's ass and peeks out from where Em draws up the material.

She knows exactly what she's doing, every single move she makes is calculated.

She's playing them all.

Let it be noted…in my wildest damn dreams, this isn't how I imagined this going down tonight. However, I don't hate my life right now. Just sayin'.

Anderson Sullivan is a creepy son of a bitch, but I already knew that. I said a silent prayer for his life the moment he grew enough balls to chastise Em about her body. I wasn't so much worried about the effect it might have on her, more so the fact that she might kill him before we get all of the information we need for the case. To his credit, he probably doesn't realize he's toying with Medusa. I mean that in the best possible way.

He better be thankful that I have a relationship with Jesus because my prayers were answered, and he lives to see another day. Although I can only imagine the scenarios that Emily probably already has in her mind for how she will inevitably end his life. She won't forget about that shit. She's been known to hold a grudge for a decade...or two. No, instead she will file it away in the dark recesses of her mind and dream of ways she will extract his nut sack from his body and make him eat it. Probably put them in a blender and make him a smoothie, Fear Factor style.

Then, in walked Mel, and things took a wild turn.

Now, I watch as Melanie Davis, the preacher's daughter, unties my woman's corset while simultaneously sliding her tongue down her throat and drinking her saliva.

If you think I'm not recording this shit to watch later with Em, you're wrong. Viewing party for two, please and thank you.

The only thing keeping me from pulling my cock out of my pants is seeing Anderson Sullivan over on the couch stroking himself as he watches the same thing that I see with a sick fascination that he has no right being privy to. Talk about a buzz kill.

Instead, I shift my focus over to Emily and Mel. I watch as Emily grips the pole behind Mel's head and rotates their bodies effortlessly.

Emily twirls out as Mel pulls the final strings on Em's corset, and it falls to the floor. Em steps over the material gracefully before twirling herself back in, sliding her ass down and over the front of Mel's body and brushing the floor of the stage with her fingertips.

Finally beginning to loosen up, Mel elongates her leg up the pole. Her skirt follows her hip as it rides up her thighs, exposing black lace underwear beneath. The two dance in unison, slowly undressing each other until they are both left completely topless. The contents of their remaining joint attire includes one thong, a pair of fishnet tights, a black lace pair of panties and two pairs of stilettos.

Emily swivels so that her back rests against the pole. She pulls Mel's body to hers, straddling one of Mel's thighs as she pulls Mel's pink nipple into her mouth.

Dark and light. They're opposites. I hate to admit it, but Sullivan was right on one count, these two together are incredible. They're every man's fantasy wrapped up in one forbidden package. Mel's skin is a porcelain white, as opposed to the dark olive of Emily's. Where Emily's nipples are a rich purple, Mel's are a blush pink. Emily grinds her pussy down against Mel's thigh as they take turns pleasuring each other.

This may be an act, just part of a ploy to get the invitation Emily feels like she so desperately needs in order to gain purchase on this case, but it's obvious that she's enjoying this. Actually, I know she's enjoying this; I can tell by the way she breaths in the speaker in my ear that she's close. So close.

She wants to come, but she's too in control of the

situation. She won't allow herself to lose that control. No matter what her body is telling her it wants. She doesn't trust the situation she's in. Therefore, she refuses to relinquish the control over her body that she is holding on to by a thread. That ability to maintain her composure is a true testament to how far she's come, both personally and professionally.

Melanie on the other hand, I can imagine that she feels like her body has betrayed her. She might dance for a living, but I get the feeling this is a little bit outside of her comfort zone. She was paralyzed when Em touched her for the first time. Now, she rides Em's thigh like she's chasing an orgasm she's afraid will disappear into thin air at a moment's notice. She wants more, and she doesn't understand why. It doesn't matter because her body is working for what it wants, despite the hesitancy of her mind.

Gripping Em's neck, she pulls her in and kisses her like, well, like I kiss her. She sucks her tongue down her throat and rides her thigh with no particular rhythm, just hunger.

What was a few moments ago a coordinated dance, has now spiraled into so much more than that.

"Mel, here, now." The desperation in Sullivan's voice breaks through what's happening between the girls as he summons Melanie. She pulls back slowly, unwilling to give up so quickly. She's not ready for it to be over.

"Now, dammit." His voice is loud, angry, demanding as he summons her for a second time. One too many. I watch the guards snap to attention, prepared to draw their weapon for any instance of non-compliance.

Emily turns towards the pole and continues to dance, like there was no interruption at all, but I see her eyes as they track back. She pretends that she's not bothered by the interruption, but she's very much aware of each and every move that's made in that room.

Mel hurries quickly towards Anderson Sullivan who slides his hand over his cock feverishly. Sweat drips from his temples as he pushes Mel to the floor between his legs and she obliges, understanding immediately what his unspoken words mean.

She wraps her mouth around his cock. He wraps his hand in her hair, fucking her mouth for mere seconds before throwing his head back and letting out a string of obscenities as he comes down her throat. He holds her head down, flush against his skin until he's fully satisfied. I can hear the intensity of her gagging from the speaker. He still doesn't let her up until tears stream down her cheeks and he's sure she has swallowed every last drop. Finally, he releases her.

"Now, go, kiss Emily. I want her to taste my cum on your lips."

Without hesitation Mel walks back to the stage and Emily meets her at the edge, pulling her to her. The bare skin of their breasts press against each other as Emily pulls Melanie's tongue into her mouth.

"Good girls. You did good. You've successfully secured yourselves a coveted invitation that, whether you admit it or not, I know you've heard about. You have forty-eight hours to prepare a routine for your debut. Go. I'm finished with you." He ushers them out of the room, not even bothering to put himself away as he leans back on the couch with both of his arms outstretched behind him, sated.

-o-

EMILY

"Mel, you good or do we need to talk it out or something? I know we've touched on this before, but I don't really have many, well, any girls that I'm friends with. I don't know how girl code applies in this particular situation. But, I get the feeling that what just went down threw you for a loop back there." I shove my corset into my locker and throw on a sports bra and sweatshirt as Mel and I stand next to each other in the nearly deserted dressing room.

One or two other girls filter through from the private rooms, but they don't linger. It's getting late. Women of this club have one job and one job only. Once that job is complete and we're no longer needed, we're not welcome here.

"Um, I'm good. I, well, that was…yeah okay, maybe we need to talk. So, you dance with other girls a lot?" Oh, sweet, Mel.

"Do I actually dance with female partners? Not usually, I'm a solo performer. Do I *dance* with female partners sometimes? I've been known to before, but if you're asking me what my preference is, well, he has a name and a dick." I snort as I laugh to myself, knowing good and damn well that Alex can hear everything I say. I really hope my preference is back at the apartment waiting for me in my bed…naked. Especially after the abrupt ending to the little performance we just put on upstairs. I'm positive I won a Golden Globe and two Academy Awards for the show I put on up there. Best supporting actress, holla at your girl, I killed it. I have to remain confident or die. It kind of makes being humble difficult. Sue me.

"So, did you know he was going to call me up there too?" Mel pulls a nineties country band t-shirt on over her head before grabbing an elastic and tying up her blonde locks away from her face.

"No, not a clue. I was pulled up just a few minutes before you. I was just as caught off guard as you were." I slip off my stilettos and pull on a pair of black leggings over my fishnet tights - better save a little somethin' somethin' for Alex - before sliding on my shoes.

"Shut up. Seriously? How did you know what to do? How were you so calm about it all?"

"Because I might look young, but I've been doing this for a lot of years, honey."

Too many years. Which is exactly why, when I hand out warnings like free candy, you should just take the damn sucker instead of thinking you know better. Here's a freebie for the day, you don't. But now's not the time for that conversation. Unfortunately, there's never a time for that conversation, and that in itself creates risk.

"This may be too personal, but was that all show for you or did you…did you come?" Oh boy, I guess we're gonna round that corner.

"Did I orgasm?" I close my locker and lean up against it with my arms crossed over my chest as Mel pulls on a pair of denim jeans and sneakers. I know what she's asking me, but I want her to say it. If she's going to have the balls to ask, she needs to use her grown up words.

From a distance I hear a door shut, and then the lights from the hallway cut out. A warning.

We're overstaying our welcome.

Time to bounce.

"Um, yeah that's what I meant. Did you, um, did you orgasm?" Mel brings my attention back to her as she closes her locker and mirrors my stance, staring at me with her bright blue eyes. She doesn't appear to be intimidated, just curious. Maybe in another time, another life, our friendship could have been something more.

"Did I want to? Hell yes. You're hot as sin Mel, and your dancing ability is commendable. Did I get to finish, though, nah. I didn't." I shrug as I glance around the room, making sure we're still alone.

Reid is still here somewhere, I'm certain he wouldn't leave knowing I was with Sullivan until Alex gave him the all-clear. I haven't heard a peep from Alex since I entered the lion's den upstairs.

"Me either. But, if I'm being honest with you...I wanted to. I was just about to come when Mr. Sullivan called my name. I didn't even hear him the first time, I was so caught up in everything that was happening." So damn innocent.

"It's okay. Your body wanted a release. It's not something to be ashamed of. Don't ever be ashamed of your body, Mel. Do I prefer men? Yes. Do I find you attractive? Also, yes. It's okay." Jesus, I did not think I'd be giving a birds and bee's talk at the end of the night tonight. This lifestyle is nothing if not unpredictable.

"Huh. Wow. Ok. So, forty-eight hours?" She asks,

seemingly satisfied with my brief synopsis of experiencing her newfound sexuality.

Forty-eight hours to go time. It doesn't sound like a lot of time, and it's not, unless you're Laura and forty-eight additional hours means the statistics aren't for finding you alive. Forty-eight more hours and we're looking at a recovery. Dammit.

"Forty-eight hours. You got your invitation." Bringing Mel along was never part of the plan. She's a liability I didn't expect to have. Just like that, there's one more person I'm responsible for keeping alive.

"Yeah, but so did you. You didn't want to go out there, did you?" Or did I?

"It is what it is. Looks like we're going one way or the other." Go time.

"Looks like it. So, he said something about a routine?" A routine that I hope we never have to perform. If we play our cards right, my hope would be an organized raid. That's one thing I've come to appreciate working with the FBI. My work is no longer a suicide mission. I've learned the value of backup and proper planning.

We need a way to take down Wilks and Sullivan at the same time. I wonder if Alex was able to gain any ground from his perspective tonight on the case.

"Yeah, I guess he wants a little more than the two of us making out and rubbing up against each other on stage. Be here early tomorrow, we need to practice. I know you like choreography, so it's cool with me if you want to go ahead and jot some ideas down. We can put something together tomorrow." Maybe this is my path to keeping Mel occupied. Keep her safe and her mind busy while I make alternative plans that hopefully save us all in the end.

"Right. Sure, I'll work on putting together a routine." I nod to her as I usher us both out the large metal door that leads to the parking lot. Mel has a small beat-up car that's seen its better days, but it's more than most of the girls have around here.

It's more than I have. I walk to and from the club, it's easier that way. Sure, maybe it's a little dangerous, but I have my suspicions that it would be far more dangerous rolling up in here with my blacked-out government-issued SUV. So, I walk and I hold my weapons close to my body, in case some fool gets the bright idea to try something. Wouldn't be a good day for him, I'm just sayin'.

"And Mel…" I turn right, toward the stretch of road that leads back to my apartment as Mel opens the door to her car. It groans in protest in the quiet of the empty parking lot. The only other cars left here will probably still be here in the morning.

"Yeah?" Pausing with her body inside the car, but her hand still on the door, she turns back to look at me.

"Make sure you don't forget to include some of the making out." I smirk as I push my hands into my sweatshirt and fight off the sudden chill in the air that came out of nowhere. The seasons are changing, but I won't be here to see the snow.

"Right, noted." She giggles nervously before closing the door to her car and cranking it up.

I smile to myself as I turn the corner to walk down the empty street, the only light coming from the streetlamps above, the ones that aren't busted out.

Each and every risk we take is wrapped up with a little insanity. With no risk there is no change. No growth. No success. Only complacency. I must be fucking insane.

She's going to get us all killed.

CHAPTER TWENTY-FOUR
ALEX

One block from the club, I stand in the darkness beside an old, abandoned garbage bin and I wait. A stray cat meows in the distance, a plea for food that I kind of hate I don't have to give. I don't know why it bothers me that this damn cat is out here alone and starving, but it does.

I gave Reid the all clear about fifteen minutes ago. I watched via remote access as he cut a light in the hallway of the club as a silent warning before he took his exit. He knows I've got it from here.

He's got work to do, a lead to follow-up on; a hunch – if you will.

Emily and Mel used the rear exit of the building, as expected, near the back parking lot. The same lot I listened to them have their earlier conversation about Laura in. Whether Mel realizes it or not, she may have saved Laura's life by confiding in Em, only time will tell.

I stand in the darkness and I wait for her. I'm not

going to scare her, I don't want to die tonight. But I couldn't sit back at the apartment and wait any longer. I needed to see her.

What is that saying? Distance makes the heart grow fonder? Whatever the hell that means. Whoever wrote that nonsense was obviously deranged. My codependency now that Em is mine is hardcore. I'm not satisfied with watching from the sidelines any longer.

I would chastise Reid for allowing her to walk home alone in the darkness every night, but it wouldn't matter. It's not his fault she's too independent for her own damn good. It's not fair to pin that shit on him, when I know good and well, she wouldn't have it any other way. And it's not like they can be seen together.

I hear her cackle through the silence of the night as she moves closer to where I wait. It's not even so much a giggle as it is a literal crazed laughter.

I let her pass. I watch as a light breeze blows through the cool night sky, and she's forced to push her hair up and out of her face. I take in the long, lean lines of her legs in her leggings and immediately remember the way she had them wrapped around Mel just an hour ago.

Stepping from the shadows, I fall in step behind her silently.

One step. Two. She doesn't slow, and I don't bother trying to catch up with her. I just follow, two steps behind as she continues a path that I know she walks nearly every night.

Kind of deep and metaphorical. I'll probably always be two steps behind her, and I'm cool with it.

"Thought you were on my couch." She speaks first.

Although I can't see her face, I hear the smile in her voice.

"Got bored waiting. Sounded like you were having more fun than I was." I kick a rock on the sidewalk and watch it skip across the abandoned roadway to our right. There's no one out this late, and if they are, they aren't the type of people we want to run in to.

"Yeah, loads of fun. Guess the definition is open to interpretation."

"How many rules you think we're breaking right now?" I ask, changing the subject. I consider the implications of us walking together like this out in the open, even if we aren't technically walking together.

"I've never been one to follow the rules much." I smile to myself at her quick-witted response.

"Me neither." I shrug.

"And yet, we both work for a unit of the federal government of the United States of America that enforces the law. Funny how life works." Indeed, it is.

"Wait, we're supposed to follow the law? I don't remember signing anything that said that." Theoretically speaking, I didn't sign a damn thing...if we're talking about legalities and shit.

"It was in the handbook." She says flatly and matter of fact.

"There's a handbook?"

"Hell, I don't know. I always figured there was some monstrosity of a handbook somewhere, but I haven't read it."

A chuckle builds low in my chest at her complete and utter disregard for following the rules.

"You walk home by yourself every night?" My eyes

scan the darkened alleyways we pass, similar to the one I stood in waiting for Emily just a few minutes ago. The closer we get to her apartment, the seedier the area surrounding us becomes.

"You creep on unsuspecting women in the dark every night?"

"Touché."

"Yeah, I walk home. But to my credit, I knew you were hiding in the alley by the garbage bin back there. I saw you when I passed by. Figured it was only a matter of time before you showed yourself."

"Shit, you saw me? I need to work on my sneak attack."

"Your sneak attack? Please. It's why I'm in the field and you, sir, are not. I heard you breathing from two blocks away. Plus, I know you talked to the damn stray cat. I don't like cats, or animals for that matter, so don't get any ideas. We will never have jointly owned inside pets." Jointly owned inside pets, this woman.

"Ouch, a punch right to the gut." I brush my hand over my chest.

"Could have been your balls."

"Can we have babies? You know, jointly owned and shit." I test my luck as we round the final corner before approaching her apartment.

She doesn't pause. She doesn't turn to look. She doesn't miss one single beat before she speaks again.

"I wanna have all your babies, Alex. I've never considered myself the motherly type. Hell, I don't even hardly remember what having a mother was like, let alone how I'm supposed to be one myself. But I dunno, I had a dream last night, and now I want bald babies. All of them. A bunch of little badasses running around breaking all the rules. You're in charge of their bad behavior, by the way, because they will clearly get those genetics from you." Shit. I'm not sure what exactly I expected her to say, but it wasn't that. My eyes itch as I consider making a family with Em. What it would be like to have a wife and children to love and care for.

I like to believe that my dad did the best that he could, but he was sick the majority of my life, still is. My dad fought against a disease that was greater than my mom or I, but at least he fought. So many times, he could have given up on life, but instead, he tried. While I hope for the best with his rehab, no matter what happens, I'll know he didn't give up. I don't wanna give up. I want to make a family with Em, and I want us to do it up right; whatever right looks like for two outcasts of society.

I've faced my demons regarding the situation. The genetics, the possibilities that I might end up in the same battle, and I've learned that the mind is a powerful thing. Limits only exist when we place them on ourselves, they exist in our minds. I'm not placing limits on my future. If I'm going to be a husband and a father, I'm going to be the best damn husband and father I can be. No limits.

"I love you, Aemilia." God, do I love this woman.

"Did you watch tonight?" She smiles slyly over her shoulder as she begins ascending the stairs to her apartment, like she didn't just turn my world up on its axis. Like I didn't just verbally profess my love for her.

"You missed the part where you reciprocate. You schooled me on that shit earlier. I'm a quick learner, now look who's already forgotten." I take the stairs two at the time to catch up.

"Shut up, nerd. Did you watch?" She pulls a key from her pocket as she pauses briefly on the landing, and I finally catch up to her.

"I did. Your toothbrush is ready and waiting for you in the bathroom. Personally, might want to use a bar of soap too, just in case." My wide hands pull her into my chest by her hips as she works against me to slide the key into the door.

"Was it weird for you?" She yanks out of my hold as the door opens. She takes in the new layout of her living space but doesn't say anything about how I've totally taken over.

"I've always watched you Em, you know that. Was it weird to watch a pervy old man touch his cock while he watched you dance? I mean, it's not something I want to watch on repeat. But, I dunno, I was feeling what you and Mel were putting down." Em drops her bag to the ground by the couch and kicks her shoes off as I close the door behind us and lock up.

"You recorded it, didn't you?" Turning toward me, she pulls her sweatshirt seductively over her head and tosses it to the couch, followed quickly by her sports bra.

"Damn straight." I stalk her. I take a step forward, she takes a counter-step back, but she never turns. Her eyes remain on mine as her smile grows the closer we get to the bedroom.

"Wanna watch it later?" She pulls her lip into her mouth as her calves hit the mattress. She's stuck with nowhere to escape.

"I'll pop some popcorn while you're sanitizing your mouth. You got popcorn, or do I need to run out real quick and go by the 7/11?" I stop when the toes of my boots hit her feet. The red polish on her toenail's peeks through the black fishnet tights that must be hiding beneath the leggings I'm about two seconds from peeling off of her.

"Of course I have popcorn. Who doesn't stock their pantry with popcorn? Blasphemy."

"Exactly what I've been telling Reid for years."

"Alex, you know this is weird as shit, right? Like for real. We're not the picture of how to build a successful, stable relationship." She continues to abuse that bottom lip as she looks up into my eyes. Like she can see something inside of them, something deep within my soul. I feel her staring into my heart.

"And yet, all I'm hearing right now is, blah blah blah you wanna build a relationship with me and let me put babies in your belly." Reaching for her chin, I gently tip it up towards me. I brush her lip with my thumb, and she releases it with a pop.

I feel the breath she's been holding as it expels over my face. Really, all that talk about sanitizing doesn't matter. I don't care whose mouth was on this mouth earlier because this is my woman. My mouth. *Mine*.

"You're right, we're not the picture of a perfect relationship. But given a choice Em, imma pick weird every time. We're both misfits of society. We're the underdogs. We're floating around in a world of social expectations that neither of us will ever meet. I don't want to be like those people. I don't want to fit the norms of society. That's got to be a boring ass life, right? Normalcy, the word even sounds square. You and I, we fit together, and that's all that matters. I want you, only you, just the way you are – murder tendencies and everything."

"Make love to me, Alex. Real love. I want to feel you up inside of my heart." Her words are the kindling to the embers that have been burning deep within my chest since the first night I arrived here. Since the night she changed my life forever.

I don't need another word, just her presence, her heart, as I drop to my knees in front of her.

-o-
EMILY

I will not cry.

I will not cry.

Damn allergies.

My chest constricts and tightens around my lungs as Alex drops to his knees at my feet.

I don't know what I did to deserve this man. After all of the hell I've endured, did karma finally come through for me? Is he my redemption from the darkness that I've lived in all these years?

I want to say yes. I want to let my heart feel what is happening between us with its entirety. I want to release the demons. But there's something buried deep in the back of my mind somewhere that's causing me this heartburn, this aching in my chest. I've lived through so much in my life. I've experienced so much loss, and I've survived because I had nothing left to lose.

Now I have Alex and the little badass babies that I haven't even met yet that I've somehow formed some strange maternal bond with.

What if it's all a trick? What if I'm being set up for my biggest downfall of all?

I won't survive it. The darkness will finally win.

But...but what if it doesn't?

"Aemilia, baby, come back to me. Don't let them steal this from us. Don't let your mind go there right now. Be here, be with me, let me love you." Alex kneels before me, the crisp denim of his jeans contrasting against the worn shag carpeting. His hands grip my hips and demand my attention. His eyes stare up into mine as he waits for an acknowledgement.

How long has he been waiting for me?

Why is it so hard for me to let him love me when loving him is so easy?

"Alex, I'm scared." The words shake as they fall from my lips.

"What are you afraid of, Em?" His hands and voice are strong, a contrast to the weakness I'm allowing myself to feel right now. If he is strong, I can be weak, even if it's just for a moment.

"I don't want to lose anymore. I want to keep you." My words are a whisper, a confession in the night.

"Together we win, Em. As long as we're together we can't lose."

"Promise?" My voice catches in my throat and burns

with unshed tears.

"Cross my heart." His lips tilt up into a boyish grin.

"Hope to die?" I mirror his smile with a watery smile of my own, remembering words I probably haven't spoken since the second grade.

"Nah, we're gonna live. I don't like needles in my eye anyways."

Leaning down, I cup his face with my hands. I feel the foreign wet drops as they drip down my cheeks onto his face, and I brush his lips with mine. It's not insistent, it's not hungry. It's pure.

He tastes like chocolate birthday cake with pink sparkling candles.

He tastes like home.

His fingers slide under the material of my leggings and, slowly, he begins to pull them down my thighs. I'm forced to pull back and straighten or risk falling over, leaving me in the fishnet tights I kept on from earlier and nothing else.

"I love you when you're dressed up, Em. I love to see you in the fancy matching lingerie sets and diamonds. I love to watch the lights ricochet from your body as you dance on stage, but I love you even more when you're in nothing at all." He emphasizes the last three words slowly as he pushes his thumb through the material of my tights, and I hear them as they rip. Then they're off, and I'm standing before him naked.

It's always about the performance. When I take the stage, when I'm working, every interaction I have is intentional and carefully planned. I thrive on the ability to control the situation.

If I'm in control, I can't get hurt.

Tonight, is different. I'm relinquishing that control. I'm willingly handing it over. In return, I'm going to allow Alex the freedom to worship me the way only he knows how.

Tonight, I'm going to allow myself to feel.

I relish in the thought that, tonight, I don't have to perform.

"Lay back on the bed, Em. Let me look at you." I obey, not because I have some obligation, but because I want to. I want to be his. I want to give myself to him fully.

He stands, and I sit back on the bed. I dangle my legs over the side and wiggle my toes in anticipation of what I know is coming.

"All the way back."

Alex steps into me, forcing me to spread my thighs further as I lay back onto the bed on my elbows.

I observe him as his eyes roam over my entire body, from the top of my head to the tips of my toes. His hands are held at his sides in restrained fists that he opens and closes on reflex in time with his breathing.

I don't think he even realizes it when his tongue darts out over his bottom lip. The moisture from his mouth glistens on his lips and mimics what I know he sees. His eyes scan over my apparent need as it drips from inside of me and gathers between my exposed thighs. His perusal is erotic and torturous all the same. I feel his eyes like a physical touch.

"Your hair, Aemilia, it's dark like your past, but shimmers like silk when the light hits it just right. It's something special and unique, only you. It's your silver lining." Reaching behind him, he grabs his shirt and pulls it over his head before dropping it at his feet.

His chest expands and contracts with each word he speaks. His abdominal muscles form divots and concaves that my fingers itch to explore. An array of tattoos cover his neck and shoulders. A reminder of darkness that he carries, a visual depiction of his past.

"Your eyes. They're the eyes of a fighter. Eyes that have seen the worst parts of the world, but also see the rainbow when others walk blind. Your eyes are your promise." He bends at the waist to take off his boots one at the time, and I watch as the muscles in his back ripple in response. The veins in his arms pop with each and every movement he makes before he stands again, straightening to his full height and towering over me as I remain on the bed.

"The subtle curvature of your cheek bones against your olive skin silently give way to the secrets you work so desperately hard to hide. You're an exotic beauty, mysterious. You don't fit in because you were never meant to." He smiles and tilts his chin towards me. "And that hidden dimple on your left cheek, it speaks of an innocence that you think is gone, but baby, it's not. You have everything left to give. More than what I deserve, but fuck if I'm not going to take it anyway. They stole your body, if only temporarily, but they didn't steal your soul. You're a warrior, Em."

They stole my body. My breath catches on those words. I repeat them in my mind and process their meaning as I force oxygen through my lungs. It's the first time Alex has really acknowledged out loud what I went through with Vito. Vito might have stolen from me, but I am not broken. I chose to fight. I won that battle, and every damn day, we work together to win the war.

With one hand, he flicks the button on his jeans and grabs the waistline of the denim material. He pulls them down his thighs, leaving him in a pair of black briefs that cling to the muscles of his legs. But I can't focus on his legs, not when his thick cock bulges in front of me, pressing forcefully against the cotton material that barely encases it.

"And this body. I wanna memorize every curve. I wanna know every freckle and every scar. I know you have a job to do, and I know what it entails. I signed on to this shit as a willing participant. At the end of the day though, your heart, your soul, your brain…this body…tell me who it belongs to. Tell me, Aemilia."

I don't hesitate, I don't have to, not when the answer to his question overwhelms me with certainty.

"You, Alex, I will always belong to you. Everything I am, everything that I have left to give, I give willingly to you. You are mine, and I am yours. Forever." My voice shakes with the sincerity in my words. Moisture continues to pool between my legs as he drops to his knees for a second time.

Leaning between my thighs, he runs his hands over my abdomen, pausing just for a moment, his thumbs brushing reverently over my belly button. "When we close this case, and we will soon, I want you to get off the pill, Em. I wanna put my babies in here. I want you to make me a daddy." There are things that I will never be able to give because of my history, no matter what Alex says. But this, this is something I can give to him.

"Yes, Alex. Soon, I promise." His hands move over my hips, down the sensitive skin of my thighs until they come to a rest just behind my knees. Lifting one leg and then the other he places my legs over his shoulders until my drenched opening hovers just off the mattress laid out in front of him.

"You're a damn snack, Em. I've been dreaming about your taste. You wanted to give my orgasm tonight to Mel, didn't you?" I feel the slow throbbing as it begins again somewhere deep inside of me. My blood hums with the vibrations of his lips as he speaks without touching. He's so close, but not close enough. Earlier, with Mel, I couldn't allow myself to lose control, I didn't have that luxury. But now, as Alex torments me, his words alone have me teetering over the ledge once more. This time, this time I can freefall.

"Aemilia, answer me. I know you're not ashamed, so tell me. You wanted that orgasm, didn't you?" His voice is more demanding, but he's not angry. He's patient with me, but his patience with himself is wearing thin, he's hungry.

"Yes, I wanted to come. I could feel her pussy against mine. I could feel her heat burning me, she wanted it too. But I couldn't, I had to maintain control of the situation."

"No, we're not talking about control tonight. Did you want to eat her pussy? The way I'm about to eat yours. Did you want to taste her?" Now he's just being an asshole. I thrust my hips forward, and he jerks back, not willing to give me what I want yet.

"Dammit, Alex. Yes, I wanted to taste her. If she was in this room right now, I would fuck you both, but she's not, and we're doing the love thing, and Jesus, if you don't put your mouth on me, I might die. Or kill you. Somebody's about to lose a life." I hear his low chuckle and then I feel it as his mouth brushes my sensitive clit, and he finally gives me what I've been waiting for…yesssss…

"Agh, thank…fuck…" I grip the sheets in my fists and throw my head back in ecstasy as he swipes his tongue from my soaked opening to the top of my clit and back again.

The relief of his touch is only temporary as desperation for a release that I've been putting off for hours continues to build inside of me.

"So, fucking good." He fucks me with his tongue as he speaks. The combination of his dirty words and dangerous tongue feeds my anticipation.

I arch my back off of the bed as I try to get closer, needing more. Responding to my silent plea, Alex moves his hand so that he can slide two fingers into my soaked pussy, curling them so that they're touching the exact spot that I didn't even realize I needed until he's there and I'm moving my hips begging for more.

I welcome the prickling sensation of the coarse hair that coats his jawline as it rubs against my thighs, a distraction from the pleasure that threatens to send me right over the edge.

His fingers create their own rhythm as he pumps in and out of my pussy, caressing that secret spot only he can find over and over again.

His teeth graze my clit, and my legs tighten around his shoulders, pulling him in harder. He might suffocate, but if he'll just get me there, at least one of us will die satisfied.

"Alex, Oh God, Alex, I'm going to come." I try to issue a warning, I'm not sure if it's more for me or for him, but I say the words all the same. When my arms refuse to hold my weight any longer, I drop my elbows and rely solely on Alex to support my hips. My hands reach feverishly for his head, looking for something to hold on to, something to ground me as my body threatens to spiral out of control into the abyss.

My body levitates from the bed as I rock into Alex's mouth erratically, taking and then taking more when I can't get enough quickly enough. His fingers curl once more as he sucks my clit into his mouth, and my body freezes. I scream out as bolts of lightning shoot up my spine, my orgasm like a physical electrocution.

I feel the warm gush I still haven't gotten used to as it drips down the back of my thighs. Alex releases my clit to slide his tongue over my opening that continues to pulse with the intensity of my orgasm.

"You could bottle that shit up, and I would drink it like a protein shake. Damn, woman." My body shakes with the aftershocks of my orgasm as Alex places my legs gently back down on the bed. The hair on his face glistens with my moisture as he smiles proudly.

"You know, I don't normally come like that. Like, I don't generally make such a mess." I consider my words as Alex crawls over me and onto the bed behind me.

"That's because you only come like that for me. Your body knows. That pussy knows who it belongs too.

Until Death

Come over here, baby." He moves behind me, scooting to the head of the bed until his back hits the wall. He looks exactly like he did last night, when I fell asleep in his arms, only he doesn't. Last night he was my shelter, my safe harbor. Tonight, his eyes are mischievous and playful as he motions for me to come to him.

CHAPTER TWENTY-FIVE
ALEX

I lick my lips and relish the taste of Em's orgasm on my tongue as I watch her crawl across the bed on her hands and knees. Her plump ass sways in the air, and I make plans for later. I want to take her from behind. I want to watch my cock as it slides effortlessly in and out of her wet pussy. A pussy that is only that wet for me. *Mine.*

I lean back into a wall of pillows that separate my skin from the cold sheetrock, and I wait for her. I see it in her eyes, I know the way her mind ticks. She thinks she's handing control over to me tonight, but she has no idea the power she holds.

She kneels in front of me and, instead of speaking, she leans forward. Her nipples brush against the exposed skin of my chest and immediately goosebumps rise up on my neck.

I hold my breath in anticipation as I wait for a kiss that never comes. Instead, her lips brush the skin on my neck.

Not just anywhere, no, her lips brush a date that will forever be engrained in my heart just as it is on my skin. The date of my mother's death. Em's way of respecting what I've lost. Her way of acknowledging my darkness.

I swallow down the emotion that threatens me, and her lips follow, over my throat and down my chest.

She takes her time marking my abdomen until her lips hover at the waistline of the briefs that I kind of wish I'd never purchased at the store earlier. I'm not a huge fan of going commando, but hell, there would be one less barrier between us right now, and my cock is begging to be released from the confines that restrain it.

Starting on my left hip, she trails her tongue across my lower abdomen. It's all I can do to suppress the groan that threatens to escape from within my chest.

Surprising me, her mouth moves over the material until she's touching my cock, only she's not touching me at all. I feel the warmth of her breath, and my cock jumps in protest beneath her lips. I'm sure she can taste the pre-cum that drips from the tip onto the thin material that separates my cock from her mouth.

I feel my orgasm as it begins to build in my lower abdomen; the tell-tell tightening at the base of my spine.

"Enough, Aemilia." I speak the words through gritted teeth. I can't take anymore. I'm going to cum in my damn briefs.

Her eyes cut up to mine and she smiles, finally pulling back and gripping the band of my briefs with her small hands. She knew exactly what she was doing to me. I lift my ass from the bed just enough to allow her to pull them down my legs. I help her out a little by kicking them the rest of the way off.

"Are all the nerdy boys packing big dicks, or is this an anomaly that's just isolated to you?" She smiles as she runs her hands back up my thighs and my cock stands to attention between us.

"I'm a prodigy, a criminal hacking mastermind. It's only natural to assume I would have a big dick." I tease her in an effort to distract myself.

"You sure do have a big...*head*." She giggles, and I start to laugh at her cheesy joke but then snap my lips closed when she leans forward and swirls her tongue over the head of my cock.

"Nope, that's not fair." I grip her long, silky locks in my hand and tug her just enough to break the seal she's created over my cock.

"What's not fair?" She pulls back and looks at me innocently, licking her lips.

"I'm too close, Em, and you're too good."

"But you got your turn?" She pretends to pout, and it doesn't help my current predicament. She's fucking adorable.

"Ride my cock, Emily."

"Yes, sir." She smiles slyly as she gives in and crawls up my body.

She spreads her legs so that a knee rests of either side of my hips and she sits up tall, elongating her spine. Gripping my cock with her hands, she lines the head up with her slick opening, and then there's that smile again. The devil.

"You want me...like this?" She teases one final time before slamming down over me and taking me into her body fully in one movement. Curse words in various languages leave my mouth as I try not to cum on impact.

"God, you're trying to kill me. Do not move, woman. You move, and I swear to Heaven above, I will spank your ass."

I threaten her, and then she does the exact opposite. I've really got to stop underestimating the extent of her rebellious streak.

"Please spank me, Alex. I want you to spank me…*hard*." She rocks forward, riding my cock and the pleasure building inside of me only intensifies. My cock grows inside of her and stretches her warm pussy.

Reaching forward, I lean up and take one of her breasts into my mouth, swirling my tongue around her nipple and then biting down. A gasp falls from her lips, so I take the hint and switch breasts, doing the same thing on the other side.

"You like the pain, Em?"

"Yes, fuck. *Please* spank me, Alex. You promised."

She continues to rock back and forth on my cock, her clit rubbing against the skin of my lower abdomen. I reach around her, gripping her left ass cheek with one hand. Using my opposite hand, I pull back and slap her ass so hard I feel the vibrations through my open palm.

"Agh! Yes, again." I hit her a second time. This time when she cries out, I grab onto her ass with both hands and rock my hips up into her. So tight, fuck. I count from ten backwards as I work to hit the spot I know will send her with me over the edge.

"You're so deep, Alex. Feels…so…good." She struggles to get the final words out. I feel the subtle shift in her pussy as it begins to tighten around my cock, and her fingernails dig into the skin on my back.

"So fucking tight. Jesus, I can barely move, woman. Come for me, Aemilia. I need you to come. Now." I can't stop. I can't hold it off any longer. I grab her ass so hard she'll probably be bruised tomorrow as I slam her down onto me again.

"Yes, Alex, yes. Fuck. I love you." Her words are barely audible, but I feel the love she pours into them, just before the contractions of her pussy pull me under, and then I'm lost to her.

I pull her to my body and bury my head in her hair as my orgasm rips violently through me, and I fill her with my cum. I'm overwhelmed with emotion and love for this woman that believes she's unlovable.

We come in unison, her body contracting and pulling every last drop from me. I feel her relax into me, coming down from her high, but I can't let go of her. Not yet. Not ever.

"I love you, Aemilia. God, I love you so much." I feel the slight quiver in her shoulders against my chest. When she doesn't move in response to my words, I pull back slightly.

I grip the sides of her face and pull her eyes up to meet mine. Silent tears run down her cheeks, staining them with the inky black from her mascara.

I don't have to ask her what's wrong, because I feel it too. I feel the same overwhelming emotion swelling inside of me.

"I love you. All of you. Every. Single. Piece." I enunciate each word as I kiss the tears from her cheeks.

"Cross you heart?" She smiles as she finally speaks. My cock immediately begins to swell again inside of her.

"Hope to live. Forever. Because I'm never getting enough of you."

"I can feel that ya know." She tilts her head back and laughs a deep, throaty laugh as she wiggles her ass on my lap.

"You're gonna be the death of me." I run my hands down over her shoulders until they come to a rest on her ribcage.

"Not before we do that again...plus, I dunno, maybe another million times, give or take." She shrugs.

"Give or take." I mimic her nonchalant response.

"But first, imma need a shower." Without warning, she hops off my lap and climbs over my legs towards the bathroom.

I smile when I catch sight of her bare ass. Just as I suspected, the imprint of my hands remain on her olive skin.

"Was that an invitation?" I lean forward to follow because I have to. It's as natural as breathing. I will always follow her.

"It was if you wanna RSVP." She throws a smile over her shoulder before stepping off of the bed and into the doorway.

"Let's go, I'm here for the party. And the after party. And the hangover breakfast." I climb the bed behind her.

"Hangover? I don't have any alcohol, Straton. I'm on the job literally twenty-four seven, and so are you, idiot." She places her hand on her hip as she pops it to the side like she thinks she wants to throw some attitude my way.

She knows better.

"Not the kind of hangover breakfast I was referring to, and no name calling." I catch up to her and smack her ass again, for good measure. Just in case she needs a reminder.

She turns, leaning into my body and lifts her finger to her chin pretending to think for a minute before speaking again.

"Oh, well in that case…you got that video too?"

"Hold up. Give me five minutes. I'll pop the popcorn."

CHAPTER TWENTY-SIX
EMILY

Beep. Beep. Beep.

"Ughhhh…" I groan out loud as I reach out blindly from my cozy cavern of blankets and man muscles in search of the beeper that demands my immediate attention from the nightstand.

When did I finally close my eyes? Thirty minutes ago?

Can a nap really be called sleep if you're merely resting your eyelids and not fully unconscious?

My entire body aches. Like deep body muscle aches. I didn't even realize I was capable of being this sore anymore, but my thighs feel like I spent my night doing squats. Well okay, maybe the reality wasn't much different, but apples and oranges…or maybe bananas. Whatevs.

Finally, my fingers hit the dated black plastic that may as well be an extension of my body and I yank it back into the cocoon with me, only it's not flashing. That's strange.

Where's the damn beeping coming from?

"Make it stop, Em." Alex whines from behind me as he speaks without opening his eyes, curling his arm around my waist and pulling me back into his chest with a grunt. I swear I could live in this little cocoon.

"I don't understand. I'm holding my beeper. It's not flashing." I stare at the piece of plastic totally puzzled.

It's not my phone.

Not my beeper.

"Great. That's because..." He leaves his arm around me but rolls over, stretching his torso across the bed and reaching towards the floor haphazardly. He fumbles around with his pants before rolling back into our secret hideaway. "It's mine."

A familiar 9-1-1 flashes in red as Alex and I both stare at a beeper that's identical to the one I hold. "Where did you get that?"

"Where do you think I got it? Who's the only person on the planet you know that likes to use ancient devices he purchases off of the black market to communicate in code?" The corner of Alex's lip tips up into a smile as I throw the covers back off of us, exposing us both to the cold night air.

"But the beeper is our thing. He didn't ask me if he could get you a beeper." I sit up straight in the bed. Alex stretches out next to me and I watch, temporarily distracted, as each of the veins in his arms come alive with movement as he stretches them out above his head. Damn, this man for being so gorgeous when I'm working really hard to be offended right now.

"Awe, Em, you wanna be jealous, don't you? But you

can't be pissy because I'm too damn adorable. Frustrating, isn't it?" He teases, finally sitting up next to me and dipping his head down back into my space to smack a loud, wet kiss on my cheek.

"No, I am not *pissy*. I didn't have a formal education, and I know that's not even a legitimate word. Stupid boys and your stupid bromance. But why is yours flashing and mine isn't?"

"Dunno. But I know how we find out."

"Oh, I do too, and I'm coming. Don't think that just because you got your own beeper that you two can have secret meetings without me. This is my case, Agent Straton." I feel his eyes on me as I climb out of the bed in search of a pair a leggings to throw on.

"I didn't even consider it. But I can tell you what I am considering, Special Agent Young." His smile stretches across his face as he stands on the opposite side of the bed with his jeans in one hand and his cock in the other. He strokes it once, then twice as he watches me pull on a pair of leggings.

Men. How? We were literally asleep three minutes ago.

"Put you pants on, Alexander. Don't even try me. Work first, then play." I grab the closest sweatshirt to me and pull it over my head.

"When we get home, I'll let you do that thing with your mouth you wanted to do earlier." He gives up as he releases his semi-hard cock and pulls on his jeans, followed by his wrinkled t-shirt from the floor.

Fully dressed, I walk toward him as he sits on the edge of the bed and finishes lacing up his boots. I stop when

I'm directly beside him and bend down to his ear to whisper. "Baby, I can do things with my mouth you've never seen. Let's go." He growls as he moves to grab me, and I squeal running from him.

He's faster than I anticipated, and the distance we cover is well, nothing, in my tiny apartment.

He catches me when I pause to grab the keys, and his hand skims my ribs as laughter falls from my lips. "Stop it, Alex! We. Have. To. Go." I pant the words as I try to get away, unsuccessfully.

"You promise to stop teasing?" His mouth finds my neck as he slides his tongue out and over my skin. I can't take it. My legs collapse beneath me as I'm overwhelmed with sensation. My skin is a live wire of sensitivity. I can't handle it. I'm dead weight as Alex holds my body up with his strength alone.

"Em, you promise?" He asks again, but it's so damn hard to speak through the laughter.

"Yes. Promise! I promise!" And just like that, the torture is over. He sets me on my feet upright and smacks my ass as he rips the keys from my hand and walks out the front door, I hurry behind him to catch up.

It's all fun and games until it's not anymore. We've got a job to do. As the darkness of the night sky settles in over us, we walk silently side by side. We turn right toward the only public transportation option available at this time of night, or morning.

Things are shifting. We're moving in on them. If I've learned anything from my time with the Bureau, it's that things always get bad before they get better.

We catch an empty bus, and within ten minutes we're

at the docks.

The moonlight ricochets off of the water as we walk hand in hand to the warehouse. It's nearing four in the morning. The moonlight will soon be replaced with the sun. A new day. A new beginning.

I run my finger over the biometric scanner located in a hidden panel on the warehouse and the door opens.

"Jesus, finally." I hear him before I see him. I let Alex lead and follow him into the warehouse, closing the door to our backs and securing us inside.

"Finally? You couldn't even bother to extend the invitation to me? Now you've got me feeling all weird, like I'm crashing my own party. What's that about, Chapman?" He leans against a steel support beam in the middle of the warehouse, wearing the same clothes I saw him in hours ago. He hasn't been home.

"Oh Em, don't get all worked up. We all know what happens when you get worked up. Your blood pressure will skyrocket and you'll start shooting at people. Do we really want to go through that again tonight?"

"To set the record straight, I never had any intentions of shooting either of you. You brought that on yourselves. Actions and consequences, Reid. Actions and consequences." I narrow my eyes at him in warning. I mean, I wasn't planning on shooting anyone tonight, but...

"Right. But I knew the two of you would be together. Two birds, one stone. Feel better?" Reid gives me his signature panty melting look with those bright baby blues. While I'm not wearing panties because time didn't allow for it, my heart still softens a little. I don't want it to soften, but it does all the same. It's like a law of nature or something.

"A little. Next time you beep me. That's our thing."

"I told you she loved me more. You owe me twenty bucks, Straton." And just like that, all is right in the world again. His arrogance is unmatched.

"That's not what she was saying an hour ago. I don't owe you anything but maybe a smack over the head for even thinking that nonsense." Alex reaches toward me, gripping my hip and pulling me into his side possessively. Men.

"Stop while you're ahead boys. I wasn't planning to discharge my weapon, but you push and you push, and then I end up pulling the trigger. Actions and consequences." I snuggle into Alex's side further with no real intentions of touching my weapon.

"Ok, so we need to talk." Reid rolls his eyes and then turns his attention back to Alex.

His blue eyes darken. He lifts a hand behind his neck and rubs the tension that I'm certain is building there. I know that look. He knows something.

"You find it?" Alex reaches into his pocket and tosses Reid his beeper to disarm.

"Yeah, your instinct was right. 49A." 49A? The exit?

"Was she there?" Laura. I look up at Alex as I try to piece together what they've yet to tell me.

"No, I couldn't find her. I didn't get inside, but I staked out the premises. I watched them come and go for hours. Sullivan's got soldiers out there. Some of them I recognized, some of them I didn't."

With each word that passes between them, I become

increasingly frustrated that I'm not in the loop.

"Hit pause. I need some frame of reference." I finally interrupt.

Alex looks to Reid and then back to me again before speaking. "I was running the data earlier while you two were working at the club. Phone records, location activity, cameras in the vicinity – anything I could get my hands on. The same exit popped up again and again, 49A. After the third time, I figured it wasn't coincidence. So, I ran some records on recent real estate activity in the area."

"49A, it's close to the club, and it's not too far from here. The best of both worlds. The interstate and the waterway, it's exactly what we suspected." I interrupt, thinking out loud.

"Right, but there's more. Guess who owns the shell company that purchased an abandoned warehouse on said exit for a smooth one-point-four million six months ago?"

Alex nods towards Reid, but I answer first. "Wilks Luxury Auto?"

"Wrong. Try again."

"I don't know, you know I hate these games. It could be any one of the criminals we deal with on a daily basis. Although, I will say it would surprise me if Anderson Sullivan had pockets deep enough to float one-point-four without going bankrupt."

"You don't hate games, you hate losing. It was Victory Properties, LLC." Reid speaks.

Victory Properties. Victory Properties. I roll it around on my tongue, but when I can't place it immediately, I ask, not wanting to waste additional time unnecessarily.

"What's the significance?"

"We were already looking at the exit. One-point-four is grossly higher than the property value, almost five times the appraisal. Something about it didn't feel right. I dug a little deeper, the LLC had to file paperwork for tax purposes during its formation, which was a mere…six months ago. No coincidences. They founded the LLC under a secondary corporation, which is owned by none other than Vito Adkins." The fuck? Vito.

"Vito is dead. I watched him die with my own eyes, Alex. You know that!" Nausea rolls in my gut and my heart races. He has to be dead.

"Em, baby, he is dead okay. I promise. We blasted that bastard so hard there was nothing left of him to bury. I've seen the death certificate, it's legitimate. His remains were identified through DNA testing. It's not Vito. Instead, someone still using his identity in order to protect their own. Someone selfish, a coward. I think it's Victor Adkins. Victor is lazy and he cares about one thing and one thing only…well maybe two – Victor cares about Victor and Victor's money. He doesn't run his own clubs; he doesn't get his hands dirty. It only makes sense that he would continue to use Vito's name to carry out the dirty work for as long as he can get away with it." Everything starts falling into place. This is the break we've been waiting on.

"Well, that party is about to come to an end. He's not going to get away with it anymore. Not if we're able to tie him to Wilks and Sullivan. We can take all three down at the same time." My words are rushed, hurried; the need to end this once and for all pumping through my blood.

"Don't get too far ahead, Em. I hear it in your voice, you want to drop a bomb on them and watch from the sidelines smiling as they all burst into flames. While that might have worked the first time, we have to consider the innocent lives that are at risk right now. They're moving women and children through that warehouse. I saw it, they're already pushing shipments. We've got to infiltrate the warehouse first. We're going to have to work this from the inside out." Reid speaks and his voice is soothing, a balm to my racing heart.

This is why we're partners; this is why we make a great team. It's also easy to see how he and Alex have been best friends for so long. Relationships in life are all a balance. I guess it takes the two of them to balance the one of me.

Reid's analysis is not wrong. My kneejerk reaction is to burn them all, but if we take a step back and think about this logically…

"I'm going in. Thirty-six hours, less now. Tomorrow night. Sullivan extended a personal invitation to Mel and I to perform." I speak up. I know that Alex is already aware of the invitation even though we have yet to discuss the specifics of what it entails, but I'm not sure how much Reid knows.

"Mel?" Reid asks.

"He wants us together, to dance as a team. But, I hope we don't have to dance at all. I think we prepare for a raid. You think we can get backup down here that quickly?" I look to both Reid and Alex. We're going to need more than the three of us and the two soldiers we've got inside. We need the ability to keep our undercover identities intact in case we don't get all three. In case this isn't actually the end.

God, I hope this is the end.

"A raid. I like it, it might just work. I'll contact Reynolds once the sun comes up and get him to prepare a team. Remember Em, this case has always been about Anderson Sullivan. Wilks is a new player in our game, and Victor, well, we never anticipated taking down the entire mafia ring. Anyone else we get is a bonus. We take 49A, we save who we can and we try to get Anderson Sullivan out of there alive. We need an interrogation; he needs a fair trial." I watch as Reid's eyes cut over to Alex after the words leave his mouth.

"Fair trial my ass." Alex chuckles, but it's deep from the dark place inside of him.

"Look, the three of us have to work together. We'll go in as a team and come out as a team. Everybody comes out alive. Then we can all take R&R on some private island. The two of you can get married, I'll be the best man, of course. We do the damn thing, and then we rest in paradise."

"Hold up. Marriage? How did we go from bombs and raids to marriage? Nobody said anything about marriage." My eyes dart between Reid and Alex, and my breathing picks up again.

"Oh, Alex, you haven't asked her yet? Em, look at him, he's got marriage eyes. I can spot those eyes from a mile away. It's the look women give me right before I excuse myself to the restroom and never return." Reid raises his eyebrow as he stares at Alex who stands next to me with a shy grin on his face.

"The question's just a formality. Marriage, babies, let's nail these bastards – I've got plans for our future." He squeezes my hip with his hand.

He thinks he's cute, *he* has plans for *our* future.

"Do I not get a say-so in any of this?" I pull back from Alex just slightly so that I can look him in the eyes when I speak. He obviously had some sort of freak memory loss and forgot who he was talking to. I cross my arms in front of my body and dare him to test me on this.

I'm going to marry Alex, and I'm going to give him all the babies he wants. But nobody said there was a requirement I make it easy on him, that takes all the fun out of it.

"Wait, you don't wanna marry me, Aemilia?" Alex takes a dramatic step back, even further away from me and presses his palm over his heart like he's genuinely concerned that I might not be in this for life; all except for the smile that he can't seem to wipe off of his handsome face.

"I already told you that I want your babies, Straton. Who wouldn't? You're the ideal candidate for procreation. I'm not opposed to the whole contractually binding marriage thing either, but you're going to have to do better than that. You can't just assume I'm going to marry you. That's not how any of this works. You ask me a real question, and I will give you a real answer. And not tonight, I'm under duress right now."

"Duress? How are you under duress?" Reid speaks up and Alex continues to smile, I see his mind working. He's already making plans.

"You know what. You two are being ridiculous.

You're obviously sleep deprived, so you're talking out of your ass. I'm done entertaining this argument, back to the case. What do we know on Laura?" I brush them both off, right now is not the time for proposals.

"First comes war. Then comes marriage. Then comes the baby in the baby carriage." Reid singsongs in the background as I shoot daggers at him with my eyes.

Emily don't pull your weapon.

Emily don't blow people up.

Emily you're being *pissy*.

Honestly, it's not my fault when they make it impossible to take them seriously.

CHAPTER TWENTY-SEVEN
ALEX

I watch as Emily's spine snaps straight and her green eyes haze over. She's not about our nonsense right now, and Reid continues to push her. He can't help it, it's engrained in him. But, from the look in Em's eyes, he's about two-point-five seconds from getting his big toe blown off.

Luckily, he sees her and realizes how close he is to pulling the trip wire. I watch his eyes turn serious and he runs his hand over his jawline looking at both of us.

It amazes me how the two of them can go from bantering back and forth playfully to life and death discussions of raids and kidnappings within seconds.

Our future family dinners will be nothing if not exciting.

"Unfortunately, not a lot. She's still missing. There's a possibility she's still at 49A. There's also a possibility she's been shipped out to who knows where. Then, the more likely possibility that no one wants to consider – she's dead." I'm banking on option three, but I don't speak that negativity into the air.

"What do we do? It will be hours yet before we're inside of that warehouse. If she's not dead yet, she certainly will be by then." Emily searches for solutions when we all know there are none that are favorable to our current predicament.

"I'm sorry, Emily. We can't risk it." Reid speaks immediately, shutting down any hope she may have had of running some sort of suicidal rescue mission.

"So, we leave her? We leave her for dead? You expect me to just accept that as a legitimate option?" Emily's voice rises and fire lights her green eyes.

"That's not what I said, Emily, and you know it. You want to blow the entire raid by waltzing up in there looking for someone that may or may not be in there to begin with? What will that accomplish? I can't tell you that you'll save anyone, but I can tell you with absolute certainty that innocents will die." Reid stares at her, the two in a standoff as Emily refuses to speak.

She and I both know he's right, but it kills her to acknowledge it.

"That's what I thought. You know as well as I do that we have to wait and hope for the best while we put together a plan that will be successful. In the meantime, Alex will be in charge of getting us inside of 49A. Sullivan's a control freak, that's a known fact. There's a feed somewhere, we just need to find it. If anyone can get us in, its Agent Straton." Agent Straton, it's sexy when Em says it, but it still feels weird hearing it from Reid.

"Sometimes this job sucks." Emily groans as her hands wrap around my waist and she pulls me in again.

"No kidding. Okay, so what else do we do in the meantime?" I look to either of them for additional direction. We have too much time, and yet, we don't have enough. Go forward or stay back? The situation is unstable at best.

Reid pulls his leg up behind him and props it on the beam to his back. "I will contact Reynolds; we'll get boots on the ground prepped and ready for the raid." He nods towards Emily. "You prepare to gain physical access inside of the warehouse. You're our bait, Em. I don't like it, but it is what it is."

"Jesus, Reid, don't call her bait." I don't like it either. Not even a little bit.

"It's cool, he's right. I'm the lure. I will get us in, and the two of you will get us out. A team."

"A team." Reid and I repeat after Emily.

"I'll keep looking for her. I won't stop searching. Now that we have the location, Reid and I will work together to get additional cameras hooked up if we think we'll need them. I need to have eyes on every angle of that place. I'll have my eyes and ears open for any mention of her. If, for whatever reason, her cellphone comes back online or she tries to contact her family, we'll be the first to know."

Emily nods slowly as our plan of action begins to take shape.

"Reid, go home. Call Reynolds, then get some rest. I'm going into the club early tonight to work with Mel on our routine. Alex will be in my ear the entire time. If we hear anything on our end, we'll contact you. You're dead on your feet right now. I need you at your best."

Emily grabs my hand and drags me behind her as she turns back toward the entrance we first walked into. She pauses as we reach the door and turns back to speak to Reid. He remains in the same spot, leaning against the steel beam that seems to be holding him up. I can see it in his eyes, Em's right, he's exhausted.

"And Chapman, if you think for one second that you're going to send out a code red, 9-1-1, on your fancy, hi-tech device there, you better think twice about who you're sending it to." She smiles as she scans her finger over the scanner and opens the door.

The sun's coming up over the horizon causing the water to sparkle over the harbor.

A stark reminder that the timer on our case isn't waiting on anyone.

-o-
EMILY

"Again."

"I don't understand. You told me to come up with the choreography, and I did. We've been practicing all afternoon. I can't even feel my legs anymore, and I still have to perform tonight. What's the deal, Emily?" Mel leans against a pole on one of the practice stages in the club in a pair of leggings and a torn t-shirt that exposes the toned skin of her abdomen.

Her long, blonde hair is pulled up high on top of her head in a messy bun that looks effortlessly gorgeous. I don't understand how other women manage to do that. I throw my hair up on my head and I look homeless. I can say that with certainty because I spent most of my life actually without a home. There is no in between for me. Homeless street chick or badass, sexy siren. You get what you get. Okay, so maybe I'm always a badass, but still.

Mel, on the other hand, is even more beautiful toned down and natural than when she's dolled up and on stage. She's the girl next door. While that's never really been my type, she's growing on me – in a sexy, non-relationship*ish* sort of way.

"One more time from the top, and then we break for the night." We've been practicing for hours. Patrons fill the front of the house, and the rookie dancers are already taking the stage. We've still got to shower and get ready for our separate performances all within an hour or so, but I push her further. One more time.

I hope to God we don't have to perform this routine. I pray that I have Mel in a safe place, and our raid is well underway before we ever take the stage. But, there are no guarantees, and I can't depend on hopes and prayers. Instead, I push her to work harder.

Sweat trickles down my spine as I lift my body from the ground for what's probably the fifteenth time tonight, but I ignore the unrelenting ache I feel in my calves. I drop my head and allow Mel's body to wrap around mine. We move as one, an erotic dance that isn't just beautiful to watch, but tells a story of love – of betrayal – of sex.

This dance is visually stunning, the choreography is phenomenal, well beyond anything those buffoons out front would ever comprehend. It's obvious Mel spent every waking moment from the time we first discussed this to now putting together this routine. Her skill level shines through each meticulous move that we make.

Choreography is where she's meant to be. I want her dream to become a reality; I want to see her succeed, but I can't encourage complacency. I want to encourage her, but I need her to harden the fuck up and fast because I don't know what we're about to be up against. I very well can't tell her that there's a very real possibility she's walking directly into a firing squad.

In order for her to succeed, this mission has to succeed. For as long as I can keep her occupied with this dance and our upcoming performance, I can keep her safe.

"You think we're going to be ready?" She asks as she places her hands on her trim hips and takes a deep heaving breath in after we've wrapped up for the final time tonight.

"I know we're going to be ready. Good job tonight, Mel." I grab my water bottle from the worn wood of the stage and chug it down, needing to rehydrate before we have to dance all over again, but this time, under the lights out front.

"Thanks, Emily. You know, it really means a lot coming from you. I don't know what I'm doing half the time, I'm just winging it and hoping for the best." If she only knew.

"We're more alike than you think, Mel. I can assure you. Your choreography isn't something that can be taught, it's something that you have to feel. I know you feel it. We might not feel it the same, but I feel it too."

"You think Mr. Sullivan's going to be happy with it?

You think we'll make some money out there?"

"I think Mr. Sullivan would have already come down here by now if he wasn't happy with it. As far as the money goes, just dance. Let your body do the work, and the rest will follow. Let's hit the showers." I cut her off, not wanting to talk about money that will never materialize. I turn towards the locker room to grab a towel, and she follows behind.

"Aemilia." I hear his voice in my ear as I open my locker. I was waiting for him.

"Not going to happen, Hood." I roll my eyes as I whisper to him, quickly grabbing my towel and turning to follow Mel to the unoccupied shower stalls.

The showers in the club are vacant and mostly unused. It's rare anyone showers here because Alex isn't the only one whose eyes are in there.

"I love you." My smile grows as I hear his laughter and think of what's to come later, when I get home.

"Love you too, babe."

CHAPTER TWENTY-EIGHT
ALEX

I'm set up at Em's kitchen table, AKA my office, in the middle of her living room peeling an orange. I'm starved, Em's kitchen cabinets are bare, and we ate all the popcorn already.

While she worked with Mel all afternoon, I spent my time searching the dark web for our warehouse. Reid saw signs of export; they're already running shipments. If that's the case, and we feel confident that it is, that means they are buying and selling somewhere, and those transactions typically don't take place on eBay.

I'm no stranger to the innerworkings of the dark web, nor am I a stranger to finding people that don't want to be found.

It's how I allowed Em to find me. It's also how I operated my not-so-legal or legitimate, but highly successful business before I was arrested and stripped of all of my toys.

I toss a piece of citrus goodness in my mouth and savor the burst of flavor. If this is dinner, I may as well enjoy it.

On the flip side, the FBI now gives me extra special toys that allow me to surf the dark web undetected, without having to worry about covering my tracks for fear of federal imprisonment. Been there, done that – nothing to write home about.

Drugs, identities, credit card numbers, people – you can find anything in the parts of the internet that the bad guys call home. If you look at it from ten thousand feet, these entrepreneurs are really not unlike any other legitimate business owner. The goods are different, but the general way transactions take place is surprisingly the same. Currency changes hands for commodity. It's simple economics if you strip it down to the basics.

To be honest, that's the way I've always looked at it, or did, until I met Em and she opened my eyes to the evil that was happening behind the transactions I was observing from afar. I see in black and white where she sees the world in color, both figuratively and literally.

After hours of running searches on two of my three monitors, the third is dedicated to Emily, obviously, I got a hit.

The footage at the warehouse isn't showing up on Sullivan's feeds because Sullivan himself doesn't have access to it.

Emily was right, there is a brothel of sorts at 49A. But, unfortunately, it's so much worse than that. Victory Productions LLC was founded in conjunction with its sister company Victory Properties. Both were formed under the umbrella of Vito's existing corporation. The production company launched a website two months ago that's gone viral on the dark web.

The website is a glorified live porn site, only more horror – less glory. Each room in the warehouse is wired up to a live feed that allows pay-per-view access on a per room basis.

The rooms all have individual themes, not unlike the rooms at Sullivan's club. However, the theming itself is a far more explicit than tiki rooms and jungle themes.

Pick your poison. Virgins, BDSM, rape and, worse than that, children. The thought threatens to send the orange I just finished right back up again.

The more taboo the room, the more expensive the access charge.

Time slots are sold in one-hour increments.

There's also a place to submit an application to attend a "live event". Along with the application, there is a deposit of ten grand required up front, with additional fees to follow if your application is approved.

I suspect that whoever is behind Victory Properties is also behind the production company. Digging down further, I've been able to find additional black links that allow shipment and delivery of the "live events," the trafficking.

My suspicions are Wilks is handling the freight. His specialty is human transport, and Victor's giving him a cut for doing the dirty work.

Sullivan is in charge of providing soldiers and dancers for the "in-house" live events, and that's where his cut comes in.

I quickly jot down notes as I watch Em perform for the final time tonight.

After only three attempts, I'm able to gain access to their system and begin searching rooms for Laura, our missing person. I try to remain impassive, looking for features that I've memorized as being distinct to her as I search. I try to ignore the pained or drugged faces I see; I mute the site volume to minimize my distractions.

I get through two rooms with no luck before a knock on the apartment door startles me out of my trance.

I glance to the monitor on my left, Em's still on stage. If my calculations are correct, which they are, I know her routines like I know how to access the Tor browser. She's within the last thirty seconds, but that means she is not the person beating down the door for the second time.

I grab the Glock that sits on the couch next to me before standing.

Taking a deep breath, because dammit if I don't want to shoot somebody tonight, I take the three steps to the door and stop. I weigh my options. There's no peep hole, this isn't that type of facility, and that's not a luxury Em thought to install. I don't have time to access her exterior cameras. I could just shoot through the door, ask questions later. Or I could open the door and hope I'm a faster shot than what or whoever is on the other side if things go sour.

Deciding to risk it, because I might be a computer nerd, but I'm a sucker for a John Wayne movie; and I'm a damn good shot. I yank the door open and prepare to take a life.

The adrenaline gives me added strength I wasn't

anticipating as I nearly yank the door of the hinges. But, instead of my life flashing before my eyes, I stare at light blue eyes and sparkling white teeth I'd know anywhere.

"Dammit, Reid. Announce yourself." I drop my weapon to my side and gulp air to slow my heartrate before I have a medical emergency. "Fuck, I almost killed my best friend."

"The look on your face, it was priceless, Alex. Priceless." Reid smiles and laughs to himself like I just told him the best damn joke he's heard all year. He clasps his hand down over my shoulder and pushes us both back inside of the apartment.

"What part of I was about to have to speed dial the coroner do you not understand?" I stare at him in disbelief, still shocked. He grabs one of the chairs from the kitchen and turns it around, straddling it, making himself comfy.

"You hesitated. We need to work on that, by the way. I'm here for personal reasons." He rocks the chair forward and then back again, complete disregard for the lifespan that chair has probably long outlived.

"Fuck if I did. My finger was on the trigger. I almost shot you through the damn door." I set my Glock down on the table and pace the few steps of the living room because the adrenaline pumping through my blood hasn't calmed enough for me to sit yet.

"But you didn't, because you're in *looooove*. Some part of you, some tiny little part of you thought maybe that was Em on the other side of that door."

"That's where you're wrong. I was watching her on the monitor. I knew she was at the club."

"Well, in that case, you're playing favorites, and that's just rude, Straton. If you knew she was there, why didn't you realize I wasn't? I'm offended."

"Because you're a big boy, and you can take care of your damn self. I had more important things to worry about. Like how the hell Victor is getting rich selling pay-per-view access to his little warehouse of horrors down by the interstate like it's the damn UFC in Vegas."

"Pay-per-view?" Reid pauses his rocking motion in the chair as he stares at me, his face turning serious.

"He's got the rooms themed up like a candy shop for pervs. It's porn on steroids. Any sick obsession you can think of, take your pick. I've scanned through a few of them searching for Laura with no luck so far. He's drugging them. They're miserable. None of it appears to be consensual." I run my hand over the back of my neck, the reality of the things that are happening just a few miles up the interstate eating at me from the inside out. The need to act is overwhelming. It's easy to see why Reid and Emily fight so hard, it's addicting.

"Shit. Do you think we can work with their access, or do we need additional cameras?"

"I think we can work with what they've got. They've got the place covered. Even if their systems go down, I'm in now, I should be able to override it to get it back up. I'll have to block their access anyway once the raid starts. Have you heard from Reynolds?"

"Yeah, he's putting a team of six agents on a plane as we speak. They should land before daybreak. Em and I will meet them down at the docks and debrief to prepare for the raid. We're right at twenty-four hours now.

Reynolds agreed that we need to keep our current undercover identities intact. That adds an element of delicacy to the situation. We anticipated the possibility of that though."

"Where will I be?" I stop in the middle of the floor as his words register.

"That's why I'm here. You can work remotely, no?"

"What are you getting at, Reid? If Emily is here, I am here. Period."

I never cared that Reid took Julie Campbell to Winter Formal. It has never bothered me that he's always been in the spotlight and I've been in the shadows, I prefer it that way. But things are different now, our dynamics are changing.

"It's your dad." And just like that, the pit of my stomach freefalls from the cliff of sanity I was barely hanging on to.

"He dead?" The words taste bitter as they leave my mouth. I hate to be this way, really, I do, but I feel like I've spent decades just waiting for a phone call. Reid said he was in a rehab facility, that he was improving, but that seed of doubt is engrained deep inside of me.

Forgiveness sits up high on the shelf next to acceptance, and it's a hard pill to swallow after years of emotional abuse and neglect.

"I hope not. I was contacted by the rehab facility. We talked about this, last time I talked to the rehab facility they were encouraged by the progress he'd made. He was granted privileges for unsupervised visitation outside of the grounds with required check-in's every hour. He left this morning, and they've been unable to reach him since." He sighs, and I feel the despair in my bones. He didn't want to tell me, I get it, it's a tough spot to be in.

"So, he's probably passed out in a dirty bar bathroom somewhere in the city." I brush it off, not willing to admit to myself that something might have actually happened to him.

"They filed a police report after eight hours. It's their policy." Reid's not smiling, he's not laughing, his face remains stoic.

"Shit." I pinch the skin between my eyebrows and try to fend off the migraine that I feel building just beneath the surface.

"That's what I said when they called me. She said they'd tried to reach me earlier, but I was tied up making some runs for Sullivan, and then I was on the phone with Reynolds. I'm sorry, Alex."

"Don't start that. This isn't your fault. You've gone above and beyond when you didn't have to do anything. You gave him a chance when he didn't have one. Always a hero. But sometimes, Reid, sometimes people just don't want to be saved. You can't help someone that refuses to get in the damn lifeboat when the Titanic is sinking. Sometimes you just gotta let them go down with the ship." I think back to his analogy and realize it's relevance to this scenario.

"I know, but I was hoping that this time, this time might be different." He shrugs, and I'm transported in time, back to the night we sat together in a cold hospital waiting room as teenagers. He was my only life raft in sea of loss and misery. Reid saved me even then.

"I can't tell you how many times I've said those words

myself, Reid. I've pleaded with the heavens; I've said a thousand prayers. You did what you could, that's it. Now, what do we need to do today?" I inhale and face my reality. I'm torn between my past and my future.

"Police are actively searching for him. There's a private jet sitting on the tarmac waiting for you. You don't have to leave tonight; it will still be there in the morning; I've got the pilot on standby. Talk to Em. Pack up what you need, and go find him. I know you well enough to know that if you don't and something happens, you'll never forgive yourself. I know Em well enough to know that, if you refuse, she'll spike your morning coffee and drag your ass on that plane herself. She's capable, I'm capable, and you'll be with us virtually the entire time. It was never the plan for you to be in that warehouse physically, anyway.

Let us do what we're trained to do, and you take care of your personal shit. When this is all over and we're relaxing on the beach sipping fruity drinks that Em picked out, you won't have this hanging over your head. You can be a part of the team and still do what you need to do to clear your conscience from across the country. Don't let your past get in the way of your future, man. Emily, she's special. The two of you have something together that I didn't even know existed outside of animated cartoon movies. What do you say?" He and I both know what I have to do. It's a decision I don't want to have to make, but it's one I know Em will respect. Honestly, I'm not doing it for him. I'm being selfish this time, and I'm doing it for me. I'm doing it for the future I want to build with Emily. I'm doing this for my mom and her memory.

"I'll talk to, Em. Thanks for looking out, Reid. You don't know…" My words trail off as emotion threatens to overwhelm me. Reid pushes back from the chair and stands, embracing me with both arms.

"Brothers for life. Defeating the evil that threatens the Universe." I smile as he speaks words that bring me back to my childhood.

"Defeating the evil and defending the galaxy. Always." We slap backs and hug like the manly men we aren't in this moment.

"I love you, Reid." I pull back and tip my chin up to Reid as water stands in the corners of my eyes.

"Love you too, Alex. I better go before Em walks in and kicks my ass for being in here and risking her cover."

I lean over to my monitor and hit refresh on her location, she's a block out.

"Hope you wore your running shoes, she's closing in." I take a step towards the couch, watching the monitor as she eats up the remaining distance to the apartment. He turns abruptly, because apparently Em's mere presence is more frightening than me at the door with a loaded Glock, and heads to the door.

"Take the SUV to the airport and leave it." He tosses me a set of keys before quickly ducking out the door and into the night.

CHAPTER TWENTY-NINE
EMILY

I take the steps to the apartment two at the time. I'm tired, and I need Alex. I just need to be in his presence. I need to breathe the same air that he breathes. Okay, and maybe touch him a little…with our clothes off. Today was a long day, and tomorrow will be even longer. Ready or not, it's go time.

I walk through the door of the apartment and drop my bag at my feet as I cross the threshold. My feet ache, my legs ache, everything aches. "Your cat tried to attack me tonight. She approached me on the dark street and attempted to rub up on my leg while I was walking home. Definite assault charges warranted. It's like she knew you and I were somehow connected, and because you spoiled her by talking to her one single time, she now thinks we're friends. We're not."

"You're thinking about this all wrong. Did you ever consider that you've now gained a bodyguard in the form of a street cat? Bet she'd throw down for you if you'd give her a little rub a dub dub." Alex sits on my couch, denim-clad legs spread open wide with his arms laid over the back like he's a damn book cover model.

"Stop it right there, I am never touching that cat. It's probably got rabies or fleas. Who knows what diseases it's carrying." My stomach growls as I walk towards the kitchen in search of sustenance. My energy is below zero, and that's unacceptable.

"Say what you want, but you were living on the street too once, and I still gave you a rub." He chuckles as I pull one of my sneakers off and toss it at his head, missing on purpose, of course. I don't have time or energy to deal with a concussion.

"Apples and oranges. Speaking of oranges, where's my dinner?" I kick my second sneaker off as I plunder the kitchen for the orange I know I left here earlier.

"I got hungry. There's nothing to eat in this house." True that.

"It's called a grocery store."

"Didn't have time."

"Oh, yeah? What's up? What do you know?" My hunger ceases as my mind goes to our case; to Laura and our upcoming raid. The hours are narrowing in on us.

"We need to talk, Aemilia."

"Whoa. Drop a damn bomb in the room. Should I just shoot you now and get it over with?"

"Calm your tits, woman. Come here." He tips his head back, motioning for me to come closer. But, my brain short circuited a few words back and imma need an explanation before I come anywhere.

"My tits are chill. Speak." My feet are planted in the kitchen as I narrow my eyes in his direction, daring him to try me.

"Reynolds is sending in a team, plane lands in the morning."

"Keep going."

"It's my dad." Well, that's not where I expected this conversation to go. I walk toward him in the living room, needing to get a closer look at his eyes.

"He's in the rehab facility that Reid set up for him, right?" I drop down on the couch next to him and wiggle myself right up on under his arm, pulling my feet beneath me and getting as close to him as humanly possible without sitting in his lap. Come to think of it, that might not be a bad idea.

"Yeah, or he was, until I guess he decided he wasn't about that life anymore. He was granted unsupervised outings this morning. Literally day one. He's required to check-in every hour. He left this morning. No one has seen or heard from him since." Alex stares at the monitors in front of us, but he doesn't see anything that's on the screens. He's somewhere else. I see his mind working, trying to find solutions to problems that he doesn't have any control over.

"Shit."

"Seems to be the reaction of the day." He answers flatly.

"You think he ghosted the program?" Wouldn't surprise me, given his history and his personality profile. Alex's father is his only living blood relative. Of course, I created a personality profile for the father of the man I plan to devote my life to. Needless to say, they don't share much in the way of their genetic makeup. Well, other than some fine-as-hell, strong Latino genes and the monstrous height thing.

"I think he's knocked the fuck out drunk somewhere. So, basically, yes." Alex sighs as he leans forward on the couch and drops his head in his hands, defeated.

"So, what's the plan? You're his only family. Don't even try to punk me right now, I know you've already got a plan." He has to go. It's hurting him, I see the pain written all over his face, but he doesn't have a choice.

Family, loyalty, sacrifice; they're the things I love about him.

Loyal to a fault.

"The police are actively searching for him. Look, Em, Reid's got a plane waiting for me, but I don't have to go. I'm not willing to risk our future because my dad can't keep his shit together for longer than twenty-four hours." I want to take the hurt away, but I can't let him stay here. Either way, it hurts. But, I can't let him risk hurting our future because he went against one of his core values.

"You risk our future if you don't go, Alex. If something happens to him and you stay here when you could have worked remotely, when maybe you could have done something, the guilt will eat you alive. I watched my parents die. I hid in a garbage bin while the only blood relatives I knew were murdered in front of me. I'm haunted by that every damn day, and every day I work like hell to vindicate their deaths. Don't do that to yourself. Don't do that to us." I want him to stay, but I have to make him go.

"That's not the same Aemilia, and you know it. You were a child."

"Doesn't matter. I lost everything, and if you don't go, I risk losing you, too. That's just not a risk I'm willing to take. Get on the damn plane. Here, I'll help you pack." I try to stand from the couch, but he wraps his arms around my waist, pulling me back in and holding me to him.

"I'll fly out in the morning. Pilot is on standby and I have the keys to the SUV."

"Son of a bitch. Reid came to this apartment, didn't he? I knew it, I knew I smelled him out there. You can smell the man from a mile away. He smells expensive, like leather or fancy old man loafers mixed with overpriced motorcycles."

"I'm not at liberty to disclose that information." Alex buries his face in my neck. He's hiding from me because I'm right. I feel his smile against my skin.

"We've been here for months, and he decides tonight is the night to risk blowing our cover." I huff out a breath, but I'm not mad, not really. How can I be when Alex's lips rest against the sensitive skin of my neck and make promises without using words.

"Go easy on him. The rehab facility called him, he wanted to deliver the news in person. I understand your concerns, and your safety is my number one priority. We're clear, I've checked everything. There hasn't been a breach." His voice vibrates against my skin causing a shiver to cascade up my spine.

"You don't leave until the morning?" I ask, needing to distract myself. I can't talk about the case right now, or the fact that I will visit Hell itself tomorrow, and the other half of my heart will be on the opposite side of the country.

"Yep." The word pops as his lips land on my neck again.

"In that case…" I pull out of his hold, taking him by surprise as I stand, turning to his spread legs so that I'm positioned between them. With his computer monitors at my back, I drop to my knees.

Tomorrow is not a promise. If anything, it's a gamble, and the stakes are high. The dealer is wild. So tonight, I'm giving everything I've got because, tomorrow, I've got to throw in all my chips and hope we come out on top when the hands are down.

-o-

I pop the button on Alex's jeans using only one hand and pull the zipper down with my other. One knowing look and a single raised eyebrow and he hovers off the old couch, just enough for me to pull down the denim that hugs his ass like a second skin. When my progress hangs up on his calves, I leave them be. I'm not trying to put up a fight, and this is all the access I need anyway.

"Impressive; that thing you did with the button."

My lips curl into a knowing smile as I pull his cock from the top of his black briefs. Already rock hard, just how I like it. Girl got game, and I take pride in it.

"Psshhhttt…you forget, I'm a professional, Alex. Hold on, and I will remind you."

His face is an odd mix of euphoria and a grimace as I wrap my hand around his length, my fingertips barely touching.

The skin is so soft, and thick purple veins bulge from the underside angrily. Maybe they wouldn't be so angry if I gave them a rub, kind of like that damn cat. I smile at the joke in my mind as I rub my fingernails over the protruding veins and watch his cock jerk beneath my touch in response.

Pre-cum pools at the tip and begs me to taste.

Sitting up on my knees, I cut to the chase, dipping down and pulling the thick head into my mouth. I savor the salty taste of the sacred elixir that I suck from the tip.

"If it feels like a professional blow job...fuck, woman." He tries to speak, but his words are cut off the second my tongue swipes the tip of his cock.

"It's probably a professional blow job." I smile around his length, finishing the sentence for him as he fills up my mouth.

I tighten my lips around him once again and grip the base of his cock with my hand, using both to work in unison together. Saliva runs from the corners of my mouth and down his length, moisturizing the skin that I can't reach and giving my hand the added lubrication it needs.

Surprising me, Alex wraps his large hand around mine and begins using our joined hands to pleasure himself. I can't say that I've ever had assistance while giving a blow job, but hell if it isn't hot knowing he's pleasuring himself with me.

I suck, and together we stroke his cock to create a rhythm that, judging by the grumbled curse words and grunts falling from his mouth from up above, is driving him to the brink of insanity.

"God, Aemilia, I'm going to fuck your mouth, and then I'm going to make love to your pussy."

"Show me how you want it, Alex. Use my hand and show me what you want me to do." I pause, looking up at him long enough to speak. His eyes remain locked on mine as he watches me from above. I want him to show me, I want him to touch himself.

"Ahhhhh, just, God, do that thing with your tongue again." I swirl my tongue around the head of his cock as he pumps our joined hands harder, our fists meet my lips brutally. I continue my rhythm of swirl, lick and suck as I feel his cock expanding even further in my mouth. He's close.

His movements are becoming wild, jerky. I've long since given up on eye contact and, instead, focus solely on pushing him over the ledge. I want him to come in my mouth, I want him to lose control. I want to take him to a place that will allow him to forget his worries, even if it's just for a few seconds.

Using my free hand, I roll his balls in the palm of my hand, lightly brushing one single fingernail over the sensitive area on the underside. I moan, deep in my throat, sending vibrations from the tip of his head down to the base of his thick shaft.

"I'm coming, Em. Fuck…agh…" His words slowly turn into disjointed groans as stream after stream of warm cum coats the back of my throat. *Mine.*

He doesn't tell me to move. It's a good thing because I want to taste all of him, every last drop.

Finally, when I feel his thighs relax beneath me, I

slowly pull off, taking one last swipe over top of his sensitive tip and nearly sending him off the couch.

"Agh, give a man a minute. Jesus, woman, that was...I don't...I don't have words. Shit." His fingers run haphazardly through the tangles in my hair, and the action is sweet. I don't even think he realizes he's doing it in his post-orgasmic haze.

"That, sir, was a professional blow job." I shrug and lick my lips, like it was no biggie. But inside, I'm damn proud of myself for that performance. I kid, but this is far beyond the level of any blowy I've ever given before, paid for or otherwise.

"I would pay every cent to my name, plus some belonging to other people, for that blowjob."

"Meh, money isn't worth anything to me. It's your heart I want to keep."

"You stole that a long time ago." Releasing my hair, he pulls me up onto his lap, forcing me to spread my legs and straddle his thick thighs.

"In that case, I'll take payment in the form of an orgasm. You mentioned something about making love to my pussy earlier. I kind of had my heart set on it." I lean forward and brush my lips against his, allowing him to taste himself.

"I did, didn't I?" Alex licks his lips and, gripping my ass with his palms, he stands from the couch. I wrap my legs around his waist to avoid falling into his makeshift desk.

He grunts as he kicks his feet out of the denim that still restrains him at his ankles. Whoops. Once he's finally free, he carries me from the living room, dropping me immediately onto the bed once we cross the threshold of the bedroom.

"Clothes off, Em."

I watch him hungrily as he pulls his shirt over his head. I strip out of the leggings and t-shirt I wore home tonight.

"Turn around. On your knees, ass up." He speaks as soon as I drop my t-shirt to the floor. I oblige because I'm desperate for anything this man wants to give me at this point.

"I wish you could see yourself, Em. You're every man's fantasy brought to life. You're my fantasy. I fucked my hand so many times to the memories I had of you in my mind. So many times I came to your presence in my imagination alone. But this, this ass in the flesh, it's better than anything I could have ever imagined." He runs his palms greedily over the skin of my ass. He's teasing. He knows what I want.

"That's what they all say." I smirk over my shoulder. I taunt him on purpose. He knows it. I know it. I want a reaction, and he doesn't disappoint.

I hear his hand before I feel it, and then my ass is stinging, but it hurts *so* good.

The skin burns, and my pussy pulses in response. His mouth is on my fiery skin before I can speak, kissing the burn away and running his tongue over the imprint of his hand. Then he's doing the exact same thing to the opposite side.

"Up. Prop up on your elbows, Em." I listen as he spreads my legs. I watch him disappear from sight as I try to glance over my shoulder. But then, his mouth is on my clit, and it's all I can do to keep from collapsing onto the bed on top of him.

"Alex. Fuuuuck, Alex." I grind down over his mouth as I fuck his face unapologetically. I need more, and patience has never been one of my more redeeming qualities.

He licks from my clit to my ass and back again before gently biting down on my clit and then sucking it into his mouth. The pattern is intoxicating. I'm floating on the precipice of my own freefall. My hips jerk each and every time he pulls my sensitive skin into his mouth until I feel my orgasm begin in the base of my stomach. The pulsing of my pussy is like the deep bass of a drum. It's a slow build, intense.

I know it's only a matter of seconds…

And then.

Nothing.

He pulls away and, in that moment, my mind immediately wonders where the nearest gun is.

I've really got to work on my reflex responses.

But then, his hands are spreading my ass again. I feel his length nudge against my soaked opening, and I can't help but lean back to get closer.

"Inside, Alex. I need you inside now." My voice is strained.

"You want me to fuck you, Em? You want me to fuck that pretty pussy?"

"Yes, please. Please, Alex. God, I'm so close." I'm panting, begging for more, and I don't even care. I'm willing to beg, borrow or plead for the orgasm that taunts me, just out of reach.

"You're soaked. So damn wet." He groans as he slides

the tip of his cock inside of me. Then, gripping my hips without further warning, he yanks me to him, filling me up and setting off a chain reaction that lights the fuse to the explosion that is my orgasm. *Finally.*

"Yes!" I scream out. Somewhere in the distance, I swear fireworks are exploding. My pussy pulses around his cock as he grips my hips and I allow him to fuck me relentlessly. He doesn't let up. I'm paralyzed, but it doesn't matter because Alex has enough brute strength for us both. He pushes me away and then yanks me back to him over and over again, taking what he needs and giving me so much more.

"This pussy is mine, Aemilia." He growls the words, staking a claim that's irrelevant because I'm already his. "So tight. Fuck, you feel so good. I'm going to come inside of you, Em. I filled up your mouth, and now, I'm going to fill up your pussy."

I can't speak. Coherent words won't come. I can't think as he pulls me to him once more and then stills. "Agh!" He roars into the darkened room as his forehead lands on my back and I physically feel the pulsing of his cock as he fills me up.

There's something so gratifying when the man you love comes inside of you. It's hard to explain, but the foreign feeling of having a piece of him inside of me…it's satisfying and addicting. I want more of it, more of him.

"I don't want to go, Em. I don't want to leave you here." His words are a confession as he continues to hold me to him, unwilling to release me.

He's so quiet. It's almost like he's afraid he'll open his eyes and I'll be gone.

"Together we win, Alex. But how can we ever win if we fail before we even begin?"

"But this isn't our beginning, Em. We've already been through so much."

"If it's not the end, then it's still the beginning. I know this isn't the end for us. So, it stands to reason that it's still the beginning."

"Now you're just making shit up." I look over my shoulder and dare him to talk back one more time.

"Argue my point then." His eyes burn a hole in my back as he stares at me in silence.

I've either baffled him or he doesn't know what to do with me. Probably the latter.

"Exactly. You can't." My elbows drop out from beneath me, finally giving way. The lack of energy is catching up to me.

"Do you need food? I think you're hangry." Alex slowly pulls out and, grabbing his t-shirt from somewhere on the bed, he cleans me up before flipping me over and pulling my body into his, like his own, personal little spoon.

"You ate my orange." Maybe I'm a little hangry, but I'm not willing to move. Starvation is a sacrifice I'm willing to make. If my attitude has to suffer a little, so be it.

"We're back to that again." He snuggles me, rubbing his nose in my hair and laughing.

"You brought it up." I yawn the words as I curl into him and make plans to soak up every ounce of love he has to give over the next few hours.

We lay together in the bed, unmoving, but neither of

us are willing to close our eyes.

My body needs sleep, but my mind and my heart just won't let me do it.

"Victor has a second company." Alex finally speaks. My stomach burns a little when I realize we can't run from our reality. We can't afford to live in our little fantasy world all night.

"Yeah?"

"Victory Productions."

"Real creative on his end." I snort as I roll over to my back so I can look at him while he speaks.

"It's pay-per-view. The production company launched the website a couple of months ago. The warehouse, it has rooms that are themed based on *specific* tastes and preferences, if you get my drift. Members are granted virtual access to the rooms by the hour. There are live viewing events and special "delivery" options. It's everything you suspected, and then some."

"He's planning to put Mel and I in a room." I knew there was more, I knew there had to be more.

"But, these rooms…they're not dancing, Em. It's sex, drugs, nonconsensual. Trafficking." I hear it in his voice, he's trying to remain neutral, but he's scared. He's worried for me, and I get it. But he's underestimating my badassery and unwillingness to lose.

I've spent my entire life surviving. Things are just starting to get good; I'm not going out now.

"Makes sense. What's Sullivan's role?" Other than being a crusty, old Italian mafia wannabe.

"He's providing bodies, basically. Soldiers, women, junkies. Wilks is freight and handling, for lack of better terminology. Victor is hiding behind his father's name stacking cash for everything else." It always comes back to the Adkins family, every damn time.

"So, we take Sullivan out, and what have we accomplished?"

"No. Don't even go there." Alex's hand rests on my ribcage. His eyes, his eyes are ready to fight. It's okay when he worries, but it's not okay when I question my own ability, huh. He props his head up on his hand so he's looking down on me in the bed. "We take out Sullivan because that's what this mission has always been about. We take him out, we take those drugs that run through his club off the streets. We sweep the illegal weapons from his warehouses down at the docks. We shut down 49A. Will they move somewhere else? Probably. But did we accomplish the goal? Yes. Then we set a new one."

We always set a new one. It's an endless cycle.

"There is no freedom."

"There is no freedom, Em. Not for people like you and me."

"But you, Alex, you are my freedom. You are my hope for more. You understand that, right?" Reaching up, I cup his cheek with my hand and run my fingers over the prickly overgrown hair. I commit him to my memory, just in case.

"I promise you, Em. We'll have more. So much more."

CHAPTER THIRTY
ALEX

"And you're sure you packed everything? You're not forgetting like some main cable that, without it, the entire mission will self-implode?" Em stands in my wrinkled ass t-shirt from last night, stains and all, in the middle of the kitchen and withholds the keys to the SUV that Reid dropped off last night.

"Cross my heart." I smile, distracting her and swiping them from her palm before she can react.

"Not that again. Hey! That was rude. My reflexes are slow before I have my coffee. Plus, you did that half-smile thing, and it's rather disarming first thing in the morning." She places her hands on her hips haughtily and it causes the soft, cotton material of the t-shirt to ride up dangerously high on her bare thighs.

"I've got everything, Aemilia. Promise. I'll drive to the airport that Reid has already pre-programmed into the GPS. I will get on the plane, and I will go rescue my father from whatever roach infested bar he's inhabited. I'll be set up and ready to go in the hotel before you guys kick off tonight. I will be there. Worst case, I don't find my father today, I still set up in the hotel, and I find him tomorrow before we hop a jet to this island Reid keeps talking about. I've heard there's a wedding I need to crash."

"Not a proposal." She states matter-of-factly.

"Wow, Em. That's pretty arrogant of you to assume." She doesn't realize I've already got plans to ask her to marry me. Real, down on one knee plans. My mother's wedding ring sits in a safety deposit box that I plan to unlock before I head back.

"Shut up, geek. Go. Get on the road. I'm tracking you on this new handy dandy watch Reid got me, so I'll be watching every step you take." She narrows her eyes. It's cute how she thinks she's the one in charge.

"You do realize I programmed that thing? It works both ways."

"Of course, you did."

"I love you, future Mrs. Alexander Straton." I back away, smiling at her until my backpack bumps the door to the apartment.

"Still not a proposal. Also, I'm not sure how I feel about changing my identity again."

"Aemilia."

"I love you. Be careful, k?" This woman will walk straight into hell's inferno and not blink, but I head out to a private jet, and she worries.

"I'm not the one preparing for battle." I remind her, and myself. Even though neither of us need it.

"Nah, you're the one we're all depending on to help us win the war."

I nod, unsure of what else there is to say. She's right. They're all depending on me to keep them safe.

In together, out together.

Only I'm not really going to be there, and the thought makes my stomach roll with nerves. I'm not doubting my ability to do my job. It's the unknown that's terrifying.

-o-

"Little Alex Straton. As I live and breathe, I can't believe it." The smell of cigarette smoke burns my nostrils, a nauseating reminder that this place hasn't changed a bit. It's been nearly two years since the last time I drug my dad's drunk ass out of this rundown bar on the outskirts of the town I grew up in.

Every single time, Benny swore he wouldn't let my dad back in here. We'd go a couple of weeks, and everything would be good, he'd get his kicks at home. Then Benny would go soft, and my phone would ring in the middle of the night again.

"Benny. Long time no see." I swear the man has to be pushing ninety. The hair on his head and beard have been white for as long as I can remember. I was sixteen the first time I walked into this bar after my dad went missing for too long. Benny helped me drag him to the car, and I drove him home. I was so disgusted. Disgusted with what my life had become. I was angry at my mom for not being there when I needed her the most. I was angry at my father's inability to step up. I was pissed at the world.

"That's on you. I've been here the whole time. Heard

you got locked up. You escape? Don't worry, I won't call the cops. Well, unless there's a reward. I'm ready to retire, boy. So, which is it?" I smile as I sit down on one of the bar stools. The black leather is worn and cracked with age and abuse. The stories these stools could probably tell.

"Nah, get your finger off that button, Benny. I got out on my own terms. It was all legal…I think."

He rubs the counter down with a wet cloth.

He knows better than to offer me anything to drink.

It's early still. I came straight here when the plane landed. The cops informed me that they didn't have a single lead on the whereabouts of my father. He's a grown ass man with a history of getting shitfaced, I can't imagine they looked real hard. I don't blame them.

"You looking for your pops?" We both know why I'm here so there's no use wasting any more of either of our time since I'm not a paying customer.

"You seen him?" Part of me hopes that he has so that he can point me in the right direction. The other part, the part that still holds a flicker of hope that my dad ran off with a woman he met on the subway this morning and hasn't thrown away months of rehab, hopes that he hasn't.

"Two hours ago. But don't look at me with those eyes boy. He was drunk when he stumbled in here. Mumbling something about going home to your momma. I tried to reason with him, but he was too far gone. I didn't give him a drop of alcohol, swear it on my grave, and I'm closer to it than you might think, given my young, boyish good looks."

"You let him leave by himself?" I try not to sound

angry. I'm not mad at Benny, it's not his fault. But that familiar disgust raises its ugly head, and my stomach feels uneasy again.

"He was in one of those moods, Alex. He's grown, and I've got a business to run. He stumbled out the door while I was serving another customer. I walked out front to make sure he wasn't passed out on the sidewalk, and he was gone. Haven't seen him since."

Momma. I know where he is.

"Thanks, Benny. I appreciate the honesty." I stand from the stool and turn to head out.

"Don't be a stranger." Benny calls from behind me.

"No offense, but I look forward to the day I never step foot in this place again." I turn back once more, smiling.

"None taken. Good luck finding your old man." I nod and duck out into the early afternoon sunshine. The clock is ticking, and I have one more stop I need to make.

-o-

A cop flies around the black car that was waiting for me when I landed at the airport as I drive down a road that I used to go out of my way to avoid.

His sirens blare in my ears as I'm transported back to that night. I never saw the scene of the accident. I'm still thankful for that, but there's a grave marker on the side of the road that marks the place she took her last breath.

I wonder what my life would be like if she was still here. Would she and my dad still be married? Would she have helped him finally overcome his depression?

Maybe I would be driving to visit them in the home I

grew up in instead of driving to pull my dad out of the dilapidated treehouse in the woods behind a house that hasn't belonged to us for years. I know that's where he is. I feel it.

Reid's parents still live in the same community, same house. But, after I graduated from high school, the bank foreclosed on my parents' home. My mom's life insurance money ran out, and my dad was forced to move into a garbage apartment that, most months, I covered the rent for.

I turn into the familiar neighborhood, and my stomach drops.

Something's not right.

Lights. Sirens. They're everywhere.

The cul-de-sac that I played basketball in, the street I road my bike down, there are at least ten of them scattered down what is normally a quiet suburban street.

Mrs. Chapman stands on her front lawn talking to a cop as I throw the car into park and jump out.

One look. Her eyes meet mine, and I know. Dad.

Reaching into the back pocket of my jeans, I grab my badge. I walk toward the chaos that surrounds the Chapman's house. It sits right next to mine. Only it's not mine anymore.

Out of the corner of my eye, I see a white playhouse with pink painted shutters. A little girl sits on the steps and watches the excitement. Where are her parents?

"Alex. Oh God, Alex. I'm sorry." Reid's mother covers her mouth with her hand, but I don't acknowledge her. I can't yet. I can't see her pity yet. I don't want to accept her tears of remorse. I merely flash my badge to the officer that tries to stop my progress as I continue through the gate to what were once adjoining backyards.

A wooden fence separates the two now. The treehouse that I used to share with Reid now sits firmly on his side of the divided property. Two paramedics stand side-by-side whispering, but they aren't moving. It's eerily silent, the opposite of the noise that assaulted my ears out front. There's a surprising lack of action considering the number of emergency responders that are here.

Why isn't anyone doing anything?

"Sir, sir, you can't go back there." A second cop tries to stop me, but I shrug him off, I'm twice his size.

"FBI." I repeat and keep moving. I don't have time for an interrogation.

One step into the overgrown woods and the scene that unfolds in front of me is like a horror movie come to life. Orange tape with black writing lines the perimeter. The area has been blocked off, secured. It's an active investigation and, in the middle of it, surrounded by various emergency responders, is my father's lifeless body.

I choke on air as my body doubles over. Fuck.

"Who let him back here?" An officer yells out as his eyes catch mine, but I barely hear him. It's like someone placed a funnel over my ears and blinders on my eyes. The world is closing in on my senses.

"Straton. Shit, man, are you okay? Hey! Somebody get him to the ambulance for some oxygen." I recognize the young guy in uniform from high school. I can't tell you his name, but he holds me upright when my legs don't want to work anymore and drags me from the woods as the darkness tries to pull me under.

The next thing I know, I'm sitting on the back of an ambulance with an oxygen mask strapped my face.

"Alex, honey, are you alright?" Mrs. Chapman rubs my leg, and I try to bring my mind back into focus. When did she get here? Wasn't she just on the front lawn?

I recognize this feeling. I'm in shock. It's strange because it's different than when my mom died. Sure, I'm upset. I'm human. But somewhere inside of me, I feel at peace knowing maybe he finally found his freedom.

Maybe, after fighting his own internal battle all these years, maybe this is the only way he thought he could win.

He wanted to be with my mom, and I have to believe that now he is. I can't fathom another alternative. I don't want to go down that road.

"Yeah, I'm good." I pull the oxygen from my face, but I don't stand just yet. I don't trust my legs, and I'm kind of enjoying sitting here with Reid's mom for a second.

"I'm so sorry, Alex. I know it's a lot. I know what you saw out there. It's something that will haunt my nightmares for years to come. I was out watering the hydrangeas, and I heard a jarring noise. Nobody's been in that treehouse for years. I thought maybe the little girl next door somehow got back there so I went to check, and he was already gone. He went quickly, Alex, he didn't suffer. I called the police immediately." Eloise Chapman is one of the strongest women I know, and even now, she stands before me with dried tears on her cheeks, but she's no longer crying. She's not crying because she's a mother, and I may as well be a son to her. She's shielding me, much the same way she shielded me the night of my mother's death in that cold ER.

"Look at me, Mrs. Chapman. You couldn't have stopped it from happening. He was determined. It was his time; I have to believe that. I'm sorry you had to see him like that."

"Me too. Are you here alone? You got here so fast. I didn't know you were living nearby."

"I am alone, but I don't live around here right now. It was coincidence that I was close by. I was actually out looking for my dad. Just didn't expect to find him this way."

"Do you want to come in? I can make you some tea or coffee. I think George has some of that expensive bourbon in his study. I could get you some of that." She tries to smile. She looks ten years younger than her age, even under all of the stress of the day. Reid got his looks from somewhere, and it sure as hell wasn't his father.

"I'm good. I need to speak with whoever's in charge here and find out what the next step is. Then, I have somewhere else I have to be." I roll my shoulders and prepare to mentally compartmentalize everything that's happened within the last twenty-four hours as well as the things I'm up against in the next.

"Tonight? You have somewhere to go tonight? After all of this?" She stares at me as if she's getting ready to call the psych ward. I don't blame her. I'm sure I look crazy, and honestly, this all feels a little bit like insanity.

"It's complicated. Look, I'm sorry for what you've gone through today, Mrs. Chapman. You were there for me the night I lost my mother when he wasn't. Kind of funny how life works; how you're here for me today, too." I stand from the ambulance and wrap her in a hug.

Holding her makes me wish my mom was here. But if she were here, none of this would have ever happened. Today is another reminder of how fragile life is. What Reid's mother doesn't realize is that tonight I hold her son's life in my hands.

I have to get them out safely. That's on my shoulders.

I can process my father's death tomorrow because tonight, they're all depending on me.

There is no place for emotion. There is no margin for error.

I can't lose anyone else. We have to win.

CHAPTER THIRTY-ONE
EMILY

"Who pissed in your cheerios this morning?" We separate out artillery and recount weapons in our warehouse down at the docks as we finish getting together the final supplies for the raid. Reid and I both have to be at the club soon. We're running out of time to prepare.

"Who asked for your commentary?" I shove a bulletproof vest into a separate stack and try not to make eye contact with him. I can feel him staring at me. He's watching me, waiting for me to crack.

"You forget to eat? Dammit, woman, you're hangry." It's not a secret, we both already know what's wrong with me. I'm wearing a giant neon sign on my forehead that screams misplaced attitude. I've been on edge since Alex walked out of the apartment this morning and took my heart with him. I have zero fucks to give today.

"No, I did not forget to eat. Get off my case,

Chapman. We've got bigger things to worry about."

"Like how your boyfriend has gone quiet on us?" Yep. That.

"You haven't heard from him either?" It surprises me that he didn't call Reid when he landed. On the one hand I'm relieved, because had he called Reid and not me, I would have been sour about it. On the other hand, that just makes the ache in my heart hurt even worse because that means neither one of us has gotten an update, and the hours have felt like years.

"Wow, that took surprisingly less time than I anticipated. I figured I'd have to push a lot harder than that to get an admission from you. To answer your question, I haven't spoken to him. But, I can assure you, he'll be here. I got confirmation from the pilot that the plane landed, and I've got a tracker on the vehicle he picked up at the airport."

He'll be here, but he won't. Not the same.

"I know, I'm tracking him too. Saw he went by your old stomping grounds." I hate to admit how many times I've looked at the tracking on the watch Reid gave me. Really, I could reason that he's moving so he's obviously alive and well. Or his plane could have been hijacked by the Italian mafia and some asshole soldier killed him, stole his watch and is now wearing it as some sick trophy. Could go either way. My brain has a very active imagination.

"I saw that too."

"Then he made a stop at a bank, and a graveyard." I hold my hand up and count off the locations on my fingers. The bank only supports my mafia theory, I'm just sayin'.

"He's looking for his dad, Em. I know you've never met the man, but he could literally be anywhere. There's a hotel reservation with his name on it waiting for him. He'll be there." Right, there…which isn't here.

"So, he hasn't checked in yet?" I don't know why I ask. I already know. My tracking device still shows him at the graveyard. Maybe that's where his dad was. Maybe he found him.

"Not yet." Reid loads ammo into weapons to my right, verifying the functionality and mechanisms as he goes. No margin for error.

"It's okay, we're good. He's good. I dunno, I'm just worried about it. I've never really had to worry about anyone other than myself, and it's weird now. I feel like part of my insides are missing. Like I can't fully breathe, and that scares me." I sit down on an empty crate and brush my hair up out of my face. We're almost done here. We've been going since first thing this morning, and our day still hasn't officially even begun.

"So, what I'm hearing is, we've been partners for how long? And this entire time you've only been looking out for you?"

"Oh, shut up. You know that's not what I meant, Reid. I've saved your ass enough times for you to realize that, in a pinch, I'm gonna have your back. I guess what I mean is, I feel vulnerable, and I don't like it. It's irritating, like an itchy sweater or something."

"An itchy sweater? When Alex comes back, I'm going to be the first person in line to let him in on how you compared him to an itchy sweater."

"Forget it, okay. Forget I said anything. He'll log on, I know he will. You know he will. Let's stop focusing on things that aren't even going to happen when we need to focus on this case. Is the rest of the team ready?"

"They're about a mile from 49A. They're prepared to move whenever we give them the signal. Are you ready?"

"To kick some Adkins ass? I'm always ready." I smile and remember why I'm here. Why I do what I do.

"We can't guarantee Adkins will even be there, Em."

"Now who's acting like they ate some *pissy* cheerios? I know, Sullivan's the target. Take out their transportation and operations. Wilks is a bonus. Adkins is like hitting the jackpot on the lottery in Vegas. I got it."

"What about Mel? She doesn't even realize what she's walking in to." He's right. We've never had a civilian directly involved like this. She doesn't have an inkling as to what she's involved in. She's an innocent bystander and, as a result, her life is in danger.

"She was going with or without us. She goes with us; she stands a chance of surviving. She goes without us; she ends up like Laura."

"You think there's a chance she's still in there?"

"Alive? It's possible, but not probable. It's been too long. Alex said there's been no sighting of her in the feed, and we haven't had a single hit on her cell." The man has searched. I found him this morning sitting back in the same spot he was in when I walked in the door last night. He must have gotten back up after I finally succumbed to my exhaustion. His eyes were bloodshot, but his mind was clear. He was looking for her. Then, when he really needed to pack up his gear, he took the time to go over the layout of the warehouse with me in detail so I would be prepared.

I don't think there's a way to prepare yourself for what's happening in that place though. The clubs are bad, I've been in and out of them for almost half my life at this point. I've seen the ugly side of this lifestyle, but this place…this place is next level.

"That's what I was afraid of. You ready to head out?" He opens the back of an SUV and begins loading in the last of our supplies. He'll take it and park it discretely for our team to access before the raid.

We'll keep a set of keys with us, our out when this is all over; if things go as planned. Honestly, I can't say I've ever been a part of a mission that went according to plan, so I don't count on seeing this vehicle again tonight after we head out.

"Yeah, Mel's probably already at the club rehearsing. I'll walk. You do your thing, and I'll see you there, Riko." I wink and slap his ass as I walk past him, and he closes the back hatch on the vehicle.

"Together we win, Em." He calls out as I scan my hand over the panel at the door.

"Together we win." I throw up a peace sign and step out into the afternoon light.

If only we were all together.

-o-

"You're awfully quiet, Emily. Are you nervous? I'm not going to lie, I'm a little nervous and excited. We're performing somewhere new. High-end clientele, deep pockets. You think they'll be celebrities there?" I listen to

Melanie's misplaced excitement as I stare at my reflection in the mirror. I stand at my locker and pretend to put the finishing touches on my makeup when, honestly, I could care less.

I feel the energy vibrating off of Mel as she fidgets next to me. It's a stark opposite to the pulsing adrenaline that forces its way through my veins.

Our night at the club is over, but my night is just beginning.

"Celebrities? Why? You got a celebrity crush that you hope to see tonight?" I humor her and try to distract my mind. Reid checked in a few hours ago. Somehow, he managed to get himself assigned out to 49A tonight, but our other two guys remain here. It's okay because the rest of our team should just be waiting on our signal. We never anticipated pulling our entire undercover team and risking their covers as well for this mission.

"You don't?" She questions me as she holds an opened tube of black mascara in her hand and raises an eyebrow.

"You do realize celebrities are just people like you and me?" I don't understand the whole celebrity thing. Maybe it's because I never had a television or went to the movies growing up, but I just don't get the hype. The rich people I've known in my life thus far have all been sadistic assholes, so there's that too. Any celebrity that might pay for access to the place we're headed to tonight deserves what they got comin'.

"Of course, but there's something sexy about the way they're untouchable. Something alluring about wanting them and not being able to have them." She sighs. Her blue eyes look every bit the innocent she is.

"Young, Mel. You two ready? Boss man said it's time to load up." We simultaneously hit pause on our conversation as one of Sullivan's soldiers steps into the nearly empty dressing room, interrupting us. I recognize the guy as one of the men that was upstairs with Mel and I the other night. He stood in the back corner, he observed, but never stepped out of line.

Mel's eyes meet mine, and I nod before slapping a fake ass smile on my face and shutting my locker door. "We're ready."

"Good, Sully's in the SUV out back waiting for you." Interesting. I didn't expect Sullivan to chaperone us himself. I guess I should have anticipated his need to control the entire situation though. We're two of his best dancers. Financially, it doesn't make since to take us and discard us…unless of course we're already sold to the highest bidder and that amount outranks what he thinks he can get out of us at the club.

The soldier walks through the dressing room and holds open the door, waiting for us.

I hear Mel inhale a deep breath before whispering something to herself and closing her locker door. She falls in step behind me as we walk through the door and into the night sky.

It's nearly two in the morning. The lights are low inside the club, and the night is coming to an end. Most of society is at home, asleep in their comfy beds. It's the time between sleep and awake when the devil comes out to play.

The soldier steps up to a waiting black SUV that looks

nearly identical to the one I helped Reid finish loading this morning and opens the door.

"My gorgeous Em Cat, and Mel. I'm glad to see you both made it." Like we had a choice in the matter. He sits in the passenger seat of the SUV. The soldier that led us here opens the driver's side door and slides in.

"Mr. Sullivan, thank you again for the invitation." Mel speaks up immediately, and I inwardly cringe. Why must she always talk so much?

"I don't want your words, Melanie, unless you're telling me to fuck you harder or your mouth is around my cock. You will not speak tonight unless you are told. Are we understood?" Sullivan brushes an invisible speck of dust from his black slacks. Mel's lips firm in silence. Wisely, she doesn't answer his open-ended question.

The SUV pulls out of the parking lot and onto the street. It's less than a ten-minute drive to 49A from here.

"I watched your rehearsal tonight, girls. Excellent performance. We've got a very special guest tonight. I expect you to put on a show. You're our star performers, and I want nothing less than perfection." Special guest. Special guest. Who is he talking about?

Within minutes we're turning off of the highway and pulling up to a seemingly deserted warehouse. There are no obvious markings on the outside of the building. It's solid metal. It's so dark out here that none of the exterior doors are visible.

Where do they park the vehicles? There's not a car in sight. The driver pulls the SUV up to, by all outward appearances, is the side of a vacant building. Sullivan opens the door and steps out.

"Out girls." The soldier speaks as Sullivan stands on the outside of the door and waits. He can't open the door for us, he would never lower himself to that level. I roll my eyes internally and relish the feel of the metal knife that hides at my waist. Your time is coming, Sullivan, and it's gonna feel so, so sweet.

I open the door and step out first, keeping my body in front of Mel as she steps from the vehicle and the SUV pulls off.

Sullivan pulls out a cell phone and punches some numbers into it as we follow him around the side of the building.

I take in my surroundings as my eyes begin to adjust to the darkness.

The highway is only about a mile through the woods that adjoin the backside of this building. There aren't any operating businesses that directly adjoin this property. Even if there were, it's the middle of the night. They're vacant. I know from the maps that Alex showed me that there is an apartment complex about a five-minute drive away and an abandoned strip mall across the street.

My eyes dart to the strip mall. Vehicles.

"Inside." Sullivan's demand jerks my eyes back to the warehouse as an entire panel on the outside of the building slides open, bathing the vacant lot we stand in with light from inside.

Sullivan slides his cell phone back into his pocket and straightens his suit coat as he steps inside, and we follow.

We stop in what looks like a foyer. It's strange. It reminds me of like a high-end spa or something. Soft music plays in the background and the lighting is dimmed. A chandelier hangs from the ceiling. There's even a sitting area with an expensive looking black velvet sofa behind us.

A woman sits on a stool at an ornate desk. The dress she wears is solid black and forms tightly to her ebony skin. Her dark hair is pulled up in a stark, high bun that accentuates her dark brown eyes. She's stunningly beautiful and looks nothing at all like she belongs here.

"Mr. Sullivan. How are you this evening?" Her voice is professional yet kind as she clicks around on a computer screen. I wonder if she has access to the cameras. Friend or foe?

"I'm fine. I have a delivery."

Delivery.

Mel stands just behind me, close enough that I hear her nervously breathing.

"Of course. Have you already arranged the drop, or do you need me to contact someone on your behalf?" Her voice is even, she maintains her professional attitude despite the rigidness in Sullivan's tone.

"I've arranged it myself. Call down for one of my soldiers. I want to hand deliver them myself." Them. Commodity. This is exactly what we needed. We're going in.

There should be a long hallway outside of this entry area, if I'm remembering right from Alex's quick tour this morning.

It's been hours since I was able to track his whereabouts. I had to remove my watch when I dressed for my performance tonight, and it still sits in my locker back at the club. I couldn't pull it out and risk it being found, so I've been relying on my gut feeling alone. I'm blind again.

I've heard nothing. I don't doubt he's doing his job. He wouldn't abandon this case; he wouldn't abandon Reid or me. He's not capable; loyal to a fault.

I feel him, but there's something off about it. Like, I feel him watching me, but my heart hurts, and I can't put my finger on why. Am I upset because I haven't heard from him? Did something happen? Am I feeling something else? All these feelings, they're foreign to me. I don't have the time right now to decipher what they mean. I have to focus on the case, all of our lives depend on it.

I have to believe that, when it's time, I'll know.

"Mr. Sullivan." The door to our right opens, and it's Reid.

"Riko." Sullivan nods because a soldier is entitled to an acknowledgement, but we're just women. Of course.

"They're ready for you." His eyes find mine behind Sullivan. They're hardened, fueled by fire. This is the first time he's been inside this warehouse; this is the first time we've been fully exposed to this operation.

Reid holds the door as Sullivan walks through, followed by me and, lastly, Mel, who trails behind nervously. I think she's already begun to realize this is more than she anticipated, and she hasn't seen anything yet.

As I pass Reid, he slips something into the palm of my hand.

I close my fingers around the small slip of paper and wait.

"Keep up girls."

Mel hurries by me as I hang back and open the slip of paper, squinting my eyes to make out the blurred ink.

My eyes quickly scan two words, scribbled on a wrinkled chewing gum wrapper.

Deceased – Laura

CHAPTER THIRTY-TWO
ALEX

I identified my father's remains.

I stared down at his lifeless body, and I...forgave him.

I don't want to carry hatred in my heart for a man that did everything he could to fight against a disease that was just too much for him to withstand here on this earth. It's not fair to me, and it's not fair to Em. So, instead of being angry, instead of allowing that hate to fill my heart, I spoke words of forgiveness.

His death will officially be ruled a suicide.

My father died by his own hands.

He was a sick man. After years of fighting an internal battle, his mind finally failed him. I don't blame the rehab facility. I don't blame myself. I don't blame anyone because everything was done, and his death still happened.

Fate.

I choose to believe he is with my mom. I'm still in

shock, I know I am. I sense it with a familiarity that I never wanted to relive. But tonight, I have a job to do.

I can't allow myself to feel all of my emotions yet.

I watch the monitor as Reid slips a piece of paper into Emily's hand. I watch as the two most important people in my life enter the hallway to hell, and I already know what that piece of paper says. I know what it says because my father's body wasn't the only deceased body I identified today.

When I arrived at the hotel, I didn't waste any time getting my equipment set up. I wanted eyes on the 49A. I wanted eyes on the club, and I wanted to test the security and reliability of this network.

I've had a facial recognition scan running in the background on the rooms of 49A since we accessed their cameras and today, I got the alert I've been waiting on. A body was being drug down a back hallway by two soldiers. When they pulled her from the room, her hair moved from her face, and that's when the scan picked her up. A thermal image scan showed her body wasn't just unconscious, it was lifeless.

I watched them pull her out the back door and drop her next to a black dumpster. They covered her with a tarp that was lying nearby and walked back into the building. Like they were just taking out the evening trash.

The team Reynolds brought in is working with the local authorities. We had a joint force conference call with them this afternoon, and everyone is on the same page. They're just happy we're here to help them clean up their streets. They've been overrun with drug problems for years, and it's no secret where it is stemming from.

As soon as I identified her remains, I sent out the alert. I was notified that they already have a plan in place to retrieve her body so that her family will have some closure. So that her little boy might one day have closure.

Em's face is hard as she reads the words to herself and then discreetly drops the paper onto the floor behind her.

The hallway is dark. It won't be found until it's too late anyway.

Em's stunning tonight. She's wearing a black, studded corset with a matching black thong that hugs her luscious hips. She picked the corset so that she could hide her weapons, not because it fits her like it was custom tailored for her body, even though it was.

She wears her signature black fishnet tights and sky-high heels that elongate her already long legs. Her hair looks jet black in the low lights of the hallway and flows down her back in a long cascade of silk strands.

Mel looks similar and yet opposite. It's obvious they attempted to coordinate their outfits for the evening. Mel's pale skin glistens against the black leather skirt that stops just at the cheeks of her ass. Her breasts sit securely in a black bra that leaves very little of her skin from the waist up open to the imagination.

They look every bit the part they're there to play. Em walks confidently, her head held high as she steps back up between Sullivan and Mel. She's trying to keep them separated. She's doing her best to keep Mel at a distance. She's protecting her, and she doesn't even realize yet what she's protecting her from. None of us do.

"Through that door." Reid comes to a halt in front of a discreet, black door.

"Stay close by, Riko."

"Yes sir." Reid nods and steps back to the far wall as Sullivan pushes open the door and ushers Mel and Em inside.

My feed goes dark as they cross the threshold into the room. It's supposed to live feed as soon as the girls walk in, but it's like the room doesn't exist on my feed. There's no restricted access, there is no access at all. The fuck?

"Riko, check in."

"Yeah, Hood."

"Feed won't come up in the room. It's like that room isn't wired. It doesn't fit the layout. Who's in there?"

"Unknown. They were inside before I arrived. I thought you knew." Shit.

"Fuck. We've got to roll. We can't waste time. I'm not leaving them in there blind."

"You got it. ETA on our team is six minutes."

"Six minutes." Laura's lifeless body being drug down the hallway flashes through my mind.

It's too long.

-o-

EMILY

Sullivan closes the door to my back as my eyes quickly scan the room. It's bare. No makeshift stage. No pole. No furniture to speak of. Nothing. Nothing but the man who stands against the opposite wall, near a door, and stares at me with a chilling, familiar gaze.

This warehouse is large. I studied the layout this morning. Enclosed entrance. Long hallway with doors on either side leading to various rooms. The rooms we viewed this morning didn't have exits. They all led back to the main hallway. The rooms were all themed, filled with various furniture, or worse, various sexual devices.

This room is different. The walls are a clinical gray, and the floor is concrete. Like when they were converting the warehouse, this room was somehow missed. Something's not right.

"What do you think?" Sullivan asks from behind Mel and I as the familiar set of eyes wanders over my legs and up my torso. He doesn't even bother to hide his hungry eyes when they linger on my chest for too long.

His father had the same eyes. He looked at me the same way. Like a trophy to be acquired. Like a prize to be held out for others to covet.

"They'll do." It's all he says as he leans against the wall in a suit that probably cost more than the entirety of Sullivan's operation. Where Anderson Sullivan is an Italian mafia wannabe, the man that stands before us is the real deal. The blood of mafia runs through his veins. He's a physical manifestation of the devil.

"These are my best performers. I swear it, Vito." Vito.

I react the moment I anticipate his movement. I see the subtle way his hand slides to his jacket. I push Mel out of the way, covering her body with mine against the wall as a single shot rings out in the room and Anderson Sullivan drops dead at my feet.

"Let's go, girls. You cost me a hell of a lot of money, and I need to collect on my investment."

Go? I wait for our team to storm the room, but nothing happens.

Did they not hear the damn gunshot? I hold Mel

upright as she shakes in my arms and stares at Sullivan's body. Blood pools on the concrete floor around our feet from a single gunshot wound to the head.

Welp, honestly, at least my hands are clean of that murder. It'll be less paperwork.

"Move, dammit."

Mel scrambles to follow, her legs miraculously regaining their strength, except her breathing is too quick. She's going to pass out if she doesn't get it together, and I need her to remain conscious.

He watches me curiously. He knows something is off. He can sense fear, and where Mel is bathed in it, I'm not. He can't figure me out. I watch him as he watches me, but I have the advantage. He doesn't know who I am, he can't. But I know exactly who he is.

He's the damn jackpot on the Vegas strip, and I'm primed for a payout.

Sullivan was wrong. He thought he was working for Vito, funny. But, Vito wasn't resurrected from the dead for this lovely occasion.

Nah, this man with the high cheekbones that kind of resemble mine and the unmistakable eyes that haunt me in my dreams, this man is Victor Adkins.

He's irritated, and he's armed, but I smile sweetly as I hold Mel's hand and we walk past him through the door. What he doesn't realize is that my insanity is a match for his.

We step back out into the darkness and are immediately forced into the back of a waiting van. Blacked out windows. No tag.

I could fight back. I could end this now, but I don't

know where the hell my backup is. Why hasn't anyone come? If Alex is watching, why the fuck am I currently being shoved into a damn kidnapper van?

Sure, I could take on Victor and win, no doubt. But I see the driver that watches through the rear-view mirror. He's most definitely not my friend.

Then, there's the young girl that sits in the passenger seat in a pair of designer jeans and black boots that run the length of her calves up and over her knees. She looks like she can't be a day older than Mel, but she's smiles slyly, like she's enjoying the show. Why does she look so familiar?

Mel's a liability for me, and I'm not willing to toss her to the wolves for my own safety. So, in we go.

-o-

ALEX

My heart hammers wildly in my chest as my fingers fly across the keyboard. It's like déjà vu, only the last time, I knew she was safe. I knew she was in control. It was my life that was hanging in the balance. I'm frantic. My brain is firing off of a thousand different synopses.

"What the fuck was that?" Reid's voice is a shock to the chaos happening inside of my brain.

"What? I can't see. What was what?" Where did the mystery room come from?

"Shots fired. Minimum of one gunshot. Check the exterior cameras. You got a read on Em's tracker?"

"Her damn tracker says she's back at the club. She must have taken it off for her performance earlier and didn't put it back on."

"What? She knows better than that."

"I've got access to a security camera across that street. Shows a black van pulling out and into our lot. I lose them once they turn the corner. What vehicle is your team on?" My eyes flicker to a second screen that shows a black van with no tag, and then they're gone again.

"Black SUV, not a van. That's not ours."

"Okay, hold on. Let me access the traffic camera at the intersection."

"I can't wait much longer. I'm about to breach the door." I hear Reid's breathing as it accelerates, preparing to act.

"SUV is less that one minute from turning into the lot. The camera picked them up running the red light."

"Where's the van?" I scan through every exterior cameras we have access to.

"I still can't see them, which means they're still in our blind spot."

"Send the signal to Reynolds, I'm going in. I can't wait any longer."

"I'm blind, Reid. You gotta talk. I need you to be my eyes. Go get her." I can see Reid in the hallway as he breaches the doorway, and then he disappears.

"Doors not locked. Shit, one body. Anderson Sullivan. Gunshot wound to the head, deceased. Alex, this room isn't like the others. There's a fucking exit door."

"Where are they?"

"The room is empty. The only blood appears to be from Sullivan." I take a deep breath. I know she's still alive. I would feel it if she wasn't. I would know.

"Your backup is pulling into the lot now."

"I'm going out."

-o-

EMILY

"Where are we going, Victor?" He stands at the door to the back of the van, unmoving, after ushering Mel and I inside.

I wait for his reaction as I use his name. He knows I know.

We're not leaving this parking lot. The force of the realization hits me with certainty.

If we were going somewhere, we'd already be on our way. Yet, he just stands in the doorway and waits. For what, I don't know.

I want to wipe the entitled smirk off the bitch's face that sits in the front seat and watches Mel and I with a knowing smile.

His lips curl up into a grin. "Nowhere, Aemilia. I told you, I need to collect on my investment." My blood freezes in my veins.

I'm paralyzed.

I've spent my entire life with my identity hidden.

How does he know that name? He's not supposed to know who I am.

I've worked too hard for too long to remain a ghost.

"Aemilia? Who's Aemilia? What's he talking about, Emily?" She's too loud. Mel speaks when she shouldn't, and this time I'm not fast enough. It happens in slow motion. She sits huddled behind me in the van, but he moves too quickly. His aim perfect.

The gunshot echoes in the confines of the van, and the splatter of Mel's blood coats my skin. She doesn't even have time to scream. She doesn't suffer. Her body slumps into mine, and then she's gone.

This is why I don't allow myself to become attached. When you're attached and you lose, you become a failure.

I failed her.

"Whoops, my finger slipped." Rage boils beneath my skin and sears my insides like fire.

"Fuck off, Victor. What do you want with me?" My eyes sting, but I refuse to let him see my tears. I am not that weak little girl anymore.

"I've got some friends that have been looking for you a long time. Years actually. Someone made a mistake and left a little girl to die in a dumpster."

"I didn't die." My words are spoken through gritted teeth.

"Because they were negligent and didn't tie up their loose ends, they lost their life. We know what you did, Aemilia. We've been watching you."

"Then you know I killed your father." I see the fire as it flashes in his eyes. The familiar fury. An eye for an eye. They killed my parents.

"I know you've been a nuisance for me for years. You're a thorn in my damn side. I normally don't bother with petty issues such as this. But, I felt it was my duty to personally find you and deliver you to those that are highly invested in making sure you finally get what you deserve."

"What do you know about my parents, Victor?" I seethe as the words leave my mouth.

"I know your mother was a cunt, and your father wasn't any better. They were traitors. Your family, they worked alongside mine for years in the old country. Your mother met your father and they turned on their blood, they disregarded their heritage. She signed their death warrant, and in doing so, she signed yours too."

"Fuck you! My parents were good, they fought against assholes like you and your family." I'm outnumbered, but I can't stop myself as my legs propel me forward. I gain enough traction as I push from the rear door of the van that I knock us both onto the hard cement.

He's momentarily taken by surprise. I use that to my advantage, knocking his weapon from his hand to the ground, just out of reach.

Pulling the knife from my waistline, I hold the blade to his neck.

Like me, he's not fearful. I guess we do have some similarities. I hold the knife at just the right angle and press it into his skin with enough pressure to watch the blood as it trickles over my blade.

"Yet, you still look like the little girl that sits in the front of that van, no? We have the same skin color, the same high cheekbones." His voice is scratchy, as the blade slips further into his neck with the vibration of his words.

"Just because we have a similar heritage does not make us the same. I don't share blood with you, Victor. I will never be mafia. I will always fight against the evil of this world, just as my parents did."

"Let him go, Em." I hear Reid's shouted words before I see him.

"I can't, Reid. He's the fucking lottery. It's his fault my parents are dead. It's his fault Mel is dead!"

Remember who are you, Emily. You are a warrior. Brave.

But, bravery doesn't have to mean revenge.

The knife shakes in my hand against his skin as he smiles at me and dares me to end his life.

"Aemilia, baby. Put the weapon down. You don't have to be the hero. Let Reid save you." Oh God, I heave a breath as I hear Alex's words. Can he see me? Where has he been?

"I need to do this, Alex." The words leave my lips on a sob.

I'm breaking.

After all these years, I can't...

I see Reid as he steps out of the shadows a few feet away, but his eyes aren't on me. His eyes are fixated behind me as he holds his weapon in position.

The gravel of the parking lot shreds my tights and cuts into my knees, and I savor the pain. I need a way to tie myself to reality. I'm losing it. I fight against the urge inside of me to kill the man that I straddle on the cement parking lot out of vengeance. I fight an internal battle and say a silent prayer that years of training win out.

"You're gonna die, bitch." Victor's smile is the last thing I remember seeing.

"Em, no!" Reid's words are a roar as they fight to be heard against the gunshots that ring out in the silence of the night.

It's strange. I hear one, and then another. Then, I swear I hear Alex.

I hear him whispering words of love, I hear his cries. Why is he crying?

And then I close my eyes and dream of pink sparkly candles on chocolate birthday cake.

CHAPTER THIRTY-THREE
ALEX

"Agent Young is down. I need fucking backup." Reid's voice is frantic as he calls for backup that isn't arriving soon enough.

I hear Em's labored breathing as she fights for a life she has yet to live.

If it's not the end, it stands to reason that it's the beginning.

Her words shake my very foundation. It can't be the end.

"Aemilia, I love you. I love you so damn much that my heart feels like it's being ripped from my chest right now, but you listen to me. You promised me that this was the beginning. You promised me that we still had time. You made promises that I intend to hold you to, so I need you to stay with me. Don't go to sleep, Em. If you sleep, they win, don't let them win."

I hear the screeching tires before I catch sight of the black van tearing through the lot.

"Apart we fail." It's a whisper. It's words of finality.

Her final words are words of defeat.

Sirens wail in the background.

"She's over here!" Reid yells, and I listen for her breathing as it continues to fade out to nothing.

The ache in my chest is physically unbearable. I can't breathe. Fuck.

"Shit, is all this blood hers?" An unfamiliar voice travels through my headset.

"Yes. No. I don't know. Three bodies. One inside that door. A second was inside the van, but I bet they dumped it. I dropped a guy over there. The others though…we lost them. Oh, God."

"I can't get a pulse. Back up. I need you to disengage yourself, Agent Chapman. Let us do our jobs."

"Somebody get me the defibrillator. We're losing her." That voice. She's too calm. How is she so calm when my entire world rests in her hands?

Why isn't she trying harder?

Try harder.

The breathing stops.

Hers.

Mine.

My world tips, and every bit of emotion I repressed from earlier, every feeling I didn't allow myself to feel, that hate that I tried to keep out of my heart, it floods my body with a vengeance. I throw my headset across the room and watch it shatter to pieces.

"You promised, Aemilia! When all else was lost, I had you. You made me a promise!" I scream at no one. At anyone. Can you hear me where you are now, Em?

I run my hand over my scalp and pace the length of the hotel room, but it's not enough.

I can't fucking breathe.

I pick up my monitors one at the time and throw them into the wall with every bit of anger and force that is suffocating me.

She's gone.

None of it matters anymore.

-o-

REID

Pick up, Alex. For the love of Jesus Christ, pick up the phone.

"How many times have you tried to contact him?" Director Alan Reynolds sits across the table from me at an undisclosed location. Because, hell, I don't even know where I am right now.

I've been put under direct orders to maintain in protective custody until I'm given clearance to resurface.

We didn't anticipate the exit.

Our timing was off.

Em's cover. It was all wrong.

"I don't know. At least fifty times, give or take." I tip back the whiskey in my glass and let it coat my throat as it rolls down and numbs the pain. It doesn't even burn anymore. It's like warm caramel, goes down smooth like candy.

"I could put out a BOLO. Technically, he's MIA." Director Reynolds crosses his ankle over his knee and chews on the end of a cigar he hasn't even bothered to light. We don't deserve cigars after that shit show.

Sullivan's body was pulled from that warehouse, deceased.

We identified Victor's driver and security, but he and the unidentified mystery girl got away. We missed them. It was Victor or Em and, in that moment...I chose Em.

I don't regret my decision. I would do it again, but it doesn't mean I'm not pissed at myself for the way it all went down anyway.

"The fuck you can. Are you insane? Then what, we send him back to prison? He was doing his job, Director. It wasn't his fault. This wasn't anyone's fault." I slam the empty glass down on the wooden table.

"I know, Agent Chapman, calm down. We aren't going to put him back in prison, he's one of us now. Which is why we have to find him."

"I'd have already found him by now if you would let me out of here." My team, our backup, they became my enemy as I fought to get in the back of that ambulance with Emily's body. They took her away from me. I was supposed to protect her, and they held me back as they closed the doors in my face and drove off with her lifeless body.

They were seconds too late. We didn't realize there was a blind spot.

They were doing their jobs. While Em was fighting for her life, our team was raiding the warehouse. Everything was according to plan, until it wasn't anymore.

Fifteen arrests were made. We have numerous pending warrants for hits on online accounts we've already been able to tie back to the website itself. We intercepted two shipments and pulled countless women and children from the building that night.

Wilks never showed his face.

We didn't fail. But it sure as hell feels like we did.

"That's not my call, Chapman."

"Since when did you start following the rules?" My words are full of malice that he doesn't deserve.

We got word from the local authorities that Mel and Laura's families were notified of their deaths today. There are no second chances for them, no more beginnings.

"Watch your mouth, boy. You don't know what you're talking about."

"I know where he is, Director. Let me go." It's not a question, it's a demand. I need access to leave. I need to find him.

"And what if I lose you both? Victor is still out there. We don't know if he saw your face. Your identity could be compromised too. It may come as a shock to you, but I'm human too, you know. I can only take so much loss." He rubs his hand over the back off his neck, and I see the dark circles under his eyes. I know he's hurting too. We all are.

"Twenty-four hours. Please, Director, I'm begging you. Get me on a plane home."

"Home?" Home.

"You heard me."

"I'll make the call, but you don't get a minute longer. Do you understand?"

"Affirmative, sir." I snort as I stand from my chair and sway on my feet. I'm going to need that plane ride to sober up.

"Go. Get on the plane before I get some sense and

change my mind."

-o-

ALEX

"Get out. This place can't hold the weight of your ego." I know it's Reid before his head pokes through the floor of the old wooden treehouse.

He's the only person that would come looking for me. He's the only person in the world I have left.

"How'd you even know it was me, you asshole?" He maneuvers his large shoulders through the opening in the floor and pulls his ass up and onto the wooden slats that we spent months painstakingly nailing together the summer before our sixth-grade year. He rests his back on the opposite wall, but our legs still touch. This place used to be our headquarters; we fought many a battle from this tiny room. Now, we couldn't stand in here at the same time if we wanted to.

"Smelled you from a mile away." I smile, but the joke's not funny. I don't have anything left in me to give. I'm tapped out.

"I could say the same about you. You forget where the shower is? I'm sure my mom would let you borrow hers if you needed it that bad." His nose scrunches up in a grimace.

The Chapmans have no idea I'm out here. This place has been taped off for the investigation of my father's death. After the case is closed, I'm certain it will be demolished. I don't blame them. I wouldn't want that reminder in my backyard either.

"Dammit, Reid. I can't breathe. It's been days, and I

still can't breathe." I drop my head into my hands. My eyes are bloodshot. I don't have any more tears left to shed.

"You've been out here for days?"

"Nah, I got here this morning."

"I heard about your dad. I'm sorry, Alex. I'm sorry for so many things." Reid's foot taps my thigh, drawing my attention up to him. His eyes are clear blue, but I see the hurt that he feels. I see the blame he's carrying on his shoulders. And part of me is happy. Happy that maybe I'm not as alone in this as I feel.

"You know, he always liked you, Reid. Said you were a good influence on me." I snort as the haunted laughter bubbles from inside of my hollow chest.

"He wasn't wrong."

"Yeah, unless you count the time you shoved a condom in my hand and told me to go get laid. I was seventeen."

"You were also a teenage hermit that was married to his desktop. I was doing you a solid. Still a positive influence if you ask me."

"You think he's with my mom, Reid?" I stare at my hands. They're still cut up from the glass of the broken monitors that I left in the floor of that hotel room. I couldn't stay there. I had to leave.

"Your mom loved your dad, Alex. Even when he struggled, your mom was there to pick him up. I know she's got him now." The certainty in his words is soothing.

"You think Em is with them? You think she found her parents?" My voice cracks despite my attempts at trying to keep it even. I haven't slept in days. I just want to close my eyes and not wake back up to this nightmare.

"Em?" Reid pauses. He looks at me like he's puzzled.

He doesn't know about her parents. He doesn't know her background. Doesn't matter anymore.

"Reid, I don't know if I can live without her. I don't want to live without her, and the thought that I'm going to have to terrifies me."

"Alex, Emily isn't dead." My head snaps to attention, and my heart jolts like I've been physically electrocuted.

"What?" I question him. He's lying.

"She's not dead. I've been calling your phone non-stop." Why would he lie? I would feel it if she were still living. I would feel it. My chest is burning.

"She wasn't breathing, Reid. She stopped breathing. They lost her pulse. She told me. She told me she wasn't going to make it."

Apart we fail. Her words have haunted me each time I've tried to close my eyes.

"And they got her back when they got her to the hospital. Bullet clipped her lung, but she's alive. Her cover was compromised, so she's currently at a military hospital under protective custody until she's recovered enough for release."

"I don't believe you."

"Alex. Don't make me give you the speech about the lifeboat again. It's not safe for you to be out here. It's not safe for either of us. I have an apartment. I bought a building a few miles from here, the old shoe factory. The apartment is still being renovated, but you can shower. Then we need to check in with Reynolds because the dude is about five minutes from blowing something up. Then, maybe, we can find a way to get you to Emily."

"I can't. I'm sorry, Reid. But I don't believe you." I want to believe that his words are true, but I can't process them.

He reaches into his back pocket and pulls out a wadded-up piece of fabric.

"You said something to Emily the other night, and now I'm going to say it to you. Let me save you, Alex. Don't do this to yourself." He tosses the wrinkled and worn fabric to me, and I catch it on instinct.

The cape. The red-letter R is faded now with time, but it's still there.

"She's alive?" My voice cracks as I ask him again. I can't keep up with the whiplash of my emotions.

"She's alive. If you think I'm scared of Reynolds, just wait and see what happens when they pull her off her meds and she realizes she's in that hospital room alone. She tried to throw down with one of the ICU nurses after she was admitted, so they've had to temporarily sedate her in order to let her body heal. But she's going to heal, Alex."

For the first time I feel the vice on my chest ease. It doesn't release me, but it allows me to consider. Consider that my string of fate may be damaged, but maybe, just maybe it's not broken.

"I'm ready. Let's go." I toss the cape back at Reid.

"You first, I don't trust this thing. The craftsmanship was subpar at best."

I peel my body from the wall and maneuver my way to the ladder.

"Reid, did you say you bought a fucking building?"
"It's a long story."
"Sign me up. I've got time for the long stories. We've got a plane to catch."

EPILOGUE
EMILY

"I thought we were doing this on an island?" I stand on the balcony of a secluded cabin in the woods. Snow coats the tips of the mountain tops behind Alex as he stares at me with moisture glistening in his eyes.

He's been staring at me since the minute I walked out into the brisk winter air in this dress. Hell, he's been staring at me non-stop for two months, starting the moment I woke up in a hospital room in a place I didn't recognize, but it was okay, because he was there. Alex is my home.

My dress, it's not white. I was never meant for white dresses. Instead, it's a soft pink that contrasts against my olive skin. The silk material forms to my body and flows to the ground, pooling on the floor and covering my bare feet. No one said shoes were a requirement. I'm only marginally concerned about frostbite.

The heated lamp on the balcony is keeping us warm

enough.

"It's not your turn to talk, Young. Hush, and let me get this right." Reid straightens his bow tie. The man is wearing a tux. We're alone in the middle of the woods, and the man somehow manages to get a tux.

"He stayed up all night practicing." Alex smiles, and my belly warms. The swarm of butterflies I've now become accustomed to takes off in the pit of my stomach. I remember all the reasons why I decided I might be willing to change my identity…again.

He's wearing a pair of fitted khaki slacks with a sleek black button down. His tattoos peek out from the buttons undone at his chest and up and over the skin of his neck.

"You his alibi now?" I smile and snuggle in under his arm. Without shoes on, he's even that much more taller than I am.

"Who me? Nah. I just heard his mumbles through the wall all night. You kept me busy enough, woman." Alex places his hand over his chest innocently.

"I know that's right. I heard you both through the wall…I swear bigfoot heard Em's loud ass panting from the other side of the mountain."

"Are you kidding? I was shot in the damn lung. Oh, by the way, surprise! Straton's baby seeds were already inside of me. So now, not only am I still recovering from a near death experience, I'm also growing an oversized Latino baby in my belly. Panting. I swear." I threaten him with my eyes.

These hormones, they don't play.

"My boy." Alex pulls his hand to my belly and begins

rubbing circles over the invisible bump, ignoring my empty threats directed towards his best friend.

Apparently, my blood work showed my hormones were elevated while I was still in the hospital. We had to wait a couple more weeks, but they finally confirmed that Alex and I are, in fact, pregnant. I tease him, but I couldn't be happier. The look on his face when they told us the news. I've never seen more pure, unfiltered joy. I wish my mom and dad were here to see this. To see us.

"He's going to take after his Uncle Reid. Just wait."

"Like hell he is. You hand my son a condom before he's thirty, and I will personally cut your balls off, Reid Chapman." I've heard the story. All I can say is, it's a good thing we all have access to the FBI database. I have a feeling we're going to need it.

"She ain't lyin'." Alex continues to rub the silk material of my dress as he smiles.

"Now, look at the two of you. Stop interrupting me. You're a distraction. You'd think you didn't want to be married." He clears his throat in exaggeration.

"Do you, Emily Aemilia Young Albani whatever your damn name is, take Alexander Wyatt Straton to be your husband?"

"I do." I smile at Alex as I look up at him to catch his adoring gaze.

"Do you, Alexander Straton, take this woman that has no true identity or proof of American citizenship to be your wife?"

Alex stifles a laugh as my eyes snap back to Reid.

"I work for the US government, Chapman."

"It's my turn, Em. Stop it, both of you. I do." Alex

slides a finger under my chin and pulls my attention back to him.

"I now pronounce you man and wife." Reid finishes triumphantly as Alex slips a ring onto my finger, his mother's ring.

"Well…kiss the hell out of her." Reid prods us. Alex and I continue to stare at each other, his goofy ass grin growing by the second.

"That's all you got, Chapman?" I speak, but I don't look away. I couldn't tear my gaze away if I wanted to, which I don't, because damn, my baby daddy is fine.

"I got my certification online. Yeah, that's all I got. Now, Alex, kiss your woman before I do." We all laugh, but my giggles are cut off the moment Alex pulls me to my tip toes and slides his tongue into my mouth. All of a sudden, I forget the entire world around us.

It's just Alex, me and our sweet baby. *Our beginning…*

"Not a fucking lesbian." I hear Reid whisper to himself as he walks back into the cabin to give us some privacy…you have no idea Reid Chapman…

-o-

Let your scars remind you of just how tough you are,
And render your love so fierce, **until death do us part**.

You are not alone.

Every forty seconds, someone loses their life to suicide.

If you or someone you know is considering suicide, please reach out. Know the signs. Understand that the need for help does not define you. The ability to recognize that need is your strength.

Take that step out and ask for help.

The National Suicide Prevention Lifeline can be a great resource to you.

800-273-8255

-o-

It stands to reason that, if it's not the end, it's still the beginning.

Reach out and start a new beginning. It doesn't have to be the end.

Don't miss Nicole Dixon's

Devil You Know

Keep reading for a preview…

CHAPTER ONE
HOLLY

"Listen, Holly, just one date. It doesn't even have to be a real date; you could just go grab coffee one afternoon or something. It would do you some good to put yourself out there again, you're not getting any younger." I rolled my eyes so hard they nearly fell out of my head as I leaned back in my office chair. I held my cell phone between my shoulder and ear, balancing it as I continued to make adjustments to the digital mock-up of the layout I was working on for my latest project. I guess I could put her on speaker phone but considering as I'm currently debating on whether or not I'm going to hang up on her, it may be a waste of my time anyway.

"Well, that was a bitch thing to say, you sound like mom. I just turned thirty last year. I'm not ancient, Tilly. And I definitely don't want to be set up with one of Kris's golfing buddies, no offense." Tilly is short for Mistletoe. Yepp, our mother has a thing for Christmas. Tilly is my oldest sister and is thirty-seven, happily married to her high school sweetheart with three kids. She wears an apron to cook dinner every night, and probably only has sex in the missionary position – if you get my drift.

I have another sister, Noel, she's thirty-four and writes sexy romance novels for a living, or you know, porn with a storyline as our mother likes to refer to it. She has an affinity for tattoos and is kind of the black sheep of the family – I think Tilly has given up on trying to tame her, and our mother definitely isn't sharing her work with her friends down at the Country Club.

"Holly, language. I've got you on speaker and the baby is nursing. All I'm saying is that your fertility clock is ticking down by the minute. Not to mention, Chet was an asshole. I can assure you, there are other men out there. Men that don't shave their arms. That was weird, Holly."

I snorted through my nose at the reminder that Chet shaved his arms regularly because he swore that it highlighted the definition in his muscles. Gag me. Show me a woman that likes day old prickly man arms. Exactly.

"I am fully aware that there are other men on planet Earth besides Chet, Tilly. Also, can I just point out that my foul mouth isn't going to spoil the mind of your infant while she sucks on your boob. She's not even listening to me, she's too busy getting milk drunk on your tits. Remind me again, how are we related?" I teased.

My sisters and I have an interesting relationship, the age gap between us is rather large and throw in the fact that our personalities are all so vastly different, sometimes it makes it hard for us to relate to each other.

For a while there, after Chet somehow swindled me into a borderline abusive relationship, I didn't see them or talk to them. I was segregated from my entire support system, and if it weren't for my group of girlfriends, I don't think I would have been able to pull myself out...without having to bury a body. Not gonna lie, there were a couple of times I considered sneaking some arsenic in Chet's morning protein shake. Sue me.

"Jesus, I ask myself that question every day. Have you talked to Noel lately?" Oh boy, have I talked to Noel lately. I talked to her last week. She was shacked up with an Italian guy somewhere in Europe. Apparently, he doesn't speak English, and she doesn't speak Italian, but there is one language they both speak and well, let's just say that's not something I'm prepared to share with Tilly tonight.

"Yeah, did you read her new release? It's still hanging on tight to the number one spot in Kindle Unlimited for the erotica genre. That scene with the guy and the other guy and the girl. Holy hell." My sister is a lot of things, but damn that woman can write some steamy sex.

"Shhhhhh....yes. Yes, I read it. Don't talk so loud, Kris is in the office with the door open."

"Tilly, it's a book, woman. It wouldn't kill Kris to take a few pointers, I'm sure. I mean, not that his swimmers aren't obviously working fine. I'm just saying. Live it up a little, take a walk on the wild side. When was the last time you did it in the middle of the week? When, Tilly?" I gave up trying to work, having too much fun playing with my sister. I know her face must be beet red right this minute.

"Now who's being a b-word? Talk to me when milk leaks from your boobs if your husband so much as looks at them the wrong way, and you have a three-year-old that screams and beats on the bedroom door the second they sense the lock is turned. The very second. Bunch of cock blockers. Oh my gosh. I can't believe I just said that. You and Noel both are bad influences. This is why Cousin Margaret is the godmother of my children." Blah, Blah, Blah…Cousin Margaret, she may as well go ahead and send her kids off to boarding school instead.

"And thank God for that really, Til. I love your little devils, but if something were to happen to you or Kris, heaven forbid, I just don't think I could do it. I'm not cut out for the parenting thing. And Noel, we won't even go there." I hate to even admit this out loud, for fear that my ovaries may actually shrivel up and fall out of my vagina – you know on the off chance I change my mind one day, but I've never wanted children. Never even had the slightest inkling that I would one day want to suck snot from a baby's nose with my bare mouth. Yes, it's a thing, I watched my sister do it. I prefer to spend my time with my one true love, design; specifically historical properties. Give me a building that has some history behind it - walls that have seen centuries pass - over dirty diapers any day of the week.

"We won't even go there. Right. Anyway, if you change your mind about the coffee thing, text me. I'm telling you, Kris has some really good-looking friends, and successful – they all have jobs, and none of them live with their parents. Well except the one, but I wasn't even going to suggest him. You don't need to stay holed up in your office for the rest of your life, Holly. Because I know that's where you are right now. I can smell you through the phone, smells like caffeine and a graveyard of ink pens." She's not wrong.

I looked around my desk at the scattered black ink pens, half of which I've discarded because they no longer roll as smoothly as the new pens do. At some point they start to skip, and if one of my pens even think about skipping, they are trashed. I only buy one specific brand and it has to be the black.

Technology has its place, and I don't know how I would do my job without it, but when I'm truly designing – when I'm feeling the stories of the people that have walked the halls of the worn and haggard architecture before me – I will always go back to my ink.

"Give the babies my love, Til. And tell Kris I said hello, and might I suggest that sex on Tuesdays is fun too."

"Night, Holly." I could physically feel her tired through the phone as I hit end on one of the longest phone calls I've had with my oldest sister in over a year. Having three children all under the age of five is killing her. Not that she wasn't a total bore before, but now she's extra vanilla.

-o-

My parents are the upper crust of the upper class, old money, handed down generation after generation. I'm not even entirely sure what my father does for a living.

Investing? Trading stocks? Real Estate? I really can't be sure, but the money – there was always plenty of it, and my mother made sure everyone knew too. Her career consists of hosting dinner parties and social gatherings, thus her love for all things Christmas. *It's the most wonderful time of the year, darlings.* I can hear her now, as she spends enough money to fund a third-word orphanage on a nine-foot-tall Christmas tree for the entrance in the grand hall.

We were raised to be debutantes, even had a coming out ball on our consecutive sixteenth birthdays. In case you were wondering, that's kind of like an auction for your fancy virginity. My mother put us in etiquette classes from the time we could walk, and we spent our summers swimming in the pool at the Country Club while my mother sipped cocktails and gossiped with her fake friends and my father played golf with his associates – or fucked one of my mother's friends in the locker room.

Not that she cared, she fucked the pool boy every Thursday at precisely three o'clock in the pool house. That's when I was supposed to be practicing my piano, but what my mother didn't realize was I could see the entrance to the pool house from the windows in the conservatory. Ms. Sicily, my piano instructor, bless her two-hundred-year-old soul, was totally oblivious to the scandalous activity I was privy to every week.

Tilly, being the first-born, was a people pleaser. She followed the rules, dated within the pre-approved circle and married for money – er, love – when she turned twenty-six. She had to wait for Kristopher to finish his doctoral program, of course. Kris is a good guy, but the man's a podiatrist. He couldn't go to medical school for something cool like cutting people open. No, he looks at crusty old toes for a living.

Anyway, I'm sure my mother thought she was golden, raising Tilly to perfection. Until Noel came along and dropped a stick of dynamite in her evening bourbon.

Noel was hell on wheels straight out of the gate. Her favorite pastime was sneaking her boyfriends into our three-story home in the coveted cul de sac of our gated community – don't even ask me how they scaled the fortress we lived behind, because those boys weren't from our side of the gates, that's for sure. And then the time she forged my dad's name on the form for her first tattoo – at sixteen and we won't even talk about the time her phone synched up to the Bluetooth in my mother's luxury SUV and began playing hardcore porn through the speakers on our way to ballet class. I was ten.

By the time I came along, well, they were just glad I preferred drawing over writing. I kept my nose stuck in history books and stayed quiet. Noel was so busy being a distraction that it was easy for me to slip by under the radar.

That was fine by me, because I didn't care for their high-class, society. The gossip and the fake smiles. Maybe that's why I fit in so well with my girlfriends now. They are crass and loud, but they're real. And sure, maybe I'm the odd man out now and they push me to date just like Tilly. But their men, the men they lean towards…well, maybe I wouldn't mind getting trapped into having a cup of coffee with one of them. Or trapped under them, I never said I was an angel.

CHAPTER TWO
REID

"Twenty-seven seconds. Twenty. Dammit, Reid. Get the fuck out of there." The muscles in my legs burned with the fire of a thousand suns as I ran, ducking for cover and then sprinting to safety. My clothes were drenched in sweat, the humidity suffocating as I gasped for air.

"Hell yeah, you beat your record by three seconds. Good work Senior Special Agent." Alex walked up behind me decked out in all black with a headset on, his voice echoed through the microscopic earpiece I wore in my ear as my chest continued to heave, searching for air that I couldn't get to process through my lungs and into my bloodstream fast enough.

"Was the rubber bullet necessary in that third room? Really, Alex? It hurt like a bitch." I rubbed my leg where a rubber bullet shot me in the thigh just as I was rolling under a synthetic fallen tree.

"Quit crying, pretty boy. How many times have we gone over this? You have to expect the unexpected, even in the simulation rooms. If you let your guard down in here, you let your guard down out there. And if you let your guard down out there, you're dead." He's right, but that doesn't make the purpling that I know is currently bubbling up on my thigh feel any better.

"The new weather control devices in here are legit, this humidity will kill me if the bullets don't." I pulled my soaked t-shirt off over my head, revealing my state-of-the-art bulletproof vest. I train in my gear, but when I'm undercover I don't get luxuries like flame retardant clothing and bulletproof vests, I just get shot. And it wouldn't be the first time. I've taken my share of bullets, but nothing I haven't lived to tell about later. And I always got those fuckers, so it wasn't for naught.

"Right, we're tweaking the simulators every day, and every day they get better. We train you guys harder, push you further. I was worried about you there for a second, thought you might be getting too old for this." Alex can poke and prod all he wants to, but I know where his train of thought is. I'm in my thirties now, and in our world that makes me an old man. The young guys training up behind me, they are counting the days until I'm pushed to a desk and told to sit down. Alex wants to see me settle down, find a wife, have kids, and buy a puppy or some shit. News fucking flash: It's not happening. I will die first.

Seventeen missions. Hundreds of women and children. Hell.

I've seen it.

I've lived it.
And I'm still here.
Every day.

I close my eyes at night and the screaming, the crying, it's all I hear. Their pleading voices echo throughout my dreams. My entire childhood I wanted to be a superhero – Batman in the flesh. I wanted to save the world. But we lose them. I've watched shipping containers full of children leave the damn harbor and I was the one that turned the lock. All because I had to maintain cover and damn it if we didn't have what we needed yet to lock the evil away.

The evil, I always knew it was out there. I could feel it, still can. It's buried in my bones, nestled against my soul. Right beside the lives of the women and children I've lost.

But I won't stop. I will not stop fighting, because each time we save one. Or we put a bullet through the skull of one of the bad guys, on accident, of course. Because you know, we're supposed to arrest them or some shit. Each time we save a life, I can breathe. Even if only for a second.

Some might call me a hero, I'm one of the good guys. Right? But I live a life of evil, and I pray when I lay my head down at night that I will be redeemed by the souls that I save in return. I'm fighting for me just as much as I'm fighting for them at this point. It's my own personal war, and I won't be defeated. I dare them to try me.

That's why I'm here today, training with Alex. I've been given notice that I've been assigned to a new leg of the case we've been building for years. I'm supposed to report next week. It's been a few months since I've been undercover. Some shit about me needing R&R. I'm itching for a new assignment. I can't sit still knowing what happens when the lights go out and most people are warm, and cozy snuggled up in their beds. I need to work. I need to fight the evil that threatens to swallow me alive.

Carlton Harbor

Book 1 – Mirror Image

Book 2 – Surprise Reflections

Book 3 – For Always

Book 4 – Starting Over

Silent Hero

Book 1 – Devil You Know

Book 2 – Until Death

ABOUT THE AUTHOR

Nicole Dixon is a Forensic Accountant with an affinity for writing sexy novels. She loves data, coffee, travel, and making sure all the voices in her head get the happily ever after they deserve. She made the decision to begin publishing her work in an effort to teach her children to never give up on their dreams, nothing is impossible.

Made in the USA
Columbia, SC
10 January 2025